AMARAH

Don't be afraid to fight
for what you believe in

AMARAH

WORLD OF LINARIA BOOK 3

L.L. MCNEIL

THREE DRAGON
— PUBLISHING —

First published in Great Britain in 2019.

No part of this publication may be reproduced, stored in a retrieval system, or transmitted, in any form or by any means, without the express written permission of the publisher except for the use of brief quotations in a book review.

All characters and events in this publication are fictitious and any resemblance to real persons, living or dead, is purely coincidental.

Amarah © 2019 L. L. McNeil
Three Dragon Publishing
www.llmcneil.com

Cover by Holly Jameson
www.hollyjameson.co.uk

For Pipkin, who keeps me on my toes by constantly tickling my knees.

ACKNOWLEDGMENTS

This book would not be complete without Garage Fiction, Olivia, and Ian. I cannot thank you enough for your unending patience, support, advice, and encouragement. Thank you.

To anyone who purchases my book, I am eternally grateful. It would mean the world and more if you would be kind enough to review *Amarah*.

SUMMARY OF PALOM

In the aftermath of Aciel's conquest, Palom, the blacksmith who forged the legendary *Valta Forinja* weapons with dragon-ore and defended Val Sharis, is hailed as a hero. He and his surviving allies—Amarah, the sky pirate, Morgen, of the Imperial Guard, and Kohl, an Arillian dragon-hunter and exile—are rewarded with gold by Princess Isa of Val Sharis and her half-brother Sapora, the new king of both Sereth and Val Sharis.

The siblings' other half-brother Tacio, accompanies Sapora into Val Sharis alongside his elite Varkain—the Cerastes. The three begin a tentative rule, allowing the hitherto despised Varkain to take up residence and work in the Val Sharis capital city: Taban Yul.

Consumed by survivor's guilt, Palom shuns the idea of being a hero. Morgen returns to Niversai, the capital of his home country of Corhaven, with Topeko, a scholar from the mage city of Berel. Amarah and Kohl, desperate to somehow restore the life of Moroda—who sacrificed herself to seal away Aciel in crystal with the power of a Sevastos—embark on a quest for greater magic that can undo the seal.

Taban Yul is full of Ittallan who despise Sapora and his rule and seek to overthrow him. Many believe that Princess Isa, more of an Ittallan than her half-brother, is better suited to rule them as queen. An uprising begins in secret, led by Lathri, former lover of Palom and daughter of a former councilwoman whom Sapora had slain prior to his coronation.

Although Palom wishes to stand by Lathri and rekindle their relationship, he is consumed by grief, shame, and paranoia, exacerbated by the cursed power of the *Valta Forinja*. Instead of joining Lathri, he leaves the city to escape his unwanted fame. He is ambushed by several Varkain and slaughters them in cold blood, turning King Sapora's attention to him. In retaliation, Sapora releases the war criminal Mateli from prison—a powerful, dangerous Ittallan—and sets him after Palom.

Kohl flies with Amarah to the Arillian floating islands in the distant north of Linaria, where she is permitted entry to his hometown of Oren by the enormous Ice Golem army which defends Arillians from outsiders. She is introduced to the Arillian magic and sees first-hand the results of those who had been under Aciel's compulsion. Their recovery seems unlikely, and she is terrified by what she sees.

In Taban Yul, so close to the crystal pillar which sealed Aciel and Moroda, other citizens are also acting strangely. Many are harming themselves and others, and several even commit suicide. Some consider it a sickness brought on by the ill-suited Varkain leader. But Sapora and Isa know better —it's Aciel's will seeping through the streets like poison. They keep quiet to prevent a panic.

Sapora requests information from the Imperial Guard and the Cerastes on an ancient Varkain treasure. He is vague about the details and refuses to confer even with Isa, whom he had promised a share of power on his ascension to the throne.

Palom returns to his hometown, a small village on the border with Sereth called Feoras Sol, and reunites with his father—whom he has not seen for twenty years. Palom left in shame, blaming himself for the death of his brother, and is welcomed home with open arms. He begins to reforge a relationship with his family, including his niece, Solvi.

In Oren, Kohl and his estranged daughter, Jato, argue over Arillian succession, what happened with Aciel, and their future. Tired of waiting, Amarah threatens Jato and the two come to blows. Although Amarah has an advantage with her *Valta Forinja*, she is no match for the Arillian General, who leaves her blinded in one eye and destroys her airship, *Khanna*. Jato then departs Oren with a handful of followers, leaving her father and Amarah behind.

Mateli tracks down Palom to the inn he is staying at, and the two battle fiercely. Palom is able to hold off his aggressor, but Solvi comes to his rescue and the two drive Mateli off. Grievously wounded, Palom begs Solvi to seek out Lathri in Taban Yul, for she is a healer educated at the University of Berel, and he believes only she can help him.

Solvi locates Lathri and begs her to save Palom. Though disheartened, Lathri obliges, and returns to Palom's side. She blames the *Valta Forinja* for his darkness, and refuses to help him any further. Enraged, Palom leaves the inn to wander the Val Sharis wilds. But as he leaves, a dragon egg he found in the forest begins to hatch. He dubs the tiny creature, *Leillu*, who immediately follows him.

The rebel movement in Taban Yul increases when it is discovered that the secret treasure Sapora is seeking is actually the Arks—ancient Varkain weapons used to slaughter Ittallan some five thousand years ago, but disappeared with little explanation. In desperation and fear, Isa calls on Morgen to help, for he is a Captain of the Imperial Guard and has some power. Despite going against a king, Morgen orders a fleet of warships to attack the palace in Taban Yul.

Sapora responds by unleashing a Sevastos and burning the fleet and half the city down. He and Tacio capture most of the rebels they don't kill—including Lathri. Isa hadn't realised he had a Sevastos under his control, for they are considered gods, and her distrust of her brother intensifies as he is going too far. She joins the remaining rebels and leads a rescue attempt to save Lathri and the others.

Having awoken missing an eye and her ship, Amarah is distraught and blames Kohl for her losses. He promises to make it up to her, and flies the two of them back to the mainland. Amarah demands a new ship from him and wishes to hunt down Jato to get her revenge. The nearest town is Tum Metsa, one of the most northerly in all Val Sharis, where she says she will await an ally's help.

Stranded by a blizzard somewhere in the north of Val Sharis, Palom and Amarah's *Valta Forinja* connect with each other and they are able to communicate. Amarah tells him to come to Tum Metsa to aid her, and Palom agrees. On the way, he discovers a small band of Arillians led by Jato are swarming through Val Sharis, slaying dragons where they see them. He knows this cannot bode well for Linaria, given Topeko's words; 'From dragon-flame begun, from dragon-flame undone.'

Realising Lathri was right and his sword is affecting him, Palom abandons his *Valta Forinja* in a snowdrift and makes his way to Tum Metsa with *Leillu*, his heart considerably lighter. The dragons will rampage now that more of their kin are being killed, and he is desperate to help after spending so much time running from responsibilities because of his cursed weapon's influence.

However, unbeknownst to Palom, by the time he reaches Tum Metsa, Amarah has already left with Kohl and the ally from her past; Traego. Amarah's help has been enlisted on a new treasure hunt—for an Ark.

1

S omewhere in the distant Karoun mountain range lay
a hidden treasure worth enough gold to buy Amarah
a fleet of airships. Whatever this "Ark" was, it had to
be one of the most valuable bounties she had ever come
across.

When her old ally, Traego, had told her the amount of
money she stood to earn on his treasure hunt, she'd struggled to maintain a straight face. Traego had a buyer lined up,
a reliable one, who had offered a vast sum to any who could
bring him reliable information about the Ark—five hundred
crowns.

Even for Amarah, a sky pirate who'd flown across
Linaria more times than she could count, such an opportunity only arose once in a lifetime. Typically, it was halfway
around the world in Corhaven—a country she'd fled and
sworn never to return to.

A bigger shame she'd have to split the reward with her
ally's lacklustre crew.

Traego's airship, *Otella*, creaked in all the places Amarah
remembered it to, its sails billowing in the cool, spring
breeze. Sure, the ship had a few more scuffs on the deck, and

the sails had been replaced since she'd last seen them—they were now an off-red rather than the amber sails of her youth —but it was still mostly as she remembered.

Otella had lived a previous life as a warship. Despite its size, it was relatively fast, and in barely a week, they'd crossed the Sea of Nami and floated among the Karoun Mountains as they travelled towards the most north-westerly point of Corhaven.

She knew of a settlement just beyond the edge of the mountains, a tiny, backwater town called Povmar, but hadn't ever visited it. She didn't really know what the town itself had to offer because the griffins that lived in these high altitudes warded off all but the most dogged travellers. Their screeches carried widely across the mountaintops, the sound somehow more piercing in the cold air.

Amarah shivered.

Griffins were vicious hunters—formidable, in fact—and they hunted in packs. This far north in Corhaven, where dragons rarely came, they were the top predators.

Traego strode along the length of the deck, his booted feet heavy. His long, curved sword hung low on his hip, and though he didn't carry his warhammer, he rarely removed its thick leather cross strap, so his belts and buckles clinked lightly with every step. He leant against the prow, where a boar's head had been fashioned out of the yellowing wood, its tusks twisted and sharp, and absent-mindedly adjusted his cuffs while staring ahead. Ever the epitome of calm, Amarah wondered if there was anything that could frighten him.

Snow-capped mountains rose around them—a far cry from the rolling plains Corhaven was famous for. The mountains had been here since time immemorial, and would no doubt remain here for another hundred thousand years, unmoved and unchanged by Linaria's strife.

2

Strange, how half of Corhaven had bowed to Aciel and his compulsion, yet this remote corner of the country seemed untouched by the Arillian conqueror.

Even the few dragons they'd seen here had drifted away on the winds—the complete opposite of those in Val Sharis that had harassed *Otella* every time they flew within sight of one. At least she still had Kohl with her. The Arillian, for all his flaws, knew dragons well and was powerful enough to see them off.

Amarah had spent her whole adult life on the run. She was used to watching her back for Imperial ships. But dragons were another matter entirely.

Since that damned Aciel and his Arillians had brought war to Linaria, the world had changed. Because of him, Jato, Aciel's fiancée, had tried to kill her.

Because of Jato, she'd lost her right eye.

Because of Jato, she'd lost her ship. Lost *Khanna*.

Jato had signed her own death warrant, as far as Amarah was concerned.

Travelling through the freezing mountaintops as part of Traego's troupe was just part of the plan to buy a new airship and get her freedom back.

Her missing eye itched in the cold, and she drew a nail underneath the patch she'd worn since leaving Val Sharis. Even if this treasure hunt of Traego's resulted in the largest amount of gold she'd ever seen, would she still be able to competently fly a new airship with one eye? She'd not flown since losing *Khanna*. It was one thing to move around day-to-day; it was another to make an airship dance with your fingertips with the same level of skill she'd always enjoyed.

'Checkpoint up ahead,' Traego called. He clasped his hands behind his back as he kept his gaze on the horizon.

Carav and Oris—the newest members of Traego's crew

—shuffled forward at his voice. They left a lot to be desired. Young and feeble-minded, Amarah didn't like them one bit.

Oris had to be fifteen or sixteen. Still a child, really. He was petulant, shadowed anyone nearby like a lost puppy, and frequently picked his nose. Patchy stubble lined his chin in his attempt to grow a beard to look older.

Carav was a few years older than Oris, and they had similarly dark blonde hair, so Amarah assumed they were siblings. On discovering she'd grown up in Ranski, Carav had taken to telling Amarah all about *her* time spent with the Samolen as a child in the hopes of bonding with the older sky thief. She wore necklaces of differing lengths—the result of her successful small-scale thievery—which Amarah had promptly told her to take off. It all made far too much noise when she moved.

Traego always had a habit of selecting the unlikeliest of people for his crews, and Amarah hoped they'd end up proving to be more useful than she suspected they were.

There was little more than wilderness out here, but considering their proximity to Povmar, the Imperial Guard had set up checkpoints along the route where the mountains were lowest, a natural valley leading to the snowy town. It reinforced Amarah's idea that Povmar had something worth taking—if you made it past the griffins.

Unfortunately, it meant dealing with the Imperial Guard and pandering to their need for paperwork.

Amarah smacked the bottom of her scythe on the deck. 'This better be the last checkpoint, Traeg. I'm sick of smiling at those damned guards.'

'Should be the last one we need ta clear,' Traego replied. He turned and walked back towards Amarah and the two younger crew members. 'According ta Antar, we'll see the shroud in another half-league or so. Then we're done.'

'I'm used to avoiding them. Don't have the patience for their questions. I know you like winding them up.'

'There's no other way through the mountains. *Otella* ain't stealthy, and their questions would be worse if we avoided their checks,' Traego said. 'Oris, got the next batch o' paper-work ready?'

The young man nodded, fishing a leaf of loose sheets from his pocket, all stamped in gold and red Imperial colours from the previous three checkpoints.

'Cap'n! They're flagging us down.' Antar called from the ship's wheel near the rear of the deck. 'I'll bring her in slowly.'

Traego nodded and clapped his hands. 'Ya know the drill. Smiles everyone. We're merchant traders, not cut-throat pirates.'

Amarah raised an eyebrow but said nothing as Antar twisted the wheel and pulled a lever to adjust the ship's sails.

Traego's pilot, a man in his late twenties, had the bold, reckless streak befitting an Estorian upbringing, yet, with his dark hair and skin, and occasionally serious attitude, Antar seemed to be Traego's polar opposite.

He reminded Amarah of herself, when she'd first joined a sky pirate's crew at fifteen years old.

Otella slowed and dropped in altitude, heading towards the large cabin built on the mountainside. Smoke rose slowly from the chimney, and a pair of small, sturdy mountain horses pawed at the ground in search of grazing. Covered in snow and made of weathered stone, the building looked as though it were as old as the mountains.

The two members of the Imperial Guard stood outside seemed half-frozen despite the thick furs lining their heads and chests, and from the scowls on their faces, were none-too-pleased to see a reconditioned warship float up.

Their own ship, a medium-sized class five six-person

scouter, resplendent in red and gold, lay a short distance away, its canons clearly visible.

'Permits and licence,' the first guard grunted as Antar gently landed the ship beside the cabin.

'Right here,' Traego said, clambering down the ladder on the side of *Otella* and handing the guard his marked papers.

The guard thumbed through the paperwork while his colleague walked towards the bottom of the ladder. 'Gotta check your cargo,' he muttered to Traego as he passed.

Traego flashed a toothy grin. 'Go ahead.'

Amarah watched the second guard scrabble up the side of the ship. She glared at Oris and Carav who were slouched beside her, and at her warning, they immediately straightened up. Amarah nodded to the guard as he climbed onto the deck, and kept her attention on him. He wandered over to the captain's quarters and left snowy footprints with every step.

She watched as he glanced over at her, held her gaze for a moment, then smiled.

It unnerved her.

He stopped in front of the closed door to the captain's quarters door and looked over his shoulder again, his eyes in the shadow of his thick, fur-lined hat. 'Amarah? Sure you're not pirating anything?'

Amarah snorted at the audacity of his statement. The fact he knew her name bothered her less. 'Does it look like we're pirating anything?' She drummed her fingers on her arms.

'No. But your reputation is what it is.' He stepped towards her with the same smile.

Instinctively, Amarah grabbed her weapon's hilt. 'Means nothing. I'm here on other business, like the paper says.' She'd send him flying with her scythe's energy if she had to.

She felt the weapon's power crackle in her grasp and readied herself.

'Wow, easy! I know it's been a little while, but you really don't recognise me?' He lifted his hat and shook out his hair. 'You've lost an eye and I still know you!'

Amarah scowled, racking her brain for any names that matched his face. Who did she know in Corhaven?

Who did she know in the *Imperial Guard*?

'Wait...*Morgen*?' It had been months since she'd last seen him. 'Isa's palace. Taban Yul? Dragons above, it's been a while!'

Morgen's grin broke into a laugh. 'Wanna put the weapon down now you know who I am? What happened to your eye?'

Amarah lowered her blade and shook her head. It was still a sore subject, and she didn't want Morgen to know she was trying to climb out of the pit she'd found herself in. She studied him, and thought he'd aged more than she'd have expected in a handful of months. He'd grown a beard, and with dark hair covering half his face, it was no wonder she hadn't recognised him straight away. Not to mention his snow-caked furs bulked up his physique more, giving him the look of a much older man.

A pang of guilt rippled through her. It was unlike her to forget a face, especially of someone she'd spent so long travelling with. 'What you doing out here? Thought you were in the capital?' Amarah asked, ignoring both Morgen's question and the stares from Oris and Carav. 'You must only see a ship once a season all the way out here.'

Morgen sighed and glanced down to his colleague and Traego. 'After everything that happened, our focus was on rebuilding Niversai. The Imperial Guard here has pretty much all been obliterated—most killed or taken by Aciel. They promoted me to captain soon as I got back—thought I

7

was gonna be kicked out after leaving to be honest—but they needed anyone with experience to help pick up the pieces. We've not located the Royal Family, either. We're a bit at a loss.' He licked his lips and glanced overboard again. When he turned back to her, Morgen dropped his voice to a whisper. 'I just needed a break from it all. So, I asked to be stationed as far away as I could. Just for a bit. They weren't happy, but it was that or I left.'

Something bothered Amarah about his hesitation. She'd been around poor liars often enough to know when people were withholding information. Besides, if he'd been promoted, surely he'd be celebrating in some tavern in the country's capital, not pulling guard in this remote mountain range. She couldn't fathom why he'd want to be put out here. She held onto the information, storing it for later. 'And Topeko?'

Morgen shrugged. 'He went back to Berel. Only stayed in Niversai a couple of weeks. But where's *Khanna*?'

Amarah ignored both his question and the longing that coursed through her like physical pain at the mention of her old airship. She tightened her grip on her scythe's handle as she imagined slicing Jato's head off in retribution for what she had done to her, done to *Khanna*.

But Topeko leaving Niversai? That didn't surprise her. The scholar was more at home in Berel than anywhere else, and didn't like to leave the University for long. She wondered whether Topeko had left due to being homesick, or because he'd discovered something in the Corhaven capital that made him flee.

She scratched her nose. 'If you wanna get away from things, why don't you come with us? We're gonna be heading out of Corhaven soon.' As soon as she said the words, she knew it was a silly offer. She, Traego, and the rest of his crew were about to steal something of incredible value, and she was inviting a Captain of the Imperial Guard to come along. And she doubted Traego would be happy about her inviting new people onto his ship.

Despite her friendship with Morgen, they were still on opposite sides of the law.

Aciel's war hadn't—and wouldn't—change that.

Morgen shook his head and put his hat back on, shivering from a sudden breeze. If he was curious about her side-stepping his questions, he didn't show it. 'Can't. Gotta stay here, and can't leave him by himself.' He jerked a thumb towards his colleague. 'Plus, the griffins here are breeding, and they've been known to take people if they're alone. You gonna be here long?'

'Hard to say. You know what trade can be like.' She grinned and shifted her weight.

Morgen gave a single, hollow chuckle, though his eyes remained flat. He glanced down when his colleague called to him. 'Looks like we're done. Safe travels, Amarah. Good to see you. Been a while since I've seen a friendly face.'

She lifted a hand to him. 'And you.'

As soon as Morgen was out of sight, Oris leapt forward. 'How d'you know someone in the Imperial Guard?' His voice was full of accusation.

'You don't work for them do you? Traego warned us about spies!' Carav echoed, backing away from her.

'Shut it, you brats. I ain't in the damned Guard! He was with us in the fight against Aciel, or don't you know nothin' about that?'

'Everythin' in order. All sorted. What's goin' on here?' Traego asked, climbing back up the ladder and rejoining the crew on board *Otella*.

Amarah folded her arms. 'Nothin'. Let's get this damned Ark so we can get out of here. I want a ship, Traego. I'm not

9

flying halfway around Linaria every time you hear about a bit of treasure!'

Traego nodded to Antar, who opened up the sails and piloted the ship into the air. 'It ain't just *some* treasure hunt, Amarah. I wouldn't bother coming meself—or bring ya—if it were. This is an *Ark*. This'll make ya as rich as Sapora.'

She shivered at the mention of the Varkain's name—the King of Sereth and Val Sharis. 'Bastard,' she muttered under her breath. 'Don't want nothin' to do with him. Dirty snake.'

'Well, sometimes ya should keep ya enemies close. Or in ya debt.' Traego smirked as the checkpoint disappeared behind them. 'Shroud ain't far now. Keep an eye out for it, okay?'

'What is this Ark, anyway? A jewel?' Amarah asked. Traego had kept her in the dark and she didn't like flying blind. Her trust in him had brought her and Kohl this far, but now they were on the cusp, she wanted to know exactly what it was they were after, and whether she needed to keep an eye on any of his crew running off with it.

Traego shrugged, his usual, easy smile on his face. 'It's something old. Something valuable—extremely valuable. Like I told ya, it's worth enough to buy *Khanna* fifty times over. Might be a bit dangerous, but what great hunt isn't?'

She scowled. 'So, you're either being shady with me 'cause you don't trust me. Or 'cause you don't have the first idea of what it is.'

'Course I trust ya. Hand-picked ya as part o' my crew, didn't I?' His smile deepened. 'Same as Antar, who found the location. Plus, my buyer knows what he wants and is good for the bounty, I promise ya that. I don't much care for the details, otherwise. We'll figure it out as we go. Always have.'

Amarah snorted. Typical Traego, racing off into Rhea knows where just at the sniff of gold.

As Carav and Oris scuttled away, Amarah walked forward and leaned over the side of *Otella*. She shoved the thoughts and questions about Morgen and Topeko from her mind as she focussed on the hunt for the shroud. For the most part, she'd grown used to having one eye, but the loss of visual range took its toll when she searched for something well-hidden and in the distance.

She was no stranger to a *Thief's Shroud*—the first trick any pirate worth their salt bought—but they were fiendishly hard to spot, particularly if they weren't your own. Damn Samolen magic.

Antar had been the one who'd made the discovery. He'd marked and hidden the location with a particularly potent shroud and raced back to Estoria to deliver the news to Traego.

The Karoun Mountains did not match the vast ranges of Val Sharis, either in height or width, but they were steep, rocky, and full of griffins. They'd had to fend off a pair as they entered the range, but since then, the skies had thankfully been clear. She suspected they had Kohl to thank for their safe passage—the Arillian was a master of the wing, and his wind and ice powers had kept everything at bay that might be a threat.

However, he'd kept his distance from *Otella* considering the Imperial Guard had orders to capture Arillians on sight. The new order had come from King Sapora in retaliation for a band of Arillians that had been destroying towns and villages in Val Sharis.

Amarah harboured a suspicion that Jato was leading the Arillian attacks. But to keep on the safe side, Kohl kept out of sight every time they approached or passed through a checkpoint.

She had grown fond of Kohl, particularly since their

return to the mainland, though she knew he was fighting his own demons.

Perhaps even more so than she was.

Amarah had not hidden the fact she wanted revenge on Jato for the loss of *Khanna* and her eye, and the tense relationship between Kohl and his daughter wouldn't help.

But Jato had to pay. She had to suffer. This excursion with Traego was simply the first step.

To her left, a short distance below, Amarah spied a small herd of mountain goats. Their large, curved horns were fair warning to any would-be predators, and their bone-coloured fur enabled them to blend into the mountain tundra. She worried their presence might attract particularly hungry griffins, and she looked skywards to see whether Kohl was providing cover on this side.

With relief, she spied the familiar cloaked figure descending, a wave of freezing air accompanying his movements. The goats scattered, racing further down the mountainside, and Kohl swooped back up, landing on the deck of the ship with more grace than she would have expected.

'Everything clear for a good while around.' He tapped his wide-brimmed hat to Traego as he reported.

'Don't this remind you of something?' Amarah asked.

'Remind me?' Kohl said.

'Heading north towards Oren? You and me, a mountain tundra below us.' She extended her arms.

Kohl adjusted his hat and cloak, loose feathers fluttering away in the breeze. 'A little. *Otella* is a much larger ship, and there are more people to consider now.'

'How much longer, Antar?' Traego called from the ship's prow.

'Just up here,' Antar called back. 'See the haze?'

Amarah and Kohl looked over the edge of *Otella*, gazes

searching for the faint shimmer layered over the face of the mountain that gave away the Shroud's position.

Amarah's smile grew. 'Just like old times.' She tightened her grip on her scythe. Whatever this Ark was, Traego had warned them that it could be dangerous, and she had no intention of being caught off-guard. After Aciel, little scared her anymore.

All the biggest hunts had some element of danger to them. For a prize as big as this one? She wouldn't be surprised if Traego lost half his crew.

If they slowed her down, she wouldn't waste time or breath on helping them.

Antar navigated them through the haze, slowing *Otella* to almost a crawl. The hairs on her arms stood up as they passed through the *Thief's Shroud*, and she shivered.

Otella hovered for a moment, then dropped gently to land on a flat patch of ground at the bottom of the valley. As the propellers whirred slowly, Antar said, 'Safer than tryin' to climb down to it from the top. You don't wanna break your neck if you slip and fall.' The pilot folded in the ship's sails and cut the engine. 'Just gotta hike up and climb the last little bit up to the entrance. But we're through the shroud now, so no Imperial Guard'll see *Otella* if they patrol.'

Amarah shouldered her scythe and followed Traego and Antar off the ship and onto the rocky ground. She frowned, reminded of the last time she was up a mountain and what it had meant for her and her companions.

Dragons.

Antar took point, leading Traego, Amarah, and Carav ahead, with Oris trailing behind. Kohl flew with them where he could, but for the most part, he had to stay grounded. There had been a path here, once, though snow and weathering had worn most of it away.

They picked their way along in single file, careful not to twist their ankles on jutting rocks.

As the path grew steeper, they shifted to climbing up the sheer rock face, grabbing onto the pieces sticking out or holding onto holes carved into the mountains.

The wind blew stronger, but Amarah dared not look anywhere except her next hold. Kohl would not be able to catch them all if they lost their grip and slipped, and she did not want to plummet to her death before she had her chance to exact revenge on Jato.

Sweat rolled down her forehead and between her fingers. Finally, just when her hands had begun to tremble, the climb was over as she pulled herself up the last short section.

They crammed together on a narrow ledge that extended from the rock face. It had been carved of smooth grey and black stone and felt very much like the porch of a large house. It crumbled in places and cobwebs covered it in a thick layer of white. Amarah shuddered at the thought of the large spiders that dwelled at these temperatures as she swept the cobwebs away.

'What is this, Ant?' Traego asked, panting after the climb and wiping his hands on his long fur coat. His dark hair was almost black with sweat. The ledge where they stood was barely wide enough to hold three people abreast, and with the six of them huddled together, she worried one of them would topple over and fall to their death in the valley below.

'Look straight in front,' Antar replied, pressing himself against the rock so as not to lean over the ledge. He unwrapped the bandana from his forehead and wiped his cheeks and the back of his neck with it. 'Something's written.'

They turned in unison, though Amarah knew it wouldn't do her any good to look.

Traego brushed away dust from the flat rock, and the grime fell away to reveal a sealed doorway carved right into the mountain itself. Amarah could just barely make out a rectangular bronze plaque nailed into the rock above the doorway.

Traego leaned up to it and read out loud, 'Veynothi.'

2

_____

T he north of Val Sharis had always endured the Everwinter, and even though it eased somewhat in spring, the cold still seeped into Palom's bones.

The village folk and nomads who lived in this harsh landscape worked twice as hard in order to push through the weather. The north of Val Sharis shared with it the bleak Everwinter found on the northernmost islands of Linaria, and life was not for the faint-hearted.

Had Palom not been the "hero of the Ittallan," nor had a young dragon following him, the residents of Tum Metsa might have laughed at him and called him soft for being affected by the lesser spring snows. After trudging through knee-high snow and numbed by cold within just an hour, he might have been inclined to agree.

His companion, *Leillu*, as he called his dragon—meaning "Little One"—had grown over the winter and now rivalled a large cat in size. He likened the hatchling to an extremely intelligent dog—not quite Ittallan—but not a dumb beast, either.

Whether or not *Leillu* would one day grow into the god-like Sevastos, he didn't know. Even if it happened, he wouldn't change the dragon's name: *Leillu* was a term of endearment in his mother tongue, especially towards infants, and names always stuck, even if they became inappropriate.

Leillu was most useful when hunting or keeping warm through the particularly bitter nights, which Palom was grateful for. Since he had given up his *Valta Forinja*—a greatsword of unimaginable power, and the legendary creation he had searched for all his life—his heart had lightened and he'd been able to think more clearly.

Yet, without his cursed *Valta Forinja*, he had lost the armour which had kept him safe as he'd traversed the Val Sharis wilds steadily north. And he'd lost his only way to communicate with Amarah, who wielded one of his other *Valta Forinja* weapons—a scythe.

Palom knew darkness still shrouded him, but ridding himself of the cursed weapon had helped immensely, as Lathri had said it would. He was beginning to rely more on his own strengths and abilities again, rather than stealing it from their gods.

A shadow overhead thrilled him—*Leillu* had returned. Flight had come as easily as walking to the dragon; it was a master of the sky. Palom wondered whether phoenixes would come, too, as he knew they trailed adult dragons, but so far, they'd been alone.

Travelling across Val Sharis by himself had seemed like a great idea to begin with, but that had been the darkness talking. In truth, he had wanted to run away. He'd wanted to disappear, so that he would no longer disappoint people, to hide his unworthiness in the distant reaches of the Val Sharis wilds. Throwing his weapon away had made that clear, hard as it had been to accept.

He'd left his friends and allies as they set off on their

own quests, turned his back on Lathri, on his father after their reconciliation.

Shunned everyone who might have once cared for him.

The guilt ate at him, but it was easier to stomach now he didn't have the dark influence of his *Valta Forinja* smothering his thoughts and pushing him to violence.

In his heart, he'd known all along that Lathri had been right. That's why he'd been so angry about it. She'd been right, and he hadn't wanted to accept that.

Since ridding himself of the sword, the weight of darkness had lifted a little. But he still had a long way to go. And the dragon hadn't given up on him just yet, either. While *Leillu* followed him, he knew he was doing the right thing and walking the right path.

Palom took comfort in that.

He trudged through the snow, feeling it crackle underfoot, as he made his way back to Tum Metsa where he waited for Amarah.

Across his shoulder, he carried a large sack of freshly chopped logs, ready to be dried and split for firewood. The axe sat at his belt beside a short knife, and a freshly-forged, two-handed broadsword on his hip.

It had been almost a week since he'd arrived in Tum Metsa, and yet he'd not sighted Amarah once. Even the villagers, so pleased to have a hero of their country in their midst, had no knowledge of anyone fitting the sky pirate's description, nor had they seen any Arillians in their village for some years.

Mentioning Arillians created a ripple of unease among the villagers, and Palom decided not to speak of their race again. He, too, harboured a barely contained hatred towards the race, and Kohl especially, for it was his betrayal that had led to the deaths of Eryn and Anahrik.

He didn't think he'd ever be able to forgive Kohl for that sin.

But Amarah? Although she was brazen, rude, and uncouth, she was true to her word, and he'd agreed to meet her in their quest to free Moroda. He hoped it would bring back some order to the chaos that hurtled through Linaria.

However, after so many days and nights, and no sign of the sky pirate, Palom was beginning to wonder whether she was even coming. Had Amarah lied? Had it been one of her elaborate pranks to lure him to Tum Metsa and then leave him there, cackling all the while?

But why would she have said Tum Metsa, of all places? It was a village only known by those who lived there—certainly not the usual haunt of a sky pirate?

Since abandoning his *Valta Forinja* somewhere in the wilderness, Palom had survived on his *meraki* alone—the innate Ittallan magic that gave him the power to shape-shift into his true form. On his return to civilisation, he needed a weapon. The village blacksmith, Parin, had eagerly accepted Palom's request to use his forge to produce a new sword for himself. Parin had to be in his late fifties, with a twisted back that made it difficult for him to work at his trade for long stretches of time.

His son, a youth of fifteen, helped him as much as he could, and both were honoured when Palom offered to assist in the village forge in thanks for letting him use their materials to craft himself a new weapon.

As far as Palom was concerned, he was simply repaying their hospitality while he waited to meet up with Amarah. But as the days dragged past, Palom became less and less certain of his allies' meeting.

Slipping on the apron and stepping back into the heat of a blacksmith's forge had reawakened memories he had spent all winter trying to bury. With muscle memory, he worked the bellows, heated the metal, used the hammer to put shape into a block of metal and turned it into a fighting weapon.

Leillu, too, had been eager to assist. Inquisitive and curious, the dragon had confidently strode in beside him, unfazed by the rich scents and forge-smoke, and watched as Palom and Parin worked the metal. Heat, sparks, and sweat filled the air, and *Leillu* took to it as easily as flight, adding her flame into the mix, and enabled Palom to build new weapons—forged in dragon-fire, but without the enchantments of the *Valta Forinja*. He'd need another shard of a Sevastos crystal for that.

He'd thought returning to the blacksmith's forge would trigger painful memories of loss and guilt. But this forge looked, smelled, and even *felt* different to his old one in Taban Yul. Palom could tap into his experience and skill as a smith to help Parin, Karvou, and the others of Tum Metsa, while avoiding the crippling shame he felt at not being able to work with Anahrik.

Even thinking Anahrik's name brought a jolt of sadness.

At least Palom had been there when Anahrik and the others were lain to rest in Taban Yul.

Hours passed by as Palom worked, assuming Amarah would meet him at night, under cover of darkness. He left the forge with a functioning weapon and a fresh welt on his wrist from loose flame.

But there had been no Amarah.

Nor had she materialised the following day. Or the day after that.

Parin and his son, Karvou, had plenty of work to be done, and Palom was only too pleased to assist. He had no idea what Amarah's plan might have been, but without his *Valta Forinja*, had no hope of speaking with her.

He supposed he could send a messenger, but there was no way of knowing where to send the message to. Amarah had said she'd lost her airship, *Khanna*, so Palom assumed she'd be on foot. But with no trace of her in the village, nor scent of her in the air, he had no chance of tracking her down.

Plus, the snow that fell here was relentless, and covered tracks almost as quickly as they were made.

No.

He had no chance of following her, if she had even been in Tum Metsa at all.

'Palom!'

Startled, he glanced up to see one of the young lads from the village charging through the snow at full pelt. Sweat stuck his hair flat against his forehead, and he still wore his stained apron.

Palom halted in his trudge uphill, dropped the sack onto the snow beside him, and drew his sword in readiness. What in Linaria could have caused such desperation on the youth's face? He blinked, and recognised the mottled apron. It was Parin's son. 'Karvou?'

'*Pali* heard reports of Arillians from Gal Etra—that's only twenty leagues from here,' Karvou said, skidding to a halt and panting, trying to catch his breath. Dirt caked his arms and smudged his face where he'd touched it.

The youth was barely fifteen, still too young to tap into his own *meraki*, but Palom would pay fifty crowns if he wasn't a hunter. He should have had the confidence and bravado of a youth coming into independence, but instead, Palom found he had the fear of the unknown and the outside as did most people in these remote, rural villages.

After everything that had happened with Aciel, it was only natural that they would fear Arillians and the death and destruction they wrought from the sky—he of all people would know. But spotting an Arillian, even a few of them, meant nothing on its own.

He recalled Amarah's warning that Jato had been seen, and thought back to the Arillians that had attacked a pair of adult dragons before he'd even reached the far north. He'd driven them off with his *Valta Forinja* then, and had somehow lost his fear of them.

Palom looked to the sky where *Leillu* circled, low. There wasn't even a cloud to distract from the blue. 'Don't see Arillians.'

'Not here, not yet. But they were seen heading this way, five of them. The eagle saw it with his own eyes. More than we've seen since...' Karvou trailed off.

Palom shrugged. 'Thank you for warning but I will be fine. Arillians do not scare me.' Having spent so long by himself, Palom's voice sounded foreign and unused even to himself. He'd never properly mastered the common tongue —Anahrik was a fast-enough talker for that—and the broken words he used felt harder than ever to work out. He tried not to swallow too many of them to avoid miscommunication, but he doubted Karvou would even realise in his panic.

'They *should* scare you! You saw what they did in Taban Yul when they had Aciel! And Niversai, across the sea! They're still rebuilding the city, and that's their capital!' Karvou continued, almost breathless with fear and fury.

'Yes. And they did same in Great War. And what Varkain did to us centuries ago. Is nothing to worry.' Palom said, holding up his broadsword. 'I have this. I have *meraki*. I have *Leillu*,' he pointed his sword towards the sky.

'*Pali* is fond of you,' the boy continued. 'Don't want nothing bad to happen to you.'

Palom allowed himself to smile, though he shook his head. 'And I am fond of Tum Metsa. Nothing bad will happen. Come. Let us walk back to your *pali* and the forge. I will tell him this.'

Without waiting for a reply, he reshouldered his sack and continued up the slight slope and into Tum Metsa, the spring sunshine warming his neck and back. He heard the lad shift his weight from foot to foot, before he ran through the thick snow to catch up.

Adjusting his hold on the sack, Palom strode on, the snow thinner on the village streets after being trampled by so many feet. *Leillu* circled as she descended, before landing beside Palom and scurrying after him, chirping happily all the while and lashing her spiked tail.

He felt free—of guilt, rage, or sadness—and did not intend to ever lose the feeling ever again.

Karvou's words did little to stir any fear in him, even if there were Arillians on their way here.

'Who is eagle?' Palom asked, as they walked through the main street that cut through the village.

Barely eighty Ittallan lived in Tum Metsa, and Palom thought he'd met them all when he first arrived—almost everyone seemed to want to shake his hand or clap him on the back. Most were amazed a hero such as he would even bother to visit them. They'd insisted on providing him a room and food free of charge in thanks for saving them from Aciel's wrath. And of course, they'd wanted to see his *Valta Forinja*, too.

Somehow, without the cursed sword on his back, he'd found it easier to manage the crowds and constant stream of questions.

But he didn't recall seeing an eagle among them.

'He's from Gal Etra, but he's cousin to Aetos and Kylos,' Karvou said. In his excitement to be able to answer a question and tap into his knowledge, his tongue continued to wag. 'Aetos is an eagle too. His sister, Kylos, is a fox. Well, a

23

vixen, I suppose. They left here about a year ago, must've been—'

Palom drowned out the noise as the youth rabbited on. Something about the names "Aetos" and "Kylos" stood out to him. He couldn't put his finger on what it was, and that irritated him.

They followed the street as it curved into a large square. A statue of a large wolf commanded its centre, jaws open and fangs bared. Palom gave it a cursory glance as he strolled past, nodding and waving to those villagers who were hurrying around, clutching weapons and shields as though they were under attack already. It seemed the warning of Arillians had whipped them up into a frenzy.

When they reached the village's only inn, Palom dropped the sack by the front door and pounded on the thick wood.

'The firewood I promised,' he said to the Ittallan who came to enquire.

'Palom! Thank you so much. You really didn't need to!'

'I promised I would. It should help for few more days,' Palom said. He carried on across the square to the loudest, dirtiest building of the whole village—the forge. Before they'd even made it halfway across the square, Palom heard the tell-tale hammering of metal against metal.

When Palom and Karvou entered the forge, they found Parin had halted in his work to talk to a customer who'd brought in a small knife that had been dented. From the gist of the conversation, Palom could tell the customer was furious the metal had bent at all.

'I don't use it for much more than work round my home!' The customer said, her voice pitched in anger. 'I'm not travelling all the way to Taban Yul every time I need a knife that works!'

Parin shook his head and ran a hand through his sooty

24

hair as he took the dented knife and inspected it through his round glasses. 'Leave it with me and I'll get it fixed.'

'By when?'

'I'll have it back to you in a couple of days. You can't rush these things.'

'A couple of days? What am I supposed to use until then? What if the Arillians attack? How am I supposed to defend myself?' Her shrill voice cut through Palom and he struggled to hold in an irritated growl.

He flushed as sweat beaded on his brow. Palom deduced it had little to do with the heat of the forge and stepped up. 'If Arillians attack, a belt knife won't protect you.'

The customer rounded on Palom without hesitation. 'Mind your own business, tiger!'

Palom narrowed his eyes. 'I am working in this forge with Parin. It *is* my business. If you want protection against anything, buy a sword.'

'I don't *want* a sword!' she shrieked.

Leillu, clearly rattled by her aggressive tone, let out a low hiss in response, tail lashing.

'And I don't want that lizard in the forge, either!' She continued, 'You've heard what they've been doing up and down the country? Burning towns and villages! What's to stop that one doing the same?' She pointed an accusatory finger at *Leillu*, who continued to hiss.

Palom sighed. He presumed her irrational fear of Arillians and dragons had caused her ridiculous behaviour. He had little patience at the best of times, but this woman was really trying his temper. 'If you want knife so badly, take mine.' He unsheathed it and held it out to her. 'I forged it myself. You know its quality and strength.'

She scowled back, as though furious he'd robbed her of a verbal fight with Parin. She snatched it from his hands and glanced it over. 'Why do I want something that's *used*?'

'I forged it when I arrived. Six days ago. I have been chopping wood since. It is new.'

She rolled her eyes and then weighed it in her hand. Clearly finding no fault with the workmanship, she attached it to her own belt and then wrapped her fur-lined cloak over herself. 'This will *have* to do, then. You need to buck up your ideas, Parin! I hope your son is better than you or Tum Metsa will never have any decent weapons again!' With a huff, she whirled around and marched out of the forge.

'I'm sorry, Palom. You didn't have to give up your own knife for her,' Parin said. He hurried forward to help Palom out of his cloak and brush snow from it.

'I am blacksmith. I will make new knife,' Palom said nonchalantly. 'Everyone will be wanting more knives and axes if your messenger speaks true.'

'You don't seem bothered by the warning?' Parin said, hanging up Palom's cloak and returning to his forge to check on the flame.

'I do not fear Arillians. Like I said to Karvou. I can fight.'

Parin licked his lips and wiped his brow with his forearm. 'Yes. But the Arillians are hunting dragons now. Normally they'd leave us alone, but...'

Palom didn't need to hear the rest of the words to understand Parin's meaning.

The villagers of Tum Metsa may have enjoyed having a so-called hero in their midst, but if it brought trouble down on their heads, they wouldn't hesitate to throw him out. It wasn't even as though he still had his *Valta Forinja* for them to admire. Palom hated the idea of *Leillu* causing them trouble and wondered whether Jato's Arillians would even bother with a young hatchling.

Parin coughed, his mouth opening to say something, then he thought better of it and inspected his fire instead, his eyes unreadable.

Leillu happily trotted after him, then leaped onto the table, sending hammers and chisels flying.

'What is matter?' Palom asked, plucking his apron from a hook on the wall, but not yet fastening it around himself.

The older blacksmith ruffled his son's hair and avoided Palom's eyes. 'There's a caravan heading south. To Taban Yul.'

Palom tilted his head but didn't interrupt.

After a pointed silence, Parin continued, 'It's villagers going to see their relatives in the capital. After Sapora's dragon burned half the city, they're sending supplies, messages, themselves. The Varkain King won't send reliable messengers, and the skies are too dangerous now with dragons and Arillians for any of us who can fly to make the trip.'

Palom read between the lines easily. 'You want me to go?'

Parin scratched behind his ear, almost guilty. 'It's Karvou. Tum Metsa is exposed. We're open to attack, here.'

'You think Karvou will be safer in capital?' Palom rehung the apron and folded his arms. Clearly he wasn't going to be doing any work in the forge today.

'Yes, I do.' Parin looked at him. 'Arillians won't attack the capital, not while Sapora has that dragon to heel. And you can take care of him better than I can, with this bad back.' He stretched and winced to prove his point.

Palom frowned.

'And...you could protect the caravan, too. You're well known. Just your presence will keep bandits off them.' Parin's voice sped up. 'And you have a dragon, too. Maybe the King will look upon you favourably if he hears of your arrival.'

Palom doubted Sapora would much care, but he decided against voicing his concerns.

'You'll be paid for your help. The village Archigo asked me about it this morning.'

'So this is pre-planned. Get rid of me.' Palom couldn't keep the hurt from his voice.

'No, no! We have to do what's right by us. This is right by my boy.' Parin held Karvou close in a half-hug. 'This is for you.' He passed Palom a small pouch, the coins within clinking. 'And you're welcome to take any weapons with you for the journey. Anything you like. No cost.'

Taban Yul. Another city he'd run away from. He'd left his lover, he'd left his niece, he'd left his father. He wondered what they would think of him, returning after months away without the great weapon that had made him a hero. Thinking about it, they'd probably still think he was a hero, *Valta Forinja* or no. Palom didn't know how he felt about that.

Leillu looked up, having sniffed every inch of the blacksmith's bench, her tail swinging gently from side to side. She chirped once.

'You think of nothing but food and sleep,' Palom scolded. Then, he looked to Parin. 'I have no choice in this. I will guard your caravan to Taban Yul.'

Parin dropped his shoulders as he relaxed. 'And...one other thing?'

Palom had been about to leave the forge when he looked back at the smith. 'Yes?'

'I'm too weak to train Karvou properly. I'm going to miss his *meraki* when he comes of age. I want to know he's taken care of. That he has a future.' His voice trembled as he gave words to a concrete decision.

'Yes?' Palom repeated.

Parin swallowed. 'I want to ask if you would take him on. As your apprentice.'

Palom held the man's pleading gaze. He had no intention

28

of taking on another apprentice—all his problems had come from trying to look after those around him, and the shame he felt when he failed.

But he understood the father's wish to protect his son. He could get him to Taban Yul, but an apprentice was a step too far.

So, he lied to protect Parin from further pain. 'I will do this.'

Then he left the forge, *Leillu* trailing behind him.

PALOM MADE his way back to the village square, and took a wide, meandering path that led to the outskirts of the village. Several large houses had been built from wood where the village Archigo and most highly-ranked villagers lived. The wide, flat area in front of their houses was a bustle of activity. Villagers carried supplies from the houses and village to the half-loaded wagons and strapped them down, ready for the long journey south.

Since arriving in Tum Metsa, Palom had chopped wood, rebuilt houses, unfrozen wells, and repaired weapons, but he'd always felt it was never quite enough, and had wished he could do more.

Today, it seemed, his wish had been granted.

The Ittallan who scrambled about to hurriedly load the wagons mostly ignored him, too intent on their own tasks. Palom counted eight wagons, all of which were covered with thick canopies to protect their contents from the elements. Several aurochs had been tied to them, no doubt commanded by an Ittallan of similar blood, for the great beasts were wild and used for food, not work.

'Ah, Palom. You received my message.'

He glanced away from the caravan to see a tall woman

stride towards him, unfazed by the snow. It was Archigo Dentra, the village elder. She'd run Tum Metsa for the past forty years and reminded Palom of an oak tree—ancient and unbending. 'Not that I don't appreciate all you've done for us,' she said.

Palom shook his head. 'I was only repaying your kindness for offering me shelter.'

Dentra nodded, her wispy hair blowing in the breeze. She watched the villagers work. They weren't just loading the wagons; many of them would be trekking south, too. Palom knew they were a hardy bunch, well-used to surviving against the elements, but he had little hope they'd fare well against a direct Arillian assault, even if he was there to help them fight.

Bandits and thieves along the way, opportunists, he could deal with by reputation alone. But an attack from the air? He didn't much fancy their chances. At least *he* could get to cover. Could disappear if needed. But a whole caravan of wagons and villagers? It'd be tough.

Regardless, it seemed he had little choice.

Without Amarah or Kohl, he had no need to be all the way out in Tum Metsa, cut off from the rest of Val Sharis. Returning to the capital, to get close to Sapora again and see if the news of his dragon was true.

And put a stop to it, if he could.

'They want to leave as soon as everything's loaded. Does that suit you? Or will you need to catch them up?' She asked, blunt and to the point.

'I can leave now,' he said. 'Parin is sending his son, too.'

She raised an eyebrow. 'Karvou? Well, I can't say as I'm surprised. It's no life here for a youth like him. He'll be able to make more of a life for himself in the city.'

Palom was stunned at her words.

As though sensing his astonishment, she continued,

'Tum Metsa is an old village. We'll still be here when the world ends, working the land and surviving through the Everwinter. It isn't right for those who still have their whole lives ahead to be trapped here. You ought to know that.'

He shrugged. He thought a life of chopping wood, building weapons, and hunting sounded perfectly acceptable.

But there was no Lathri here.

He scratched his head, coming to understand her sentiment. 'Any news from Taban Yul?'

'Nothing we can reliably take. Sapora has a dragon. A Sevastos. Rebels attacked him, and he retaliated in fire. I just hope the whole city hasn't been taken over by Varkain by the time you arrive.' Bitterness rang clear in her words. 'I don't know what'll become of Val Sharis under him. I thought the Princess Isa could keep his violence under control. But I suppose he is too much even for her.'

Palom recalled Princess Isa—despite her relation to the Varkain, he knew she cared for the Ittallan and cared for the country of her people.

He sighed. As the villagers prepared to travel towards the capital, Palom hoped his princess had not been caught in Sapora's slaughter.

3

Isa squeezed her eyes shut in the hopes of drowning out the screams that drifted through the palace from the dungeons.

Tacio, her half-brother, seemed to have made it his mission to cause misery and torment everywhere he went, and had argued that it was is right as Head of the Cerastes to do as he wished to prisoners of the crown.

It was the same thing, every morning, every afternoon, every evening.

She'd thought Tacio would grow bored of the "sport," as he called it, but he seemed to have a knack for thinking up new and interesting ways to elicit fear and pain from his prisoners. But despite his brutal methods, and to Isa's continual wonder, he could not break Lathri.

Lathri had provided no more information on this day than she had the morning before.

Thrice, Isa had asked Tacio to cease his torture of Lathri —a well-known and liked healer in one of the city's districts known as Little Yomal—and thrice she'd been laughed at, pushed out of the way, and told to leave if she couldn't stomach what needed to be done to keep their land safe from usurpers and would-be vigilantes.

What kind of queen did she hope to be if she couldn't handle the punishment that went with the title?

Isa forced herself to stay in the cell with Lathri while she was tortured. It happened most mornings, and though it was almost unbearable, she had to stay. After all, Lathri's capture had been her fault. She'd betrayed her half-brothers and joined Lathri's resistance against them.

She'd been caught with rebels trying to free Lathri from the dungeons, and had saved her own skin by claiming to have apprehended the intruders. It was deceitful, she knew, but it was also the only reason *she*, too, was not on the receiving end of Tacio's torture. Of course, Tacio still suspected her, and it took every bit of wit and skill to keep him from discovering the truth: that she had betrayed her half-brother, the king, and joined the rebel movement against him.

Lathri had been captive for two weeks, now, and her torture had ramped up following the failed escape attempt. Isa had done her best to help with the rescue mission, but Tacio was too sharp, his reactions too swift, and he'd managed to leap into action before the break-out could gain any traction.

Within minutes, the palace had swarmed with elite Varkain guards—Cerastes—loyal to the king's half-brother, and it had all been Isa could manage to do to help them get away before being caught herself with another rebel called Kylos.

Thankfully, the Cerastes had not seen her involvement, but Tacio viewed her with even more suspicion than before, and now, Isa couldn't leave the palace without having her movements watched.

She remained on watch in a corner of the cell, trying desperately not to look at Lathri.

'Don't lie to me. It's treason to lie to royalty, you know. I'll sever your pretty head from your body.' Tacio twirled a small hatchet in his right hand, and Lathri's face and arms bore the marks of his latest tool of persuasion—as he called them. Isa had to admire Lathri's resilience.

If she'd been on the receiving end of Tacio's blade, she knew she'd have given up everything by now. Thank Rhea their positions weren't reversed.

'I have...nothing more to tell you.' Lathri's arms were chained to the wall behind her back, and she knelt on the cold, stone floor in a puddle of her own blood and urine. Her unkempt hair was loose and knotted as it fell about her shoulders in limp waves, and her skin was sullen, lacking the lustre Isa had always seen on the healer.

But despite her skeletal appearance, Lathri would not break.

And Tacio was not permitted to kill her, so at their painful impasse, they waited for Tacio to grow bored, or King Sapora to release her.

Until then, Isa remained by her side in the mornings—partly for moral support, and partly for Tacio to have fewer suspicions of her—kept Tacio in check as much as she could and hoped to discover an opportunity to get the leader of the rebels away in one piece.

But, after so many days, even Isa's resolve was wavering, and she looked away as Tacio marked Lathri's elbow with a particularly deep gash, and spilled fresh blood.

'My gut tells me you're still not giving up what you ought to give up.' Tacio crouched in front of her, using the bottom of the hatchet to lift Lathri's chin so he could look her in the eye.

Isa shuddered. The Varkain spoke in a lazy drawl, as

34

though he had better things to do than his appointed tasks. Tacio had removed his rings and rolled up the sleeves of his jacket to save them getting dirtied by blood or grime, and his perfectly slicked back hair showed nothing out of place.

He let out a low hiss, and though Isa couldn't see his face, she wouldn't be surprised if he'd extended his jaw to show off the double row of ivory fangs.

Tacio delighted in his power and the terror he caused.

Lathri remained defiant, her mouth pressed into a thin line despite the pain that must have wracked her body.

The other two Cerastes stood still and silent in the corners of the cell. Isa glanced to them and shuddered at their impassive faces.

'I'll admit, you've done well to deny my questions. But I think a new tact, perhaps,' Tacio spoke again. He stared at Lathri, but she remained guarded. Tacio snorted, then turned his head slightly to speak to the Cerastes behind his right shoulder. 'Bring her in.'

Isa's eyes widened. This was new.

This was unexpected.

Her heart raced as she looked to the door, where the Cerastes stationed nearest exited the cell. For several long moments, Isa was only aware of her pulse in her ears. She forced her breathing to remain slow, lest Tacio picked up on her panic, and she hardly dared look when the Cerastes re-entered the cell with another person in tow.

'Lathri!' The newcomer screamed, as soon as she caught sight of her.

Isa froze.

It was Kylos.

From her disheveled looks, she'd been man-handled a bit, but otherwise seemed unharmed.

Isa glanced back to Tacio and flinched. His eyes were

locked onto hers. She whispered a quick prayer to Rhea that he'd not seen her reaction.

Her heart pounded harder, and she realised he could probably hear that, too.

She swallowed and held her gaze to his as the Cerastes pushed Kylos towards him.

'You're dismissed,' Tacio said, finally looking to the two Cerastes and standing up to face Kylos.

As soon as Kylos was out of the Cerastes' grip, she widened her stance, glaring at Tacio as light engulfed her body. Isa stood as Kylos used her *meraki*, her limbs shortening and body lengthening as she transformed. Within a few seconds, a vixen stood proud on the cell floor, ears back and teeth bared. She wasted no time, crouching then leaping forward to attack Tacio with a snarl.

Perhaps in any other palace, in any other cell, the growl would have brought a dozen guards running. But in the royal palace of Taban Yul, home to King Sapora and his half-brother, nothing stirred.

Tears threatened to spill, but Isa forced them back. She wasn't allowed to.

She couldn't give away her allegiance.

'I'll ask you again. Who gave the order for the rebel attack on the palace? Who flaunts their treasonous actions in Niversai? How many rebels have joined the cause?' Tacio asked, darting left and right, keeping easy reach out of the vixen's lunges, his movements almost lazy.

Isa had grown up knowing the Varkain, and her trained eyes and heightened senses enabled her to keep track of him, but his speed frightened her even so.

He was just delaying the inevitable.

Isa screamed internally for Kylos to flee. To run and make her escape.

'I don't know, Lord Tacio,' Lathri replied, her head

drooping low even as Tacio retaliated to Kylos's attacks, nicking the vixen with his hatchet here and there.

Isa leapt back as the two fought, charging around the small cell and knocking into weapons, keys, and buckets, sending everything flying. She watched Tacio grow suddenly bored of the game and make his move, darting forward and plunging the weapon into Kylos's thigh, dropping her.

The princess had seen death and battle before, dealt a lot of it herself, but attacking in cold blood made her sick.

Lathri wailed as Kylos whimpered on the floor, and Isa's heart bled for her, for her situation, and for how little she could do to help.

She looked to Kylos and half-rose to her.

The vixen shuddered as she transformed back, screaming as she clutched at the hatchet embedded in her right thigh. Tears streamed from her eyes, and she looked up, as though noticing the princess for the first time.

Isa whirled around and strode towards the door.

Tacio had had his fill. He'd leave Lathri alone until the next morning, she hoped. 'I need some fresh air.'

Throwing herself at the door, she shoved it open and raced along the corridors of the lower palace, running past stationed guards and nobility—both Ittallan and Varkain— as she sought to escape from Tacio's torture.

She didn't understand how Sapora could let it happen. She supposed he thought an entertained Tacio was easier to manage than a bored Tacio. They didn't have thralls in Val Sharis as they did in Sereth, and it appeared Tacio was creating his own blood sports to fill in the gaps, in the guise of serving the king.

Neither of her half-brothers had lived up to her expectations since coming to power, and she grew more fearful of them with every day that passed.

Sapora.

Some king he was. He spent half his waking time in the palace libraries, poring over tomes and bringing up books on the histories of the Varkain and the legendary Arks, and the other half, stalking through Taban Yul to spy on his subjects personally.

She shivered as she ascended a flight of stairs. This was not their agreement.

This had never been the plan.

Yet, everything she had wanted—acceptance and power —was both hers and not hers. Regret burned deeply in her breast and she tried to push it away. Her emotions fuelled her, and she loped up the stairs three at a time.

She pushed through the door at the top of the stairs and stepped into sunlight seeping through the stained glass windows. It was one of the long halls that connected two parts of the palace together, and had been lined with tapestries of past kings and queens. To the left, the hangar lay mostly empty and still, having not replenished the warships lost in the siege against Aciel. To the right, she could enter the main palace and either steal into the kitchens, her rooms, or perhaps make her way to the top of one of the many towers.

Isa took a moment to gather herself and regain her composure. She was a princess. She was of royal blood. And yet the terror which filled her veins in Tacio's presence turned her into what she feared she really was—a scared little girl who had no right to rule.

She walked to the left, her eyes drawn to the elaborate tapestries hanging on the wall. Sapora's tapestry was obviously missing, the blank space where it had been, standing out like a sore thumb. She paused and looked up to the empty wall, one thumb nail between her teeth as she pushed her fear away.

In her mind's eye, she could see her own portrait there, as the Val Sharis Queen.

There hadn't been a queen for eight generations, and she'd desperately wanted to fill that space. It had been all she and Sapora had talked about whenever he'd visited her as a prince. He'd scowled when she'd told him of the teasing she endured at the hands of the Goldstones in the palace. She was a bastard, the offspring of some silly Ittallan woman who'd bedded the Varkain King after he'd conquered their country.

What right did a bastard have to live in the palace?

Why should she have access to her people's coin and luxury, when she should be on the streets like the verminous cat she was.

If she'd been fathered by anyone else. A random Varkain. A drunkard Ittallan. She'd never so much as set foot within the palace's walls.

And now she was trying to enforce her claim to power? To the throne?

Preposterous.

Even the Council had dismissed her.

It had only been through their fear of the Varkain King, Vasil, that she'd grown up in the lap of luxury, and only through the continuing fear of Sapora, that she'd remained at all.

Even now, the memories pained her.

After everything she and Sapora had been through, after everything they'd promised each other, he was turning his back on her in his own pursuit for power and legends.

'I hope you're suffering from the spring flowers, dear sister. It's most unlike you to cry.'

Isa whirled around at the cool voice.

She hadn't heard Sapora approach. Hadn't been aware anyone had been nearby.

He wore gold at his throat and wrists in contrast to the black and grey tailored vest, its cut worked to show off his leanness.

Isa saw a hint of his true form every time she glanced at him, and suppressed her fear. She shook her head. Lying to Sapora was not the same as lying to Tacio. He knew her too well, and could see through all her fibs. 'The torture was too much.'

Sapora narrowed his eyes. 'Tacio can get carried away, I suppose.'

She wiped away any residue of water on her face.

'I was on my way to speak with him, actually. Is he still...occupied?'

Isa shrugged. 'He'll be done now, I'm sure. Is something wrong?'

'Vasil wishes to come to Taban Yul.'

That was unusual. Their father preferred the tunnels in Sereth to Val Sharis. 'Oh,' she said.

Sapora exhaled through his nose. 'Summercourt. Apparently it's not something I can argue against.'

Isa swallowed. If Sapora hated the tradition, it would be doubly bad for her. Especially as her Varkain blood didn't show in any of her features. At best, she'd be ignored. At worst, it would be like her childhood all over again, except with her father's snakes biting at her.

'Must he?' she asked, a note of desperation in her voice.

Sapora nodded.

Perhaps Summercourt would keep Tacio occupied long enough to work out an escape plan for Lathri, Kylos, and the other rebels that her brothers had captured.

If they were lucky.

'I'll leave you to speak with him, then,' she said, excusing herself and darting past Sapora lest he deduced what she was planning.

Isa was light on her feet, her wildcat *meraki* giving her a swiftness most could only dream of, and she was at the top of the palace tower before she even realised where her feet had carried her. The windows were wide open, although most were just holes through which those small enough could slip through, and she glimpsed the city below in the rising sun.

How many thousands of people had their lives upheaved and destroyed because of the power-hungry greed of Sapora and Tacio?

Ittallan who'd lived in the city for generations had been uprooted by Varkain emigrating from Sereth to the richest city in Linaria. Sapora had torn up trade agreements and written new ones, and when met with challenges, Tacio and his Cerastes would quieten them. Tacio was even worse than Sapora—a full-blooded Varkain with an ego to match his royal blood, he undermined Sapora and Isa at every opportunity. But Sapora believed keeping their half-brother close was better than letting him run riot in Sereth while Sapora attempted to establish a new order in Val Sharis.

And, of course, that was to say nothing of those who'd burned in the Sevastos' fire at Sapora's command when the palace had been under attack by Imperial ships turned rogue by Lathri's rebels.

She had been the one who'd written to Morgen.

She'd implored him to turn against Sapora, to put an end to the suffering he'd caused her people.

To put an end to his quest to bring back the Arks.

As she reached the roof of the tower, Isa climbed up the last few stairs and stepped out into the cool spring air. The wind was strong so high up, and a tickle ran along her bare arms as she saw the world open up all around her. Normally, she'd have transformed and skulked around the city until sleep brought her back and she could forget everything she'd seen Tacio do—at least for a while.

But Taban Yul still bore the fresh scars of dragon-fire, and that would take months to heal. Seeing her marble streets blackened, statues toppled and homes burned out or melted, pained her as though she'd been the one to endure the flames.

When Sapora had released the Sevastos, she could hardly believe it. Even now, looking at the blackened streets and buildings, it felt like a dream. A nightmare.

She'd not turned her back on Sapora to join the rebels, but had also turned her back on them to save herself when Tacio caught them.

Now, she had no-one to turn to, no-one who didn't view her with suspicion because of her fear and selfishness.

Today, she needed to get away.

Stepping off the edge of the tower, Isa dropped to the battlements some ten feet below. She landed in a crouch and sprang back, stepping forward and past the Cerastes on watch duty. It had been bizarre to see Varkain in the red and gold livery of the Imperial Guard. Their uniforms may have shouted Imperial Guard, but they reported to Tacio first and foremost.

They knew of her excursions and she often brought them gold or trinkets to keep them from running their mouths to Tacio—an arrangement she disliked, but was far safer than having Varkain trail her through the city, or beyond.

Picking her way along the battlements, Isa leapt and climbed from wall to wall, tower to tower, until she reached the tower on the north side of the palace, where her own rooms were hidden within. Scaling the wall, she clambered up and onto the wide, flat roof, where she'd parked her two greatest treasures: two small, swift, single-seater airships.

They were class fives, built for speed, and gave her a sense of freedom she'd sorely lacked since Sapora had come to power.

It was funny how he'd taken her freedom then given it back.

Of course, she'd leant him one of her ships when he'd asked, and he'd used it to investigate one of the Arks he'd been convinced was in Val Sharis, but true to his word, he'd returned it again to her once he was finished with it.

Before she got into one of her ships, she looked over Taban Yul once again. The initial shock of the new king and regime was settling, and though there was still a great disturbance—which she blamed herself for in enlisting Morgen's help to use warships against the palace—the citizens were able to get on with their lives and trade. At least, until another of Sapora's new rules went into effect.

And now Summercourt was coming?

That, too, would give the citizens respite, at least.

Isa shuddered suddenly, worried what Tacio might have gleaned from her in the dungeons.

As much as she wished to get into one of her ships and fly away, she knew she shouldn't. She couldn't run from her responsibilities. Many of those still loyal to Lathri lived in the city, and they'd need to know about Summercourt.

They'd also be expecting her to report back on what was happening to Lathri, Kylos, and the other captured rebels. Isa knew they were tallying up those friends and comrades who had been killed at Tacio's fangs, and she knew many of them would hold her personally responsible.

She didn't blame them.

After all, she was free to move about as she pleased, while they'd been forced into hiding lest Tacio or his Cerastes caught them.

It would be futile to explain she was a prisoner in her own palace.

Convincing them that she wasn't in league with her brothers was an impossible task, so she'd opted for ignoring their accusations and keeping to her side of the bargain as much as she could. Keeping them updated, and working out when and how they could free the captured rebels.

She sat on the tower's roof, her legs dangling over the side as she watched the city move about its day. A shadow passed over her, and she glanced up to see the Sevastos.

Isa braced herself at the blast of wind from its beating wings washed over her. The dragon, her brother's slave in all but name, appeared to have returned from a hunt. The Sevastos was one of the oldest creatures in Linaria, certainly the most powerful, and Sapora treated it like a trained dog. Seeing a creature as old and powerful as that, as strong as the Goddess Rhea herself, always took Isa's breath away. Its immense wings brought night prematurely to Taban Yul, guarding the city from any who might threaten it, or Sapora. A god bound to the Varkain by an ancient pact.

And Sapora wouldn't divulge the details of how.

He was far too clever for that. He wouldn't trust anyone with that knowledge, least of all her.

Even she was mesmerised by the dragon's power, and yet Sapora still quested for the Arks. All she knew was that Sapora hungered for information on them more than anything she'd ever known.

Her mind wandered back to Kylos and the hatchet in her leg. Isa admired the Ittallan's determination and strength, her fearlessness in the face of the snake's jaws. She deserved better than what Tacio gave her. Lathri deserved better.

With Sapora's obsession over the Arks, and even a fleet of warships incapable of standing up to the Sevastos, Isa feared there was nothing that could touch him. And it was madness to think he could bring back the Arks, those ancient weapons.

It was impossible.

The Sevastos suddenly let out a bellow that carried over the city and goosebumps rose on Isa's arms as the sound washed over her.

Perhaps not so impossible.

Sapora could do it, if anyone could. The realisation of his obsession stirred a primal fear deep within her. He was family. He had always stood by her, when everyone else walked over her, pushed her around, or treated her as if she were invisible. She'd never had cause to doubt Sapora, or his intentions, and everything had gone exactly the way he'd said it would.

But now? All they'd planned had been what needed to happen to get him into power. This was beyond anything they'd discussed. Ant Tacio was another spanner in the works.

Of the three siblings, he was the most vicious, the most power-hungry, the most wild. Sapora was cool and calm— she'd only ever seen him lose his temper once. Tacio, however? Everyone walked on eggshells around him, and she was sure he and Sapora would come to blows before too long. Or perhaps she would.

A shame that Sapora needed him to retain the support of the Varkain.

For all the power at his control, Sapora's hold on his throne was tenuous at best.

And it wasn't enough. It would never be enough.

Sapora had wanted to be king of not only Sereth, as was his birthright, but to move his power to Val Sharis and build a greater legacy than Vasil, their father and warrior-king. Yet at every turn he was rebuffed if not by his people, then by the Ittallan, and if not by the Ittallan, then their

Council and Goldstones, and if not by them, then by Tacio.

No matter what he did, how great, how terrifying, it was never enough.

The Arks would bridge that gap, she could see his thinking, but surely that would be too much? Where did you draw the line when you were forging ahead into the unknown?

If it was respect and admiration that Sapora craved, he was going to shatter all chance of earning that if he continued on this path and succeeded.

She sighed and ran a hand through her hair, loosening her braids. She'd promised to help Lathri in her resistance, and help free her, but the palace was too well-guarded. And even if by some miracle she did free her and they escaped with their life, then what? She was Princess Isa of Val Sharis —her home *was* the palace. She'd have nowhere to run to— hiding underground with a group of mismatched rebels wasn't a long-term plan.

Of all the power she had, it paled in comparison to Sapora's. She was in an inescapable corner.

And of course, by far the worst of her problems, was Aciel—whatever was left of him. Sapora knew it too, and claimed that was what drove him to seek out the Arks and restore them. Aciel: the Arillian conqueror who'd brought war and bloodshed to her land, who now lay sealed in the crystal from Moroda's Sevastos on the edge of Taban Yul.

The crystal had darkened over the months since his entrapment, and even the most thuggish of Cerastis refused to stand near it for fear they'd be brought to their knees by intense pain. Blood would pour from their mouths and noses, and they'd die in a crumpled heap.

Those strong enough to withstand whatever Arillian magic was killing the others would slowly lose their minds,

46

disobeying orders and seemingly deaf and blind to all around them. Worse, it affected those living and working in the city, prompting Sapora to evacuate the districts nearest the crystal.

In life, Aciel had the power of compulsion. Now, his powers were seeping out from his grave. Sapora hadn't reacted, but had simply taken note of the reports from Tacio's Cerastes.

Moroda's peaceful end to the fighting—her sacrifice—had only delayed the inevitable. Sealing away did not mean dead and gone.

And that notion fuelled Sapora's quest to find and resurrect the Arks.

4

Amarah followed Traego down the tunnel, keeping about three paces behind him. He held a torch high, flames lighting only a short way ahead and leaving the majority of the cramped tunnel in pitch dark.

Unease tugged at her, and her heart pumped a little faster than she would have liked. Regardless of how valuable Traego said the Ark they hunted was, her blood ran cold in the darkness.

Mountain caves and tunnels were natural things with uneven rock and irregular formations. But this tunnel seemed too smooth, too regimented, as though it had been deliberately carved into the rock. Their steps echoed cleanly, bouncing off the floor and walls and making it sound as though a small army trampled down the steadily narrowing tunnel.

Her gut had never been wrong before, and she'd been in plenty of dangerous places in the twenty years or so she'd been a sky pirate. From Goldstone manor houses to small castles, jungles to deserts, she'd scaled the breadth of Linaria in her continuing hunt for gold and that which would earn her more coin.

But there was something about this tunnel that chilled her to the bone.

It was almost as if they were walking down the gullet of some enormous, ancient predator.

Unwilling to show any fear to her allies, Amarah took a tight-lipped approach and even stopped berating the two youths who accompanied them. Kohl brought up the rear, but the Arillian was as stoic as ever, and even she couldn't tell his true thoughts about being in this place.

The tunnel was cool, shielded from the biting mountain wind, but it reminded Amarah of a crypt more than anything else, especially with their lengthening shadows on the walls.

And if it was, whose crypt exactly were they walking into?

Despite the sense of dread which grew with each step, Amarah breathed out her fear and slipped back into the familiarity of treasure hunting, taking her cues from Traego as the troupe moved together silently, as a single unit. Only Kohl stood out as not being part of their crew, but she'd seen him bring a dragon down single-handedly, and had no concerns about him should they find themselves in a brawl.

'Veynothi. It's an ancient name,' Kohl said after a time, almost making Amarah jump. He trailed behind them, just on the border of the torchlight. 'A thousand years old. Perhaps two?'

Amarah glanced back at him, curious as to what he might know, but too on edge to give words to her thoughts.

Kohl continued, 'A phantom, that's what it is. The most powerful creatures in all Linaria.' His voice wavered slightly.

Traego and the others said nothing in response, though their pace slowed as the tunnel curled round to the left. Captain Traego was a master at hiding his emotions and masking his expression. He'd always been laid-back, with a

49

carefree attitude to life. And he was an incredible talker. But Amarah could sense his unease. To see him quiet meant this was serious.

Her stomach tightened at Kohl's words, and the younger troupe members, Carav and Oris, giggled nervously.

The Arillian continued, as though their silence invited further explanation. 'As old as the ice golems. Amarah, I do not think we—any of us—should be here.' He sent a gentle breeze of cold air along the tunnel, causing their flames to flicker.

Traego halted. 'This treasure'll make us richer than any Goldstone. All the pirates in Estoria, Val Sharis, heck, in all of Linaria would be on their way here if they knew where *here* was.'

Amarah raised an eyebrow.

'Antar's message is less than a fortnight old, and I got Antar here,' Traego continued. 'So, we got a head-start on whoever else wants a piece o' this pie. Be good ta split it between us. But everyone wants this all for 'emself, so we gotta be first.'

'Traego...' Kohl whispered.

'Our lot ain't the most...well, there's plenty nasty pirates out there. We don't want one o' them gettin' their fingers on this prize. Rhea knows what could happen if they do. Basir, Ipot, even Cyd would be a problem.'

Amarah glowered as Traego reeled off of the pirate captains. She had vivid memories attached to each one. She kept her eyes on Kohl as she tried to read his expression. If the Arillian wanted to reply, he gave no indication. He bowed his head to Traego and made no move to stop him when he continued to lead them on.

Her stomach was in knots—adrenaline in anticipation of a life's work in one haul, the uncertainty of what they sought, and terror at what might happen if any of their rivals were to get hold of it—whatever *it* was. There'd be no flying off into the sunset for them. No. They'd lay waste to Estoria, kill any rivals, and claim the tropical paradise as their own private playground.

And yet Kohl made out like the Ark, Veynothi, was a creature, if not a person.

How could a whole person be treasure?

Traego hadn't mentioned anything about a kidnapping, and he knew she didn't roll with that, anyway. Perhaps that's why he'd been so shady when she'd pressed him for answers.

But something ancient?

Something kept in what looked suspiciously like a crypt?

A sudden wave of panic rose in her gut, and Amarah clenched her stomach against it.

She licked her lips and thought of the new ship she'd get once this hunt was over. It was the only way she could distract herself from the fear which gnawed at her. Her scythe flashed a wave of blue light as though in response and she smacked the bottom of it on the tunnel floor, the crack echoing all around her.

The sharp noise always comforted her, reminded her she wasn't alone, and of course this particular weapon was unlike any other. Forged by master blacksmiths Palom and Anahrik in response to Aciel, they'd managed to use the power of dragons to enhance it a hundred-fold and bestow it with enchanted powers. The *Valta Forinja*.

Her scythe glowed pale blue in the dark, a trick that had come in useful during her travels, and saved her holding a torch.

Quite how Palom had managed to tap into Linaria's greatest power, she wasn't sure, nor did she care to know the details. It had kept her safe against the Arillians during their attack, and in every battle she'd fought since.

Almost.

She thought of hunting down Jato and making her pay for what she'd done to *Khanna*. For what she'd done to her.

The tunnel narrowed suddenly, their path blocked by a stone door.

The group set to work without orders or pre-amble, attempting to heave the door open—she and Traego on one side, Antar and Oris on the other, with Kohl and Carav ready to react if anything jumped out to attack them. When their shoulders proved fruitless, Amarah used her scythe as leverage, the blade channelling power as a force that she felt through her fingers.

The door came suddenly loose with a worrying crunch, pebbles and dust falling out from the walls surrounding it as the hinges disintegrated at the touch of her *Valta Forinja*.

She leapt back, weapon at the ready. Without both eyes, her peripheral vision had reduced, and she felt truly vulnerable for the first time since her fight with Jato. Desperation kept her there.

Traego and Antar tried to lower the stone door gently, but it fell from their hands and crashed to the tunnel floor. Amarah flinched at the noise and dust, terrified they'd announced their presence to everyone within fifty leagues of the cave. Her *Valta Forinja* pulsed and sent out a flash of blue light, responding to her terror.

They all froze, waiting with bated breath in case anyone —or anything—approached them after their loud entrance. But aside from the settling dust, the tunnel was as quiet as it had been when they entered, though Amarah was sure the others could hear the pounding of her heart.

She swallowed.

A long minute passed.

Traego breathed out. 'Let's go.' His voice was barely above a whisper, as though speaking aloud would bring the whole tunnel collapsing upon them. 'Here, Amarah. I'll teach ya a new lesson. The real riches come from ancient treasures, not the modern trinkets ya're used ta thieving.'

The captain's voice had picked up. He was excited.

It did little to still the adrenaline coursing through her, but she followed him into the dark room. Antar, Carav, Oris, and Kohl followed, their torches held high, but their meagre flames could not light the entirety of what appeared to be a cavernous room.

The floor and walls were stone, seemingly built into the sheer rock of the mountain. It had been intricately carved, and a smooth, flat path led to a plinth at the back of the room. On either side of the path, several deep, narrow wells had been carved into the floor—each leading to the waist-high plinth. Amarah counted twelve on each side, but their torchlight didn't reach beyond the plinth itself, so if there were more, she couldn't see.

Unlit sconces lined the walls, and the same, intricate detailing as on the floor curled around each one. It seemed runic, as they danced much in the way letters of written script did, but whether it was for decoration or some deeper meaning, she had no idea.

Amarah was convinced now. It had to be a tomb.

She'd seen some elaborate crypts before, but stealing from the dead left her with a bad taste, and after the first handful of grave robbings in her youth, she'd given it up, never wishing to stoop to that level again. She'd also been certain she carried a curse for nine years after her last one, having picked up more broken bones then than at any other time in her life.

But she'd never seen anything like this before.

'What *is* this place?' Carav asked, her eyes wide as they drank in their surroundings.

'Damned creepy is what it is,' Antar replied, walking

along the path and approaching the plinth with an outstretched hand.

'Maybe you should've come in and had a look around before shrouding it and bringing us down here!' Oris said in a huff.

Amarah followed Antar while the others split up to investigate the room, searching for anything of value. She peered down one of the wells that lined the path, but it was too dark to see the bottom. The room smelled of must and decay, as though it hadn't been visited since whenever Veynothi had been buried here.

She really didn't fancy the idea of stealing from a thousand-year-old corpse's tomb, if Kohl was to be believed.

'So, Traeg, what's the treasure, then? Where is it?' Oris called as he ran a hand along the underside of a wall sconce and waved his torch high, the light throwing grotesque shadows on the walls as it moved. 'Just rocks and sconces, here. That ain't worth nothing! Where's the jewels? The weapons? The Ark what you said would make me rich?'

'Keep your voice down,' Amarah said in little more than a stern whisper. 'You'll wake the dead if you yell like that!'

Traego crouched before one of the wells, his own torch held above it, no doubt trying to see if there was anything in the bottom. He didn't reply to Oris, and seemed content to let him and the others explore at their own pace instead of responding to his crewmates' growing frustrations.

Amarah shivered. Antar had to be wrong. There wasn't any treasure here. There was no Ark. Best to get out while they were still in one piece. She held her scythe high, the blue light brightening the room, and looked for Kohl.

The Arillian stood stock-still in the doorway, his eyes staring at the back of the cavern.

Amarah whirled around, following his gaze, and her breath caught in her throat.

A woman of stone had been carved into the wall some ten paces behind the plinth.

Veynothi had been sculpted into the mountain itself, her face forced into a grimace, fangs bared and eyes wide in the purest of rage. Her clawed hands reached out to the room, but her legs were swallowed by the wall as though she were trapped half-in, half-out of the rock. Her vertical slit pupils were frozen in stone, but Amarah would recognise those eyes from halfway around the world.

A Varkain.

Veynothi was an ancient Varkain.

Which meant that the Ark was a Varkain, or at least, a statue of one.

Amarah tightened her grip on her scythe as it pulsed another flash of blue light in response to her building adrenaline. She swallowed again, forcing her fear into her usual angry defence and stepped towards the plinth, pushing herself through terror to investigate. Only when she stood before the plinth did she notice the sword hilts buried deep into the stone. 'There's six swords here,' she said.

The others appeared by her side, Traego last of all.

Amarah's eyes were locked on Veynothi's. 'She's a *Varkain*, Traego. A fucking Varkain!'

Traego drew his sword, perhaps spurred on by her outrage, and the room filled with Kohl's freezing wind.

'I'm a thief, Traeg. A damned good one. But a good burglar knows when she's out of her depth and I swear to Rhea herself, that's this place, right now!' She said, her voice rising in panic. 'I ain't staying here for no snake. Don't care how much it's worth.'

The ceiling cracked, dusting them all in white grit. Amarah flinched, but raised the blade of her scythe instinctively to meet anything that appeared.

The ground trembled and a second later, their torches

blew out, throwing them into the eerie blue light that Amarah's scythe emitted.

Kohl's wind disappeared.

'What the fuck is going on?' Carav yelled into the darkness, her fear fuelling Amarah's panic. Trapped in a snake pit. A tomb. A damned Varkain's tomb.

Veynothi must have cracked the ceiling and blown out the sconces, surely. It was a warning.

She clutched the handle of her scythe with both hands and stared at Veynothi, ready to fight.

The stone didn't move or respond to Carav's words, and they stood for several long moments, on the edge of fleeing.

Traego let out a sigh. 'The mountain moves. Wind. Griffins. Dragons. Other ships,' he said, though Amarah heard the slight quiver in his voice. Perhaps his excitement was rightly turning to fear. He shrugged. 'Nothin' ta worry about. Carav, ya bring anythin' else ta light the torches?'

'Nuh-uh.' Her voice trembled openly.

'I still wanna know what this treasure is, Traeg! We can't bring back a stone statue!' Oris said, his voice loud either through bravery or foolishness.

Amarah thought him stupid, but she wondered what Traego had dragged them into a Varkain crypt for. The snake shape-shifters weren't known for their love of gold, and she'd seen no treasure or casket of any kind in the tomb —if that was what they were after.

Heck, she hadn't even known that Varkain were buried outside of their own country. What was the snake's crypt doing all the way out in Corhaven?

'Don't like being in a dead thing's place,' Carav said with a whimper.

'Dead things can't hurt you,' Antar replied with bravado. 'The thing's swords are buried blade-first in stone. Ours are in our hands.' He brandished one of his daggers with a grin.

'It isn't dead.' Kohl's voice cut through the air. 'Veynothi...Varkain...Ark...Whatever she is. She's alive. The same power as in our ice golems is in her, too. Even moreso. This...this...Ark. It's as powerful as they come. We must leave at once. And pray to your Goddess Rhea that you are not cursed for disturbing what lies below this mountain.'

Goosebumps rose at his words and she rounded on the captain. 'Traego, what in Rhea's name have you led us into?'

'Thought ya were hardened fighters an' skilled pirates. It might not be dead. But it ain't alive, either. Ain't moving. Wouldn't let us stroll in here otherwise, would it?' Traego said.

'Cap'n's right. Plus I ain't afraid of no snake. Thousand-year-old one'd move pretty slow, wouldn't it?' Antar agreed.

Amarah shook her head, angry at their stubbornness. 'If Veynothi is an Ark, then this treasure hunt is over. The Ark ain't a jewel we can swipe and escape with. It's not a tapestry or a type of wine. It's some fucking dark snake magic and I don't want nothin' to do with it! I don't care how much bounty you've been offered.'

'Oh, so ya want Cyd or someone worse ta have it instead?' Traego countered.

'Do not bicker! We must leave. Now.' Kohl's voice was strained, tinged with urgency. He filled the chamber with his cold wind, the force of it whipping up Amarah's hair. His all-encompassing fear served only to worsen hers, and she took a few steps back towards him.

Amarah continued, 'I ain't grave-robbing, Traeg! It's damned bad luck! Antar, you'll have to find a new hunt for us—'

Kohl let out a gurgled cry and dropped to his knees.

'What's happening?' Amarah gasped.

The Arillian panted, dropped forward and braced his hands on the ground. 'The wind...'

She raced to his side and crouched down beside him, one hand on his shoulder, just above where his feathered wings protruded from his cloak. 'Kohl? Tell me what's goin' on?'

The wind intensified, the freezing blast biting into her flesh and numbing her lips.

'I can't control...She's...What is she *doing*?' Kohl screamed, the icy wind crashing around the room, tearing cloaks and hats from bodies and picking up the loose stones from the floor to career them into the walls in a freezing hurricane.

'Dragons, above, Traego! Help me!' Amarah yelled over the wind as the others forced their way against the gale to them, arms covering their heads against the loose debris being hurled around.

Kohl's wings twisted and bowed, and he clenched his hands into fists, dirt digging into his nails where he dragged them across the floor. His body convulsed once, twice, sending a wave of ice in all directions, and then he fell forward and collapsed onto the floor, the gale disappearing.

'Kohl? Kohl!' Amarah shook him, but the Arillian had passed out. Terrified and confused, she grabbed him by his upper arm and pulled him up. Between the five of them, they turned him onto his back, then dragged him to the wall where they sat him upright.

'I ain't never seen nothin' like that,' Oris said, brushing ice from his arms and chest.

'You sure he's on your side? Arillians are tearing up Linaria now,' Antar said, his dark eyes on Amarah. He pulled a chunk of rock from where it had embedded in his padded jerkin. 'This one ain't a spy?'

'He's an ally, I swear to Rhea herself. I don't have a clue what happened.' She pushed herself to standing as she tried to calm herself.

As she leaned over to grab her scythe and send some light into the cavern, Amarah saw a pair of golden eyes glaring at her from within the stone on the back wall, bright in the darkness. They *definitely* hadn't been there before. 'Vey...Vey...' she choked.

Traego was on his feet in a heartbeat, striding purposefully towards the statue, sword drawn, his confidence either bravado or sheer, greed-driven stupidity. 'Come on, then, snake. Kill us for breaking inta ya lair!' His tone belied what Amarah believed him to be feeling, but nothing happened to meet Traego's challenge. 'Ya don't scare me, snake. Ya're locked in stone and we can't get ya out. And that means ya can't get us.'

Amarah and the others listened in shock as Traego met Veynothi's gaze head on. Insulted her. Stood firm, exposed, and waiting.

And nothing happened.

Amarah let out a shaky breath, having been convinced Traego was walking to his death. But if Veynothi didn't react to Traego's taunting, had she been responsible for knocking Kohl out? Her scythe continued to flash, almost in time with her pounding heart.

The uncertainty of it all left an acrid taste in her mouth, and she wanted nothing more than to flee the snake's tomb and take a long bath to cleanse herself of the stench.

Fear sweat beaded on her forehead and she angrily wiped it away with an arm.

Kohl let out a soft groan, and she knelt beside him to put a hand on his chest. Aside from gentle breathing, he wasn't moving at all.

She tried again to get them moving. 'Traego? One of your crew's down. Can we get the fuck out of here, now?'

The captain turned back to the others. 'She must've absorbed his power, somehow. Some kinda defence mechanism the Varkain put in this room to stop thieves. No threat ta us. Ya all want treasure? Don't think we'll be the ones ta get it unless we spring her from stone.' He laughed and shook his head. 'Yeah, I think she's definitely the Ark they want. No wonder he was willing ta pay so much gold...'

'What d'you mean?' Antar asked. 'Release her? That even possible?'

'Why would you even want to?' Carav yelped, voicing Amarah's thoughts.

'The wells.' Traego pointed to the nearest one with the tip of his sword. 'Varkain have their blood magic, right? Reckon a lotta people hafta bleed ta death in here ta get her out. So unless ya wanna cut off ya arm, I say we grab what we can and get back ta Estoria. I'm sure that'll be worth at least part o' the bounty. It won't be a wasted trip.'

'I wanna get out,' Amarah said. She didn't care about maintaining face. Didn't care that she had her *Valta Forinja*.

Being in the tomb of a Varkain was one thing. But Veynothi had beaten Kohl—the strongest fighter she knew —somehow. While she was trapped in stone and without any visible weapons of her own.

Antar nodded. 'Me too. In and out, nice and quick. Thief's way, right Traeg?' His eyes twinkled in the semi-darkness.

Traego sheathed his sword at his hip. 'People who wanna find Veynothi'll pay a pretty penny. People who wanna free her'll pay even more. We need proof. See if ya can get one of them blades out the plinth. That should be good enough. The people who're in the know about the Ark'll know about those.'

Amarah held her scythe high to provide more light as Antar led the way to the plinth, Oris following rather reluctantly considering his earlier fury. Antar drew a pair of flat daggers from the many strapped across his chest, and Oris brandished a hand-axe. They selected one of Veynothi's swords and began to hack away at it's stone prison, chipping at the crumbling plinth and creating far more noise than Amarah was comfortable with.

Traego stood quietly while the two worked, watching them with eagle-like intensity. Amarah saw his gaze dart occasionally to Veynothi. Amarah had once joked if he was an Ittallan, he'd have been an eagle. A king of the skies, wry, intelligent, fearless, and with talons more vicious than any she'd met before.

The entrance to the cavern had been hidden by a shroud, and so far as they knew, the only person to have discovered the cavern's location was Antar—paid by Traego's own hand. Perhaps no-one else would come here to claim the Ark and free her.

Kohl groaned, and she willed him to wake up.

Veynothi was a Varkain, of that she was certain. While she knew Varkain dabbled in blood magic, she knew almost nothing about it, and so didn't have the first idea of what it could or couldn't do. Traego had called Veynothi an Ark. Kohl had said Veynothi was as old as the Arillians' ice golems.

This was deep magic. Ancient magic. The likes of Moroda and her Sevastos.

World-changing, life-stopping magic.

Amarah shuddered. All she had wanted to do was take her pick of Linaria's wealth and finance her way through life. Have a home, a comfortable one, far away from Gold-stones and guards on a beach in Estoria. Eat whatever she liked whenever she liked, and sail the skies of Linaria as she chose.

She didn't want to wait another second in Veynothi's presence.

'Traeg, I'm going. I'll fly *Otella* myself if I have to,' Amarah said. She was done. 'Let's go.'

She needed to get a new ship and get her own back on Jato for everything she had done and taken away from her. Then, she needed to hunt down the final Sevastos—the only way she could think of that might be able free Moroda from her crystal prison. Gold was needed for both tasks, as were allies.

But this? This was more than she'd signed up for.

Far more than she wanted to take on.

There had to be other ways to get a ship. Other ways to raise the money. Traego wasn't her only ally—in Estoria, there were half a dozen former comrades and crewmates, all of whom she could pull in to get the gold she needed for a new ship.

In her right hand, her *Valta Forinja* scythe glowed, lighting the room in ethereal white-blue. It buzzed slightly, as it always did, but it felt stronger, this time.

The weapon pulsed, and with a sudden wave of energy, the wall sconces burst into blue flame, filling the cavern with bright light and chasing the shadows from the corners.

'This is beyond anything...' Amarah said, words dying on her tongue. 'Traeg, this ain't somewhere for us to be. Help me carry him out, let's go. Find something else. Gotta be a Goldstone country house out here we can take a look at?' She hated the pleading tone in her voice, but this was not like any other job. This was something much more.

Traego shook his head. 'Just wait. They nearly got this blade out. Once we get what we came for, we head straight to Estoria and lie low for a bit.'

Amarah bit her tongue. Estoria was safe, but it was on the other side of the world. The thought of carrying something of Veynothi's so far was bound to attract attention.

More chunks of stone crumbled away from the plinth as

Antar and Oris's weapons picked away at it. Amarah saw Traego's eyes widen in anticipation of his prize.

She took a shaky breath and asked a question she knew the answer to already. 'Your buyer. The one who's after this Ark. He's a Varkain?'

Traego's face split into a smile as one of Veynothi's swords finally came away from the stone plinth. Antar grabbed it before it clattered to the floor.

Amarah ignored Veynothi's intense gaze from across the cavern.

The captain looked over his shoulder at her with a smirk. 'The richest snake of them all.'

5

I t was full dark before Morgen returned to Povmar, his
base while stationed in the Karoun Mountains. The
griffin's piercing shrieks echoed loudly as dusk fell,
and he knew from experience their singing would continue
long into the night. The sound no longer gave him chills, but
tonight they seemed particularly shrill.

The outpost at Povmar didn't offer anything near the
luxuries of Rosecastle. The Imperial Guard was able to
enjoy boasted five or six single-room buildings mostly used
as sleeping quarters, and a larger communal building where
food was cooked and mead was poured in vast quantities.
The forest pressed in around them, and beyond, the mountains rose vast and foreboding.

Thankfully, he'd not been stationed here in winter—
he'd hate to think how bleak it would be then—and it was
unpleasant even in spring. But it was better than the alternative: Sapora finding him.

He'd taken to drinking most evenings just so he could
fall asleep, if passing out could be called sleep. It was the
only way to quench the constant fear that plagued him. The
fear that Sapora or one of his Varkain would find him

sooner or later, and then he'd be bitten, paralysed, poisoned, killed.

Whatever the Varkain King wished to do to him in punishment for his betrayal.

Almost every night, he'd screamed through terrifying nightmares of Sapora breaking into his room. Sometimes he took his cobra form, and Morgen's bed sheets would suddenly change from cotton into snakeskin.

Just the memory of that nightmare made him tremble.

So, he'd turned to mead to numb his mind and smother his dreams, and all the days rolled into each other while he hid in the middle of nowhere.

Seeing Amarah today had both been a fantastic surprise and a stark reminder that the rest of the world went on outside of Povmar. Her words—and the company she kept —weighed heavily on his mind. She'd spoken of freedom and treasure while he hid, cornered in the same place, following orders he didn't believe in for a cause he didn't care for, because he was simply too afraid to do anything else.

If anything, he was now in an even worse position than before he met Moroda and Eryn back in Niversai.

The colleagues he had stationed with him were either too young and inexperienced to work at Rosecastle, or too old to. Morgen had been promoted to captain and put in charge of the lot of them—seven vagabonds who wanted to be there even less than he did.

Still, it was better than being Sapora's pawn.

And yet, if it hadn't been for what he'd done, Val Sharis and likely Corhaven, too, would be under the snake's thumb. He very much doubted his actions would put a stop to Sapora, but if it delayed him for a season or too, long enough for Princess Isa or someone else to bring him under control, then that was a positive. And at least here, in the farthest reaches of Corhaven, he was away from Sapora and his spies.

Morgen sat down at one of the long wooden tables in the communal hall floor, a flagon of mead and a steaming bowl of goat broth waiting for him. He pulled out his folder of paperwork and lay it on the table. One small sheet of paper stood out from the rest—darker in colour and folded over several times.

He glanced up to ensure no-one was nearby, before he unfolded the odd paper and held it close to his face as he re-read it for what must have been the thousandth time.

MORGEN,

People are suffering. Dying. I can't help them alone.

The nest is taking over and my influence has faded under their fangs.

My city bleeds under their poison.

Is this your world?

Help us. I beg you. Send Imperial aid and help me free my city.

These dances are always written in blood.

MORGEN SMOOTHED the paper over as he read it and his fingers trembled. He vividly remembered talking to Princess Isa on a palace balcony, only a few days before Aciel's attack. Remembered every word she'd said. Remembered about dances written in blood.

She'd risked so much in sending him that message. And so had he, when he'd responded.

'Hey, captain!' One of his called, the slur in his voice giving away the fact he'd already worked his way through three or four flagons before Morgen had arrived. They

66

treated him like any other grunt, which he was fine with. He didn't feel he deserved his promotion, and they could sense it.

Morgen didn't look up from the paperwork, but nonchalantly refolded Isa'a plea and returned it to the stack. 'What is it, Graff?'

'What you think of that Traego?'

'Who?' He asked, pulling out a pot of ink and one of his good quills as he prepared to mark off this week's reports.

'Traego. The captain of that ship that came through today. Ain't like there's loadsa ships come through for you to get mixed up with?' Laughter echoed around the room, the crackle of fire drowned out for a few moments. Four of them were huddled around the bar, helping themselves to far too much mead and keeping themselves warm by the hearth.

'What about him?' Morgen asked, beginning to add his notes to the day's report.

'Seemed dodgy? I swear I heard about a pirate Traego what got mixed up in some antique thefts a while back? Got away free 'cause he ran to Estoria?'

Morgen paused, rolling around the statement in his mind as he re-inked his quill. Estoria. Where had he heard that before? He didn't need to ask anything as the drunken soldier continued unprompted.

'You know? Must've been a year or so ago? Before Aciel. I guess you were babysitting the king in Rosecastle back then, right?' More laughter echoed, but Morgen didn't rise to the brait. He'd been in the Imperial Guard long enough to know the banter, and how to avoid it or invite more of it on you. He took a sip of his mead and swallowed it down, then continued to write. 'Estoria? That's near Val Saris?'

'Yah. It's south. Few big islands near the border of Val Sharis and Sereth.' Graff seemed pleased with himself.

'Independent state, right? No Imperial Guard? No royalty?' Morgen asked, shoving the completed papers to one side and pulling a new report near him.

'That's the one. Should we grab Traego on the way back?'

Morgen read the page in front of him three times before he realised he wasn't really reading anything. He was bored with reports, numbers, and quantities. Bored of the conversation. Bored of hiding. 'He's all right. Nothing out there to worry about, and his ship is from Val Sharis. If Sapora wants him, he can get him himself.'

'Captain?'

'You want to be on the end of his fangs if you catch someone he's given special treatment to? I'll sign your name on this report and you can explain it to the Varkain when they come looking for what happened to their smuggler ship.'

Graff snorted, but didn't argue back. Despite his drink, he still had some sense.

Morgen turned around to face him. 'Have some water and get your head down. Griffins are what you need to worry about up here, not Val Sharis pirates.'

The laughter stopped and the sound of crackling wood and spitting fire filled the hall. He held his gaze with his subordinate.

'Right, sir.' Graff muttered, putting his flagon down.

'Good. I need to get these reports checked off, signed, and sent back to Niversai before the sea boat leaves the harbour.' Morgen swallowed down the rest of his mead as he returned to his paperwork, thoughts of Amarah, Traego, and their sky pirates filling his mind. He knew full well they were pirates, and knew they weren't out near Povmar for a holiday.

They were up to something, whether that was smuggling something into or out of the region. But as a last favour to his friend, he'd held his tongue, stamped their trade papers, and let them pass. He'd moved out here to get away from real work. He had no desire to stir up trouble with the pirates of Estoria, especially considering they would be out of his jurisdiction when they returned to their base.

Of course, thinking of Amarah made him immediately think of Palom, Anahrik, Kohl, Moroda, and...Eryn. The travellers whose company he'd shared for so long, grown so close to...

And who were now gone.

He'd hoped desperately that Sapora could do something to help, tap into some deep magic to bring Eryn back, like he'd assured Morgen he'd be able to. But the Varkain had lied, just like Amarah always said he would. Morgen felt so helpless in Niversai, surrounded by destruction. He'd taken orders in secret from the Varkain King, reported what he could, found out what information there was in Niversai. Searched for the thing he'd said Rosecastle would have information on. All for nought.

And when he'd answered Isa's call for help, he'd sealed his fate against the Varkain.

Moving out to Povmar was the first thing he'd done for himself since leaving Rosecastle, and he hoped it wouldn't be a mistake. It had been very dull, and the endless days of snowy skies and griffins' shrieks had given him plenty of time to think on the past and consider his future.

One thought, in particular, kept coming back to him.

Dragons were the source of everything. The power and poverty, the creation and destruction.

Linaria, and the magic that ran through the world, came from them.

Topeko and the Samolen in Berel had said as much during his brief time there. And he still had his ring, for what little good it did. He'd not been able to tap into the magic inherent in all life as Moroda had—Topeko had said something about his training in sword and shield blocking access to his own magic. He'd written it off as a farce, but when he'd seen what Moroda had done on the battlefield against Aciel, when the crystal pillar had been left—all that remained of both her and Aciel—he'd struggled to shake the feeling that perhaps he just needed more knowledge and he'd be able to access magic.

And, really, what was to stop him doing so? From taking his knowledge of magic a step further, and learning more? All he'd need to do would be fly to Berel and seek out Topeko, or any of the scholars at the university, surely?

It would mean leaving the Imperial Guard, though. For good. And at a time where numbers were so thin on the ground, he couldn't imagine such a request being accepted.

He still pondered it as he signed the bottom of each sheet of paper, then blew carefully across the ink to help it dry. Once satisfied it wouldn't smudge, he rolled them up, bundled them with twine, and stood from his bench, stretching his arms out above his head and letting his back crack. 'I'm getting these sent back to Niversai. They'll want to make sure we're all still alive out here and doing our jobs.'

He was answered with a grunt from the others, and Morgen slipped his cloak and gloves on. Moonlight streamed in through the windows, and he would be glad to get out of the hot, smoke-filled room and breathe in some fresh air. With a quick nod to his colleagues, Morgen crossed the hall and pushed open the heavy doors.

Snow crunched underfoot, and the sharpness of the air almost burned his lungs. He inhaled deeply several times before he headed off down the well-worn path and into Povmar.

Buildings sat nestled among large snow drifts and in between trees on either side of the path. Morgen walked past them all and headed down the narrow mountain path. Povmar was home to barely a hundred people, mostly hunters and woodsman, but it was company more than the drunkards of the Imperial Guard. And he needed to clear his head.

The sky above was clear and bright with stars, all three moons fully risen. Two were swollen and the third waned, but they provided plenty of light for him to see his way to town without the need for a torch.

Povmar was secluded, half-hidden at the base of the Karoun mountains before they touched the frigid sea, and surrounded on all other sides by thick forest. The wolves and bears which lurked in the trees were nothing compared to their Ittallan counterparts, and Morgen found himself strangely unafraid. Before, he'd have refused to wander alone at night in such a wild, remote part of Corhaven.

Now, having fended off half a dozen griffin attacks, it was no different from strolling through the town itself.

So far north, the usual rules of trade closing at third moonrise went out the window—all three moons were visible for most of the day almost all year round. The towns-folk of Povmar bundled themselves in furs and boiled leather, were big boned and long-haired, and lived a hardy life Morgen was slowly coming to understand.

A few of the townsfolk had bred and trained a number of wolfdogs, mostly to warn them of griffin attacks, and do what they could to defend against them. Morgen heard their yowling as he approached the town centre. Children ran along the streets in the darkness, many carrying short knives. Morgen smiled a little. In Niversai—in any other city in Corhaven—children of their age would have been tucked up in bed hours ago.

The people of Povmar lived by their own rules. It was the only way they could survive.

His colleague's words echoed in his thoughts as he made his way through town towards the harbour, where the weekly ship would be setting sail for Niversai in the morning. In another life, he'd never have let Amarah pass. Any fool within a hundred leagues could see who, and what, she was. Whatever papers they carried were forged. Good forges, maybe, but forges all the same. Amarah had too big a history, too large a reputation to just let slide. He'd even arrested her in Niversai himself not all that long ago.

He wondered whether Sapora really had given her and Traego special pass to come here and do whatever it was they were here to do. Piracy was illegal in both Corhaven and Val Sharis. He'd not heard the Varkain King had permitted it yet.

Perhaps they were simply good pirates and had avoided the Imperial Guard in Val Sharis.

A sudden chill took him.

What if Sapora had *expected* the Corhaven Imperial Guard to catch Traego and turn him in? What if Sapora would punish those who let Traego pass by, unhindered?

No.

Morgen shook himself out of the brief panic which rose in his gut. Sapora was a law unto himself. The Sevastos he had under his control was testament to that. A god of Linaria, reduced to little more than a trained dog, so the snake could keep people in check.

It sickened Morgen.

He turned a corner onto a street bustling with activity— shops and traders, both. A new shipment of furs had arrived, it seemed, and half the town was out looking for a bargain. With spring coming, there would be little need for thick furs, but everyone seemed to buy a year in advance when prices were more favourable.

Considering he was to be stationed at the outpost for the

foreseeable future, and now he'd had wages paid regularly since returning to Corhaven, Morgen decided to have a look for himself to see if he could make his stay in the remote mountain region slightly more bearable.

With fewer regulations out here, slightly more unscrupulous products also made it onto the trader's stalls for sale—he'd seen phoenix scales and dragon claws—as well as exotic foods and wines from far and wide. Morgen turned a blind eye to items that ought to be licenced, uninterested in causing a commotion. In such a small town, offending the wrong person could make your life a misery, especially as he was captain of the guard here. Plus, he didn't particularly believe in the laws he was trying to uphold. How hypocritical would it be to condemn someone for breaking the rules when he cared so little for them?

He shook his head. He'd spend far too long with Amarah. Now he was starting to think like her.

Morgen shuffled along to the another stall, pushing past the throng of people huddled around the shipment of furs.

'Oh shit!'

Morgen glanced to his left as a thickly set, heavily bearded trader tripped on his own feet in his haste to sweep some small, glass bottles off his table. When he resurfaced, he placed folded piles of linen and cloth where the bottles had been.

'What was that?' Morgen asked, curiosity piqued.

'Nothin', nothin',' the trader said, pulling up the sack where the bottles clinked within. He drew the string tight and placed it in a heavy crate behind him, where several identical sacks rested. 'Somethin' special but, uh, papers ain't come through yet so shouldn't have 'em out, you know. Didn't mean to. Just unloaded everythin' all at once.' Sweat beaded on his forehead despite the chill.

He was probably the worst liar Morgen had ever come

across, but he shook his head to show his neutrality. 'Sell whatever you need to. You're a man of business with a job to do.'

'Uh, yeah, sir. Thanks.' He made no move to withdraw the bottles.

Morgen added, 'I'm off duty.' He held up the bundled report papers. 'Need to send these off with the boat before it leaves.' But Morgen was curious—most traders didn't seem to care whether he saw their wares or not. What had this one been so keen to hide? He was more interested in discovering *what* they were, rather than fining him for selling them. 'Let me see?'

The trader let out a sigh, his shoulders rolling. 'Shipment arrived from Ranski a couple of hours ago. Pretty high demand for this stuff. Excellent at keeping griffins back.' He grabbed the large sack and fished out a few bottles from it. 'Can do anythin' you want. You just put in your order and a few weeks later...' He waggled his eyebrows.

'Can you show me?'

'Of course, of course. What d'ya wanna see?'

Morgen shrugged again, still clueless as to what the man traded. 'Anything.'

The trader picked up a small, red vial, dwarfed in his nad, and carefully uncorked it. A small flame appeared as the cork was removed, and disappeared just as quickly. Morgen watched, transfixed.

'This one isn't so popular no more, but I still get an order every now and then.' The trader tipped the contents of the bottle onto the table. It wasn't quite a liquid or solid, it was a kind of glutinous mass without form or shape, and it glittered red in the torchlight. 'Just needs a second to warm up. Cold ain't so good for it here. S'pose that's why it ain't so popular—'

Morgen had stopped listening.

He was fixated by the contents of the bottle. In the few seconds since it had been tipped out, it had writhed around, twisting and turning, as if sensing something. It rolled towards the edge of the table, and began to rise very slowly, expanding and stretching until it was as thin as a sheet of paper, and as tall as Morgen.

'There it goes. See? Just needs a bit of time,' the trader babbled on.

Morgen struggled to keep his mouth from dropping open. In front of him no longer sat a red blob, but a replica of himself. A clone. A mirror image. Complete down to the snow that had landed on his cheek.

'It won't move or nothin', it just stands there. They're great decoys. Griffins can't tell the difference so people put them out where they don't want griffins to be. Then they can get on with their work.'

'Where did you say you got this from?' Morgen stared at the mirror of himself, horrified and amazed at the incredible detail. Every hair, every freckle, every piece of clothing and armour. The mirror even carried a sword.

'Ranski.'

Morgen nodded. 'This is Samolen magic. Bottled Samolen magic.'

'Somethin' like that. Don't ask too many questions as long as I get what's ordered.'

Morgen blinked, turning his head this way and that, but the mirror remained still as stone. He looked down to the trader's sack and saw dozens of other bottles, all of varying shapes, sizes, and colours. 'Whatever you want, you just order it,' Morgen repeated, his mind slowly turning. 'What do the other ones do?'

The trader pulled out several bottles and lay them on the table, clearly no longer concerned over Morgen's presence. 'Ah, well, mostly people like 'em to hide things. Some to trap things. Great help hunting when there's not so many of us, you know? There's so many. Whatever you want, they can do, if you don't mind waitin'. Ranski's a long way from here.' He erupted into a laughter Morgen thought was unnecessary.

Morgen reached for a tall, slender bottle in navy blue, when the trader hurriedly snatched it back. 'Ah, can't let you touch that one,' he apologised. 'That one's bought and paid for already...'

Morgen scratched his nose. 'I can't see it?'

The trader licked his lips. 'Let's just say it's called "dragon's breath" for a reason.'

Dragons.

Why was it always dragons?

Morgen folded his arms and whispered aloud, 'it's just energy.'

'You okay? Sir?' The trader asked.

He blinked, realising he'd been lost in his own thoughts for Rhea knew how long. His mirror image had disappeared, but the red magic remained sat on the table as if awaiting further instruction. He thought to the Samolen ring from Topeko, and the *Valta Forinja* from Palom. Both had magic fuelled by dragons and were locked in a crate of his personal belongings.

'I'm fine,' he said. He suddenly craved the warmth of his bed and a roaring fire. He'd not considered leaving Povmar for a long while—at least a year, or however long it took for Sapora to settle down.

But, now?

Anahrik. Moroda. Eryn.

He thought of his fallen friends, of what they had gone through because of Aciel. Because of what the Arillians had thrust upon them.

He'd wrapped up his *Valta Forinja* sword the moment

he'd returned to Niversai, and left it in the armoury of Rose-castle—or what was left of it. He'd only retrieved it along with his belongings when he'd flown here, convincing himself he would avenge Eryn and the others with it.

But with Aciel sealed away in crystal, revenge wasn't so easy to work out anymore.

He didn't know what to do, what was needed.

Now, he wondered whether he should travel to Berel and seek out Topeko. Ranski was a peaceful nation that took no part in the wars of Linaria's people. Although a dragon-forged weapon would not be welcome there, he considered Topeko a friend.

He couldn't go with Amarah, so perhaps he'd seek out one of the few friends he had left. And he'd be just as safe from Sapora there as he was in the middle of nowhere.

And if he was refused leave? He supposed that's why he had the *Valta Forinja*.

No-one would follow him. No-one would know where he was going.

He decided then to return to his quarters just as soon as he shipped the reports, and unwrap his *Valta Forinja* and the Samolen ring.

Perhaps he could now discover a use for them both.

6

A marah sat on the deck of *Otella*, the wind warming more her the further south they travelled. She'd been exhausted after discovering Veynothi, but adrenaline still pumped through her, preventing sleep.

Retracing their steps through the checkpoints had been easy enough—Morgen had seen to that. Traego put on his typical grin, but Amarah couldn't ignore his quietness. With the captain on edge, so was she.

They wouldn't be the only hunters after the Ark, not with a bounty that size on it, but her gut told her that the "treasure" was not something that should have ever been disturbed. She didn't need Kohl's superstitions to see that. The Arillian himself had recovered enough by the time they'd left to fly the short distance to the ship, which relieved Amarah more than she cared to admit.

Not to mention the fact that Veynothi was *very* much alive, and her resting place seemed little different from a tomb. Amarah had no intention of bringing ill fortune upon herself, and even if she didn't truly believe in either the Goddess Rhea or in Arillian lore, there were too many deities wielding too much power for her to risk pissing one off by grave robbing from something that ancient.

Carav and Oris were pleased with themselves for having freed Veynothi's blade; Antar remained stoic as he flew south and then east towards the Sea of Nami, and Traego was unreadable. Amarah had spent a great deal of the flight watching her captain, looking for any hint of his true thoughts.

She'd not known him to be so guarded, but she'd also not known him to stumble across a treasure hunt that stood to make him quite as rich as this one did. Although the fact the promised gold came from Sapora sickened her.

Now it made more sense as to why he flew with such a skeleton crew. Taking the bare minimum with him meant fewer mouths could talk. Carav and Oris were too new to this lifestyle to be much of a threat, and though Antar was a seasoned pilot, he seemed loyal enough to Traego.

She assumed he had a decent share in Sapora's bounty. As would be her own reward.

But would buying a new airship with the snake's money be worth it? She'd never worked for or with a Varkain—certainly not by choice, anyway—and now she found herself hurrying to Estoria with a piece of treasure the snake king wanted. The dilemma tore at her.

Amarah huffed to herself as she looked at Veynothi's blade, turning it slowly in her hand. She'd never seen anything quite like it, and she fought with a *Valta Forinja*, arguably one of the rarest weapons in all Linaria.

The Varkain blade was old and brittle, and had either been made of stone or turned into stone by whomever had sealed Veynothi away.

She could still picture those piercing gold eyes watching her every move in the dark chamber, and she suppressed a shiver. The stone was almost green with age, covered in a fine layer of whatever algae had strength enough to grow at such altitude and in such barren conditions.

Amarah held it close to her eye, frowning a little as she studied the details.

What Sapora wanted with the blade, with Veynothi, Amarah shuddered to think.

He already had a Sevastos at his command, an ancient dragon of incredible strength. What more could he possibly want? To amass the world's power? Perhaps it was a guarantee of a quick death if everything went wrong. A smirk grew on her lips at the thought.

'What're ya grinning about?' Traego asked, walking up to her and resting on one knee. 'Not seen ya smile since ya first saw me. Didn't realise ya'd been *that* put off pirating!'

'Never,' she replied, 'just thinking is all.'

'About...?'

'Our favourite snake. And whatever that thing was in the chamber. I'd rather it was in there than out here. Maybe she'll kill him.'

'The one who frees her? Nah.'

'No?' Amarah handed the old sword to Traego, hilt-first. 'Something tells me that *thing* does whatever it likes, whether or not a king frees it.'

Traego took the blade from her and glanced at it. 'Veynothi...Whatever it is, it has a weakness. It feels fear. Nothin' likes bein' locked up. Whatever sealed it away could seal it again. Sapora is a hell of a negotiator. He has leverage. Ha. I could use him in my crew!'

Amarah thought he'd made a giant assumption about the Ark. He'd always been somewhat reckless. Perhaps this hunt was pushing him to the edge of madness. 'Sail with a Varkain aboard? You've lost your mind, Traeg.'

The Sea of Nami opened up underneath them as Antar powered them along at a fair pace. Amarah had never once heard of Traego being picked up by the Imperial Guard while on *Otella*, and she supposed his decision to base himself in Estoria was a large part of his success.

The sun burned high above them, bringing much needed warmth. From their bearing, Amarah looked to the horizon as Antar steered them south-east, waiting to see the western coast of Val Sharis as they approached.

Traego replied, 'Believe it or not, I worked with a pair of Varkain in Corhaven a year back. They've a grudge against everyone. Cheapest security ever. 'Course it brought the Imperial Guard on us double-quick. Lucky I was faster than them.'

Amarah's smile fell from her face. 'I say again, you've lost your mind.' She'd never trusted the Varkain, not even Sapora, though he'd been a reluctant ally for some time. They always had their own agenda, and blood always seemed to be part of it. 'Damn snakes.'

'Ya still can't stand 'em?'

Amarah rolled her eyes. 'Would you, if you'd been through what I have with them?'

Traego yawned and scratched the back of his head with Veynothi's blade. Amarah scowled at his disrespect. Traego said, 'Grudges weight ya down. Slow ya—'

'Drive you on,' she snapped. 'I told you why I need a new ship. This ridiculous Ark hunt of yours ain't gonna change that. I'm gonna get Jato back for what she did to me. What she took from me.' She glared at Traego, all rage fuelled into her stare.

He was so close she could see her own reflection in Traego's eyes, and saw the patch that covered her right eye socket—a stark reminder of what she'd lost. She knew she was lucky Jato hadn't killed her. Amarah balled her hands. She was going to make damned sure Jato regretted that mistake.

'Such fierceness. Ya oughta be a bounty hunter, not a humble thief.' Traego stepped back and stood up straight. 'Maybe a bit o' time in Estoria'll do ya some good. The weather's fine all year round. Clear blue seas and empty skies far as ya look. Sunshine does everyone good.'

Amarah snorted again but said nothing. She'd been to Estoria a handful of times and knew what to expect. She looked back over the side of the ship at the vast sea below. Kohl was little more than a dark smudge in the distance, scouting ahead as always, despite his battle with Veynothi.

At first, she'd thought he just wanted to make himself useful. But the more time she spent with Kohl, the more she understood him. Now, she believed he simply disliked their company. Then again, she was on a vendetta against his daughter, and they'd all partaken in some very deep magic. Traego had promised them all equal share in whatever reward the blade fetched, but Kohl wanted nothing to do with it.

'Always honourable, aren't you?' Amarah whispered to herself, casting her mind back to his less-than-honourable behaviour in the past. His abandonment had turned Palom against him, and even she hadn't been completely comfortable when she'd found out he'd left Moroda, Eryn, and Morgen to fight alone against Jato and her Arillians. Whatever ethic he worked to was his own, one he was unwilling to share, and he now seemed set on redeeming himself.

Amarah only hoped the Jato element of his ethic had been cut out.

She didn't want an enemy of Kohl, but would face him, if it came to it. Her scythe had cut down Aciel's Arillians easily enough. He'd be no different.

A chill breeze broke her thoughts as Kohl returned to land on deck. He spoke without preamble, 'There are two ships that've been trailing you a while. They're putting on speed and gaining.'

Amarah got to her feet, scythe in hand, and peered back out to the blue sky. She felt the thrum of *Otella*'s propellers somewhere beneath her, and squared up. Two medium-sized airships approached them in tandem. They were sleek and narrow, and looked to be class fours, the same class *Khanna* had been—built for speed and maneuverability over anything else. They might have been couriers or postal vessels once upon a time, but had been stripped of any identifying features, marks, or assigned colours. They flew blue-grey sails which were hard to see clearly against the bright sky. And if they were the same class as *Khanna*, they'd have six cannons.

'Look alive. Told ya we weren't the only ones out this way,' Traego barked. He shoved Veynothi's blade into an oversized sheath on his belt. 'If they've been followin' us, they reckon we've got something worth having.'

'What's your plan? Say nothing?' Carav asked, a hint of panic in her voice. It was clearly her first altercation with other ships while out on a flight.

'No point lying. I like ta be honest. They ain't taking our treasure and we've got an Arillian on our side if they wanna push the matter.' He glanced at Kohl, and Amarah couldn't help but assume the captain was testing Kohl's loyalty.

'Do not bring me into your thievery.' Kohl ruffled his wings indignantly. 'I want no part in it.'

'Ya don't gotta be part o' anything. Just have our backs if things turn ugly, right?'

Kohl fluttered his wings again but said nothing.

Traego clambered up the footholds etched into *Otella*'s central mast, almost halfway up to his now defunct lookout platform—thanks to Kohl—and shielded his eyes from the sun as he gazed into the distance. The wind picked up and he leaned into it, his sure-footedness and experience on his ship letting him stay comfortable. 'Can't see no Imperial colours. They aren't traders, neither. Definitely sky pirates. Oh, shit. Might be Cyd, actually. Oris! You wake up those cannons. Kohl, any chance you could slow 'em down? Blow 'em off course?'

'Certainly not!' Kohl replied.

'It'd save people dying here,' Amarah said, knowing just the spot to poke to get a reaction out of the Arillian. For a former leader of his people, Kohl had no clout. 'These guys shoot first then search. Wanna help make that *not* happen?'

If Traego was correct in his guess and Cyd was aboard one of the two ships, blood would definitely be spilled.

Kohl huffed. 'Give them what they want, and there'll not be any bloodshed.' He took to the wing and hovered a short way above *Otella*, watching the two ships approach.

'Amarah, what ya been doing travelling around with this guy?' Traego jumped down and landed heavily on deck, his curved sword drawn and held up. 'This'll get ugly. *Otella* can't outfly Cyd's two, and we'll be in range soon. They might not be built for fighting, but they can pack a punch. Oris! Ya got them damned cannons ready yet?'

Adrenaline coursed through Amarah's body, and she wheeled around on her toes, suddenly wishing Traego had brought more man power along for the journey. Her scythe could attack from a distance, sending out a wave of power to incapacitate. The less chance they had of coming aboard, the more chance she, Traego, and the others had of staying alive.

Being a sky thief certainly had its less than glamorous side to it.

'They're firing!' Kohl shouted, flapping his wings and gaining height.

His warning gave them only a few seconds to duck as

cannonfire slammed into *Otella*, shaking the ship and splintering wood from the side of the hull as it impacted squarely.

Definitely Cyd. He always attacked first and spoke later.

'Oris! Let loose!' Traego yelled, and immediately *Otella* lurched underfoot as four of its twenty cannons shot one after the other, leaving a thick plume of grey smoke—evidently the only ones Oris had had time to make ready. Four blazes of distinctly dragon-shaped fire roared as they flew towards the enemy ship, red, gold, and yellow flames rolling into one another and lighting up the sky to almost blinding levels of brightness. Amarah could have sworn she saw one of them beat a pair of wings to speed itself on, before she squinted her eye shut as they tore through the first ship's hull with an explosive crash.

When she looked back, she saw its sails had taken to flame immediately, the wood burning and black smoke filling the sky, blotting out the brightness of the fire. She heard a reptilian growl echo from the fire, the noise rumbling out and causing her knees to tremble involuntarily.

After several moments, the smoke lifted slightly, giving Amarah a better view of the two ships. The nearest one had no middle mast left, and the other had taken damage to its starboard propeller—Traego's attack clearly powerful enough to leap from one ship to attack the other, although the dragon-shaped fires were already beginning to shrink in the short minute since they had been set loose. Both ships were aflame and their crews so concerned with dousing the rapidly spreading flames they didn't shoot back.

The second ship, the one with the damaged propeller, dropped back several feet, and Amarah saw people scrambling over one another to get the fire under control.

She grinned. *Dragon's breath.*

This was why Traego had such a reputation among thieves, why he'd been able to build and run his ship on a skeleton crew, hold a permanent base in Estoria, and was nigh untouchable by the Imperial Guard.

Forget calling him an eagle. He was a magpie, with more tricks up his sleeve every day—he didn't strike hardest or fastest. He just struck where it was most efficient, and only when he had to.

Amarah looked straight up to see Kohl still hovering above them, and scowled at his reluctance to participate. He'd been adamant in helping her reclaim a ship, saying he felt partly responsible for what Jato had done, yet he wasn't willing to join in all that debt encompassed.

'Hold fire,' Traego called. He surveyed the scene and calculated his next move. 'Looks like one of 'em's sending over an envoy. We'll blast both ships into the sea if they make a move against us.'

Amarah looked up to see a tiny, two-person ship take off from the larger, less damaged of the pair, its single sail billowing proudly in the warm, southern wind. She scowled. 'I don't trust 'em. Traeg, wanna give me Veynothi's blade if that's what they're after?'

'All good. Don't want them ta see me giving ya nothing. Weapons ready. Kohl, if ya fancy helping out, I wouldn't mind ya landing down here,' Traego said. 'There's only three of 'em squeezed on that boat, but they could have anything. I'm not the only one ta buy bottled magic.'

Amarah didn't need telling twice.

The two ships separated even more as smaller dragon-shaped flames split from the four main ones, and continued to leap about and bite down on anything flammable. The remaining crews hurriedly attempted to get the fires under control. Amarah wondered whether they'd be able to, or if Traego would end up rescuing their crews, too.

'Cap'n Traego!' A man yelled out as the envoy ship drew near. 'Gonna land an' have a nice chat with you!'

Traego squared himself. 'Ya're welcome ta land. But whether ya leave or not again is ta be decided.'

Otella's crew held their breaths as the small ship circled and slowed, landing on the wide deck with a thump. Amarah glanced at Antar, who left *Otella* hovering in place and darted over to the newcomers, one of his daggers raised and pointed at them.

'No sudden moves!' Carav cried, her small axe in hand.

Amarah exhaled through her nose and tried not to shake her head. Inexperience caused deaths out here, but Traego had a knack for picking up urchins and training them up. After all, it was how she had ended up where she had.

But she had to admit that Traego's ability to pick out promising youths had waned over the years.

Her captain strolled leisurely over to the envoy ship, hands in his coat pockets as he looked over the three arrivals. 'What brings ya aboard my *Otella* on this fine spring morning? I do hope ya didn't mean ta shoot us.'

'Alright, Traeg.' One said, clambering out of the ship and stepping onto *Otella*.

He'd not eaten in a week, from the look of him. Amarah wrinkled her nose slightly and leaned back against the side of the deck. 'So sorry. My gunner's a bit sensitive to the Imperial Guard.'

Traego raised an eyebrow. 'Imperial Guard? On my ship?'

'Yeah. That one,' he nodded to Amarah, 'is friends with 'em. We saw in Taban Yul.'

Amarah snorted but didn't interrupt. This was for the captain to sort out.

'Pretty damned rude o' ya ta say something like that. Ya

know I don't stand for rudeness, lad. Say something else like that and ya won't be able ta say anything again,' Traego said. He spoke jokingly, as though he chatted with a close acquaintance. But that was his way—he'd fool you into thinking you were his friend, that he didn't realise what was going on, and then he'd strike.

A master of disguise, persuasion, and ambush.

Amarah narrowed her eyes and watched, tense for when the inevitable fighting kicked off. She was interested in whether they'd randomly decided to try their luck, knowing whose ship it was, or whether they'd heard something about the Ark hunt and wanted part of it.

'Sorry, Traeg. Didn't mean nuffin' by it. Was just sayin' is all...' he trailed off and dropped his gaze. His two companions got out of their ship, one waited by it, and the other walked up to Traego and his apologetic comrade.

'I got it on good authority you got somefin' aboard worth five hundred crowns.'

Amarah straightened up. This one was more direct, cleaner, with slicked hair tied back down his neck, ears and nose full of gold rings to distract from his disfigured and burned skin.

Cyd.

Anxiety coiled in the pit of her stomach. She shot a glance to Kohl, who still looked decidedly uninterested in the events unfolding below him.

'In Estoria, everythin's fair, Traeg. Nice, even split. Ain't that what you always say?' Cyd asked, his gold rings jingling slightly as he spoke. There was an ugly tattoo on the side of his neck which snaked up his chin to his cheek, an elaborate display of swirls and dots in black-green ink.

Amarah shuddered. If that was Cyd's Thief Ink, she bet he was richer than half the Goldstones in Corhaven. And

88

she could hardly believe he had the audacity to show them in full display.

It had been years since she'd last seen Cyd, and thought he'd died at the hands of an enraged dragon during a hunt gone wrong. His bulk had only grown in the time that had passed, the tattoos and jewellery masking the scars he carried as a reminder of that hunt.

Traego replied, 'Course it is. For my crew. Ya ain't on that. Not since ya backstabbed me over those damned dragon eggs.' His voice had cooled.

Amarah wiped her palms on her tunic and then re-gripped her scythe. It was going to come to blows, no question. It always did with Cyd. She waited for the tell that would precede the explosion of movement.

'Ya still sore over that? That mutiny *you* kicked off?' Cyd spat at Traego's feet. 'You weren't spending fair then an' you ain't spending fair again. Hand it over and we'll head off. No blood spilled.'

'That's rude, Cyd,' Traego said. 'Rude ta come on my boat and start talking ta me like ya're the captain. Especially when yours is half on fire.'

His words hung in the air, and Amarah refused to wait any longer.

She swung her scythe, sending a blow of blue energy to the third pirate who waited by the envoy ship. He was knocked clean out, the knife in his hand dropping to the deck.

Traego reacted on reflex, the sword in his hand plunging through the belly of the first pirate who'd spoken, Cyd having somehow sidestepped the strike and drawn a pair of daggers in one swift move.

'*And* you stole my warhammer. Don't think I don't know about that!' Cyd snarled, his eyes gleaming.

'Fire!' Traego bellowed, making good on his threat of blowing both ships out of the sky if they made a wrong move. He lunged forward and went toe-to-toe with Cyd in a blaze of steel. The echo of their blades rang out, and Amarah rushed ahead, slashing with her scythe and joining the fray.

Beneath her feet, the ship rocked as Oris unleashed *dragon's breath* on the two ships once again. The fast reaction helped—their flames smashed into them before either crew knew what was going on, while Antar ran back to the wheel to maneuver *Otella* out of range of any counter shots. The wind changed, blowing the smoke back towards them, and stench of *dragon's breath* filled the sky: a disgusting burning scent that reminded Amarah of rotten eggs. It was a good bit of magic, but it left her wanting to gag.

It seemed Traego didn't want anyone talking and wasn't taking any chances.

Cyd lunged at Traego, faster than the captain moved. Amarah couldn't leap to his defence, her weapon was bulky, inaccurate, and she'd have just as much chance of taking Traego's head clean off as she did Cyd's.

An explosion rang out from one of the ships, the force of the blast sent shockwaves of energy pulsing through the air and everyone dropped to their knees. Oris must have fired again. Thick smoke wafted across to them. Amarah squinted, her one eye watering heavily, and the stench of *dragon's breath* burnt her nose and throat. Coughing, she staggered to her feet and tried to get clear of the smoke blowing across the deck.

Antar snapped to attention and *Otella* powered away, turning violently and tilting to hasten their escape from the putrid smoke. Amarah's feet slid at the suddenly steep angle underfoot, and she ended up pressed against the ship's side, clutching onto the edge and her scythe.

The temperature suddenly dropped and she shivered

involuntarily. Her vision cleared as Kohl descended, arms outstretched, wings splayed. Freezing wind shot from his fingertips and cleared the air of the acrid smoke. Amarah would have been thankful, but as the smoke lifted, she saw Traego in a headlock—Cyd had him pinned against the mast, a knife at his throat.

'Traego!' Amarah and Carav yelled in unison.

'Last chance, Traeg. Give me what I want, and you leave with your life. You can swim, right?' Cyd said, grinning through bloodied teeth. 'You took my ship once. I'll just kill you and take yours.'

'Not happening ya piece o' shit!'

Cyd grunted in response. He flipped Traego round, pressed his back to the mast, and raised the knife. 'Big mistake. You know corpses are easy to search. I can get rid of every one of your crew, easy. *Otella* can be flown alone, you always brag about that. I fancy me this pretty ship, now. 'Specially as you got rid of mine. It's only fair.'

Before Cyd could bring an end to the fight, both he and Traego were hit square on with a blast of freeing air. They went flying and landed face first on the deck, weapons rolling away from them. Kohl sent forth another gust of icy air, and Amarah raced forward, her scythe at the ready.

She saw Veynothi's blade on deck beside one of Traego's daggers and darted towards it. In her peripheral, Cyd was on his feet and also charging towards the blade. Amarah cracked a wave of energy towards him, skidded to a halt, and snatched up the blade from the deck.

'That's mine!' Cyd snarled, recoiling from her attack and slashing at her with his knife.

As Amarah rose to meet him, he brought his dagger down on her arm. Instinct made her pull it back, but his weapon sliced into her hand and he shoved her roughly into the side of *Otella*, grabbing for the sword. Searing pain shot through her hand and she lost her grip on Veynothi's sword. In a split second, it plummeted into the sea below.

'Look what you've done, you fucking idiot!' Cyd roared, looking over the edge as the water swallowed the blade.

Amarah didn't hesitate.

Ignoring her bleeding hand, she clambered onto the side and leapt off.

7

Palom and *Leillu* retraced their steps across the great ice plains between Tum Metsa and Gal Etra. When he'd come to Tum Metsa, he'd hoped to re-join Amarah. Now, he left with new allies, and an equal sense of trepidation. They fell into position with the caravan as it travelled east to pick up extra supplies and people from Gal Etra before the long trek south to the capital. They'd been assigned a large covered wagon for their supplies, which they shared with Karvou and another Ittallan called Yfaila, an old weaver who wanted to bring her wares to the capital in the hopes of making a small fortune.

He'd seen some of her rugs while the wagon had been loaded and didn't think much of them. But he had noticed she'd created several with Varkain and snake designs on them, and it was clear she'd planned ahead to cater to a new strain of customer.

She was older than he by a few years, but held herself with the poise of a young Goldstone. She spoke little, and bluntly, and cared for none of the luxuries many of the other villagers enjoyed. She ate from her own supplies and shared nothing with the other dozen or so members of the

93

caravan, and her hermit-like behaviour meant none of the others encroached on their wagon more than was absolutely necessary.

Palom found Yfaila's manner, abrupt as it was, a welcome break.

He'd left Taban Yul in the midst of anger and misery, had turned his back on his former lover, Lathri, and her allies. Had fled from his niece, Solvi, his father, Manilo, and everyone in the village of his birth. And now, the capital had truly fallen to Sapora's claws. If the Varkain king really had unleashed a Sevastos dragon upon his enemies, Palom wasn't sure anyone he cared for would have remained in the city.

And if they did, he had no idea how they might react to his return.

He walked near the middle of the caravan as they moved, the better to dart ahead or drop behind should anything trouble them during the journey. Many Ittallan walked, too, with only the very elderly opting to ride in the wagons. Palom overheard most of the conversation, but tuned it out to little more than background noise while he kept alert for threats.

'I don't care what he says. A snake is a snake.' One of the Ittallan barked suddenly, his voice raised in clear frustration.

'A snake he may be, but he's also the king. And the capital offers safety. Protection. Call it cowardice if you feel better for it. I'd rather live.'

Palom glanced over to see a pair of Ittallan in the middle of an argument. One was broad and bearded, the other was a lanky youth bundled up in furs. It was the youth who seemed to be more trusting of Sapora than any Ittallan had right to be.

'Rubbish. Whole city is cursed now. I had word just last

week that my cousin threw himself off a bridge and into the river. Whoever heard of such a thing!'

The youth sighed heavily. 'Snakes can't make people do that, even with their blood magic! Your cousin probably had too much to drink and lost his step. Everyone's turned to something to numb the pain of change.'

Palom swallowed any words he might have retorted with and kept his gaze forward, eyes scanning the trees as they passed through the dense forest towards Gal Etra. The heavy, rhythmic trudge of his boots in the deep snow served to keep his focus. He turned around to check the rear of the caravan, and watched as *Leillu* leapt forward, diving into the snow and wriggling back out with chunks of it stuck to her rich, blue scales. He suppressed a grin at her simple enjoyment before continuing onwards several paces behind the arguing duo.

He very much doubted there'd be anyone or anything out here to trouble them, and his services wouldn't truly be needed until they were on their way to Taban Yul. But he took his work seriously and didn't want to be seen as cutting corners, so kept his watch as thoroughly as he would any other time. He knew there were only so many paths through the extreme northern regions, and fewer still that could accommodate a travelling caravan of such size.

As the light began to fade, he wondered whether they would end up going back past where he had abandoned his *Valta Forinja*—buried to its hilt in the depths of the trees. He'd left it just outside Gal Etra, before he'd hurried to Tum Metsa to catch up with Amarah, though that had been fruitless.

Palom couldn't help but think of the sword, and whether the magic within the enchanted blade would call to him, still.

It had been a power unlike anything he'd ever experienced.

The blades he'd forged during his brief stay in Tum Metsa with *Leillu*'s flame were beautiful and deadly, but they were nothing like the legendary *Valta Forinja*. Now his mind had cleared of the sword's influence, he wanted to study the lore and see whether there were any texts that might explain what he'd managed to create in such a foolhardy manner.

Palom knew he would not be the only smith to visit the University in Berel, and if they knew even half of what went into the blade, he wouldn't put their recreation past a person with more ambition. Discovering and wielding the *Valta Forinja* had been his boyhood dream. There'd be others who felt the same way, he was sure.

He knew he'd been downcast following Aciel's defeat—who wouldn't, after having lost so many friends and allies. But the sword had somehow made everything worse. Darker. Twisted. The sword had clouded his vision to only his own misery and guilt, and he'd paid the price for his self-induced isolation.

Of course, had it not been for his *Valta Forinja*, he'd never have discovered *Leillu*.

Other than Sapora and his Sevastos, who were clearly an exception, people and dragons didn't mix. They were wild animals, apex predators, and highly respected. That respect usually meant people kept a healthy distance from them.

And while many looked upon him and his dragon companion with interest, no-one truly knew what it meant, or how he would cope as she grew. Palom himself assumed *Leillu* would fly off to live her own life as she chose, and perhaps seek out others of her kind. But so far, the dragon had followed him everywhere like a puppy.

For the most part, Palom hadn't worried about it. He

simply took each day as it came, and would deal with any problems if and when they appeared.

But what he *had* to consider were the fully grown dragons attacking towns and villages throughout Val Sharis.

They seemed bent on revenge following Aciel's slaughter of them to harness their powers, and wasn't helped by Jato continuing with her fiancée's work. Would *Leillu* somehow be affected by their anger, too?

He wondered whether she would turn on him in the night and attack.

It was a grim possibility that Palom disliked thinking about, but he had to prepare for that possibility—if and when it came.

For now, the young dragon seemed perfectly content to follow alongside him and get herself involved in whatever work he was part of, and Palom had no problem with that. And he had to admit the younger Ittallan was right—if they were safe in Taban Yul, it would be silly to not travel there.

No dragon, no Arillian, would dare attack the capital while a veritable god stood guard.

As they passed the quarter-league sign to Gal Etra, Palom stopped. The trees around him looked much the same as the trees they'd passed on their way there, but he knew his *Valta Forinja* was hidden here...somewhere. He'd plunged it deep into the ground, but even if it hadn't been snowing every day since, he doubted he'd have been able to physically see it.

There was no flash of light, no pulse of energy.

Nothing that called to him. No pull.

His shoulders dropped in relief, and he watched as the caravan passed by, the wagons travelling single-file to navigate the narrow path through the trees.

If anything, he'd have liked to discover it again if only to reopen his communication path to Amarah, but he wasn't sure speaking to the sky thief would be worth the pain of once again possessing the cursed weapon.

No.

She was off doing whatever it was she did. He had his own goal—to ensure the safety of the caravan on its journey to Taban Yul, and, by extension, keep Karvou safe, too. When he reached Taban Yul, he could decide for himself whether to seek out his former comrades, or perhaps he'd just speak with Princess Isa and see if there was anything he could do to aid her.

Karvou's father had wanted Palom to take his son on as an apprentice, and had asked with such desperation that Palom would have felt terrible if he'd refused.

The fact he had no intention of taking on an apprentice was something he had omitted from the conversation, and he was now left with a young lad, not yet able to tap into his *meraki*, looking to Palom as some sort of idol. And he didn't have the first idea of what to do with him.

Of course, he could always set up a new forge in Taban Yul. He was certain Princess Isa would permit it, despite burning down his old one and no doubt significantly damaging other buildings in Trader's Alley. And his reputation as a hero of Val Sharis would certainly bring him customers. But after everything that had happened, Palom wasn't sure he wanted to go back to blacksmithing.

That had been his life, once. And now that things had changed so drastically, he wasn't sure whether he could return to it ever again.

His dragon-forged sword, his *Valta Forinja*, had poisoned him—mind and body. It had sapped his strength and cleared his thoughts of all reason. The darkness had been extreme and absolute, and even now, traces of it still lingered deep within him. Casting away that weapon had lifted such a weight from his chest he'd felt as though he'd been reborn.

He sighed in his reminiscing as the last wagon trundled past. Palom remained where he was, keeping an eye out for anything that might follow them with ill intentions. He'd been about to continue on, having decided the way was clear, when he saw Yfaila shuffle onwards.

She limped and used a stick to help her walk, but Palom hadn't realised how far she'd slipped behind, and cursed himself for being more interested in memories of his *Valta Forinja* than his current task. He hurried over to help her. 'You should be riding in wagon,' he said, in a harsher tone than he'd meant.

Yfaila scowled up at him, her tightly braided hair coming loose with sweat, evidently offended. 'I'm not dead yet.'

Taken aback, Palom offered her his arm, but she shoved it out of the way with her stick and carried on. 'You will lose sight of caravan at this speed,' he said. He took a moment to gather himself. 'I cannot let this happen.'

She snorted. 'Your job is to look after them, not me.'

'You are part of travelling group. I look after you as well as them,' he replied. He was used to her brusque nature, but her words were rude more than anything else, and he bristled at them.

'I'm just fine. Anyway, I can't stand listening to them argue over snakes and Arillians. This way, I get my peace and quiet.' She looked pointedly at Palom, as though he were disturbing her.

He walked beside her, despite her rebuffal of his help. Leillu had stopped some way ahead and looked back at them quizzically. 'Have you visited Taban Yul before?' Palom asked. 'I do not think you will get peace and quiet in city.'

'That's different.' Yfaila huffed.

Palom bit his tongue for a moment as they made their way along the path, following the tracks in the snow made by the wagons. They were due to reach Gal Etra by nightfall, and with the sun slipping below the horizon, it wouldn't be long until they reached the town and could rest.

He decided to try again with Yfaila on what would be a more neutral topic. 'We are almost at Gal Etra. Do you have family there?' He wanted to help her, but he was at a loss as to how, when she refused his assistance.

'I know your former business partner was a falcon, but I have no interest in fraternising with a tiger,' she snapped. 'My business is my own. I don't need anyone shoving their nose where it isn't wanted!'

Palom raised his eyebrows. Most Ittallan, especially those in rural locations like the far north, kept to their own cliques more than most. Having spent so long in the capital, where people mingled freely, he'd almost forgotten that.

He didn't know what Yfaila's *meraki* allowed her to transform into, but from her icy response, he assumed it was some kind of bird. If she didn't want his help, that was down to her. But he was being paid to ensure everyone's safety, whether she liked it or not. 'When we leave tomorrow, you can sit in wagon.'

Yfaila opened her mouth to reply, but Palom's patience had disintegrated, and he cut her off before she had the chance to say anything. 'Everyone walks. So you will have your peace in wagon as you will be only one in it.'

She pressed her lips together to show her displeasure, but she didn't argue.

Quite what he had done to annoy her—other than be a tiger—Palom had no idea. Aside from a few customary greetings when they'd first met, he hadn't spoken with her until now.

Anger smouldered within him, but he hadn't yet lost

sight of the last wagon, and he kept his gaze on that to keep from snapping at Yfaila again.

She stumbled suddenly, dropping to one knee, her stick falling into the deep snow.

Palom looked down at her. If he helped her up, she'd rebuke him. If he stood and waited, she'd rebuke him. He sighed, knowing he'd get another verbal attack whatever he did, so he picked up her stick and offered it to her when she got herself back to her feet.

She took several moments to brush snow from herself before grudgingly taking her stick off him.

He waited for a thank you, but received a sharp nod, and then she hobbled on. She passed *Leillu*, who had sat against a tree to wait for them, but she ignored the dragon. After a moment, Palom followed, patting *Leillu* gently on the head, and keeping several paces behind Yfaila so as not to give her more reason to complain.

~

BY THE TIME YFAILA, Palom, and *Leillu* reached Gal Etra, it was full dark. Torches burned high and bright by the town's gates, and Palom was grateful for company of a more cheerful sort.

An older Ittallan approached the caravan and went to great lengths to shake the hand of every one of the travellers. When he reached Palom, he clasped his hand with both of his. 'Palom, the great tiger. Such an honour to have you with us. Your strength will serve us well, I'm sure.'

'Thank you, sir.'

'I apologise. I'm Odi. My mother is the Gal Etra Archigo. I hear your father is now Archigo of Feoras Sol? Do you see much of him, now?'

Palom shook his head. 'Not so much now. But I hope to return soon. When things are...more settled.'

Odi nodded slowly, a knowing nod. 'Let us pray that Rhea settles things sooner rather than later. I'll be coming with you and the others. Summercourt is one of the last remaining ways we can have any influence in Val Sharis, now.'

Palom shrugged. He didn't care for politics and ruling. 'I will see you in morning, then.'

Odi understood the dismissal and took his leave, turning to greet the other Ittallan.

The wagons had gathered just within the gates, with most of the travellers sorting through their belongings as the townspeople of Gal Etra came to greet them. Palom made his way to his own wagon and peered inside to find Karvou fast asleep under a heavy blanket, huddled against their supplies. 'Karvou. We are at Gal Etra,' Palom called gently. 'There will be hot food for you.'

When he saw the boy stir, he retreated, only to find a small crowd of people surrounding the wagons. One person stood out in particular—a short Ittallan with a slight hunchback.

'Palom? Palom yeh've come to Gal Etra!'

Palom groaned inwardly as he recognised the fast-talking voice. 'Jek. It has been a while.'

He'd met Jek in Taban Yul back when he'd still had his *Valta Forinja*. The other Ittallan had been irritating with his non-stop talk, but he'd also witnessed Palom slaughter several Varkain while on their way to Feoras Sol, and had quietened significantly after that.

Time seemed to have helped, and Jek didn't hold back in his greetings. 'It sure has! How've yeh been? I didnae know yeh'd come so far up north! This is my neck o' the woods, this is! I'm a Gal Etran, born and bred!' The Ittallan raced up to him, arms wide as though wanting to embrace him.

Leillu leaped forward with a snarl, and Jek pulled up short.

'Sorry. *Leillu* is not fan of sudden moves. Especially towards me,' Palom said.

'Oh, right,' Jek said, holding out a hand tentatively towards *Leillu's* inquisitive blue nose. '*Leillu*? It's okay, *Leillu*. I'm a friend.'

Palom watched as the young dragon's snarl softened into a chirp, and she folded her wings tight against her body almost as if she were permitting Jek's presence. 'I have not seen her do this before,' he admitted.

'It's sweet of yeh to call her *Leillu*. She is nae much of a little one any more, though!' Jek said, brushing the dragon's nose with the back of his fingers. The dragon's shoulders came up to Jek's waist and her growth showed no sign of slowing.

Palom folded his arms. 'I know. But names stick.'

'Yeh not wrong,' Jek agreed. 'I suppose yeh've heard about the dragons attacking towns in Val Sharis?'

'I have.'

'And Arillians, too?'

'I have. It is why I am here. Guarding caravan to Taban Yul.'

Jek nodded, thoughtful. 'I'm heading to the capital, too.'

Palom shrugged. Between Jek and Yfaila for company, his journey would be a long, long trek.

Jek continued, 'Of course Taban Yul seems tae be on a bit o' a knife's edge. What with King Sapora tryin' tae bring back the Arks and everything.'

Palom's blood turned cold at the casual mention of the Arks.

Lathri and her companions had hinted at them when

he'd last been in the city. It had been the trigger which had made him leave. To hear another report from the other side of the country somehow made it more concrete.

He knew well the destruction the Arks had wrought during the war between Ittallan and Varkain all those years ago. His childhood had been full of the histories, and even speaking their name created a primal fear deep within him. They were most powerful weapons the Varkain had ever unleashed—a force created to annihilate the Ittallan, and nothing else. Palom shook his head at the thought. The idea of returning to the capital brought back memories of why he'd fled it in the first place. Although this time, he didn't have his *Valta Forinja* muddying his thoughts and heightening his fears and negative emotions.

This time, he was acting with a clear head.

'You are...sure?' Palom asked, though he braced himself for Jek's enthusiastic nod.

'I am. Every town has an Imperial Guard post, right? King Sapora, well, Tacio, I suppose, sent a couple of Cerastes along with the last courier. So we had it straight from the Varkain's mouth. Sapora's offering gold tae anyone who can bring him information on the Ark's locations.'

'So...he does not know where they are?'

'Guess not.'

'How much money is he offering?' Palom pressed.

Jek scratched his chin thoughtfully. 'Yeh know what it's like. These things dinnae remain clear. They get exaggerated. But last I heard it was five hundred crowns.'

Palom couldn't conceal his reaction. His mouth gaped open. 'Just for *information*?'

'Yep. Thing is, Sapora seems tae be betting on the fact the Arks are ancient history. They're forgotten even among many Ittallan.' He shrugged, and made way for a small group of townsfolk as they brushed passed. 'And even those who remember? That's a lot of money to make you consider...'

Palom shook his head in disbelief. *Leillu* rubbed her nose against his leg, as though sensing his discomfort. 'Five hundred crowns...' It was enough money to do anything. To start a new life anywhere in Linaria. 'Surely...Surely it is impossible. The Arks are gone. Lost to the Varkain. No?'

'Who knows. Like I said, it's a fair bit o' gold tae make yeh wanna look, right?'

Palom shook his head again. He glanced up to see Yfaila bundling a small parcel in her linens as she made her way into town, while Karvou clambered out. He threw a satchel over his shoulder, and hurried over to Palom as soon as he spotted him, his smile wide and eyes bright despite the hour.

Jek immediately turned to the youth and struck up an unrelated conversation while Palom allowed his thoughts to torment him. He'd hoped that Lathri's comrades had been wrong in their estimation, but had left the city on the off chance it was true.

Now, he felt he was walking straight towards death by Varkain.

He watched Karvou happily chat with Jek, all innocence and naivety, and frowned. Rhea help them all if Sapora succeeded in bringing the Arks back.

8

I sa had always found speaking with Sapora easy. In fact, she delighted at the palace servants' clear uncomfortableness while she strode up to her brother and spoke easily.

But in the weeks following his ascension to power, and also Tacio and his Cerastes moving into the palace, things had become...complicated.

He still trusted her, she thought, but Tacio seemed to see right through her lies, and had her watched with greater intensity since the strike on the palace. Quite how he was able to tell, she wasn't sure. Perhaps he was simply suspicious of her having never seen that much of her before now, and harbouring an innate suspicion to anyone who was—or appeared to be—an Ittallan.

Herself included.

When she'd seen the servants carry out word of the king's bounty on, "an ancient Varkain treasure," she hadn't thought much of it. But since she'd set up a tentative friendship with Lathri and her rebels, Isa had come to realise that her brother really was after the Arks. With the Sevastos at his beck and call, adding Arks to his arsenal was overkill, surely?

She'd tried to broach the subject as delicately as possible with Sapora. 'Are you sure you should be trusting common thieves with something as...' Isa struggled for the right words, 'as...*valuable* as this?'

Sapora shrugged, his attention on yet another map laid out on the table before him. 'All thieves want one thing: gold. It's about trusting in what they *want*, rather than trusting them. And I have plenty of gold.'

Isa frowned. She couldn't argue with the logic that all low-lifes and criminals were interested only in filling their own pockets. But the thought of just anyone stumbling into an Ark...she didn't have the faintest idea of what might happen.

Sapora continued, 'I'd go myself, but it's better if I stay in Taban Yul. Although if everyone keeps drawing a blank, I might need to send Tacio to do some digging.... I've lost my eyes in Niversai, too. Morgen has vanished.'

Isa saw him scowl but said nothing on the matter. Sapora didn't yet suspect her involvement in the strike on the palace, and she was keen to keep it that way. Quite how Lathri coped under Tacio's relentless torture, she didn't know, but she was grateful for her silence.

It kept her safe.

'I imagine Morgen is busy with the rebuild of Niversai. I hear the city was damaged rather badly following Aciel's strike there,' she said. 'They've sent several requests for gold, materials, and resources to help with progress. Rosecastle is almost fully restored, but the rest of the city...' Isa trailed off.

Sapora wasn't listening.

He'd become increasingly distant since the strike on Taban Yul, and though he'd always played his cards close to his chest, this was more than she'd ever seen before.

Although he didn't question her, she feared he no longer trusted her.

If that was the case, any power her voice held was diminishing.

With a sigh, Isa stepped away from her brother and the maps. 'I'm going into the city. Rhea knows they need motivation to rebuild what the Sevastos damaged.' The barb came out quickly, but Sapora seemed either not to notice, or not to care.

She huffed and whirled around, hastening out of the council tower and out of the palace.

∼

ISA LOOPED Little Yomal three times before she dared cross into the residential district. She knew Tacio's Cerastes followed her, and they were getting harder and harder to lose. The damned snakes were masters of stealth.

She'd left under pretence of helping the citizens, and that had been the truth. She'd simply omitted the fact she was also visiting *other* citizens who'd happily see Tacio and Sapora's heads severed.

Isa was over an hour late by the time she was certain she'd lost any tail who had tried to follow her, but she refused to apologise to Aetos, Solvi, and the other rebels of Lathri's group. She'd made it clear that she was continuing to put herself in direct risk by helping them, and now they'd failed to free Lathri, she'd be watched more closely than ever.

Thankfully, the one who would reprimand her the most fiercely, Kylos, was already locked up. Kylos's brother, Aetos, looked up at Isa the moment she entered the room through the balcony, having clambered up the building's side. His eyes held hope and frustration in equal measure, and she knew both emotions were directed at her. She reported immediately, 'Kylos is being kept in the palace dungeons alongside Lathri and a handful of others. Sapora won't permit them to be killed. Don't worry.'

Her words felt hollow and bitter, and even as she spoke them, she felt as though she'd somehow betrayed their trust. She no longer recognised the myriad of faces crowded into Lathri's townhouse. Many still recovered from injuries sustained either during their strike, or from Sapora's retaliation, and the deep stench of burning filled her nose with every breath she took.

Isa swallowed and leaned against the wall, for Lathri's furniture had been taken up by other Ittallan who were in more need of rest than she. She drummed her fingers against her bare arms as she surveyed the scene.

Lathri lived in relative comfort, with a large living space full of cosy furniture, a balcony that gave unparalleled views of the northern half of Taban Yul—including the palace—and a bedroom which currently served as a recovery suite. Isa had forbidden any healers to attend the injured during the select hours of the day and night that she might visit, as she hadn't trusted any to not run to Sapora with news of her collaboration. This way, Isa could share information and remain hidden from all but the most necessary eyes.

While unwilling to sacrifice the skills of healers, Aetos had acquiesced, knowing that should Tacio or any of his Cerastes discover Isa's trips to the house, they'd all be dead before sunrise the next day.

But seeing so many ill and injured pulled at her heartstrings.

These were *her* people. And they were suffering.

Aetos, acting leader in Lathri's absence, nodded at Isa's brief update, his golden eyes blinking back whatever emotion threatened to spill, and turned back to changing the bandage on a woman's shoulder.

The home was now a bedhouse for Lathri's followers to rest and recover, and Isa blamed herself for the need. In fact, the only person who didn't seem to look at her with suspicion and doubt was Solvi, the niece of her ally, Palom, who'd thrown herself in with Lathri the moment she'd learned the healer wanted Sapora off the throne, and Isa put on it.

The young Ittallan had only just turned eighteen years old and able to tap into her *meraki*, and they shared a similar true form, resulting in greater camaraderie between them. Despite being half-Ittallan, half-Varkain, Isa had grown up in Val Sharis, and thus leaned more towards the Ittallan's cultural nuances than she did of the Varkain.

'King Sapora also wishes to bring Summercourt back,' she announced, once the room had settled again. She knew Sapora personally didn't want to do it—the request came from Vasil—but it wasn't worth the effort of explaining the details to the room of Ittallan rebels.

Solvi glanced up from her plate of food and caught Isa's gaze with a worried look of her own.

'I guess he'll try to get some of the Ittallan back on his side. He's too far gone for that. Not after all the damage that dragon of his caused to the capital,' Aetos replied.

Isa was pleased and relieved that his reaction held fewer teeth than she'd expected it to. She replied, 'He already has somewhat of a Council. This'll just make the decisions and any alterations more formal. Of course, it means Vasil and his entourage will be coming.' Better to warn them.

'Great. More snakes.' Aetos shrugged, then tied off the replaced bandage. 'He'll fill the palace full of them. I don't know why we don't just leave the city.' He ran a hand through his short, dark hair and walked to the balcony. He gripped the rail and leaned forward, sighing deeply.

Isa knew he would fly again today, to keep eyes on the palace, perhaps. Or he'd scout further along, to the border between Val Sharis and Sereth. Whether it was habit or he didn't trust her information, she didn't know. And with his sister locked up, she didn't want to rile him up any more than he clearly was.

'Course it's not gonna be fair, is it? Just another way to show off his power.' Aetos whirled around and watched them from the balcony. 'Pretend to have Ittallan join in service of the palace but give all the positions of power to more snakes. Dragons above, what's next after Summercourt?'

'The Arks...' Solvi said in a quiet voice.

Aetos snorted. '*That* is no joke. Bring one of them back, or all four of them—Rhea forbid—and we can kiss Val Sharis goodbye. All of Linaria, in fact.'

Isa squirmed. She'd not told them how close Sapora had been to freeing Malashash, the Ark who'd historically defended Sereth, and suddenly wondered whether there was more to Vasil's visit than Summercourt. Vasil never travelled lightly; he always brought a handful of his personal Cerastes; his queen, Savra; her servants; thralls for their entertainment and menial duties... and a Valendrin.

She'd only met one of the Blood Mages once before, when she'd been ten or eleven years old, who had accompanied her father on one of his rare visits to the palace. While she'd been excited to see her father, Vasil had only time for the Valendrin, the council, and a brief lunch with herself and Sapora.

That lunch had been a frightening experience.

She'd grown accustomed to the Cerastes who accompanied her father and their severe manner, as well as the Varkain who made up most of his entourage. But the Valendrin had been another creature entirely. A Varkain who never transformed, who became so utterly consumed by their magic, she'd been certain their reptilian features simply pushed through the thin flesh covering their body. It left them looking like a sort of skeletal half-creature, or someone who'd been trapped by their *meraki* mid-way through a transformation.

While there were plenty of tales of Ittallan who'd gone feral by remaining in their true forms for far too long, she'd never known the opposite—except in the case of the Valendrin.

Whether it was their nature in general, or just the one who'd visited the palace with her father that day, she didn't know. Nor did she particularly care to.

Ever since she'd been able to tap into her own *meraki* at eighteen, and her father had seen her true form, she'd been ignored. Invisible at the best of times, and bullied at the worst, it had only ever been Sapora who had stuck by her and treated her with the respect her royal blood commanded.

After Vasil had ceased travelling to the palace, the snub-bings had lessened. Summercourt would bring it all back in one, long, formal event that she'd be unable to escape. And if Summercourt *was* a pretence, and Vasil travelled with another Valendrin that Sapora wished to consult with, then her brother was getting desperate in his quest to discover and restore the Arks.

And a desperate king was a dangerous one.

The woman Aetos had been bandaging shook her head and let out a wistful sigh. 'Taban Yul. The richest city in Linaria, our capital, reduced to a ghost town full of Varkain squatters, bribery, and death. Not to mention blackened and burned by our very own king's command!'

Isa didn't reply. The woman was right. Her beloved city was a far cry from the bustling place she remembered from her childhood. And that was before taking Aciel into consideration. Whatever he'd done, whatever he was doing, had triggered a change slowly being realised across the whole city. His poison was worse than Sapora's—slower, more insidious, and sickening the residents.

In fact, she could hardly stand to be within sight of the crystal pillar which loomed on the edge of Taban Yul. Even the bravest, most loyal of the Cerastes now refused to stand guard over it, and the city's north gate had been sealed on a semi-permanent basis to prevent others from travelling too close to it as they passed into or out of Taban Yul.

She and her fleet of warships had beaten the warmongering Arillian, and yet his remains continued to mock her.

Solvi stood and took her empty plate to Lathri's sink, breaking Isa from her thoughts. Summercourt and Arks. While she couldn't prevent the formalities of palace life, she would do her best to stop the Arks from coming back. She had to.

But as to exactly how, she'd only drawn a blank. She needed the stars to align perfectly to have any hope of influencing Sapora.

Sapora seemed to trust her, still, or at least didn't concern himself with what Tacio thought he knew. But Tacio was more of a threat than Sapora. Suspicious of everyone, he was a pure Varkain through and through, and detested the Ittallan as their ancestors had detested one another.

The thought of a half-breed on the throne rubbed a lot of people the wrong way, and for all Sapora's claims of bringing the two races together and uniting them, all that seemed to have been achieved since he'd become king was alienating both.

Aetos continued to rant about Summercourt and the state of Val Sharis. If it wasn't Sapora and his Varkain, it was the sickness in the city caused somehow by Aciel. And if it wasn't the crystal, it was the Arillian attacks moving steadily further south towards them. And if it wasn't the Arillian attacks, it was the dragonfire lighting up the eastern coast of Val Sharis in their furious onslaught.

Isa rubbed her temple. She couldn't do it alone. She needed the support of her people and of a competent council. If she could somehow influence Summercourt, somehow ensure those loyal to her could join the Council...

She had one goal first and foremost—to free Lathri.

The fact she was still alive went showed that Sapora, at least, did not want her dead.

And Lathri's mother had been an influential member of the Council before her death. Lathri's knowledge of power, politics, and the love she had of the Ittallan people, made her an ideal ally. One that Isa would be foolish not to work with.

Her fellow rebels' complaints grew louder and more heated, and Isa watched as Solvi returned from the kitchen, wiping her hands dry on the front of her tunic.

Isa frowned. Solvi looked up to her, with a generous dose of naivety, but she still thought the world of her. What kind of a princess let down her followers? Who gave up when things became difficult?

She refused to be responsible for crushing Solvi's beliefs, too.

Isa glanced out to the balcony and noted how the sun had tracked across the sky. Tacio's Cerastes wouldn't be long in searching all the districts looking for her. Better she get out and on with her rounds before she would rouse suspicion.

'Do not give up. I am with you. Val Sharis will get through whatever threats Sapora unleashes, believe me. I won't let him destroy us. I won't.' Although it was far from a stirring speech, it was all Isa could offer right now. She slipped out the front door, her footsteps echoing away.

~

ISA HAD ALWAYS STRUGGLED to belong.

She'd been born in the palace to a Goldstone—a woman she couldn't even remember—and brought up by those in the council after her mother's death. Sapora had been born almost a year prior to another Ittallan Goldstone, and they'd been raised together as palace children, offspring of King Vasil following his conquest of the nation. Of course, the warrior king rarely departed Sereth, so she and her brother were left largely to themselves and their carers.

If anything, those early years had been the happiest, most carefree times of her life.

Although she and her brother received regular tutoring to ready them for royal duties, and she'd even studied at one of the best colleges in the city to widen her education, Sapora always received more attention. He was the elder of them, and he was being brought up as the crown prince. She was just another bastard whom they had to cater to because of her blood.

It wasn't until she reached eighteen and could tap into her *meraki* and see what her heritage was that she had been shunned. Sapora had joined his father in Sereth having shown his true form to be that of a *naja*. She, on the other hand, was a cat.

Vasil lost interest in her, but she could not be thrown onto the streets. So, Isa lived in the palace, never permitted to wield any of the power that should have been hers, and treated as a worthless bastard by the nobility. Caught between two worlds and never belonging in either.

All that would come to the surface again with the return of Summercourt.

Isa shoved the thoughts aside and walked lightly across the city streets, with no clear destination in mind, simply allowing her feet to guide her. As she crossed from Little Yomal east, towards the Food Quarter, she passed butchers and bakers, and relished in the scent of warm bread baking, the sweet sugar and caramels from the confectioners, and the fresh fish brought in from the docks, caught that dawn.

It was the thought of food that grabbed her attention more than anything, and she slipped along a slightly elevated side street to join the throng of people gathered by the fishmongers, ready to snag themselves a bargain.

Reaching into her pocket, she pulled out her bag of loose change and took out five half pennies. Many people said things in the city were expensive, but that was only true if you went to the tourist areas. In certain places, you'd be charged double or triple, depending on what it was worth, and how gullible you were. But in the lesser known areas where locals and families had run businesses for years, you could always get a good deal.

And having spent all her life in Taban Yul, Isa knew exactly where she could get a good deal.

Although she could technically have anything she wanted for free, she chose to pay for most things as a way of supporting the citizens and warming them to her.

As the crowd thickened and the smell of fish grew, Isa stopped, leaning forward on her tiptoes as she tried to make out what was causing the commotion while keeping herself relatively out of view. It was always a busy time at the beginning of the day, when the morning's catch was evaluated, weighed, and priced up. But today there seemed to be more bodies present than usual.

Frowning, Isa lingered on the edge of the crowd,

watching for anything that might have caused the disturbance. She wished to transform and leap onto the rooftops for a better look, but that might have drawn attention to her.

Shouts carried from the shopfront, bodies were pushed and shoved, and finally, a young child was thrown from the throng, where he stumbled and toppled over in the middle of the street. He grazed his palms on the cobblestones and wailed loudly.

'Bastard!'

Isa kept out of the way, observing, as the child's mother stormed over to him and picked him up. She dusted him off and kissed his hands where they bled. He couldn't have been older than four or five, and he clutched his mother's long hair as she held him to her breast. 'Every morning for ten years, I've come here! Every morning! You can't just do this to us!'

'Orders from the king, pet,' a condescending voice replied, old and grating. 'You got a problem, you take it up with him.'

'He ain't no king of mine! Even Vasil gave us our rights! You can't double the prices without notice! Some of us have families! I've got six children to feed!' She was close to tears in her frustration and hysteria.

He looked disdainfully down at her, then spat, causing a ripple of anger in the crowd. 'Then maybe you should stop breedin' if you can't afford them.' He stepped forward, a large knife in one hand, wearing a thick apron covered with fish blood and guts. 'And watch your tongue. "No king of mine?" That's treason, that is.'

He was clearly a Varkain—his skin as grey as his apron —and his lip curled to reveal several pointed fangs.

Though not as regular as the woman seemed to be, Isa had visited this fishmonger several times and had never seen him before.

'*My* family owns this alley now, and every shop on it. Maybe you'll have better luck in East Cross. We don't give handouts to no-one.'

Indignant with rage and clearly upset by his insult, the woman spun on her heel and stormed off. The crowd parted to make way for her, her son bawling his eyes out all the while.

'For any of you creatures what didn't hear that, this shop has been taken over. Stock all the same, but different owners and prices as King Sapora has amended the tax laws. New prices on the door. Anyone got any issue, go get yourself an audience with the king. I hear Summercourt is coming up. Make your case there. Till then, if you ain't buying anything, you get off our property.' Two other Varkain appeared at the door behind him, both broad, their frames filling the doorway. They looked like brawly Varkain who were raised to fight, rather than to fish, and were probably put there by Tacio or his Cerastes rather than being related to the one who'd thrown the woman out.

Isa's appetite left her and she slunk away before the rest of the crowd could stampede, trying to figure out how to word her complaints of the Varkain's action to Sapora when she returned to the palace. Plenty of people had been put out of action with the Varkain exodus had come to Taban Yul. First, they'd taken up abandoned and derelict buildings. Then they'd started seeping into the slums, pushing out the poorest families. About a third of the city had become Varkain-only districts, but now they were forcing business and trade out...Isa worried there'd be a civil uprising outside of the rebel efforts if Sapora and Tacio let it continue.

A shadow passed overhead, and she flinched, looking up.

The Sevastos.

She'd bravely tried to talk to it, once, but it had either ignored her or refused to speak.

It did not attack unless commanded to by Sapora.

It did not hunt unless commanded to by Sapora.

The ancient dragon was treated worse than a dog—just a presence to put off any would-be attackers. Sapora claimed it protected the city and the people in it, but it was clear the dragon only protected the Varkain.

Aciel was the real threat, his rot festering and spreading throughout the city, and it appeared not even a Sevastos could do anything about that.

Isa shuddered and hurried away from the fishmongers.

The darkness Aciel had brought to Linaria hadn't gone, it had merely shifted. A festering wound in the most prestigious city in the world, leaking poison and corrupting those who dared go near it.

Traders' Alley was always busy, and she picked her way through the customers and traders both. Coins littered the streets, trapped between cobblestones from overzealous customers or lucky pickpockets. Beggar children shuffled along on their hands and knees, pocketing change where they found it.

They were mostly shingles—coins the wealthy Goldstones gave no worth to—but there was the occasional half penny, too, and she saw a particularly swift handed boy grab a silver florin from between a crack.

If you were a Varkain, you were rich—or certainly would be, if you moved to Taban Yul. You could do exactly as you wished and nothing and no-one could touch you because you had the backing of the king. But everyone else? They had to make do, scrounging from what the Goldstones left and the Varkain tossed out.

That was *not* the life for someone living in the richest city in Linaria.

She sat on a bench opposite a pair of tall, slender, flat-leafed trees and watched the crowds of morning shoppers mill about their business. More than half of everyone there was Varkain.

Isa sighed, thinking about how the city had changed, how the people—more than just the rebels—wanted things to change. Not necessarily to back the way it had been, even she knew that hadn't been the best, but something had to give.

It was unfair for the city to be given to the Varkain simply because Sapora allowed it. But with a Sevastos at his command, there was a worrying, growing number of Ittallan who believed him a god himself.

She didn't blame them. After all, Rhea and her dragons had been worshipped since time immemorial. The University at Berel existed to study the goddess, the dragons, and their magic. To have the oldest and most powerful of Rhea's children at the command of a king?

That was something holy.

Something divine.

And it was why she had joined with Lathri and her rebels. Someone had to take a stand and fight back, even if it was futile.

She needed to do something to change it.

She needed to make Sapora listen. There was no way he'd be able to enjoy a long rule if he isolated half his subjects and bled them dry.

Isa rubbed her temples again she she considered what she'd say to her brother, and how she'd phrase it.

'Make them bleed. Destroy their homes.'

Isa was on her feet in a heartbeat, a short dagger grasped in her left hand. 'What?' The throngs of people milling about glanced up at her sudden stance, but otherwise paid her no mind.

'Paint the city red with their blood.'

A shiver ran down her body. The voice carried on the wind, fading as the breeze died. Isa stood stock still, listening, straining for any sound, but she could only hear the gentle thrum of conversation from the morning crowd.

'Disgusting. Creatures. Vermin.'

Isa whirled around and chased after the distant voice, racing through the streets and barging past the crowd. With her blade in hand, most declined to pursue her, and she was perfectly fine with that. She didn't want a crowd following her and finding her with whoever spoke.

It had to be Aciel's influence again.

She'd never forget the cool wind and compelling voice when she'd come face to face with it, even if it was spoken through unwary citizens.

Isa came to a small bridge leading back into Little Yomal, the water underneath splashing gently. The last traces of the voice had disappeared, but she saw a couple leaning over the bridge, their hands entwined as they stared into the distance with unfocussed eyes. The city's double wall lay directly ahead, and beyond—the field of fighting, where the crystal pillar lay.

Isa took in a deep breath. 'Excuse me?'

'No more. Leave nothing alive,' the couple said, their voices monotone.

'Stop!' Isa yelled, but they ignored her.

As she looked on in horror, the two stepped off the bridge to plunge into the water. Isa ran to the edge and looked into the river, and watched, helpless, as their bodies were swept away.

9

M

urky. Cold. Dark.

Seawater smothered Amarah as she dove into it, her eye focussed on her prize—the thin, grey, chipped blade that was sinking fast.

Damn that Cyd!

Orange coloured the top of her vision as the two airships that had attacked them crashed into the sea above her, both still aflame from Traego's attack. The water slowed their descent but she could still hear the roar rushing in her ears. Though she was a sky pirate, she had no qualms about being on or in the water, and she pushed out all thoughts from her mind that did not relate to catching her prize.

As the momentum of her dive wore off, she kicked out, powering deeper into the gloom, the blade just out of reach and sinking quickly. Arms outstretched, she propelled herself forward and down, closing in on the blade. Her hand still bled from Cyd's dagger, leaving a small stream of red, but she ignored the pain and pushed on. Dark shapes darted out of sight—fish, probably—as she drew close to the treasure. She'd been through too much over it to just let it sink to the bottom of the ocean because of Cyd and Traego's stupid behaviour. With one final kick, she powered down several lengths and grasped the hilt of the blade before it was lost.

A jolt ran through her, almost like electricity, and she flinched, nearly letting go of the sword. Her fingers trembled and went numb. Steadying her wrist with her other hand for a moment, she whirled around, her chest tight as her breath began to run out.

When she was sure she wouldn't drop the sword, Amarah swam upwards as quickly as she could, grateful she'd taken off her heavier furs for the flight to Estoria. Several more chunks of wood thudded into the water above and around her, the heavier bits of debris sinking, sending great streams of foam back to the surface. Amarah avoided them, navigating past anything that might harm her as she used her free hand to help her swim.

Breaking the surface, Amarah gasped. She gulped down great lungfuls of air, her hair plastered to her face, her right hand clutching the ancient blade. Around her, she saw the wreckage of the two airships—a bit of hull, a torn sail, barrels half-blown apart. Wiping her face clear, and inadvertently smearing blood across her forehead, Amarah paddled way from them, looking for open water.

A swell rose up, and Amarah bobbed underneath as the waves cascaded overhead. She floated as much as she could, putting as little energy into treading water as was possible and letting the current move her. If anything, she hoped the water would carry her further from the still-flaming debris.

Just as she was about to break the surface and take another breath, something grabbed her across the waist.

Almost gagging in surprise, Amarah brought her elbows down instinctively, her left one thumping into something solid that tried to press itself against her. She kicked out against the thing and shoved herself to the surface.

She gasped once before the thing grabbed her foot and pulled her back underwater. Amarah squinted and opened her eye to see one of the crew from the other ship grappling with her. He was incandescent with rage, his arms locked on her boot as he pulled her further and further down. She could barely make out the features on his pale face in the gloom and had no way of identifying him.

Amarah thrashed, kicking with her free leg to loosen his grip on her. Bubbles rose furiously all around them, masking her view almost as much as the natural murk of the seawater. She cursed losing her dominant hand through clutching onto Veynothi's blade, and scrabbled in the water to try and prevent being pulled away from the surface.

Her assailant was stronger than her, and had gravity on his side, as he pulled them both deeper and deeper into the gloom. The bright orange light from the ships' fires dimmed as he pulled and swam, desperate to keep her underwater.

She grimaced—surely he couldn't hold his breath indefinitely? Did he mean to drown himself and pull her along with him?

Panic began to rise in her gut, but she forced it down. Her kicks made his grip even more determined, and with nothing left to lose, she lashed out with her right hand—and the blade.

The ancient sword struck him clear across the forearm, and blood gushed from the gaping wound.

Amarah had no time to check how badly she'd hurt him —his grip loosened immediately, and she kicked away, powering herself up to the surface where she gasped in several lungfuls of air. Her chest stung as she took more breaths, and she hadn't realised how much it had hurt while she'd been terrified of being held underwater.

She span about as she treaded water, keeping her head above the surface. The remnants of the ships seemed to span in all directions, most of which were still ablaze, blotting the sky above with thick, dark smoke.

Cold seeped into her, and Amarah began to shiver. She swam towards a particularly large piece of debris whose flames had been put out either by the crew's frantic efforts before the ship fell from the sky, or by the seawater. She wasn't sure she could get back to the surface once more if her enemy had enough strength to attack her again, and getting onto something that could float seemed the best move.

Amarah grasped onto the edge of the debris and, with some difficulty considering her wounded hand and her tiredness, pulled herself up onto it, never letting go of the blade. She coughed up a bit of seawater and spat it away as she righted herself to sit on the wood, scooting back to be as close to the centre as she could be.

Once the smoke had cleared and she could see *Otella*—and the crew could see *her*—she'd make her way towards it. For now, she was better off waiting here while she caught her breath back than flailing around in the water and getting weaker.

Licking her lips and tasting salt, she wiped her face with a sodden arm, shivering more vigorously now she was out of the water. Not a moment later, the man resurfaced, blood pooling in the water around him. He tried to swim, but the arm she had cut appeared useless, and he couldn't get in a full stroke as he headed towards her.

Drawing up her knees so her feet were clear of the water, Amarah brandished the blade at him. She didn't say anything, but surely he could see it was the same weapon she'd used against him and wouldn't approach.

Something broke the water's surface with a splash to her left, and she glanced over to see another body. From the severe burns she could see, Amarah assumed the *dragon's breath* had killed him, or had certainly weakened him enough for the fall to do the rest of the job. The pungent stench of the attack still filled the air, which didn't help with the burning sensation in her chest.

The first man carried on swimming towards her, and she scowled. Whether he was trying to attack her again and steal the blade, or simply get onto something that floated, Amarah wasn't having it. 'Stay back!' she yelled, though her voice cracked. He didn't seem to hear or he decided to ignore her warning, and carried on towards her regardless, sinking down every few strokes as his dead-weight arm dragged underneath.

Even from where she sat, Amarah could see the blood trailing from his wound, colouring the water. More bubbles burst on the surface as other bodies floated up—most of which were dead. She wrinkled her nose, but there was nothing to be done for them. They had been stupid enough to fire on *Otella*. Surely they had to expect some kind of reaction.

'I'm warning you!' Amarah yelled, as her attacher drew within a handful of strokes of the debris. Her fingers squeezed the hilt of the blade in readiness. More movement caught her eye, and she saw something grey protrude from the water several feet behind the man.

A moment later, and he disappeared underwater with a sharp gurgle of surprise.

More bubbles burst on the surface, but he didn't reappear.

Amarah trembled, and it had little to do with the cold.

One by one, the other bodies which floated nearby were pulled under, disappearing with little more than a flurry of bubbles that foamed at the surface. Other bits of debris also vanished, though they popped back up a short distance from their original location.

Clutching the hilt of the sword, Amarah watched as pieces of hull disappeared all around her, one after the other. Panic swelled. Sharks? Giant squid? Something else entirely?

She tensed, waiting with dread for whatever it was to pull her under, too. She spared a glance overhead, but the sky was still thick with smoke. Although she could hear *Otella's* propellers, she couldn't see the airship.

She opened her mouth to speak a half-hopeful prayer to Rhea, when the piece of wood she was sat on cracked right down the middle, and Amarah was plunged back into the sea.

She span wildly as she was sucked underwater, losing all sense of direction and movement. When she managed to open her eye, she saw a waiting row of yellow fangs smiling at her in the darkness.

Amarah couldn't make out much colour underwater, but its face seemed a mass of green and black scales, and she could only barely see where it was in the murk. Its sinuous body moved swiftly, coiling overhead and underneath. Amarah knew of sea creatures that lurked in the depths, great monsters of enormous size, but hadn't spent enough time by the water to understand which were truth and which were fiction.

Her first thought, that a shark had been attracted to the blood, was dashed.

Whatever this creature was, it dwarfed even the largest sharks.

Something thumped into her back, and Amarah saw more of the creatures' body had coiled around her, like an enormous, scaley, eel. It moved easily, fins cutting through the water as it circled Amarah in gentle loops. She saw sharp barbs protruding from the tips of its fins, and instinctively pulled herself in, lest those barbs caught her by the leg or arm. The creature had limbs which helped it move in the water, but it swam too quickly, and the light was too poor, for her to count how many.

It lunged away suddenly, breaking the water's surface and coming back under with another body between its teeth. Blood darkened the water all around it as the creature shook its head violently, the body coming apart in its mouth as though it were a child's doll.

Amarah made a break for the surface, managed to take a quick breath, and went back under in time to meet the smiling teeth once again. She didn't want this thing to grab her without warning, and though it terrified her, she'd rather keep her eyes on it.

It hovered near her as it ate, letting out a deep rumble that vibrated through the water. She felt the noise in her bones as much as in her mind.

'*Veynothi.*'

Her heart pounded. Did this sea monster think *she* was the Ark?

She did hold one of Veynothi's swords, after all.

The creature swam closer, teeth disappearing as it closed its mouth to swallow the last remnants of its meal. It then turned to face her and swam forward as gently as a creature of that size could. It nudged her body with its squat, round face, which was easily ten feet wide, and Amarah saw it watched her through four black eyes.

The panic which had for so long threatened now burst, and she kicked it in an attempt to get back to the surface and away from whatever it was. She was comfortable in the sky, a ship's deck underfoot. She was not comfortable lost at sea with a monster encircling her.

Breaking the surface, she looked up to see a patch of clear blue sky through the *dragon's breath* smoke. Just beyond, she saw *Otella* floating low to the surface of the sea.

It was too far away for her to make out Traego or any of the others, but she flailed anyway, waving both the sword and her free hand.

Most of the debris still floated around her, the monster having tried to eat them and spitting them back out, and she swam towards the closest one in an attempt to get away.

If the thing thought she was Veynothi, perhaps she was safe.

She very much doubted she'd remain safe if it figured out she wasn't the Varkain.

Water broke beside her as the creature's fins appeared, the barbs shining wickedly black in the sunshine. She powered off to the side and toward another piece of debris, only to find her path blocked again by the creature's tail as it splashed in front of her, covering her in foamy spray.

Amarah dove to find the monster's teeth waiting for her, and she swam off in another direction to get away. The creature rumbled again, more loudly than before. Words that meant nothing echoed in her head and disoriented her again.

She thrashed around with the blade, hoping to catch it off guard or at least dissuade it from attacking her.

The rumbling stopped and Amarah managed to reach the surface again. Dizzy, she whirled around, and found she'd swam a fair distance from the larger pieces of wreckage—only several smaller bits of wood and debris floated here, none of which she could use as cover.

Cursing, she headed back to the wreckage. There was no way she could outswim the creature in open water, even if Traego was able to spot her straight away. She had to take her chances among the wreckage and hope the creature didn't decide to just eat her and be done with it.

She felt more rumbling from underneath, but couldn't make out the words while she was on the surface. Amarah paid it no mind, anyway. Whatever language it spoke, she didn't know it. She had no hope of trying to communicate anything to it, and decided it would be best to just keep out of its way as best she could.

Just as she approached a large enough piece of wood that she could fit onto, the creature's tail emerged from somewhere to her right and slapped her hard on the back, knocking the breath out of her and shoving her underwater again.

Amarah rolled away, almost losing her grip on the blade, as she avoided the creature's sharp barbs, which extended all the way down to the tip of its tail.

'*Veynothi.*' The rumble came again, more angrily.

Terrified her time was up, and already losing strength from the exertion, Amarah faced the creature. She shook her head, though she didn't know if it would mean anything, and raised the blade to it.

The monster rumbled again, the vibrations intense as they cascaded through the water and slammed into her. More words in the same language. She squinted, trying to hold onto both her breath and consciousness. It lunged forward, two of its forelimbs extended.

In her semi-conscious state, Amarah thought how funny its webbed claws looked before they smacked into her chest, sending her backwards. The tail lashed at her next, drawing blood where the barbs sliced into her cheek, but the blow sent her back to the surface. Amarah took several breaths and her vision came back. She saw her torn eye patch floating some way off and felt hot blood on her cheek, stark against her cold body.

Arms going numb, she attempted to swim away, only to have the creature slam into her again from underneath. Amarah was thrown back in among the wreckage, where she grasped onto a barrel to keep herself from sinking.

She'd always thought she'd die in the middle of a heist, having bitten off more than she could chew. She'd never thought she'd be eaten by some creature of the deep.

She looked down to see the creature powering towards her, jaws wide, for another attack or to swallow her whole.

Amarah took a deep breath then let go of the barrel, sinking back into the water. She held Veynothi's sword out, the tip facing the creature. She braced herself for impact, and then the blade connected with the monster's scales. It drew blood as easily as it had the pirate who'd grabbed her earlier.

With a roaring squeal, the creature dove away immediately, leaving streaks of oily blood in the water.

Amarah forced herself up to the surface, only to find the barrel had floated off with the current. Shivering, she looked skywards again, and her heart lifted when she saw Kohl appear, blowing the smoke away with his frigid wind and clearing her view to *Otella*.

The sight gave her renewed strength, and as *Otella* dropped close to the surface of the water, she made a beeline for it, swimming as quickly she could, lest the monster returned.

'Amarah! Grab on!' Traego called, casting a rope overboard.

When the ship was close enough, the bottom almost touching the water, Amarah threw herself onto the rope and heaved herself up out of the water with Traego, Oris, and Carav pulling her up.

She was so relieved when she was back aboard the deck she could have kissed it.

'Couldn't resist a swim, could ya?' Traego asked, taking Veynothi's blade from her with one hand, and pulling her to her feet with the other. 'All ya had to do was ask and I'd've had Antar put *Otella* down on one of the islands!'

'Very fuckin' funny, Traego,' Amarah panted. She leaned forward, her hands on her thighs, water dripping from her body and forming a puddle underneath. Her arms continued to tremble, and her face felt oddly exposed now she no longer had the patch covering her eye. 'You ever see anything...like that before?'

Carav shuffled forward with a couple of thick blankets of wool, and she handed one to Amarah. It was old, scratchy, and smelled stale, but Amarah gratefully wiped her face and hair with it. She gently dabbed at the slash across her cheek from the monster's barb, desperately hoping it wasn't venomous.

'Like what?' Carav asked.

Amarah frowned. The creature had been enormous, how had they not seen what it was?

The thought struck her. The monster hadn't ever come to the surface—certainly not its main body, anyway. Only fins and the tip of its tail had broken the surface, and smoke had masked most of the battle. It was no wonder they'd not seen.

Amarah hoped that if they had, they wouldn't have been so slow to pick her up.

She fought to stop her teeth chattering. As she got her breath back, she glanced around and saw Kohl flying over the wreckage of the two ships, using his wind to blow the debris and remaining flames away from Otella.

'At least he's helping out now,' she muttered.

Carav shrugged and handed Amarah another blanket along with a strip of bandage for her wounded hand. 'Dunno why you travel with him.'

Amarah snorted, using the smaller blanket to wipe down her arms and legs while she wore the larger one over her shoulders like a shawl. 'He saved my life. I'm not stopping him from flying off if he wants. But he wants to keep an eye on me.'

'What for?' Carav asked.

Amarah glanced at Traego and grinned, throwing a sodden, bloody blanket back at Carav and taking another fresh one. 'Because I'm going to kill his daughter.' She said, some of her old self coming through. She hobbled across the deck to the other side, wiping her face and mouth with the edge of the large blanket. She was grateful she could feel the warmth of the sun on her face now she was out of the sea, and already her shivering had lessened.

It was an experience she wouldn't soon forget, and she'd certainly pay the sea more respect from now on.

Traego followed her, and handed over her scythe.

She nodded, grateful, and swapped Veynothi's blade for her own weapon. Now safe and warming up, exhaustion threatened to overwhelm her, and Amarah leaned against the side of the deck as Antar lifted *Otella* higher and away from the ruins below.

'You feel anything...odd when you hold that?' She asked the captain as he sheathed Veynothi's sword.

'This? Nah. Why? Did ya feel something?' He asked.

Amarah shook her head. Traego had kept most of them in the dark over this treasure hunt. She had no intention of giving away her knowledge so soon. 'Works like any other sword. Cut up some of Cyd's crew easily enough. Even in the water.'

Traego nodded. 'Speaking of, we got him locked in my cabin. No sense in killing Cyd, not when he's more useful alive.'

Amarah shrugged. That was Traego's call. Personally, she'd have cut his head off and kicked him overboard. But she was on *Otella* and as the ship's captain, Traego's word was law.

Amarah was just beginning to dry off completely when a breeze of cold air preceded Kohl's arrival. She scowled at him. He'd have been able to pluck her from the water easily, if he'd bothered to get involved.

It seemed the Arillian was also angry. He spoke even before he had landed, 'Traego, that was unnecessary. There was no need to destroy those ships. Look at the danger you put Amarah in.'

'Amarah put herself in it,' Traego replied. 'And there was plenty of need. They're rivals. Ya rather they shoot *me* out the sky? And my crew? And Amarah?' Traego turned away from the Arillian and looked back out to sea. 'It's a cut-throat world out there and striking fast is the only way to survive. Thought ya'd know that, spending enough time 'round Amarah.'

Kohl fluttered his wings as he cleared his throat, but he said nothing. Amarah had seen him back off enough times when challenged. For all his abilities, he didn't have that much strength—Jato had probably seen to that. For one who claimed he was interested in her safety, he seemed averse to helping her out.

Traego wasn't one to press a battle where it wasn't warranted, so the captain and the Arillian kept quiet as Antar sailed them further south, the burning wreckage soon little more than a dark smudge on the horizon behind them.

She decided it wasn't worth mentioning it. She didn't want Traego or any of his crew thinking she needed the Arillian to look after her. Dragons above, she could look after herself.

And it wasn't as though Kohl had been able to see the mess she'd jumped into.

But if she hadn't they'd have lost the sword and the chance at Sapora's bounty. Not that Traego or the others had even thanked her for what she'd done.

Amarah sighed and pulled the blanket around her shoulder even more tightly. The patch she'd lost had been a gift from Kohl, too, and he hadn't even mentioned it. He'd been more interested in having a go at Traego for how he chose to run his ship.

'Where's Cyd?'

Traego shrugged. 'Antar took care o' him while ya were in the water. We tossed him overboard.'

Amarah glanced at Kohl, and the expression on his face told her Traego was telling the truth.

Once, she'd have pitied Cyd. Now, she just wanted to watch him burn.

She shook her head. They'd be in Estoria soon enough.

She'd get her cut of the bounty from Traego and use the funds to get herself a new ship—one she could run *exactly* as she wished—and then she could get her own back on Jato.

And then, once *Khanna* had been avenged, she could turn her sights on Moroda and seeing what she could do to bring her back. If that was even possible.

Amarah had seen so many things in the past few weeks that she wasn't even sure what was or wasn't possible anymore. From ice golems to floating islands, ancient Varkain and sea monsters that could talk.

Perhaps bringing Moroda back was truly possible after all.

She allowed herself a smile at the thought. She'd love to see the look on Topeko's face when she shattered previously held knowledge and beliefs about his dragon Goddess and her magic.

But despite her goals becoming more real, her blanket, and the warmth of the sun, Amarah couldn't shake the chill in her fingers from where she'd clutched Veynothi's blade.

'Blood magic...Damned Varkain,' she whispered.

10

H eat smacked Morgen square in the jaw when he stepped off his cruise class airship and onto the desert sands of Ranski.

He had almost forgotten how humid the place was, and he'd last visited on the edge of winter. Now Linaria was turning into spring, the heat in the desert country was far harsher than he'd realised it would be.

Morgen immediately shrugged out of his cloak and loosened his belt to prevent the leather chafing against his skin. The place was poles apart from Povmar, and he wondered whether the extremes of temperature would have an adverse effect on his body.

As he filed out of the airship and through the Samolen guarding the entrance to Berel, he stripped off more layers until he only wore his thin linen undertunic. His papers marked him still as part of the Imperial Guard—it was the only way he'd be able to enter the city with his weapons and armour—despite having officially resigned and wielding no such power any longer.

He'd not followed proper procedure, of course. Yes, he'd sent a letter of resignation alongside his latest reports, but by the time his superiors in Niversai received and replied—no doubt with their refusal—he'd be long gone. And he very much doubted they could spare the resources needed to track down one man.

Morgen had sailed by boat around the west coast of Corhaven to a harbour town called Cashlin, from where he'd chartered an airship all the way into Ranski, and the country's capital: Berel. The whole trip had cost him twenty crowns, which was a significant chunk of his money. But he'd paid more for speed than anything, as he'd arrived only four days after leaving Povmar.

Berel was certainly the largest settlement in Ranski, home to the University, a fully functional airship dock, and residents from all around Linaria. Most tourists came to see Berel New Town, which held the University, to speak with the scholars who lived and worked there.

The country was separated from the rest of Linaria by its own laws. It had no King, Council, or Imperial Guard and was forbidden to take any part in any wars or struggles taking place across the world. It meant the country was a safe haven, and through its border with Corhaven, was near enough to Niversai for those who needed to quickly return.

Morgen shouldered his bags as he left the dock, and made his way down a wide staircase into the New Town. He vaguely remembered the way to Topeko's residence, and knew he needed to get to the Old Town first.

The streets were bustling with people, many of whom were robed scholars, their coloured cheek jewels glinting in the hot, desert sun. Many gave him smiles or polite nods, which Morgen was sure to return. He felt immense relief that he'd dug out the ring Topeko had gifted him and wore it proudly as he made his way through the New Town.

Memories flooded him as the dust and heat beat against his exposed skin. How young and naive he'd been the last time he'd visited Berel. It felt like a lifetime ago. Since his last trip, he'd crossed the Sea of Nami and flown to the far corners of Val Sharis, killed more people than he'd ever wanted to, and lost many friends.

And yet, somehow, it felt *right* to be here. Certainly it was better than freezing in the middle of nowhere halfway up a mountain. He'd all but lost his earlier trepidation, and was pleased with his decision to travel here. He'd deal with any consequences of leaving the Imperial Guard later.

His finger was warm where the crystal ring sat, and he was determined to put all his efforts into learning the Samolen magic Topeko offered. After all, Sapora had no idea where he was, and he had all the time in the world to learn and perfect this new way of fighting.

Morgen ran a hand across his beard, resolving to shave it back, if not off completely, at the first opportunity. Sweat beaded down his face and arms, causing the dust and sand from the streets to stick unpleasantly to his skin. He ran a hand over his face and through his hair as he made his way steadily towards the large bridge that connected the New with the Old Town.

The hangar his airship had docked at was a large one in the centre of the New Town, no doubt to cater for tourists and other visitors. The smaller one he remembered landing in when he had arrived at Berel before on Amarah's airship, *Khanna*, had been in the Old Town. It had more than likely been for private use than anything else. But he didn't begrudge walking through Berel to re-familiarise himself with the city, if he was to be staying here for a while.

Of the Samolen he did see, most had one cheek jewel that shimmered purple. Morgen recalled that had been the colour for the teacher, and so assumed these were scholars. He saw a few with pale blue jewels, and one with white, but there were by far more tourists in Berel than Samolen.

He supposed it was the middle of the day, and many native Samolen would be at the University, or otherwise working, and he wondered whether he'd have to wait until another time to see Topeko and ask for his help.

Morgen continued to ponder his options as he passed under the archway at the head of the bridge. It linked the town's two halves, which were separated by the lake. Morgen had crossed the bridge on his last visit and found the lake just as breathtaking as the first time.

The lake wasn't one of water, but it shone in the sunshine as if it were. The lake was pure, unfiltered, magic. "Rhea's breath," they had called it. It gave the Samolen their natural affinity for performing magic, and they used it to create their ornaments and artefacts—including their cheek jewels—to harness and direct their own innate abilities.

He grinned at how much he remembered, but it also led to more questions—questions that hadn't occurred to him the last time he'd been here but were now of utmost importance.

Morgen took a few minutes to enjoy the sight of the lake of magic—as did several other tourists who leaned over the side of the bridge for a better look—before continuing into the Old Town. As he made his way along, he began to see familiar buildings, which reassured him that he was heading in the right direction. It didn't take long before he heard music pulsing through the streets, washing away his weariness and re-energising his steps.

Try as he might, Morgen couldn't see where the music was coming from, but heard strings and drums play together softly, as though seeping from the buildings and street itself. He picked up his pace, even the intense heat no longer giving him as much trouble, excited to see Topeko and understand the nuances of Samolen magic, and how he might tap into it.

The street narrowed somewhat, and the buildings became larger and spaced further apart. In place of tiled or thatched roofs, coloured fabrics draped over the tops. His heart picked up as he recognised one house draped in purple and red sashes, the material blowing slightly in the light breeze drifting through the street.

Steeling himself, Morgen approached the building and took a long minute to study it. The last thing he wanted to do was barge in on the wrong house, but he was quite certain it was Topeko's home—the place he and the others had stayed for several days while they discovered more about Aciel, the dragons, and the magic of Linaria.

Once certain, he stepped up to the entranceway, then paused. With no physical door to knock on, he was suddenly unsure of how to announce himself, and didn't know enough about Samolen customs to take a guess. Morgen lifted a corner of the fabric and poked his head through, cautiously calling, 'Hello?'

'Topeko's at the university for a while. You'll need to come back tomorrow.'

Morgen didn't recognise the voice, but hovered half inside the entranceway while he debated. His eyes adjusted to the dim interior, and saw the large, circular foyer was as lavishly decorated as he remembered it.

His bag's strap dug into his shoulder, weighted down by a large quantity of books borrowed from Topeko's library, as well as the ereven sphere ornament gifted to Moroda so long ago.

He couldn't leave, not with so many valuables, so he simply cleared his throat to show he hadn't left and wasn't going to.

'Waiting there won't do any good. I told you, Kalos Topeko is at the university.'

Morgen glanced up as a youth walked into the entrance

foyer, a dishcloth over one shoulder and a small chalice in his left hand. There was something familiar about him, but Morgen couldn't quite put his finger on who he was.

The youth placed the cloth and chalice on a sideboard, then faced him. 'Morgen? It can't be!'

Morgen blinked, suddenly putting two and two together. 'Andel? Wow...You've grown.'

The last time Morgen had seen him, Andel had definitely been a child. He'd only been twelve or thirteen years old. It seemed Andel had enjoyed a growth spurt quite recently—he had to be a foot and a half taller than he remembered.

Andel bowed low, his arms outstretched. 'I'm a Kalosai now. Topeko's taken me properly under his wing.'

'That's great!' Morgen replied, truly happy for Andel, even though he was unfamiliar with the terminology. 'Can I come in?'

Andel straightened and hurried to the entranceway, pulling the fabric open wide for Morgen to walk through. 'Of course, of course. You're a guest, still.'

It then occurred to Morgen why he'd not recognised Andel immediately. 'Oh! You're talking now!' He rolled the bag off his shoulder and placed it on the floor. 'You finished your silence?'

Andel grinned, the freckles on his face having darkened somewhat as he'd aged. 'Indeed. Kalosai can talk all they like, you know. But when you're training to be one, that's when you do your year of silence. Something about self-control.' He shrugged as though apologetic, but he still grinned widely. 'Let me help you with your things.' He made his way across the room to Morgen's side, and hefted up his bag with one hand, belying a physical strength as well as mental.

Stood so close, Morgen could see Andel's cheek jewel

shimmering in the afternoon sun—half purple, half clear, depending on how the light hit it.

'It's good to see you again, my friend.' Morgen slapped Andel on the back.

Despite Andel's youthful strength, he staggered under Morgen's greeting, stumbling slightly in his robes. Andel coughed and smiled. 'Ah, I forget you all wrestle with each other just to say hello. A hug is just fine.' He stepped back to embrace Morgen for a long moment in a gesture that mirrored Topeko's when Morgen had first met the scholar. 'Welcome back to Berel. Will you be staying long?' Andel tightened his grip on the bags handle.

'I'm not so sure. I need to talk to Topeko. I wanna learn more of your magic,' Morgen said. He lifted his hand to show Andel the ring he wore. 'I never got the most from this. Relied too much on my sword. It's hard to overcome years of training by using a power you don't really understand.'

Andel nodded. 'I'm sure he'd be happy to discuss that with you. I can have a room prepared if you'll be here a little while?'

'Thanks. I appreciate it.' Morgen hurried after Andel, who left the foyer and made his way down the hall. 'So, when did you start talking?'

'Only a month or so ago. My training has intensified now I've chosen my path. I'm going to be a healer. Requires a different type of learning.'

'Different type?'

'Yes. You see the different jewels we wear? It signifies a different specialty. To develop talent in these areas, you need a different training regime. Don't forget, all magic is innate —but wild. Training allows us to understand, harness, and control Rhea's breath.'

Morgen nodded, thinking back to the lake. 'Makes sense.

142

I forgot you called it all that. I thought it just applied to the lake.'

'"It"?' Andel raised an eyebrow and stopped by a door—a solid one made of wood. 'Linaria's life blood. The very essence of our world. A sacred, potent power. Yes, we call "it" Rhea's breath.'

Morgen swallowed and nodded. Though Andel's tone was still jovial, he realised he'd stepped on a nerve. He'd have to be an imbecile to miss Andel's offense, and he'd be sure to guard what he said when Topeko returned. The scholar was used to Amarah's brusque tongue, and he doubted he'd be able to truly offend him, but it was better to start a new training schedule on the right foot. He wanted to remain here and learn, and to do that effectively, he needed to mind his manners.

Morgen felt his ears go red in embarrassment. 'Sorry, Andel. I didn't mean it like that.'

Andel slapped Morgen hard on the back in an imitation of the earlier gesture. 'It's fine. I also wanted to say I heard about what happened in Val Sharis. Topeko told me everything when he returned.'

Morgen's throat immediately tightened.

'I can't believe you were all there, in the thick of it...fighting Aciel...'

Cool anger rushed over his skin, and Morgen was suddenly acutely aware of his heartbeat. 'Not...not all of us were there.'

Andel unlocked the door using a small set of gold keys and didn't reply. Whether he hadn't heard him, or didn't have anything to say in response, Morgen wasn't sure.

Morgen grabbed his bag back off Andel and pushed the door open. 'Will Topeko be back tonight?'

'Yes, but not until long past midnight. You'll see him in

the morning,' Andel said. He hovered in the doorway, as though unsure whether Morgen needed anything else.

Morgen was about to bid him farewell as he rested, when the weight of his bag caught his attention. 'Oh. These are yours, by the way. I wanted to bring them back. Moro...She...We said we'd return them.' He swallowed thickly as he fought down his flaring emotions. He lifted the bag's top and withdrew several large tomes, alongside a small sphere wrapped in soft linen.

'Morgen...' Andel stepped into the room and gently took the books from Morgen with both hands. 'Thank you so much. I cannot say what this means.'

Morgen shrugged. 'They're yours. Well, they're Topeko's, I guess?'

Andel gazed at the books almost in reverence before shaking his head. 'Thank you very much, Morgen. Are you hungry? Thirsty?'

He was, but he didn't want to put Andel out any further, and he needed to calm his emotions at the mention of his fallen friends. 'No, I'm fine. I'll get my things settled here, then look around town for a bit, if Topeko isn't around?'

Andel held the books close to his chest. 'Of course. Please, make yourself at home. I shall prepare a meal at sunset. You'll know when to return, the music will change.'

'I remember. Thanks again, Andel. I'll see you later.'

When Andel had left the room and closed the door, Morgen carried his much lighter bag to the bed against the wall. Silks covered the open window, blocking the intensity of the sun, but still allowing light to flood the room.

He rooted through his belongings and pulled out the short sword Palom had made for him. His *Valta Forinja* had been wrapped pommel to tip in several layers of linen and stored away since the battle with Aciel. He'd had plans to avenge the others with its sheer power...avenge Eryn.

But after returning to Niversai, working for Sapora, and then betraying the Varkain, he'd left it hidden in his belongings and hadn't so much as peeked at it since. Now, he'd brought it to a nation that looked upon conflict with disdain, and hoped to learn what he could of their magic to use it against Sapora and any Arillians he came across to somehow do justice to Eryn and the others.

And if the trader in Povmar was to be believed, Samolen magic could do a lot more than he could have ever imagined.

Perhaps resurrection was among those skills.

Morgen changed quickly, swapping his travelling clothes with a lighter shirt, then exited Topeko's house. Even if Topeko wasn't around, he could still visit the University like any other tourist.

He wondered whether Topeko and Andel lived alone, whether Andel was his son or just a student—a Kalosai, was it?—and how Amarah was mixed up with them all. The sky pirate apparently had Samolen heritage, but he'd never seen her perform any sort of magic, and she was so unwilling to speak of her past, he'd never learned any more about her than what she was happy to show.

As Morgen stepped back out into the bright sun, he let his feet carry him back towards the New Town and the University. He wondered if he'd need to choose a discipline of magic, like Andel had. Was that even possible for a non-Samolen? Or did he simply have to take what he could get?

The crystal on his ring hummed, warming his hand almost to an uncomfortable level.

He didn't know what would be possible until he tried, but Moroda and Eryn had learned much.

His heart pounded again.

Eryn.

It had been hardly more than a crush. When she'd

smiled a certain way, fiercely defended her sister, and faced her fears until she could do nothing else but flee...Morgen shook his head.

He didn't want to go down that train of thought. It led him to the palace of Val Sharis, the grand ball, and Sapora's cobra form which still gave him nightmares.

They were travelling companions, the same as everyone else. They'd all been in it together, had been so much and pulled through despite the odds being stacked against them...except at the final hurdle. That damned Jato and her Arillians.

Kohl's flight could be forgiven—who could ask anyone to attack their own flesh and blood?

But Jato was cold. Merciless. Just like Aciel.

The pair of them needed to rot.

He balled his fists as he crossed the bridge back into the New Town.

Several buildings made up the University, and Morgen headed for the main courtyard. Many people had gathered there, tourists and Kalosai, both. Although the lake was invariably the jewel of Berel, a sight thousands travelled the world to glimpse, the University held treasures more valuable even than that.

The five dragon stones stood on a raised altar, mirroring in all but colour the one on the outskirts of Taban Yul, which held both Aciel and Moroda. They were willingly given from Sevastos dragons thousands of years prior. Those ancient beasts had deigned give the Kalos' of Berel their power, so long as it was used to protect and defend, and never attack.

Morgen had found the notion strange, that the most power in the world had been gathered here, and was studied, not used for domination or destruction. He sat on the low wall which surrounded the courtyard, and looked up at the pillars. Each had to be eight feet tall, and they all glistened in different colours as the sunlight passed through them. He wondered if any of these stones held people's souls within, or if Moroda's Sevastos had been the only one to seal life away.

He slipped his ring from his hand and rolled it around in his fingers as he looked up at them, the sun providing a very pleasant warmth on his face as he relaxed.

It had been a shock, returning to the Imperial Guard after the battle. Suddenly having to follow orders again and complete reports. It all seemed so trivial.

So utterly pointless.

People all around the world were scrambling to recover from Aciel's war. Many had lost family if not in death, then to the Arillian conqueror's compulsion. Tens of thousands had been present in the battle above Taban Yul. Most had been in airships blasted out of the sky, but there had still been ground troops crushed by the Arillian's enormous storms.

Even now, a distant rumble of thunder would set him on edge.

He'd collected his reward money from Princess Isa, then flown back with Topeko to Niversai, the Corhaven capital. On his return to Rosecastle, he'd been thrust back into repair duty, helping to rebuild the city and get the citizen's lives back on track...all the while responding to Sapora's orders in addition to his own.

Of course, he'd been relieved when Aciel and his army had been defeated, but he wasn't sure he'd actually been on the winning side. Having lost so many friends, Morgen wasn't sure he'd do it all again if given the chance.

And now Sapora had a Sevastos of his own. One with as much power as the dragon Moroda had bargained with. As much power as the crystal stones sat here, in Berel.

He pulled a folded sheet of paper from his pocket and read Princess Isa's writing again. It was the justification for sending Imperial ships to Taban Yul.

The justification for all those who had died if not at Sapora's fangs, then in the dragon-fire unleashed by his Sevastos.

He tried to put their deaths on Princess Isa's head, instead of his own. He'd issued the command, but she had been the one who'd requested it. He was just following her orders.

He wondered what Taban Yul was like now. Had it been half destroyed by the dragon, as Niversai had been? Had Princess Isa sent another request, begging him to come to her city and help rebuild *that*, too?

If she had, her message would go undelivered. Though his comrades at Rosecastle knew he'd been sent to Povmar, none there knew where he was now. He'd been sure to keep them in the dark, lest any snakes came hunting after him.

He wondered whether Topeko, in his wisdom, would be able to get a message to her, though. Whether even sending such a message would be wise.

No.

Better to remain in isolation.

If no-one knew where he was, he could get his training underway without fear of being pulled away again. And Sapora had no chance of finding him here.

Even if he knew where he was, the laws of Ranski forbade conflict. Ranski wasn't part of the Sapora's rule, and the Varkain wouldn't be able to attack him so long as he remained here.

Of that he was sure.

Morgen sighed, refolding the paper and pocketing it again. He watched as a Kalos and trio of Kalosai hurried past, each carrying a fist-sized iron ball. He tilted his head to keep them in view as they crossed the courtyard, but lost them when they disappeared into one of the many University buildings.

Samolen magic could do things he'd thought impossible. The variety and scope had been clear to see from the Povmar trader's haul. Right now, he didn't know what he didn't know, but he trusted Topeko enough to teach him what he could. If the scholar assented.

After all, he'd returned the books. He still carried the ring. He had the gold to fund himself.

All he needed was the power, and the knowledge to wield it.

11

The archipelago of Estoria sprawled along the horizon in long, sweeping curves.

It had taken another four days of flying before land came into sight, and Amarah almost longed to have solid ground under her feet again. The coastlines of most countries were jagged, sheer cliffs, but Estoria's islands were smooth and inviting. Lush green foliage filled the land, and deep, white beaches kissed the turquoise sea.

Amarah thrilled at their approach, as she had the first time she'd travelled to the place—also aboard one of Traego's ships, come to think of it. She'd been in her teens at the time, and green as to what a life of thieving would truly mean. After all, what was the point of stealing gold and items if you had nowhere secure to store it or sell it on?

Estoria had become a haven for all sorts of miscreants. While many bold sky pirates had settled here, at least temporarily, the lush, tropical islands were also home to many Goldstones who wished to avoid the Imperial Guard —or at least paying their fair share of taxes. There were several old families who were Goldstones through owner-ship of land or inherited wealth. But there were far more who gained their riches through less than savoury means, and Amarah had always found it ironic how they were still treated with courteous respect in cities across Corhaven or Val Sharis, yet she was looked upon with disdain.

At least she was honest about what she did. The majority of Goldstones were worse than snakes.

As *Otella* approached land, she saw the towering trees and large, wooden buildings constructed within the highest branches. While some wealthy Estorians lived in these tree-tops, most of the larger buildings were Goldstone homes or places of business, built from the finest materials or as safe houses for some of their more valuable possessions. Many Goldstones paid the abundant pirates to prevent them from stealing, and others paid far more for the pirates to actually protect their valuables.

It felt like layers upon layers of corruption, with the sky pirates generally coming out on top.

Estoria was not governed by any king or council, and a myriad of Goldstones owned the archipelago. They'd originally bought the lush, tropical land when it had been discovered by early cartographers and explorers.

It offered freedom in the truest sense, with few laws to uphold, but also meant that Estoria was chaotic, with the strongest or loudest generally enjoying the best life. And that was why Amarah never stayed longer than a few weeks, if she could help it.

She much preferred to live on her ship, always on the move, travelling where she fancied, when she fancied, without worrying about whether the next sky pirate would stab her in the back for her latest haul.

Troupes formed quickly enough, and each one carved out their own patch among the islands. While skirmishes weren't uncommon, many respected one another enough to let each other be—unless there was a transgression of some kind. If that happened, then there'd be all out war between the troupes. Favours would be called in and there would almost certainly be deaths unless the proper apologies were made.

Nervous excitement coursed through Amarah. It had been a long time since she'd returned to Estoria, and she didn't want to remain here any longer than was needed to acquire a new airship. Then she could get her revenge on Jato, and turn her attention to freeing Moroda.

Berel seemed a likely place to gather information. After all, Topeko knew more about dragons than anyone else, and might be able to help her in her quest. Whether she needed to find another Sevastos or Topeko had other ideas, she'd follow it through to the end, and repay her debt to Moroda.

The rough waves below them gave way to a calmer surf, disturbed only by enormous shoals of fish bubbling at the surface of the sea. Gulls called relentlessly, darting out of *Otella*'s way only at the last minute as they shrieked their indignation. They were larger here than anywhere else in Linaria—almost the size of eagles—and Amarah remembered being mobbed by a gang of them on her first visit to Estoria.

The thought reminded her of the sea monster, and she shuddered. Clearly everything was larger near Estoria. She had no idea what that creature was, or why it hadn't eaten her immediately like it had the bodies of Cyd's crew. And it had *spoken* to her.

Somehow.

It had said Veynothi's name. It had known who the Ark was.

The idea of selling Veynothi's blade to Sapora made her blood run cold. Any bounty of that magnitude had to have serious repercussions. Would they all be cursed? Would they all drop dead? Would Sapora himself kill them?

Amarah didn't have the faintest idea of what an ancient Varkain weapon might or might not do, but the fact there was some enormous sea monster following it about made her more uneasy than ever, and she decided right there and then to never enter the sea again.

She found herself glancing often to Traego, who carried Veynothi's sword at his hip, and remembering her numb fingers when she'd grasped it. He'd said nothing like that had happened to him, and Amarah wondered if it had something to do with being in the water.

She knew from experience that Samolen magic was capable of many things. It stood to reason that Varkain magic might be equally able. But her lack of understanding put her at a disadvantage, and she disliked wading into the unknown.

The early morning sun was already hot, and the wind carried salt-sweet air. Amarah inhaled deeply. She'd almost forgotten the humidity of Estoria. She leaned on the side and peered overboard as Antar slowed *Otella* and brought the ship over land.

Many people were already up and about, getting on with their day's work, and she heard their shouts to one another clearly over the airship's propellers. Kohl had remained on board since they'd spied land, and he walked over to her.

'This is probably the closest place I have to a home,' Amarah said. She kept her gaze on the island below as Antar navigated the ship per Traego's orders. 'Couldn't be further from Oren, could it?'

'Quite.' Kohl tipped his hat, but didn't remove it despite the sweltering heat.

Estoria was where she had truly become a sky pirate. Where she had learned the tricks of the trade and bottled Samolen magic, where she'd met allies, made enemies, and of course, where she had bought *Khanna*.

Her stomach lurched at the thought and was quickly replaced by hot, raging anger.

Jato was going to pay. No power in Linaria would stop Amarah from exacting her revenge on the spoiled Arillian and all she stood for.

Amarah glanced at Kohl, but he was as silent and stoic as ever. Even now, after all this time, she struggled to read him. He followed her out of guilt, she knew that. Jato had been responsible for destroying *Khanna* and blinding Amarah in one eye. He'd been there and hadn't acted quickly enough to stop it.

And then Jato had disowned him and left.

Perhaps it was less out of guilt and more out of shame that he followed her.

That, and the fact she'd said he owed her a ship for his daughter's actions.

But while having someone in your debt was always a nice position to be in, Kohl's reluctance to get involved had become tiresome, and Amarah wondered if she wouldn't be better off on her own, like she usually was.

Kohl had lost his daughter, though he still loved her. She knew he hoped to reconcile with her, somehow. Until that happened, he moped around in misery and refused to be part of his own future.

She couldn't figure out what he wanted, couldn't figure out how she could get him to actually be useful. She needed to know his leverage.

Maybe she needed to cut him some slack and see if that helped him along.

'Landing now. Grab everything ya need, I'll be heading ta base with the sword and our travelling companion,' Traego said. He marched across the deck, counting out florins from a heavy purse. 'Job's half done, but ya get ya pay for being part of it. Twenty florins each, as agreed.'

Amarah took her share and inspected the silver. 'Thought it was fifty?'

'Always been twenty, Amarah.' Traego grinned. 'I'll give ya fifty if ya wanna be messenger and let our interested party know we've found what he wants.'

'Fifty florins to see Sapora? You'd have better luck with crowns!'

Traego laughed as the ship dropped in altitude, and Antar smoothly maneuvered *Otella* to rest in among other ships along a wooden dock still in sight of the sea. 'Maybe if the messenger took the blade with 'em, I'd consider more gold. I just need a runner and a fast ship. Don't wanna hold off this payout any longer than I need. Plus, I'm outta *dragon's breath* so need ta restock.'

At least with her few florins she'd be able to get something to eat and a new eye patch. Already the tender skin itched terribly in the sticky Estorian heat, and covering it again would ease her discomfort.

Oris and Carav scrambled away from their posts and threw themselves over the side, clambering down ladders, rigging, and onto the soft sand. Antar followed the two youngest crew members, with Traego bringing up the rear, Veynothi's blade still tied to his hip.

'Coming, Kohl?' Amarah asked, grabbing her *Valta Forinja* and following Traego off the ship.

'I have no choice.' The Arillian fluttered his wings as he lifted off the deck gently. 'Will you get a new ship here?'

'That's the plan.' Amarah pulled herself down the side and into the dappled shade of the palm trees, their long, thin trunks and wide, flat leaves blowing gently in the wind. She rolled her shoulders. 'Feels good to be back.'

She and Kohl followed Traego and the others along the shoreline. Though the sand was soft underfoot, there was the occasional crunch of a shell or pebble, or, as Amarah realised a fraction before it was too late, the tip of a discarded knife. Kicking it away, they walked onto the main beach where a large number of Estorians were gathered, all heavily sun-kissed and closer in spirit to the sea than to the land they walked on.

Several children chased each other through the surf with sticks, their screams and laughter filling the surrounding air. Most kept clear of the docks, where the pirates seemed to frequent, and the sand they ran on looked to be clear of any danger. The locals seemed to keep to their own areas, following invisible lines which divided the islands into different territories.

Amarah stopped when Traego pulled up to speak with a group of people picking fish from their nets and throwing them into buckets, cutting off the heads with sharp knives as they did, and discarding them. Gulls screeched overhead, occasionally swooping down to grab a fish. Other Estorians stripped to the waist dragged longboats onto shore, their holds bursting with fish, crabs, and seaweed.

'You're lucky to have such a close friend as Traego,' Kohl commented. He surveyed the scene with curiosity.

Amarah shook her head. '*Friend*? Don't be stupid. He's an ally, that's all.'

'The difference being...?'

She rolled her eyes. 'We have a common goal. We don't stab each other in the back until *after* we get what we both want.'

'He came to your aid when you needed help in Tum Metsa. If that isn't friendship, I don't know what is.'

She shook her head again. 'Nah. He came and got me 'cause he's got a better chance of winning this treasure hunt with me. That's all. Traeg's like everyone here. Cyd's the same.' She gestured to the island around them with wide arms. 'We're all ruled by how much gold we can fill our pockets with. We're all tools for each other. If I weren't such a damned good thief, Traeg would've left me.'

'No. There's more than that. I've seen how he looks at you, speaks to you. It isn't as black and white as you say.'

'Of course it is. If I needed someone competent, someone I could rely on for a job as big as this, I'd make sure I got *me*, too.' She cackled. 'Soon as I ain't useful, I'm dumped. That's our life. Besides, look at Carav and Oris. Antar is decent, but those two? Fodder.'

'And I thought you kept some honour...'

Amarah scratched at the old scar under her left eye and thought about his words of honour. 'You like to see the good in people. Guess you had to with a daughter like Jato.' The insult rolled off her tongue before she'd even realised it, and she bit her lip.

Kohl didn't reply, and Amarah huffed. Her jibes always went straight to the core. That was probably a large part of why she didn't have friends. And perhaps explained a little of Kohl's reluctance to swoop in and get involved.

She surveyed the view and tasted sea salt on her lips. The last time she'd been arrested, she'd been in the Corhaven capital, Niversai. She'd met Moroda, and the Goldstone's sister, Eryn, had freed them all. It had been a stroke of luck, but then she'd felt indebted to Eryn because of it. Everyone in Estoria tallied up favours owed to one another, and it was a habit she couldn't get out of.

When Morgen had caught up with them later on, she could have handed over Moroda and Eryn to him and saved her own skin. Most of the sky pirates she knew would have.

But Eryn had freed her from the cell. She'd owed the sisters, and refused turn them in.

She *did* have her own sense of honour, regardless of what Kohl thought.

Long-legged dogs padded across the waterfront, tongues

lolling and wiry fur carrying the scent of the ocean. They sniffed eagerly at anything edible, licking rocks clean of seaweed and nibbling at the leftover flesh of crab shells long after they'd been picked clean by gulls.

Amarah made her way over to Traego to see what the hold up was. She desperately needed something to eat and to figure out whether *Otella*'s captain would provide it or if she needed to sort herself out.

He was talking to a fisherman whose white hair blew around his face in the wind. He bit onto a pipe as he worked the fish, occasionally pointing to his comrades to give instruction or correct what they were doing. When he took his knife to a fish head, Amarah saw a faded line of *Thief's Ink* across his wrist. 'If it's got scales or a shell, I know what it is, an' how to cook it. An' how to avoid being eaten by it, if you're out for a swim.' The old man laughed, his mirth quickly descending into a lengthy coughing fit. He removed the pipe from between his teeth and spat a gob of dark phlegm into an empty bucket beside him.

Amarah's lip curled, and she took a step back.

'Good ta know.' Traego's wry grin never left his lips. 'What about sea slugs?'

The old man chuckled again, having recovered from his coughing, and replaced his pipe. 'Now they're not for eatin' but they're good for farmin'.'

'Just tell me where ta look.'

The fisherman stood up and stretched his back, lifting his sun-beaten face to the sky. 'You'll have the best luck on the north side. Just past Fallice.'

Traego nodded to him and flicked a half florin in the man's direction before heading off up the coast, his crew in tow.

When they were far enough away, Kohl leaned in closer to Amarah. 'What was that about?'

'Traego's finding us a safe spot to go over the next part of the job. Fallice is a small district, a bit like a market town.'

'I thought this was your home? Aren't you all safe here?'

Amarah laughed and shook her head. 'Kohl, this is Estoria. Pirate's Paradise. Home of Thieves and Miscreants. Nowhere here is safe. With a bounty this big, Traeg ain't taking any chances.'

Kohl raised an eyebrow and dipped his hat to her.

'Word'll soon get round of Cyd's capture and his two ships going down. Traego ain't exactly the most popular guy around here, so we need to get things in motion then head off soon as we can.'

'Perhaps he would not be in such a rush to escape if there had been no death and destruction to begin with,' Kohl said.

'Kohl, are you even awake?' Amarah snapped. 'Aciel might be gone, but your damned daughter is still tearing about, and to top it off, we've got King Snake in charge of things in Taban Yul. Linaria is going downhill, fast. It's everyone for themselves. If you don't know how to cope with that, you're as good as dead already.'

The Arillian glowered at her words. 'Did you learn nothing from Moroda?'

'Just how to not make stupid mistakes that get you killed.'

The icy wind that hit Amarah was not Kohl cooling off. It was a direct attack that send her flying across the beach. She landed with a thud, sand in her air and eye, and she rolled onto her hands and knees, coughing and spluttering. Half-winded and half in shock, she drew her scythe and levelled it at him. 'What in Rhea's name...?'

'How *dare* you show such disrespect to the dead.' Kohl said in a measured tone.

'Dead? That's new!' She took a staggering step forward.

In her peripheral vision, she saw Traego and the others had stopped and were watching them intently. 'You told me she was sealed, not dead! That your Ice Golems could resurrect her from that crystal pillar!'

'That's not what I meant.'

'Then what *did* you mean, Kohl?' Amarah swung the scythe loosely from side to side, feeling the perfectly balanced weight. Blue energy crackled around the blade as though tense and ready to spring forward towards her aggressor. Her scythe seemed just as eager to attack him as she did, and she relished the chance to vent her frustrations.

Kohl said, 'You do not insult those who are no longer with us.'

Amarah spat into the sand and took another step forward, planting her foot solidly in front of her. 'No-one tells me what to do. I'll swear and insult and praise whoever I damn well please! Don't like it? You've got all of Linaria to fly away to!'

Kohl opened his mouth to speak and appeared to struggle with what to say. After a moment, he looked away. 'I apologise.'

'You *apologise*?' She was angry now. Her scythe crackled with energy, reflecting and heightening her rage. 'You know what, Kohl, why don't you just fuck right off? You ain't done anything to help me since we left Oren! All you do is whine about what we do. You owe me for this!' She jabbed a finger at her face, her missing eye in full view now she had lost her patch. 'You owe me for this!' She pointed the same finger at the sky above them, where airships floated lazily along. 'If you ain't willing to pay that debt, then hold still and I'll strike you down right here, right now.' Amarah tightened her grip, and several small waves of energy careened away from the scythe, blasting sand back.

She was angry that he hadn't come to help her when she

was in the sea. She'd been terrified that some creature of the deep would swallow her. And if she'd avoided being eaten, she'd come close to losing Veynothi's blade, and everything would have been for nothing. Why couldn't he have used his wind to blow the smoke away and grab her? Or frozen the surface of the water so she could float on that and stop the risk of drowning?

She was angry that he did nothing.

She was angry that he was a coward.

Kohl lowered his wings and hands and shook his head. 'I know I am in your debt, Amarah. I *will* assist you. Forgive an old man through his grieving.'

She snorted, considering his words and whether or not he would be of help to her.

She'd never had a child. Never had someone she cared so deeply about. And so she couldn't fathom his hurt at losing Jato.

It wasn't as if she didn't have feelings. She was just as angry and upset at how the world treated her, when allies betrayed her, and when simply surviving seemed impossible. But sitting around and being upset about it never did anything, and it grated at her when she saw someone with as much strength as Kohl throw it all away in cowardice.

They'd argued a lot during their travels, and he had helped her from time to time. But since travelling with him, she'd lost her ship, lost her eye, and was no closer to finding a way to free Moroda.

In all that, he'd lost the friends he'd made through his betrayals, seen his home town full of sick Arillians recovering from Aciel's campaign, and lost his daughter—the only family he seemed to have left.

Amarah span the blade as she came to a decision. 'We're here on Traego's hospitality. Let's try to not ruin that, yeah?' She glared at him as she walked past, her long strides quickly shortening the distance between herself and Traego. Rage still flared within her, but she held it down.

'Okay?' Traego asked, his voice a whisper.

'All good,' Amarah whispered back. She noted he quickly sheathed his own sword. Perhaps Traego wasn't so selfish after all.

'Our base is just up here. The long building. We've got it for a week at least,' Traego said, as Carav and Oris ran up to it. 'Amarah, if you want him gone, there's bounties on Arillians you know. Twenty crowns for each one delivered to the palace, dead or alive. And the pits were busy even before I left Estoria last.'

She ignored his casual mention of the drowning pits that had terrified her when she'd first come to Estoria, and tried to push thoughts of Kohl out of her mind. 'I can look after myself.'

Traego nodded. 'I know. Just offerin' is all.'

Amarah sighed and followed Carav and Oris.

She still bristled from Kohl's attack and didn't trust herself to say anything more. She dreaded to think how Kohl would react when he discovered the bounty on his kind, or the pits themselves.

The tiniest pang of pity rippled through her.

The inside of the lodge was well furnished—far better than any of the hideouts she remembered—and Amarah settled down on a plush chair piled high with thick cushions. Kohl remained standing while the others found their comfort in seats, rugs, and chairs. Antar returned from a back room, evidently having hurried ahead with Cyd, and Amarah noted him discreetly wiping his bloodied knuckles on the back of his tunic.

Cyd wouldn't be a threat for some while, it seemed.

She wondered whether Traego would send Antar to

Taban Yul as his runner. Antar certainly had experience flying, and could defend himself. But perhaps Carav or Oris would make a better choice—neither was old enough or experienced enough to have a reputation, and both were faceless in a crowd. And if they died, they were easily replaceable.

Traego followed after and immediately went to pull himself a bottle of gold rum from the dusty shelf against the lodge's back wall. He held the bottle to the others, who each declined in turn, before he uncorked it and took a swig. 'Nothin' like a drink after a good day's work!'

Amarah shook her head and rubbed at her eye again. She hadn't realised how much losing the patch would irritate her skin.

After a few more large mouthfuls, Traego restoppered the bottle and put it back on the shelf. He pulled Veynothi's blade from his hip and inspected it closely. 'All right, scrubs. Not a bad job. Not only did we get what we went for, we knocked out Cyd and his two ships, and no-one's the wiser for what we got. But our work ain't over yet. I got a run for ya. Not too far, but ya need to get ta Taban Yul without the Imperials picking ya up.'

Amarah frowned. It would take even a fast ship a few days to reach Taban Yul and get back. And there was no guarantee Sapora would even meet with a pirate from Estoria, much less give them any money. He might keep them waiting several days, too, before he deemed them worthy of an audience.

Then there'd be more back and forths with negotiations or threats, and she doubted Sapora would pay any of the bounty until he'd seen Veynothi for himself. Amarah thought of all the processes and the timeframes for each scenario, trying to consider all the setbacks they might experience along the way.

Getting paid would be months away, *if* everything went to plan.

She'd never get her ship at this rate, and she didn't have the patience or luxury of time to wait for Traego's hunt to bear fruit. She needed to get Jato and then get on with her hunt to free Moroda.

To do that, she needed a ship. And stealing from anyone in Estoria was suicide.

There was no alternative. She had to go to Taban Yul.

Cursing herself for her luck at having to be near Sapora again, she lifted her chin to speak. 'Get me a ship and I'll do it for you.'

'Amarah?' Traego couldn't mask the shock in his voice. Clearly his earlier words had been in jest. He swiftly recovered and fished in his pocket for a moment. 'This is the payment for this run.'

A half-crown.

Carav and Oris shuffled forward like magpies at the glint of gold, although Antar was stoic enough to keep his face impassive.

Amarah snorted. It wasn't enough. Wasn't nearly enough. But if it got her to Taban Yul, she could start making some real money. There were plenty of Goldstones in Val Sharis.

She'd take the ship and whatever money she could steal in Taban Yul, then start hunting Jato.

She shrugged. 'Money is money. I ain't flying *Otella*. It's too well-known. I'm sure someone you know has one I can borrow. Or even buy something cheap. Only needs to be a two-seater, right? Something small and fast?'

'Ya know, if this were any other hunt, I'd let ya. Give ya any ship and ya could be there and back nice an' quick,' Traego said. Amarah sensed a "but" coming and braced herself for disappointment.

'But I need ya here right now. So I'll pass on ya this time.'

She scowled. Didn't he trust her to come back? Or did he actually need her for something else?

Either way, it annoyed her that she couldn't get back into the air as quickly as she'd like, and instead had to sit around and wait in Estoria at Traego's convenience.

'I'll fly me and Oris,' Antar said. 'My sister has a ship she don't use much. *Narbiot*. Pretty sure it ain't ever been outside Estoria, so no chance of the Imperial Guard recognising it.'

'That's more like it. I'll give ya another half when ya get back.' Traego handed the gold to him and placed a piece of folded cloth in his other hand. 'Give this ta the king. Only the king. Mention the Arks and he'll see ya. I promise.'

Oris's eyes went wide as he watched Antar take the gold, then he hurried to the pilot's side.

Amarah suppressed a pang of jealousy.

'Quicker ya go, the quicker ya can get back.' Traego apparently thought better of putting the rum away and grabbed the bottle off the shelf again.

Amarah watched as Antar and Oris headed out of the lodge and fought the urge to scream obscenities at Traego. She'd leapt into the sea to retrieve Veynothi's blade for him. None of his crew had done that. She'd fought a damned sea monster over it! Why had Traego passed up the chance to send her? He was the one who'd picked her up from Val Sharis and asked her to be part of his stupid treasure hunt in the first place.

Whenever she'd worked with Traego, she'd been his second-in-command. The one he turned to for advice. The one the crew followed when Traego was indisposed. While it was clear he treated Antar with a similar level of trust, it irked her that Traego had allowed the young, inexperienced Oris to go with him instead of sending her.

And now she had to wait until Rhea knew when for a sliver of gold.

'I wanna be ready to move as soon as Antar gets back,' Traego said, wiping rum from his chin. 'Get some rest. We'll get our heads together ta plan later.'

Amarah decided getting annoyed at Traego wouldn't work. It never had. The angrier you were at him, the calmer he became. It had infuriated her in her youth, and she had no intention of being frustrated in the same manner again. So she gave him a quick nod that she hoped didn't betray her simmering annoyance and made her way outside again with the intention of finding something to eat. It was easier to focus if she had a full belly, and being fed always made a shit situation more tolerable.

Considering Traego wasn't in a hurry to divulge his next steps with her, she thought she might as well get used to being back in Estoria, and figure out how to get away.

12

As the caravan left Gal Etra the next morning, they followed a narrow road which swung south-west to the River Feor. Large parts of the river were frozen over, but the fast current kept at least some of it clear all year round. Palom knew they'd follow it as it meandered south-west through the Rio Neva forest, before the last part of their journey through an open valley south to Taban Yul. So long as they kept the Feor Mountains on their left, they wouldn't go far wrong, even if the road became indiscernible after being snowed over.

A herd of elk several hundred strong watched their passage with impassive, unblinking stares from gaps in the trees, and *Leillu* snarled at them as they passed. Palom gave them little more than a cursory glance. An eagle screeched somewhere above them, and he looked up to see its dark silhouette against the clouds.

Snow wolves were the main predators this far north. He heard their chilling howls echoing off the mountains as they passed. He first saw their tracks about a league away from Gal Etra, each paw print almost two feet wide—one could give Palom a run for his money even in his true form. But they seemed as wary of the caravan as the Ittallan were of them, and Palom never caught so much as a glimpse of fur as they travelled slowly south.

If anything, Palom was more worried about Arillians. The villagers of Tum Metsa had been in a panic at the mere mention of them, and they could fly, of course. It meant they could cover ground far more quickly than the wagons, and Palom hated being a sitting duck. But if the Arillians were only interested in hunting dragons, then as long as he kept *Leillu* out of sight, the caravan would be okay.

He hoped.

True to his command, Yfaila sat in their wagon as it trundled along, staring moodily ahead but keeping silent. He felt her glare at him but ignored it. If she wanted to make herself miserable, she was more than welcome to do so. As long as she didn't interfere with his job or upset the other travellers, he couldn't care less.

Jek and Karvou chatted away happily as they made their way south, which was a stroke of luck more than anything else. Palom had been wondering what he would say to Karvou, or how he would broach the topic of the lad becoming his apprentice. Thankfully with Jek's mouth running faster than the river, it was a challenge he didn't yet have to face, and Palom was left to guard the caravan without distractions.

Shortly before the sun began to set, the caravan slowed.

Palom hurried forward to see a small village just beyond a rise in the land. The tiny settlement was more of a hamlet, and although it was ringed by a tall wooden fence, Palom counted fewer than thirty buildings within.

'It's much too small to accommodate the caravan.'

Palom looked up as an old Ittallan approached him; Odi. He had to be in his late fifties and was related to the elder of Gal Etra. Odi acted as the one in charge of the travellers—he set the pace, looked after their supplies, and ensured everyone had what they needed for the journey.

'It is too small,' Palom agreed. 'I did not know there was village here.'

Odi shook his head. 'I'd wager there are half a dozen settlements in northern Val Sharis that are unaccounted for. Most Ittallan only care for the cities with gold. These hamlets tend to be rural folk who don't get out much.'

'Where do we rest, then?' Palom looked back to Odi as he tried to get the measure of the man. He'd been introduced, briefly, along with dozens more faces in Gal Etra, but had paid little attention. Palom was being paid to guard the caravan, and that was all he cared about. So long as they weren't attacked and no-one fell behind, the names and ranks of those he travelled with were unimportant. Odi had to babysit them. He would be paid five crowns to guard them all. Once they were in Taban Yul, his troubles would begin.

Odi turned back to look at the caravan. The first wagons had stopped and were waiting for the end wagons to catch up. 'We passed a clearing a little while back. Might be a tight squeeze, but it's better than taking over that village.'

'It is only for one night.' Palom shrugged. 'There will be enough space, I think.'

Palom could easily have continued on through the night —their pace was painfully slow—but he reminded himself he travelled with village folk, woodmen, and few hunters. They needed frequent breaks to keep up their meagre pace. He hated their vulnerability, but there was little he could do to speed things along. Even when the weather had been on their side—little more than a brief flurry of snow—they still struggled along at barely more than a crawl.

As the sun began to set, the caravan pulled into the large clearing to rest. Palom circled the clearing while the Ittallan set up their cookpots and stretched their legs. The children immediately set to play, scooping up snow and hurling it at one another, their laughter echoing through the trees.

Leillu shadowed Palom, and he wondered if—or when—her independence would come and she'd leave him. For now, *Leillu* rarely let him out of her sight. She got up to follow him if he moved, and would happily wake from sleep to investigate something he did that seemed out of the ordinary.

For Palom, she was another pair of eyes, alerting him to movements sometimes before even he realised people were there.

By the time he returned to the clearing, having confirmed they'd not been tracked by any bandits or opportunists, Palom made his way to his own wagon. Yfaila had selected a tree stump to sit on, and sipped at a mug of something steaming. It smelled sweet, but she ignored him when he looked over.

Fighting against the urge to roll his eyes, he walked past her and to his own supplies on his side of the wagon. He'd been intending on checking up on Karvou and Jek, when a sudden blur of movement from above caught his attention. He leaped forward, sword at the ready, as a dark shape dove into the centre of camp towards where Odi spoke with a handful of Ittallan.

'Odi!' Palom roared in warning, lunging forward to cross the camp as quickly as he could.

The elder looked up and smiled, unafraid.

Palom was confused, but had already committed to his attack—his sword brandished towards the black eagle that twisted in mid-air to avoid his strike.

It landed awkwardly, having had to change course at the last second, and immediately transformed in a blaze of light.

'Dragons above, Palom, would yeh put that bloody

sword away!' The Ittallan yelled. He struggled to stand and wiped away the snow on his arms and shoulders. 'Yeh very nearly clipped meh wings and then where would I be?'

Palom straightened and studied him. The man's face had reddened somewhat, and his dark hair was plastered to his forehead with sweat. 'Who are you and what business do you have here?' He didn't hold his sword up, but there was enough challenge in Palom's voice that he hoped the new arrival wouldn't try anything.

'Palom, please,' Odi said. He stepped forward and put a hand on the new Ittallan's shoulder. 'This is Aetos, one of our messengers.'

Palom blinked. He knew that name. He recognised the face. 'Aetos...?' He tried to remember where he knew the eagle from.

'Nice teh see yeh again, too.' Aetos's voice was anything but welcoming. 'I didn't think I'd ever see yeh again after yeh left Taban Yul in such a huff! Are yeh finally coming to the capital? Rhea knows we need yeh help.'

It hit Palom all at once.

Aetos had been one of Lathri's comrades. One of those rebels conspiring against Sapora.

It had been Lathri and her rebels that had spooked him into leaving the city.

And by Aetos's words, the rebels didn't seem to be having much luck against the Varkain.

A cold dread seeped through him. He'd heard there'd been an attack on the palace, on Sapora himself, and the king had imprisoned everyone he hadn't killed. But since then, Palom had focussed on meeting up with Amarah, and then helping out Palin in Tum Metsa.

Seeing Aetos in the flesh brought back the very real war that Lathri and her friends fought without him. Something for him to focus on, something to care about, beyond his current, singular task.

'Lathri...?' He almost choked the words out. He forgot about Odi, about Karvou, about the caravan. Aetos was his link with Lathri, the woman he'd left to fight Sapora alone.

Aetos held his gaze for a moment, as though deciding what to tell him. Eventually, he said, 'She's alive, but not well, I fear. But if yeh aren't worried about the city, yeh should be. Princess Isa reports when she can, but the snakes have her under lock and key. For Isa's position, there's no' a lot she can do. And Sapora's quest for the Arks is—'

'The Arks!' Palom's breath caught. He'd left the capital at the *idea* that Sapora was after the Arks. To hear them spoken aloud, as though they'd been confirmed...

Leillu growled low by his heels, and Palom shook his head, remembering where he was.

He looked warily to Odi and the handful of others who had gathered to meet Aetos. He swallowed. 'Aetos...should you not...I do not think this is right place to be speaking about these things...'

Aetos's irritation seemed to fade away in an instant, replaced by a grin. 'Why not? I'm reporting to meh comrades and allies.'

Palom blinked. 'Your...allies?'

Odi clapped a hand on Palom's shoulder. 'Why do you think we're all travelling to the capital, Palom? You're guarding the rebel cause!'

Palom span around, jaw half open. He rushed to the nearest wagon and saw shields, spears, and more blades than he could count hidden behind their food and clothing supplies.

Had he been so unhappy with his latest task that he'd completely missed just who he travelled with?

'I'd have had a chat with you about it before we reached

the capital,' Odi said, coming to stand beside him. 'Most of us *do* want to see friends and family in Taban Yul. But all of us despise the idea of a snake on the throne. Vasil let us govern ourselves. Sapora has blown everything apart and re-written the rules in his own ink. We would see Isa crowned as our queen.'

Aetos came to stand on Palom's other side. 'It's true. And he's put out a huge bounty on information of the Arks. Subtle this snake is not. It's why I fly up and down Val Sharis as often as I can. Teh see what the situation is and report teh those inside and outside of Taban Yul. Sapora's preparing for something, and I don't think it's just the dragons burning up the countryside.'

Palom frowned and looked at *Leillu*. The young blue dragon had curled up by his foot and watched him with golden eyes. He recalled Jek's warning about the Arks when they'd arrived in Gal Etra and shivered. 'I heard something about this.'

Aetos shook his head. 'So has all of Val Sharis. Whatev-er's going on, we need teh stop it. Taban Yul might be safe from the dragons because of the Sevastos, but that doesn't say much about the rest of Linaria.'

Odi added, 'Don't think us Ittallan will fare too well. Of course, Sapora loves playing protector. He's bringing in more Varkain, and even Ittallan from further afield are coming to the capital looking for shelter.'

Palom remained quiet.

Aetos continued, 'Sapora's also bringing back Summer-court. Perfect excuse for Odi and the others to come to Taban Yul. All the elders have to be present for it, yeh know.'

It was a good ruse.

Odi turned to the messenger. 'When we left Tum Metsa, we received reports of Arillian sightings. Looks like they aren't finished with us yet.'

Aetos shook his head. 'And I thought we would be done with them once Aciel was sorted out.' He sighed. 'There's too many enemies and too little time. Our numbers are low. Morale is at rock bottom following the attack on the palace. Something has teh give and I don't think it'll be Sapora.'

Palom's mind raced. By the time he made it to Taban Yul, it might be too late for Lathri.

Aetos went on, 'Tacio's patrols come every day and every night. They follow the princess, but haven't yet found our base, thank Rhea. We've still so many injured. It's a wonder they aren't just following the scent of blood.'

Palom shuddered at the thought of being trapped in your own home, hunted by Varkain. He wanted to get to Taban Yul faster than ever. Wanted to be there to make a difference, to help, to repay Lathri and seek her forgiveness. He needed to. 'I am coming back to Taban Yul. I am coming back for Lathri. Sapora will not win.'

'Did yeh ever think it possible to see a Sevastos in your lifetime? Let alone have one patrol Taban Yul under a Varkain king? With Sapora, anything's possible. Don't underestimate him.'

'I will not.' Palom shook his head as though to cement the fact. He knew Sapora, and knew what he was capable of. A fine ruler, perhaps, but of his own people. Not the Ittallan. His thirst for power would be his undoing, as it was of every tyrant in history.

Leillu growled suddenly, and Palom looked at her. The ridges along her back stood up and she leaped into the air, flapping her wings and gaining altitude quickly.

'What's the matter with the dragon?' Odi asked.

'I...not sure,' Palom muttered, squinting as he looked skywards. Thanks to her colouring, *Leillu* was tricky to spot in the darkening sky, and he struggled to see her.

A strong breeze blew, and Palom raised his sword again,

readying himself to face any threat as long as he had a weapon in hand. The roar which followed the wind almost dropped him to his knees, and he staggered as an enormous shadow flew overhead, the beating of its wings keeping him forced to the ground.

When he had strength enough to stand, he saw the vast creature was a dragon—fully grown—and flying straight as an arrow due south.

'*Leillu!*' Palom cried out, hoping the young dragon hadn't been caught up in the hurricane of the older creature's flightpath.

'I'll see,' Aetos said.

Before he could object, the Ittallan had transformed again, the light which engulfed him almost blinding Palom. The black feathers of the eagle were even harder to spot now the sun had dipped below the horizon, and Palom suddenly wished he had his *Valta Forinja* to cast some light into the darkness above.

'Has she seen older dragons before?' Odi asked, a gentleness in his voice that assuaged Palom's fears. 'Perhaps she's just investigating.'

Palom swallowed. He wasn't convinced by the elder's words. 'Once. A few days before I came to Tum Metsa.'

'Aetos will keep an eye out for her. Come on. Let's get something to eat.' Odi turned to lead him back to their temporary camp, but even the smell of cooking food wasn't enough to distract Palom from the unease that gnawed at him. *Leillu* was tiny in comparison to the older dragon. One flick of the tail, one strong beat of the wings, and *Leillu* would be lost.

And what Aetos could do to help, Palom had no idea.

He remained where he was, staring into the night, looking through the trees above for any sign of movement; a roar or hiss of dragon-fire.

But there was nothing.

'Palom!' Odi called from several paces away.

He supposed Aetos could report back what he'd seen, if nothing else, but he didn't want to look away and miss seeing *Leillu*.

He always knew the dragon would leave him at some point. At least, he'd always assumed she would. But her flight had been so sudden, and he'd been completely unprepared for it, that he didn't know what he was supposed to do.

Palom turned to walk back into the camp, hoping neither Jek nor Karvou would spot him. Right now, he didn't feel up to any kind of conversation.

The eagle's shrill cry brought his attention back to the sky.

'Aetos?' He gasped.

The noise had been a warning. But Palom hadn't realised it.

A bolt of lightning ripped through the sky and smashed into the trees just beside where the wagons had parked, the resulting explosion ringing in Palom's ears and whiting out his vision.

Reacting on instinct, he dove for the ground, hands covering his head.

Thunder rumbled almost immediately after, shaking the ground and deafening him.

Long seconds passed, and he smelled burning wood and flesh. He gingerly opened one eye to see the Ittallan in chaos, screaming and racing around as they attempted to douse the fire that had sprung up at the base of the trees surrounding them.

Arillians.

He forced himself to his feet and picked up the sword

he'd dropped, before looking around and above them for the Arillian who'd attacked.

In the darkness, he saw several silhouettes and felt their wind buffet their camp.

Light flickered around them as they prepared to launch another bolt of lightning, but the attack never came. Confused, Palom watched as a sudden, tiny flame lit them up.

Leillu.

'Get away from them! They will kill you!' Palom screamed.

He ran from the camp, trees whipping past him as he powered along, calling to *Leillu* all the while. He had no idea if the young dragon could outfly the Arillians, but he needed to lead them away from the camp at any rate.

As he burst from the trees into another large clearing, Palom skidded to a halt and looked skywards again. Full dark had almost settled and though the three moons were bright, he struggled to see the Arillians above him.

'*Leillu!*' He screamed again, his heart pounding at the thought of his companion hurt—or worse.

Another small flame showed Palom where his dragon was, and then he saw her whirl away and dive towards him, narrowly avoiding the bolts of lightning flung in her direction. Adrenaline coursed through him as he tightened his grip on the sword and widened his stance. It had been a long time since he'd fought Arillians, and he'd had a distinct advantage back then with his *Valta Forinja*. Briefly, he wondered whether he'd put enough distance between the camp to keep them safe, before he dismissed the distraction, eyes locked on the Arillians as they descended after *Leillu*.

When they flew lower, he saw them more clearly—there were four. At least the reports from Tum Metsa had been exaggerated. The fewer Arillians he had to deal with, the better.

The Arillian in the centre landed, her wings ragged and torn, her armour plating scuffed with use. She glared at him with grey eyes full of spite.

He'd recognise her anywhere. 'J...Jato?!'

'How dare you address me,' she hissed. As her three companions landed beside her, Jato flicked her wrist and sent another bolt of lightning towards Palom.

He lifted his sword to block the strike, and the electrical energy glanced off to the side where it fizzled out in the snow. As he recovered from the initial surprise of seeing the Arillian General right in front of him, his anger took hold. 'Jato! You killed Anahrik! Eryn! My friends!' He gripped the sword with both hands as fury seeped through him.

'Meaningless.' Jato looked past him. 'I only care about that beast. Give it to me now, and I'll spare you.'

'*Leillu*?' Palom narrowed his eyes but didn't take his attention off Jato.

'The dragon!'

'She is not mine to give.' He looked at her three companions, who didn't seem in any hurry to attack, instead waiting on Jato's instructions. 'You are the ones who will leave, and *I* will spare *you*.'

Jato balled her hands into fists. 'Then we'll kill you and be done with it. Now!'

Palom roared his fury and charged forward, slashing with his sword before they had a chance to get a single attack out. The tip of his blade caught one of the three followers, cutting into her wrists and removing her as a threat. The other two leaped into the air with Jato, changing their focus from *Leillu* to him, which suited Palom perfectly well.

Without hesitating, he took a step forward and threw the

sword after the nearest Arillian. He had no doubt it was a tactic they weren't expecting or had encountered before. The blade cut into the Arillian's wings before landing in the snow a short distance away.

Palom lunged forward, rolling in the snow as he reached for the sword, narrowly missing being singed by another lightning strike. A roar from behind told him *Leillu* had got herself involved in the fight, and a wave of heat washed over him as she unleashed her fire again.

A second Arillian crashed into the snow, his wings aflame, his screams echoing in the chill night sky. Palom grabbed the sword and rushed at him, dragging the blade across the downed Arillian's chest as he did.

Palom rolled away from another blast and found himself near the Arillian whose wrists he'd cut. She was shrieking, tears rushing down her face. He stood beside her, hoping her proximity would dissuade her comrades from attacking, but Jato sent another lightning bolt down. Fear twisted in Palom's gut as he saw what his enemy was prepared to do to get what she wanted.

With two enemies negated, it left only Jato and one other. They were out of reach now, having gained height quickly. Palom held his sword towards them, ready to deflect their attacks, one eye on *Leillu*.

The young dragon roared, breathing more flames towards them, but Jato and her comrade beat their wings and flew out of range.

'*Leillu*! Save your fire!' Palom called, though he didn't know whether or not *Leillu* actually understood his words.

Palom dodged and deflected lightning attacks from above as the Arillians forced him further and further away from the campsite. Electricity stung him several times, numbing his limbs where he'd been caught, but he slipped into an instinctive fighting mode where every movement was a reaction rather than a considered choice.

He could barely spare a thought for *Leillu*, but every time he saw blue scales in his peripheral vision as she flew near, or felt the wash of heat as she breathed fire in defense, he sighed in relief that she was still okay. The dragon wasn't large enough to do any real damage or threaten the Arillians, but she was certainly quick enough to keep Jato at bay, and agile enough to avoid her lightning attacks.

The snow underfoot had long since melted, given the heat of fire and electricity, and the hard ground turned into slush. More than once, Palom slipped, losing his footing in the terrain, and it didn't take long before he panted with the effort of keeping up a defense while unable to land an attack of his own as long as they stayed in the air.

Bright, flickering light from Jato caught his full attention, and Palom gritted his teeth as he saw her create a ball of lightning. Electricity crackled with it and careened around her. She raised both arms above her head as though preparing to throw it at him with all her strength.

She was unhinged, and Palom wasn't sure his sword could deflect her rage-fuelled attacks. He braced himself and held the weapon out, but then saw with horror that the tip had been blunted and the edges melted from the Arillian's attacks.

He had nothing left to fight with.

He dropped the sword and turned to flee, light engulfing him as he tapped into his own *meraki*—shifting into his true form in a matter of seconds. Everything in his vision narrowed as he raced away, the enormous strides of the tiger covering ground faster than he ever could on two legs. He heard the familiar wingbeats of his dragon following him.

The mushy ground gave way to thick snow as he reached the edge of their battlefield, and his paws gave him traction as he sped away. The land sloped upwards and he powered on, but no matter how fast he ran, wings were always faster.

Jato and her comrade dropped to the ground in front of him, and landed on the crest of the rise. Jato's face glowed white in the reflection of her lightning, and she threw the ball at him with a fury he felt in his bones. Palom and *Leillu* split off in opposite directions, narrowly missing the blast.

He heard an eagle cry again, but even Aetos's warning could not get him out of the way in time—he was hit full on the side by a bolt of lightning which sent him careening over, landing in a heap of fresh snow.

Electricity rippled through his body, his muscles spasming and unresponsive.

'Just another dumb beast!' Jato laughed, the noise echoing across the snow. 'Aciel was right to attack you. Wipe you from the face of Linaria.'

Palom snarled and pushed himself to his feet. He could never get away quickly enough, they'd just catch him. He took several deep breaths and then limped towards her. He gained speed slowly as his body recovered from her attack, widening each stride until he was almost at a full run. Jato stood confidently in the snow, hands raised and ready to meet him.

With a roar, he jumped, kicking away from the snow and pounced towards her, claws drawn.

Another bolt of lightning smacked into him and knocked him from the sky. Another soon followed, and then a third.

Palom lay in the snow, panting from exertion and pain. He felt warm blood trickle down his side, and he tasted the iron tang of it. Dimly, he heard the eagle shriek from somewhere above, but his head pounded so much it sounded as though Aetos was a thousand leagues away.

He shivered and twitched, the lightning wounds burning across his body.

Snow began to fall and blurred his vision slightly.

Palom closed his eyes to the pain, angry for not being stronger or faster, angry for letting *Leillu* down.

His head hurt so much he thought it had split open, and his breath came in short, shallow gasps.

This was it. This was his end.

His body cooled under the falling snow, and he tensed, bracing himself for the final attacks that would finish him off.

But no further attacks came.

Had he died?

He forced his eyes open and saw red colouring the snow around him. He felt the ache in his body and the pain of open wounds. No, he couldn't be dead.

Dizzy, he looked around for signs of the two Arillians or *Leillu*, but he saw nothing aside from a vast, snowy tundra and the darkness beyond.

Then he felt the ground move under him.

A small tremor at first, then a larger shake.

He lifted his head and saw *Leillu* several paces away, her back to him. With great effort, he heaved himself to his feet and half-crawled to the crest of the hill, where *Leillu* looked off into the distance.

He struggled towards her, his body threatening to collapse with every breath, until he finally pulled himself through the melted snow to *Leillu*'s side.

Palom dropped to the ground, exhausted, and released his *meraki*. His legs were slashed and bleeding, and he had a vicious cut on his neck, but he had no energy left to do anything about it. He shivered in the sudden cold, more apparent now his skin touched the snow where he lay on his front. '*Leillu*...?' He coughed, but the dragon didn't respond.

With great effort, he turned his head to look down at the ridge and to the small hamlet, where the same fully grown dragon from before stood. It had landed and approached the village with slow, pointed steps, the snow melting where its scales touched it. The creature's scales were a dark blue, with a paler underbelly, and several large horns crowned the back of it's head. It took Palom some effort to make out the details in the darkness, but he knew the dragon was an apex predator.

Jato and the other Arillian with her blasted the dragon with electrical attacks, but it appeared they'd tired during their battle with him, and the dragon hardly seemed to feel their lightning.

It raised its wings and beat them several times, rearing onto its rear legs and letting out another ground-trembling roar. It lashed its tail, sweeping away snow from under it as it watched the hamlet.

The village gates were a formality rather than a deterrent to keeping people out, but the villagers opened them anyway and charged the beast with spears and swords. Palom heard their battle cries, and panic rose in his chest.

Then the dragon opened its mouth.

If dragon-flame could be compared to anything, *Leillu*'s fire was a candle that flickered gently. This creature's was a volcano eruption. The raw power it spewed forth engulfed the village in a single blast, its breath searing flesh from bone in moments.

At the sight of the dragon's power, Jato and her comrade turned and fled, flying higher and further until they were nothing more than a distant speck in the sky.

The dragon didn't seem to even notice them. When it ran out of breath, it fanned its wings again, pushing the flames to take hold of every structure in the village. The screams of the residents sickened Palom as he could do nothing but watch. He heard the beast take another breath, and closed his eyes as flames washed over the settlement again. Smoke blotted out the sky, ash blew on the wind, and the acrid scent of burning filled the air.

Twice more, the dragon breathed fire. It didn't fly overhead and loose a stream of flames, it simply stood at the gates to the village and destroyed everything it could see, permitting none to escape. The wooden fence surrounding the buildings caught alight, trapping everyone within.

Those who attempted to race from the gates ran straight to the dragon's waiting jaws, where it engulfed them in flame and roasted them where they stood. Wood cracked in the heat, metal oozed and melted, and only when there were no more screams did the dragon cease.

When it had finished, it turned around and looked at Palom and *Leillu*, who watched in horror. Embers from the dragon's flames floated in the dark air all around it, and the crackle and spit of burning buildings filled Palom's ears. The orange light of the flames behind it tinged the dragon's blue scales, and against the night sky, it looked every bit the god many Linarians claimed them to be.

Palom locked his gaze with the dragon and knew he would have no chance of survival if it loosed its flames upon him. He had not even the strength to stand, much less run away from the creature.

The dragon watched him for a long while, as though considering whether to add two more lives to its count for the night.

When Palom couldn't stand to look any longer, the beast lifted its head to the black sky above. It raised its wings and flew into the darkness, leaving the unmarked hamlet nothing more than a pile of embers smoking in the ground.

13

The palace of Taban Yul had been constructed with acres of marble and gold to show off Ittallan riches to the rest of Linaria who came to visit the city. The palace grounds boasted vast gardens and a thick stone wall which provided privacy from those who couldn't afford to enter. At frequent intervals around the palace walls, much like the city's walls, large golden statues depicting famous Ittallan from history had been constructed; cartographers and merchants, ship-builders and captains, researchers and elders.

The palace provided a meeting ground of sorts for the country's nobility, and many Goldstones would come to eat in the dining halls surrounded by Val Sharis' history. Isa could remember when tourists from Corhaven and Ranski would fly in to tour the lower halls of the palace while servants explained what happened in what part of the palace, how things were run, and how it had changed over the centuries. It made a fair amount of money, too, and even though the tours had lessened somewhat, plenty of Goldstones still came to dine and survey the city from the palace's tall windows. And the palace was also home to the governing body of Val Sharis; the Council.

Or it had done, until Sapora had disposed of them shortly before his coronation.

While Isa had completely supported Sapora's slaughter —she'd stood by her brother while he had killed them—the next part of Sapora's promises hadn't come true. She hadn't been given the power she'd been assured. And Sapora seemed to hold the rest of the Ittallan in contempt as much as he had the old Council.

She should have known Summercourt would come along sooner rather than later. For all his words, her brother couldn't rule alone. Val Sharis was a vast country with many towns and settlements. Whatever happened in the capital affected them, too, and Isa knew from experience that the elders who lived in those towns and villages throughout Val Sharis were more often than not quite vocal about their needs.

Sapora and Tacio couldn't simply kill them all. Every Ittallan in the country would descend on them and there'd be no way to win.

No, they had to play at politics to some degree. With Vasil and the Varkain present, though, Isa was worried any discussions would be tense.

She wandered through the palace, remembering how things had used to be. They'd been terrible for her, of course, but at least she'd been free to go as she pleased without being watched. She had been safe in her own home.

Though not a castle designed to protect against attack, the palace had been Isa's fortress.

It was now her prison.

In a few days, when Summercourt was in full swing, it might very well become her grave.

Isa paced through the halls and corridors in search of

Sapora. Having more and more Varkain move into Taban Yul was one thing, but taking over streets and forcing residents and traders out under threat of violence was something else. They were a highly cultured, civilised people. Not savages.

The Varkain behaviour in the city was doing little to fight against the stereotype.

Seeing the young couple throw themselves into the river unnerved Isa more than she cared to admit. Sapora needed to take his attention off Summercourt, off his Ark hunt, and focus it on the country's capital. He was supposed to be a king, after all.

What was the point of having all his weapons if the capital of Val Sharis fell under his watch?

She'd *make* him listen to her.

Her city depended on it.

Isa approached Sapora's rooms on the west side of the palace. He'd shut off the entire wing to any but his most trusted Varkain, led by a Cerastes called Roke, who was seldom away from Sapora's side.

She suspected Roke had some mixed blood in his lineage which had warmed him to Sapora rather than Tacio, who led the Cersates aside from Sapora's few, selected individuals that made up his Royal Guard. Roke himself certainly seemed less severe than the other Varkain who'd moved into the palace, and Isa wasn't sure if it was because of their lineages or because Roke respected Sapora's command enough to respect her, too.

He'd lost his right hand and ear during some skirmish in his youth, and his grizzled appearance kept many of the palace servants away. He'd fought when Lathri's rebels and Morgen's warships had attacked the palace and added a few more scars to his repertoire, but his demeanour hadn't changed at all.

He was about the only high-ranking Cerastes who didn't insult her with nicknames such as, "the kitten princess," which was a relief more than anything. And she could trust Roke to be frank with her.

She saw him standing guard at the top of the hallway leading to Sapora's chambers and slowed her approach. He held a spear, the tip pointing up, but she knew he carried a variety of other blades, too. Long weapons weren't especially useful in close quarters.

She wondered if he'd have to test that before everything was all over.

Roke inclined his head to her in respect, but remained silent, watching her with a cool gaze.

'I'm here to see my brother,' Isa said out of courtesy rather than to ask permission. 'There are urgent matters I need to discuss with him.'

Roke held his spear across the hallway, blocking her passage. 'He is not within, Princess Isa. He left instructions to forbid any from entering his chambers during his absence.'

Isa drew up short. 'Where is he?'

'He didn't tell me. Just that he would return later, and that he would not permit any to enter his chambers until then.'

She sighed. If Sapora was in the Council Tower—where he usually was, if not in his rooms—then Tacio would likely be there, too. Dismissing Tacio would not be easy at all. She bit her lip, irritated that her chance of speaking privately with Sapora had slipped away.

'Would you like me to pass on a message when he returns?' Roke asked in an attempt to be helpful. 'Or send for you?'

She shook her head. 'That won't be necessary. Thank you.' She added her gratitude almost as an after-thought—

she didn't want to squander Roke's respect towards her—and then headed back into the palace towards the Council Tower.

~

'No, Princess Isa. I have not seen him,' Koraki said when she cornered the head steward some while later. He was up to his neck in preparations for Summercourt and spoke to her so curtly it bordered on rudeness. 'The tower has stood empty all day, in fact.' Despite his role as chief of the palace staff, Sapora and Tacio seemed to use the raven Ittallan as their personal punching bag. He had more scars across his face since they arrived in the city than the majority of the Cerastes who came with them.

He alone of the old Council had been spared from Sapora's slaughter at the ball.

Isa had at first wondered why, for he had been among the most insulting to Sapora while they had been growing up. Now, Isa believed her brother was exacting his revenge on him over a longer period of time.

Koraki's words troubled her, and she chewed the inside of her lip. Sapora rarely left the palace. If he wasn't in his rooms or the tower, she really had no clue where he might be. She supposed he could travel wherever he wished whenever he wished, but she'd never seen him act on it.

He'd always been too focussed on his Ark hunt or the Sevastos.

Perhaps it was something in preparation for Summercourt? It was the only thing that had changed in the past few weeks.

As she turned to walk off, a thought struck her: the tower had been empty all day, which meant Tacio wasn't around, either.

A sudden, desperate, and dangerous idea that conflicted with her common sense built at the realisation of her opportunity.

Tacio and Sapora were both out of the palace.

Perhaps she could use her rare piece of luck and make it up to Lathri now.

Against her better judgement, she made up her mind, and returned to where Koraki lingered near the entrance to the palace dungeons. A pair of maids approached him, each carrying two large buckets of water, and he barked an order. As they scurried off, Isa followed. They rounded a corner, no doubt on their way to the ballroom where the majority of Summercourt was to be held, and she hurried after them, heart thumping in fear and excitement at what she was about to do. 'Stop where you are.'

They halted immediately and glanced nervously at each other before looking at her. Both were quite young, and obviously Ittallan. Both had brunette hair tied back into severe buns, and one was far taller than the other. Isa took one of the buckets from the nearest maid, the shorter one, whom she thought might have been younger and more timid. 'I'll be needing this. You carry on.'

'Yes, Princess Isa. Of course.' The younger maid bowed her head slightly before scurrying away after the tall one. She didn't even look back at her.

Isa waited until they'd passed through a large set of double doors before returning to Koraki, weighed down slightly by the heavy bucket. The door to the dungeon was closed behind him, and beyond—Lathri.

When she saw him, she took a deep breath, and in her most commanding voice said, 'Get the guards down there away from their posts.' There was no going back now.

Koraki lifted an eyebrow. 'Excuse me?'

'I don't have much time.' Her voice had turned harsh,

some element of her rank seeping through. 'Summercourt draws near, and I want to ensure the prisoners are well presented. I don't trust the maids to do a good job, and I demand privacy from the Cerastes.'

Somewhat flustered, he turned to open the door. Pausing, he glanced back over his shoulder, but she kept her hard gaze on him. 'Isa...'

'They can receive new orders from Roke in the meantime. I don't wish to be disturbed.'

He buckled underneath her words and hurried down the steps to where Tacio's Cerastes stood guard over their prisoners.

Isa heard muffled talking through the thick stone, followed by hasty footsteps as the Cerastes followed Koraki back to the main hallway. She stood aside as the door burst open and the three of them charged away.

Isa swallowed, then slipped through the door and down to the dungeons, sure to take her bucket with her. She had minutes at most.

She moved as quickly as she could, no longer worried about how much noise she was making now the guards had left their posts. The water sloshed around in the bucket, some of it splashing over her as she hurried along. The plush carpet underfoot ended and cold flagstones chilled her feet as she practically ran down the passageways and flights of stairs until she arrived in the main dungeons.

She grabbed the set of keys from the nail on the wall where the Cerastes had stood guard only moments before, and strode off. Individual cells split off on either side as pathways mazed through the palace's lower floors, but Isa knew exactly where she was going.

To Lathri.

There were other prisoners, too. Those who Tacio or his Cerastes has picked up during their time in the city. But Isa wasn't interested in those. It was Lathri and her rebels that she needed to free, that she needed on her side.

She reached the correct cell and skidded to a halt, dropping the bucket on the floor to alert Lathri of her presence. 'Lathri! Lathri, I'm here. It's me, Isa!'

The other woman looked up slowly, her long, blonde hair scraggly and dirty from her time in the dungeons. Grime had pressed into her knees where she crouched on the cell floor, and at her elbows. Isa said, 'I'm getting you out, now!'

Lathri blinked and seemed to take a few seconds to understand what was being said. '...No.'

'What? Yes, I am. I'm here.' Isa brandished the keys that she'd plucked from the wall.

'No. Save the others. Save Kylos...' Lathri's voice was hoarse.

Isa didn't understand. Lathri was the leader of their cause, the most influential and important of them all. She *had* to free her.

Lathri continued before Isa could retort, 'Kylos is opposite me. Get her out. Please. Save the others before me.'

Isa bit her lip. She wanted to do what Lathri asked, but she didn't want to leave her in the cell. She didn't have time to instrument an entire jailbreak, and the Cerastes would be back any moment when they realised she'd lied and Roke had no orders for them.

'Go, Isa,' Lathri said.

The princess whirled around to face the other cell where Kylos leaned against the bars in darkness. Her right thigh was wrapped in a heavy bandage, but there was no fresh blood. She'd evidently overheard. 'Lathri, you've been in here longer than me. You need to get away!'

'I will leave when everyone is free. Or I will die here.' Lathri's voice weakened as she spoke.

'I'm not going to let you die,' Isa snapped. She plunged the key into the lock and twisted it violently. Wrenching open the cell gate, she hurried to the wall and unlocked Kylos's chains from the stone.

'Can you run?' Isa asked.

Kylos nodded. 'The snakes haven't broken me yet.'

'Good.' Isa refused to think of her betrayal against her brothers.

The Ittallan followed Isa out of the cell, and she turned to face the others, hands reaching through the bars in a desperate plea for freedom, voices begging to be released. Isa was about to unlock the next nearest cell when she heard footsteps along the flagstones.

Her time was up. She dropped the keys and ran off. 'Kylos! Follow me!' Isa hurried to the end of the passageway and turned down another dark one, away from the approaching steps.

'Wait! The others!' Kylos called.

Isa rounded on her. 'There's no time! Come on!' She didn't wait for a response and raced deeper into the dungeons. If Kylos had any sense, she'd follow her, else she'd have to face the wrath of the Cerastes when they came down to check—she knew it had been a stupid decision, but she'd been out of options and up against it for time.

And she needed to do *something*.

Explaining her way out of this one would be nigh impossible, but without Tacio or Sapora there to see for themselves, she hoped she could get away with saying Kylos had freed herself. If she could help the Ittallan escape the palace, her brothers wouldn't know of her involvement.

The Cerastes might have been under Tacio, but if she could have Roke deny her involvement; have Roke back up her story, then she might be able to get away with it.

She heard footsteps after her, but they were Kylos's soft

193

shoes and not the Cerastes' armoured boots, and Isa put on a burst of speed, leading the Ittallan through the lower dungeons. It had been too long since she'd last been down here, and her heart thudded as she followed her memories.

After a minute of running, during which time Isa tried to lessen the amount of noise she made lest the Cerastes heard and followed—and then compromised her secret route— she reached a small wooden door hidden in the stone. At first, she thought she'd taken a wrong turn and ended up at a dead end, but the wood had simply darkened with age and it had taken her eyes a moment or two to adjust to the low light in the darkest part of the dungeons.

'Where do we go?' Kylos asked, catching up to her and limping slightly.

She'd forgotten the other woman had probably had only a tiny amount of food in the last few days and would tire quickly.

'Nearly there,' Isa said. She stepped forward and put a small key into the rusted lock of the door. Relief flooded her when it clicked and she heaved it open, sending dust and splinters floating to the floor.

Isa led them up the steep wooden steps—careful to leap over a few that had rotted away to nothing after years of abandonment—and arrived at the edge of a narrow passageway. The wall at the end was soft, and when she touched it lightly, it gave way.

'A tapestry!' Kylos exclaimed, her voice just above a whisper.

'Yes. One of the old places I used to hide in as a child,' Isa whispered back. 'No-one ever found me.' She poked her head around the tapestry and looked into the grand ballroom. It was a bustle of activity as servants carried chairs, plants, and large pieces of formal furniture in preparation for Summercourt. Maids scurried around them, dusting and mopping as they went. 'Good. It's busy. We won't be noticed,' Isa said. She looked to the far wall where the windows had been opened to air the room.

'I still smell blood here,' Kylos said. She glared at the floor.

Isa swallowed. The last time the ballroom had been in use was when Sapora visited before he'd become king— when he'd slaughtered the last council and those who disagreed with his rule. The event had been a bloodbath.

She'd been part of that, too.

It had been a necessary tragedy, and she stood by Sapora's decision to do it. But she knew that act would not be without consequence. Lathri and her followers were testament to that.

'Ignore it. I'll walk you as quick as we can to the window. You can get out through there,' Isa said, trying to keep her mind focussed.

'Are you insane? They'll see me!'

Isa shoved a handful of rotting wood into Kylos's hands. 'Carry these. A quick glance and you'll look like you're clearing out rubbish. Then you'll be gone before anyone realises otherwise.'

They didn't have much choice, anyway. And at least the ballroom was far enough away from the traditional entrance to the palace dungeons that she might not be immediately suspected.

So long as Koraki kept his mouth shut.

Isa took a breath, silently prayed to Rhea for luck, and then stepped out from behind the tapestry into the ballroom.

'No. Bring it here,' she commanded Kylos, slipping into her ruse as the servants already in the ballroom shuffled away from her.

195

Kylos followed, holding the stack of wood against her chest and keeping silent.

No-one gave them a second glance.

Her heart pounded in her ears. She tried to ignore everything other than getting Kylos out.

The window had to be fifteen paces away. She could see the blue sky through the wide gap, smell food carried on the warm wind drifting through.

She risked a look back to Kylos, who kept within two steps of her. The other servants paid them no mind as they focussed on their own jobs.

She felt sunlight on her arm as she stepped up to the window, less than a handful of paces away now. Whatever happened to her, at least Kylos was free, and she'd cemented herself as an ally to them. They would trust her, regardless of what Tacio and his Cerastes did.

'Isa. There you are.'

She froze.

Tacio.

She wanted to bolt. The window was only a handful of steps away, but Tacio's voice carried such a threat on it that she didn't dare do anything but hold still.

'And...well, look here. Isn't that one of my prisoners stood with you?' His voice was casual, playful almost.

Her eyes darted to the side where Kylos hovered, poised on the edge of fleeing.

Any witty retort, any words to defend herself left her as fear took over. He'd be able to smell her sweat, hear her heart pound, and know he had her perfectly cornered.

Exactly where he wanted her.

'Isa, it's rude to ignore someone. Especially a prince.'

With great effort, Isa turned to face her brother. The bubble of activity throughout the hall had stopped. Everyone watched either Tacio or Isa, waiting to see what would happen, waiting to see if they would need to flee—clearly the carnage of the ball still fresh in many minds.

A young maid peered out from behind her brother and Isa narrowed her eyes. She'd been the timid one who Isa had taken the bucket of water from. Isa glowered at her, and the maid promptly disappeared.

Isa couldn't deny the knowledge that Kylos was a prisoner. She'd been in the dungeons when Tacio had her tortured.

She couldn't lie to him when her behaviour screamed that she'd been caught.

Her only defence was to be bold. To continue down the path she'd chosen for herself. 'She isn't a prisoner...anymore.'

Tacio sneered and began to walk towards her. 'Well she will be just as soon as I put her back in her cell.'

Three Cerastes appeared behind him, their spears held aloft as they followed Tacio towards Isa.

Isa balled her hands. She wouldn't draw her own blade against them and escalate the situation.

Tacio wouldn't kill her.

He wouldn't.

She was...blood.

But when she saw the murderous gleam in his eyes, her logic fell to pieces, and she no longer believed her life was safe.

'Tacio...' she whispered. 'You're mistaken.'

A smile crept onto his face. 'I don't think I am, Isa.'

'You're meant to lead the Cerastes, not bully me and undermine me every chance you get!' Her confidence grew a little as she lashed out at him. '*That's* your job! Leave me out of it!'

His smile deepened, a few fangs poking over his lip. 'Well I wouldn't be very good at my job if I couldn't weed out and catch the rats in the palace,' his eyes flickered to Kylos, 'or the city.'

The insult stung.

Tacio addressed the Cerastes with him, 'My captains.' He stopped walking about halfway along the hall, and the servants who remained between Isa and the Varkain darted out of the way. 'Would you be so kind as to retrieve my prisoner and return her to the dungeons. I shall deal with Isa myself.'

They nodded and marched past Tacio towards Isa and Kylos.

Isa heard Kylos let out a squeak of fear. She could do nothing to help her.

She didn't know what to say or do; whether to beg, plead, feign indifference. She trembled, her confidence leaving her as quickly as it had come.

'Stop where you are!'

Isa whirled around to the sound of a new voice from somewhere behind her.

Sapora stood at the south entrance to the ballroom, his clawed hands covered in soil and mud, sweat dripping down his face. It looked as though he'd been digging through the gardens on his hands and knees all morning. His eyes were blazing fury, and Isa felt her stomach drop.

'Brother,' Tacio said, unaffected by Sapora's rage, and for once not curling up his nose at Sapora's dirty appearance. 'I was simply retrieving a prisoner who somehow escaped my Cerastes. I think Isa might be able to explain how that happened.' He idly scratched his cheek.

Isa's eyes widened. She couldn't think clearly let alone form words. She looked to Sapora, her whole body trembling.

Caught between two orders, the three Cerastes held their ground a few paces from Kylos.

Sapora looked at Isa for a long while, his pupils dilated, eyes unreadable.

Isa was sure he would command them to seize her, too. She prayed silently to Rhea, wishing for a swift death, if that's what it would come to.

'I pardoned her.'

Isa almost fell over at Sapora's words.

Tacio, too, seemed shocked. He stammered an inarticulate gurgle of noise.

Kylos didn't need telling twice. She transformed in a burst of white light, and a lithe, lean fox scrambled the last few steps across the floor and out the open window.

Isa looked back to Sapora, the highest ranking of them all, the one whose orders she would have to follow. Behind him, lingering in the doorway, she saw Koraki.

Her eyes widened but she said nothing, too afraid of what might happen and too stunned at what had happened.

Sapora glared at the open window, then back to her, and lastly to Tacio. In an icy voice that permitted no arguing, he said, 'Tacio. Get your Cerastes back to their posts. Continue overseeing preparations for Summercourt. I'll not have any delays, do you understand? Isa. With me.'

He spun on his heel and marched from the ballroom, peeling off his dirtied jacket as he went.

Isa felt Tacio's eyes bore into her, and she all but ran after Sapora, a dread like she'd never felt before washing over her.

14

Amarah sat in the damp sand, the sea lapping at her feet, while she attempted to cool down in the midday heat. Gulls cried overhead while terns dove into the surf and came up with beaks full of fish. After what had happened with the monster, she'd sworn off seafood and had settled for two fried vegetable cakes and a spiced, garlic pork skewer to sate her hunger.

She hurled the wooden skewer into the water and reclined slightly, her belly full and content.

It was the closest she'd come to peace in as long as she could remember and listening to the waves brought her some comfort. A brief respite from the constant plots and schemes of the thieves and pirates who made Estoria their home.

But as hot as it was, the fear of that sea monster prevented her from even getting waist-deep into the water, which somewhat tarnished her peace.

She doubted her peace would last, anyway. She'd been in the tomb of an ancient Varkain, had stolen something from her, and had met Rhea knew what in the sea.

If anything, she was amazed she was still alive to tell the tale.

Traego had kept hold of Veynothi's blade, of course. And as keen as she was to see whether the monster was after her or the sword—regardless of who held it—she didn't want to risk Traego being eaten by the creature if he was to go into the sea clutching the blade. If Traego disappeared, she'd have no chance of getting any gold, and the whole damned journey would have been for nothing.

On the horizon, fishing ships bobbed gently on the waves and airships loomed in the sky above, their bulky shadows passing overhead like clouds. Amarah saw a mix of cargo ships, transport vessels, sleek scouters, heavy fighters, and tiny, personal ships that the Estorians used to quickly travel between the islands.

Many sky pirate ships hovered in wait for merchant vessels—or particularly brave Imperial ships—to approach Estoria. They'd swoop in and either attack or take ransom payments for safe passage, and it was one of the easiest ways the largest troupes earned their money. Some of them didn't even need to leave Estoria to make a fortune for themselves.

It would be a particular troupe on top one week, and then another the next. They would constantly be fighting with each other over who would be able to guard the most lucrative sections of Estoria's many coasts, until one backed down. Blood was spilled more often than not, but someone actually dying was a rarity. Most would rather run and live to fight another day than lose their life over a piece of territory that moved and shifted as often as the sea.

Of course, seeing the airships made her think of *Khanna*. Or to be more precise, of *Khanna*'s replacement. Amarah didn't see the point of getting anything much bigger than *Khanna*. Something like *Otella* would be too bulky for her to really be happy flying. That, and it stood out like a sore thumb. Although *Khanna* had been somewhat recognisable, it had also been small, sleek, and fast enough to disappear when she needed.

And she didn't really need—or want—the firepower of a bigger ship, anyway. Fleeing and keeping far enough away from trouble had worked well enough for her so far, and she saw no reason to change that.

Plus, with Traego's experience and recommendations, she could purchase some bottled Samolen magic that would suit her needs going forward.

Speed was non-negotiable. She was certain of that. She doubted she'd find another ship as agile or maneuverable as *Khanna* had been, but taking on a ship that leaned more towards speed than power would be a plus.

It was unlikely there'd be anything new about. Sky pirates never parted with their ships, unless they were damaged and someone wanted to salvage parts from it. No, she'd have to find an Estorian or—and she hated to admit it —a Goldstone who wanted rid of one of theirs. She'd been lucky to buy *Khanna*. She very much doubted she'd be so lucky again.

Especially not if she'd been cursed following her grave-robbing antics.

Amarah sighed. Technically she owned a warship in Taban Yul, one that Princess Isa had given her before the battle against Aciel, and it had served her well enough then. But a warship needed a crew—she couldn't fly that alone. Getting a decent crew of competent, reliable people was hard enough, and recruiting for one would be nigh impossible with the skies as dangerous as they were.

Only the very brave or the very foolish were risking their ships—and lives—by flying in Val Sharis now. No-one in their right mind would sign up to a ship with Arillians and dragons on the warpath. She had to laugh as Antar was counted in one of those two groups while he delivered Traego's message to Sapora. No. She had to sort herself out alone. Her warship would have to wait for the time being.

A small, red crab scuttled across the sand and bumped into her ankle, breaking her thoughts.

Amarah lifted her leg to allow it to pass underneath and continue on its way. Not too long ago, she'd have just kicked it into the water, away from her. She wondered what had changed, and when she'd grown soft.

She heard heavy footsteps approaching and tilted her head slightly to face the noise.

When she saw who it was, Amarah looked back to the sea with a smirk. 'Not flying no more?'

'Your friend, Traego, told me it would be unwise,' Kohl said.

'Hardly friends,' she said. 'And anyway, today he's an ally. Might not be tomorrow.'

'Sounds exciting.' His voice was flat. Kohl kicked sand from his shoes and lifted his hat to run a hand through his hair.

'Why's he say flying's unwise?' She knew the answer, but wondered what Traego had told him.

'High bounty on us Arillians, it seems.' He sat down in the sand beside her, his heavy cloak covering his wings from view.

'Is that right?' The truth, then. 'Well I suppose you'll want to head off? Get away from Estoria and us criminals?'

Kohl sighed. 'I said I'd help you. Let me help.'

Amarah snorted but didn't reply. He'd made similar promises before and she had no reason to believe him this time. Or maybe he'd keep his word this time. Then she'd finally manage to track down Jato and get her revenge on everything the half-crazed Arillian had done to her.

Her original plan had been to find another Sevastos and

use Kohl's experience and skill as a dragon-hunter to track one down. If a Sevastos had sealed Moroda, perhaps another would be able to unseal her.

But without a ship, she had no chance of finding any dragon, much less a Sevastos.

And before all that, she needed to get her own back on Jato.

'You won't turn me in?' Kohl asked.

The question caught her off guard. 'What? Why would I do that?'

He shrugged. 'High bounty on Arillians. You're a sky pirate...'

'Don't mean anything. My sights are on a bigger prize.' Although whether Traego or anyone else on his crew thought the same thing, she wasn't sure. Kohl had flown with them and warned them about Cyd's approach. Perhaps that would be enough to dissuade them from trying to claim their bounty on *him*. For the time being, at least.

She picked up a pebble from the sand and threw it across the water, watching it skip along the surface.

'I'll admit, it's uncomfortably hot here,' Kohl said after a while. He waved his fingers and sent ice crystals floating in the air. They drifted gently on the wind and melted immediately where they touched Amarah's skin.

She shivered and rubbed a hand on her arm where the cool water dripped down. 'Lucky you can do that. Give it a few months and Estoria's unbearable to be outside in the day. Summer's a killer.'

'Indeed.'

They sat in silence for a while, the waves and calling birds keeping them company. She heard distant shouts from Estorians some way behind them as they got on with their day's work, but it blurred together into background noise that Amarah tuned out.

Her thoughts wandered back to her airship, and what it would be like. But until she had the gold from her share of this ridiculous bounty in her pocket, it was fanciful thinking. It would take days for Antar to reach Taban Yul, and as much time coming back to Estoria.

Her eyes flicked over to where Kohl sat, jealousy rising in her chest. He could fly whenever he wished, wherever he wished. He was powerful enough to create ice out of thin air. He had so much and squandered it all.

'Why didn't you help me before?' Amarah asked all of a sudden. The thought had only been half-formed in her mind before her lips had blurted out the question. She kept her eyes locked on the waves at her feet.

'When?'

Funny. He'd failed to help on so many occasions, he needed her to specify. 'On *Otella*. When I was in the sea.'

Kohl didn't reply for a long while, and Amarah turned to check he was still paying attention.

'Traego and the others were still fighting Cyd,' he said. 'I tried to prevent more needless slaughter. The other two ships were going down, and their crews along with them.'

Amarah didn't understand why any of that mattered. 'I could have done with your help back then.'

'I thought you could swim?'

'I can. But being in open water with airships falling out the sky on top of you, fire everywhere.... Plus stuff that's *in* the water....' She stopped short before mentioning her encounter with the sea monster.

Kohl adjusted how he sat, clearly uncomfortable. 'I thought you would be fine. I know all I seem to do is apologise, so I won't insult you by doing so again. Traego's airship would pick you up. I tried to lessen the damage in the meanwhile. I hadn't thought you were in any danger.'

Amarah nodded. She always put on a brave face,

whether she was confident or terrified. It was no wonder he hadn't realised her fear. Then again, she hadn't been afraid when she'd leapt overboard.

It was only when the monster had appeared that her confidence had left her.

If she didn't say anything, he'd never know. But she didn't like the idea of other people knowing what, for the moment, was information that was exclusive to her.

In her line of work, knowledge was always valuable.

Perhaps it was her own fault that Kohl was less than helpful. She did have a natural mistrust of those around her, after all, and rarely told others what she thought or her worries. He didn't know what was going on—not truly—because she didn't tell him. She just expected him to keep out of her way and do as he was told. She wondered who was treating who like a child.

In the end, she held her tongue and shrugged, bravado slipping back into place. 'I guess.'

'You were okay, weren't you? You were laughing as soon as you were back aboard *Otella*.'

'Of course I was.' A defence, similar to her insulting aggression. But she didn't say that, either.

'I'll be sure not to leave you in that kind of situation again,' Kohl said, a little desperate. 'At least you retrieved Veynothi's blade.'

'I just need Sapora to pay Traego then I can buy my next ship.'

'You aren't going to steal one?'

She laughed at that. 'Just because I'm a sky pirate doesn't mean I don't buy stuff with honest gold every now and then. Plus, stealing an airship from sky pirates is stupid.'

'So, what are you going to do?' Kohl asked. 'It may be some time before Traego receives the gold.'

Amarah looked at him and met his piercing grey gaze

face on. He was stating the obvious, and she didn't appreciate being spoken down to. 'Well, I'll just have to be patient, won't I?'

'Patient? You never struck me as the patient type, Amarah.'

She remembered her impatience in Oren, Kohl's hometown, when she had all but knocked down Jato's home with her *Valta Forinja* in order to speak with Kohl after being kept waiting for a couple of days. That had kicked off her fight with the Arillian General and lost her both *Khanna* and her eye.

Jato had taken those from her, so Amarah still blamed her, rather than herself. 'I won't sit and do nothing,' she clarified. 'But I'll have to wait. Unless you have a handful of crowns you've been hiding all this time?'

Kohl smiled and looked away. 'No, I don't.'

'I'll have a wander. See what I can get. So I can be ready to go straight away.' She stood up and stretched, shaking the sand from her boots.

'I thought you liked it here?' Kohl followed suit and spent a while wiping down his cloak.

'I do. But I like being on my own ship better.'

AMARAH WALKED along the sandy streets, Kohl beside her.

She didn't remember much of this part of Estoria. Buildings were erected and knocked down on almost a seasonal basis, and with so many proprietors changing, it was though she'd never been here before.

Unfortunately it meant she took twice as long as she would have liked to find anything, and she needed a new eye patch soon. Being unable to read also didn't help, as the shop signs were meaningless to her unless they contained a recognisable object or symbol.

She found herself peering into every shop and stall she passed in an attempt to locate a seamster.

Kohl would have struggled with his hat and cloak if it weren't for his Frost-touch, and although most people they passed looked at him curiously for being so heavily dressed, none seemed to realise he was an Arillian.

Traego's warning about the drowning pits had sent a shiver down her spine, and she didn't want to end up anywhere near there again. If any opportunists learned what Kohl was, Amarah would put money on him being attacked before the next day.

Estoria had plenty of eccentric Goldstones living there, and to see someone in heavy clothing was not completely unheard of. Amarah supposed as long as he kept his wings covered and didn't get too close to anyone, the Estorians and sky pirates would simply think he was an Ittallan Goldstone and leave him to himself.

She hoped.

'Amarah!'

She stopped and looked back the way she had come to see Carav running down the street towards her, kicking up sand with every footstep. The young woman had taken Amarah's advice and removed the long, dangling pendants and necklaces, and as a result made far less noise as she moved.

Carav skidded to a halt when she reached her, panting heavily. 'Traeg's asked for ya!'

Amarah shook her head and carried on. 'I'm busy at the moment. He'll have to wait a bit.'

'What you doing?' Carav asked.

Amarah wanted to snap at her to mind her own business, but before she could say anything, Kohl replied.

208

'Looking for a seamster. Amarah needs a new patch for her eye.'

Carav's eyes lit up. 'Oh, I know! I can show you a great one.' She bounded off without waiting for a reply.

Amarah couldn't be annoyed at Kohl, but something about Carav's too-eager manner irritated her. She gave a short huff and followed the blonde woman as she wove through the crowds of shoppers and locals until they turned down a small side street.

'Here you are,' Carav said, hands on her hips, looking up proudly to the storefront.

Amarah turned to see a wooden board with a spinning wheel etched onto it protruding from the shop's front. 'Well done,' she said.

'Told ya I could help!' Carav beamed.

Amarah nodded but didn't praise her. She didn't want to encourage her further. She opened the door to the wooden shop and immediately regretted it. Fabrics and clothing lined every inch of available space, and the stuffiness was suffocating. Amarah coughed. 'Hello?'

Carav and Kohl followed inside, the former hurrying to Amarah and the latter lingering near the door.

'Yes? Can I help ye?' A short Estorian woman appeared from behind a basket of mismatched linens. She had deep blue eyes and wore a dress of red in sharp contrast, and grinned widely when she saw Amarah and Carav.

'Got a spare bit of cloth for this?' Amarah asked, pointing to her missing eye. 'Lost mine on the flight here.'

The woman easily navigated the clothing and piles of materials until she reached Amarah, where she roughly grasped her shoulder and pulled her down to a height she could inspect.

Amarah suppressed a surprised yelp but held still under the woman's firm grip. She closed her good eye as the woman whipped out a measuring tape and wrapped it around her face, then across her eye socket, and then between both her eyebrows.

'She's with me and Traego,' Carav said, watching as the seamster held Amarah firm and continued to take her measurements.

Just as suddenly, the woman let go and walked off, staring at the tape and muttering to herself.

'Well? You got something?' Amarah asked, rubbing her forehead where the woman's thumb had pressed into her skin.

The seamster made a wild gesture with her hand that Amarah took to be dismissive. 'I make ye something.'

'I don't need you to make anything special. An off-cut will do. I got a handful of pennies and I just need—'

'Come back tomorrow, I have something for ye.' The seamster sat at her low desk and started scribbling numbers in black ink on a spare sheet of parchment.

'She's good,' Carav said. She ran a hand along the fabrics hanging from a rail along the length of the shop.

Amarah looked to Kohl, who hovered awkwardly near the door. He shrugged, and Amarah returned the gesture. 'I'll see you tomorrow, then?'

The woman didn't look up from her notes and simply repeated the hand gesture.

It *was* a dismissal, that time.

When they all stepped back out into the sunny street, Amarah ran a hand over her face and rubbed her good eye. 'Well, that was easier than I thought.'

'Is that not how business transactions are usually carried out?' Kohl asked.

'Normally they ask more questions and want a lot more money. Not that I'm complaining,' Amarah added. 'Just unexpected is all.'

'You're welcome!' Carav quite easily accepted the compliment as personal praise. 'Back to Traeg, now?'

Amarah wasn't in any particular hurry to return to Traego's lodge. She hadn't yet seen what airships she might be able to procure for herself and hadn't fully explored this part of the island.

The street had thinned in the few minutes they'd been inside, and it took Amarah a second to notice people running off to its far end.

'What's the commotion?' Kohl asked.

Amarah knew the drowning pits were in that direction, and suddenly going back to Traego seemed the better idea. She tried to redirect. 'Could be anything. Probably a couple of kids in a scrap. Or maybe someone dropped a purse of coins.' She began to walk the other way.

'Shouldn't we help?'

'We need to get back to Traego,' Carav said. She grabbed Amarah's elbow and started pulling her along, half-dragging her through the street.

Amarah forced herself to take several more steps, but had to stop when Kohl didn't follow. He stood in the same spot, looking at the crowd gathering at the end of the street as though transfixed. They could hear shouts of fear and anger, now. 'Kohl. Let's go.'

He ignored them and headed off towards the crowd.

Amarah watched him go. 'Oh shit.'

Carav darted off, and Amarah had no choice but to follow, calling for Kohl all the while.

By the time she and Carav reached the crowd, Kohl had been lost in it. Amarah could just barely pick him out given his height and his hat, but with the majority of the crowd waving their hands and shouting, even following his hat became tricky.

'Kohl! Come on! We need to go!' Amarah called, but he

ignored her and continued to push his way through the crowd.

She closed her eye and shook her head. It wasn't going to be good.

She shouldered her way past the packed Estorians, Carav trailing her like a dog, and it didn't take long for them to reach the front of the crowd.

Several paces ahead of the gathered Estorians, the land disappeared in a sheer, twenty foot drop. The sea writhed at the bottom of the pit. A mesh of metal criss-crossed the top of the pit, joined by thick chains to a large metal wheel. Four burly Estorians pulled at the wheel, the chains rattling as the metal lid opened slowly, exposing the pit and the sea below.

Amarah and Carav glanced across the crowd of people, but Kohl seemed to have vanished.

On the far side of the pit, a small group of people huddled together, waiting. Amarah could see the metal cuffs holding their hands together, and sickness filled her.

She knew exactly what they were and what was going to happen. 'Split up. Find Kohl and get him away, now.'

Carav nodded and tore off in one direction, while Amarah headed in the opposite. She didn't call his name now, she doubted she'd be heard over the raucous cheering, but she kept her eye out for her companion.

How could she have lost sight of him so quickly?

The wheel clicked as it held the lid open fully, and a hush grew over the crowd in anticipation of what was to follow.

Amarah had reached the end of the crowd and hadn't seen him yet. She angrily ran a hand through her hair, scratching her scalp as she peered over the faceless bodies, looking for Kohl.

Finally, with the crowd no longer moving, she spotted

the familiar hat about halfway along the line. Without hesitation, Amarah made a beeline for him.

Before she could get close enough to be within earshot, the small group of prisoners screamed.

She glanced across the pit to where two of the Estorian guards shoved them forward, ripping away their cloaks and revealing the prisoners as Arillians. Their wings had been bound with rope, and another coil trapped their knees. She looked away again. She'd seen this happening plenty of times before. She didn't need to see it again.

She focussed on Kohl and getting to him as quickly as possible. Even from several paces away, she could see his stricken expression as he watched the group shoved to the edge of the pit.

The guards were babbling something to the crowd about their dangerous captives and the safety of Linaria, but Amarah wasn't listening.

'Kohl. I told you to go.'

She reached him as the first guard shoved one of the Arillians. Kohl tensed and Amarah gave in. She looked to see the Arillian—a young woman from her appearance—scream as she hurtled down into the pit and the waiting sea below.

The other two Arillians followed shortly after, and the cheers from the crowd drowned out the splash as they hit the water. The sickness which had welled up almost exploded, and she fought to keep her trembling under control.

She couldn't look away, and she saw the Estorians return to the wheel and slacken the chain, lowering the metal to cover the pit opening. If the Arillians somehow freed their wings, there'd be no way they could fly back out.

'I told ya ta get back ta my place. I didn't want ta have ta come all the way out here ta look for ya.' It was Traego.

'I tried,' she whispered. Tears welled in the corners of her eyes at the senseless murder. She didn't need to look at Kohl to know how he felt.

Dimly, she noticed Carav returning to their group as the crowd continued to cheer all around them.

Traego spoke coldly, 'While ya're here, I'm ya captain. And ya do as I say. Or leave, if ya want, and forfeit ya share o' the bounty.'

15

Morgen tried to ignore the sweat dripping down his nose.

The harsh desert sun pounded on his bare skin, and although a sheet of fabric covered the window, Morgen still felt the burning heat on him. He took a slow breath in through his mouth, his eyes closed from the distractions of the room around him, as he attempted to regain focus on his task.

Meditation had never been his forte.

He'd lost track of time, but given how his muscles ached, he assumed he'd been at it for over an hour so far. His legs cramped and his knees throbbed, but Andel remained cross-legged on a rug beside him and seemed perfectly at ease. Morgen could hardly hear him breathe.

And still, he had to continue.

It was only the beginning of Topeko's training, and the scholar—the Kalos—had refused to begin teaching him properly until he learned the appropriate level of self control. Morgen had no time to spend years in silence as Andel had. He needed an intense course of training that would put him on the same level as any Kalosai in less than a quarter of the time.

Topeko hadn't been pleased.

But when Morgen had offered him gold in advance, he'd relented. And then Topeko had thrust half a dozen dusty tomes into his hand and advised him to read up and study the theory.

Morgen had glowered at first, and then convinced Topeko to begin his physical training through the day if he promised to read at night. That had displeased Topeko even more, who'd gone on as close to a tirade as was possible for the mild-mannered teacher. Apparently the theory alone was so intense that to consider physical training alongside it was madness.

Morgen had convinced Topeko to let him try, and if he found it too great a drain on his mind and body, he'd step back.

Unfortunately it meant the training was less physical, but Morgen knew he needed to improve his self-control if he was to have a hope at achieving the magical proficiency he dreamed of. And he knew Topeko wasn't being difficult. He'd taught *Ra* for years. Clearly there was a reason why it was taught in the current manner. Trying to find shortcuts wouldn't be easy.

Topeko had questioned him thoroughly on his motives for returning to Berel and learning the art of *Ra*. He'd asked the same questions over and over, often just worded slightly differently, and Morgen had wondered what the problem was.

In the end, Topeko had agreed to teach him firstly due to the gold, and secondly as a favour to Amarah.

'I saw her just before coming here. Less than a week ago?' Morgen had said when Topeko joined him for breakfast the day after he arrived.

Andel must have warned him, because Topeko didn't seem surprised in the slightest to see Morgen at the breakfast table helping himself.

'She's almost the same as always,' Morgen had continued. 'Aside from her eye. She's lost that...oh, and *Khanna*, too. Been in the wars, it seems. But she's in good spirits. Nothing'll get her down. I think she's on her way to Estoria.'

Topeko pursed his lips together as he digested the news. 'She lives such a dangerous life. I'd hoped she'd have calmed down somewhat after travelling with Moroda and Eryn.'

At the mention of Eryn—which of course reminded him of what he'd lost and how he'd messed up—Morgen's anger had been sudden and all-encompassing. He slammed his spoon down on the wooden table and pushed himself to his feet. 'It's because of Moroda, Eryn, and Anahrik's sacrifice that Amarah's been pushed on to greater purpose!' His hands trembled, and he took a moment to gather himself while Topeko and Andel looked at him in stunned silence. 'It's done the same for me, too. I want...I want to do some good in the world. I won't be able to if I'm stuck in the Imperial Guard for the rest of my life.'

Morgen remembered the hushed words Topeko and Andel had shared with one another, and for the past few days, Andel had hardly left his side—the younger lad becoming something of a personal mentor while Morgen began his studies.

Though he had never felt anything less than welcome in Topeko's home, following that breakfast, Morgen wanted to leave as soon as he possibly could, and as soon as he'd learned the bare minimum from his lessons. As soon as he could make a difference and challenge Sapora.

As soon as he could avenge Eryn, Moroda, and Anahrik.

He was so lost in his memories that Morgen didn't hear Topeko approach until the Kalos spoke.

'That's your two hours.'

Morgen blinked and opened his eyes, a sudden wave of panic flooding him. He glanced around and saw Andel slowly open his eyes and exhale, as though waking from sleep.

'Here, drink this.' Topeko offered them both a clay bottle.

Morgen took it and unstoppered the cork, drinking the cool water in several large gulps. 'Thank you, sir.' He put his head down and let the water run down his recently cropped hair and along the back of his neck. The relief was heavenly.

Topeko smiled at the formal address and helped them both to their feet. Without any preamble, he began the morning's lesson, 'You are of course familiar with the art of *Ra*, and its counter, *He*?'

Morgen nodded, wiping his mouth dry and stretching to relieve the stiffness in his knees from being sat down for so long.

'They both exist, though we Samolen, and those who study in our schools, only have access to *Ra*—to life and creation. *He* is beyond us. Loss. Destruction. Death. But it is important to have an understanding of this darkness if one is to truly comprehend *Ra*.'

Morgen had no idea what he meant, but nodded anyway. It sounded like the comparison between a sword and shield, and stating you could only use a shield. Surely they were both important? 'In Corhaven, there are loads of myths about Samolen magic. If you can teach me the truths....'

'Yes, I can,' Topeko said. He circled them, arms folded behind his back, his robes skimming the wooden floor. 'The Dragon Goddess Rhea created Linaria, and bestowed upon her children her innate magic. This chiefly refers to the dragons, but also us. You and me.'

Morgen listened intently. He shifted his stance to stretch his other leg.

'We are all Rhea's children, and so we all have the ability to harness the innate magic within us. Many of the...more advanced powers are found within us Samolen, and you will not be able to access them, no matter how hard you try, Morgen,' Topeko said. He paused in his walking and looked directly at him. 'I shall attempt to teach you all our abilities to see what you can do, and what you can focus on. Andel will help.'

Morgen couldn't stop the smile from growing on his face. Now he'd cooled down and loosened himself up, he was ready to dive straight into the proper training, and discover all their limitations. 'What are the abilities, Kalos Topeko?' He was sure to keep the formal name at the tip of his tongue. If Topeko confirmed the resurrection magic, then he'd be on the right track.

'Andel?' Topeko said, turning to his other student.

'There are six branches of Samolen magic,' Andel said at once. 'Kalos, Kalosin, Kaloset, Kalosuk, Kalosol, and Kalosai.'

'Um,' Morgen said, his motivation and confidence suddenly deflating. They might as well have been speaking the Ittallan Old Tongue. Morgen could read, just about, but he'd never had any formal education or schooling other than what you learned with a sword in your hand and an angry captain barking orders at you. He had no idea what any of the magic branches meant or how they differed from one another.

'Correct, Andel,' Topeko praised with a clap. 'Kalos is the teacher. Kalosai is the student.'

'I get those...' Morgen mumbled, glancing from Andel to

Topeko. He supposed he knew something, when they reminded him.

'The healer, Kalosin, is what Andel will be on completion of his studies and training,' Topeko said. 'Kaloset is the musician. You've felt their power every day that you've been here.'

Morgen remembered the music that played in Berel every morning and evening and nodded excitedly. It had been his first ever experience of Samolen magic, and it had been wonderful. The magic in those sounds could rejuvenate you after a hard, harsh journey. It could wash away your aches, and restore your energy, ready for another day.

'The final two.' Topeko's voice grew sharp. 'Kalosol, the shaper. A more advanced form of the magic that you, Moroda, and Eryn used when you were last here. The most common of all Samolen magic: the movement and manipulation of the energy that is all around us,' Topeko said. He raised a hand to the candles which burned brightly on the table behind them. With a short gesture, the flames extinguished, and then reappeared in the sconce at the far end of the room a moment later.

'I remember,' Morgen said. Moroda had managed to create a small shield from the energy around her. The possibilities had seemed endless, and hope filled him as he thought of learning all that could be done with energy. 'And...the final one?'

'The conjurer. Kalosuk. It is almost the opposite of the Kalosol. A Kalosuk can create and wield energy that is *not around us*. It is produced from within, and thusly one of the hardest to master. This is what takes the greatest strength, the greatest self-control. A Kalosuk who has poor control is likely to kill themselves as much as wield their magic.'

Morgen swallowed. There was nothing so close as resurrection magic than the last one, and he was sure to keep his face impassive as Topeko explained each one. Creating energy that isn't around us, creating energy from thin air, surely meant limitless possibilities. He tried to broach the subject indirectly, 'Kalos, the teacher, is purple. Like your cheek jewel? And blue is Kalosai, for students?'

'It is,' Topeko agreed.

'That's why my ring...the rings you gave us...all had blue crystals in them? Because they're for Kalosai?'

Topeko smiled, some of his defensiveness ebbing away. 'Also true. Kalosin, healers, have white stones. Kaloset, musicians, are green.'

'And Kalosol are yellow. Kalosuk are red,' Andel added, rounding off the fifth and sixth branches of magic. Morgen thought to all the Samolen he'd seen. He'd known they all wore a coloured jewel in their cheeks, and some of them—like Topeko—even had two. But he'd not given more than a passing thought as to what the colours meant. He'd just assumed they were chosen based on how pretty they looked and little more.

To learn that they all meant mastery of a particular branch of magic suddenly made them far more interesting. He considered the branches, but reached a decision fairly quickly. Becoming a Kalosuk would be his goal, with a Kalosol as a backup if he was unable to harness the conjurer abilities. It would give him the flexibility and breadth of opportunity that he needed.

'I shall work through each with you, one at a time, though I fear you will make no Kalosin. The healer is the rarest and most difficult to master of all *Ra* magic,' Topeko said.

Morgen glanced at Andel, expecting a smug grin as he would expect with any of his comrades in the Imperial Guard who used a particularly tricky weapon that no-one else could manage, but Andel's face remained neutral.

'Most Samolen are shapers. They are Kalosol. It is the easiest to learn for everything you need to use it is all around you. Life energy is abundant, which is why *Ra* is easiest for Kalosol.' Topeko resumed circling them, pausing occasionally to glance out of the windows as he passed each one. 'I shall not presume what you could be, if indeed you could be anything, but I shall do my best.'

'Thank you, sir,' Morgen said. 'I wish to protect my friends, to help in this war.'

Topeko flinched at the insinuation of battle.

Morgen immediately recognised his transgression and held his hands up defensively. 'What I mean is...is to look after those I care about. I can't really stop a war that's already going on, but if any fighting comes near...? I want to be able to stop anyone from getting hurt. From dying.'

Topeko pursed his lips. He didn't seem convinced, but Morgen didn't want to push his luck, so he kept quiet. He'd always been better at picking out the liars rather than lying himself.

'Perhaps a shield?' Andel chimed in.

Morgen couldn't have been more grateful. 'Exactly. A shield. A wall. Something to keep loved ones safe behind.'

Topeko mused the notion for a little while longer before accepting it. 'Well, a shield is not such a difficult thing to shape. Firmly in the branch of the Kalosol, but also with some potential crossover to the Kalosuk, depending on how advanced a level you reach. We'll see how you get on with both approaches. Perhaps, if you are adept enough, and given time, you may be able to obtain a cheek jewel of your own to signify your mastery.'

Morgen couldn't help but delight in Topeko's words. Though he spoke with many hidden caveats, chief among which was to not use this magic for violence, Morgen was confident in his abilities and what they might grow to. He'd always approached his training with the right attitude and had excelled. He didn't see how Samolen magic could be much different.

And he'd kept his *Valta Forinja* safely hidden with his belongings. In fact, he hadn't dared to even open it since arriving in Berel.

If he had been a completely lost cause, Topeko wouldn't have agreed to train him, he was sure. And Morgen wished he and the others had had the time to learn more from him before taking on Aciel. Perhaps they'd not have lost so many people to him, or Jato, had they trained in *Ra*. If they could competently defend themselves, perhaps no-one would have died at all.

Although his final goal was resurrection, a shield would be a good enough starting point. Keeping aggressors back was always useful, and if he could figure out how to manipulate a magical barrier enough to *push* them away, then all the better. If he was going to be training towards mastery, he might as well learn everything he could along the way.

'You'll keep your ring on until you can work *Ra* without the aid of the crystal,' Topeko said. '*Ra* is innate, of course. But to master it, you must eventually be able to tap into it without the booster.'

And so Morgen began to train.

He spent the early mornings, before breakfast, in deep meditation with Andel. Sometimes Topeko joined them, sometimes he didn't. While Morgen had initially found the sessions to be rather boring, he quickly discovered how much it sharpened his mind and focus.

Food was given frequently throughout the day—short meals of only a few mouthfuls, which Morgen thought were hardly enough to keep a child satisfied, let alone an adult, and in the desert sun he lost any excess fat he'd gained while tucked up nice and safe in Povmar.

He quickly grew used to the heat in his hand from the crystal as it worked with his innate life magic—*Ra*, he reminded himself—and had begun to show progress far more quickly than he'd assumed he would. He'd thought Andel would be forgiving, considering he was still a Kalosai and had gone through the same type of training not too long ago, but Morgen couldn't have been further from the truth.

Kalos Topeko was kind, patient, and understanding.

Kalosai Andel seemed un-satisfied until Morgen collapsed with exertion.

Tapping into *Ra* felt less like a conscious choice with clear motions, and more of an instinctive hope that he was pulling at his energy in the right way. The first few times, Morgen had been left sick and dizzy with exhaustion, but the ring certainly acted as a booster. Morgen likened it to stabbing an enemy in total darkness. He had a rough idea of where they were, but the ring acted as a beam of light which clearly showed him the right way forward. He still needed to step through the light, of course, but it was far easier when he knew the right direction to move in.

Every time he did particularly well during a lesson, Andel clapped him on the back with progressively more and more force, until Morgen had to brace himself every time he was praised. He'd even commented that Andel's actions were bordering on painful, and wasn't becoming of a Kalosai of Ranski.

Andel had been sure to push Morgen twice as hard the following day in response, and seemed to delight in Morgen's challenge.

The first time Morgen had managed to create a shield— almost a week after he'd first begun to study properly, he'd been so surprised at this achievement that he'd dropped all the energy he held and fainted.

When he came to a few minutes later, Andel offered him some water and then demanded he recreate it.

Through it all, Morgen was grateful for his drills in the Imperial Guard. He had no idea how anyone could cope with the constant demands on their body and mind when it came to harnessing the energy around himself.

Ra was supposed to be innate. Supposed to be easy.

He knew he didn't have a drop of Samolen blood in him, so he was at a disadvantage, but he had rather intense one-on-one tutoring. He thought he'd be able to pick it up quicker than he had been, or at least recover from the exertion faster.

He dreaded to think what the effort would be like if he had to conjure magic out of thin air.

The thought of becoming a master conjurer, a Kalosuk, suddenly felt like an impossible dream that would never be within his reach. That defeat, even hypothetical, spurred him on to work harder at what he knew he *could* do.

Although he'd given into his fear of Sapora and fled to Povmar, Morgen didn't think of himself as a quitter. If he couldn't go through, he'd just find a way to go around.

Morgen strained to mould his shield and shape it into something solid and useful—to cover himself, others, and even move it at will to protect something at a distance. He remembered during that fateful battle against Jato that Moroda and Eryn had produced a similar shield, but their lack of training and endurance meant it was unsustainable, and it hadn't taken the Arillians long to cut through it.

The shields he'd always used had been made of wood and metal. Most were circular or oval discs that he could kneel behind and protect himself from a sword blow or an arrow strike. The shield he produced through *Ra* was shapeless and hung in the air until he gave it form.

It was also invisible, which made manipulating the energy that much harder.

Morgen had never been an imaginative child, and trying to form something with his mind, something that he couldn't see, was extremely difficult. He had a vague idea of its shape, for when Andel attempted to reach through it and touch his face, Morgen's shield prevented his hand from making contact. It was more of a thin wall of magic that covered his body and moved as he did, rather than a large square or circle that was locked to his arm.

He supposed it made the magic more versatile and useful than a physical shield could ever be, but Morgen still had to get used to creating the thing and keeping it strong. He could barely hold it for thirty seconds before Andel's determined hand pushed right through it.

But it was something he could work on. Something to build on and progress from.

And even more impressive and inspirational was Andel's own training. In between Morgen's exercises, Andel carried on with his own studies, moving from healing grazes and headaches to bleeding wounds and bruises.

A number of Samolen would arrive at Topeko's home through the day, and no matter how tired he was, Andel would always greet them with a smile and a healing hand. There were some things he couldn't do yet—after all, he was still learning himself—and a broken wrist was beyond his capabilities, but Andel's sheer strength of will was something that Morgen found inspiring, if nothing else.

Morgen wanted to ask Andel about his *Valta Forinja*, and whether any of the *Ra* magic he was learning could be combined with his sword. But given the Samolen's firm stance against violence, Morgen wasn't sure he could bring up the subject with his fellow student.

That, and he didn't completely trust Andel not to tell Topeko of his sword.

With his training beginning to show some results, Morgen didn't want to put his relationship with Topeko or his welcome in the country at risk.

~

'YOU KNOW, Amarah's mother is half-Samolen, and her father is full-Samolen, but she has absolutely no innate ability to tap into magic,' Topeko said. He spooned broth from a simmering pot in the centre of the table into each of their waiting bowls.

Morgen looked up from his place at the table. He'd been savouring the break—he was seldom allowed them—with a half-doze while he waited for food to be ready.

'On the other hand, Moroda took to it far more easily. I wish I knew why some people are better at it than others.' He handed Morgen his bowl of food and then ladled out more for Andel. 'I suppose it's like you explaining whether someone is better with a sword or bow.'

'It's a tool to be practiced before it can be wielded effectively.'

Andel took his bowl and slurped at it immediately. 'Yes. It's why the university was built—not only to house ancient relics and texts of the past, but to hone us in the knowledge of *Ra*, so we could better protect Linaria with these powers.'

Morgen could understand that. But he was also nothing like Amarah or Moroda. He'd push himself further and harder than anyone else he knew. Samolen magic might focus on life and creation, but it could sting as well. He sported a number of bruises and cuts when he dropped the energy he held, or tried to control too much—far more than he was capable of.

He knew what to do. It was simply a question of whether his body and mind would let him.

Topeko, though sticking with him, seemed to be warning him against doing anything stupid. Though he knew the Kalos probably had good reason to caution him and question his motives, it was Morgen's memory of Eryn, Moroda, and Anahrik that kept him going. It made him push on through the pain towards a point where he could harness *Ra* in such as way as to put a stop to Jato and the dragons. To stop Sapora.

And to a point where he could resurrect those lost to Linaria.

16

Sapora marched through the palace like a man possessed, leaving mud and soil on the pristine marble floors with every step.

Isa all but ran after him, careful to avoid stepping in the mess lest she smeared more of it along with her and gave the maids even more work to do. She hadn't relaxed since leaving the ballroom, and her sense of dread grew with every passing minute. It didn't take long for her to realise that he was leading them back to his own chambers, though he didn't say a single word as they marched on.

She had never seen him this angry before, and she was grateful that she couldn't see his face as she hurried after him.

Sapora always had a cool anger. An anger he'd been perfectly in control of. In fact, she'd never known him to even raise his voice—even when the palace had been under attack.

But this? This was a bright hot bubbling anger that threatened to explode, and she wished she didn't have to be near him when that happened.

Roke inclined his head to Sapora as they approached but wisely said nothing. Either it was in his nature to remain silent unless addressed or he could sense the king's simmering rage. Isa averted her eyes as she hurried past Roke and through the large door into Sapora's personal chambers.

Sapora stopped in his circular antechamber and Isa took a breath, ready to face whatever he said. But Sapora simply plucked a burning sconce from the wall, reached a hand behind the tapestry of himself—he'd had it relocated from the gallery to his rooms shortly after moving into the palace —and revealed a hole in the stone wall.

Eyes wide, Isa followed him through the hole and along a narrow passageway, her feet echoing off the stone steps leading down. She guessed it had been a cellar for a previous ruler—she could still smell aged wine in the stone —but knew now wouldn't be the right time to mention it.

The torch in Sapora's hand flickered, the light not quite illuminating the vast cellar. Isa's eyes adjusted quickly to the dimness, and when Sapora stopped by the wall to light the sconces there, she finally stopped and looked around. Her brother moved slowly and methodically along the walls of the room, lighting each of the sconces as he went. Bookcases and stone tables lined the edges of the cellar, and an enormous oak dining table dominated the centre. On every surface and nailed against every bit of clear space on the walls were mirrors.

Mirrors of every conceivable size and shape.

Isa looked around, half in awe, half in horror. What seemed peculiar—other than the fact Sapora must have had over fifty mirrors squeezed into his secret cellar—was the fact that every single one had a shard of glass missing from it.

'What is this place?' She asked, walking slowly through the room, her fingertips brushing the mirrors as she passed them. When she touched the glass, a tiny shiver ran up her arm. 'Is it...is it blood magic?'

'Varkain communication,' Sapora said, lighting the last wall sconces and bringing clarity to what would have been a dark cellar. Another reminder of how much she and Sapora had grown apart. He knew of things she couldn't fathom, had lived a life she could only dream of. They had been raised together as a prince and princess, and yet their paths had diverged so wildly, it was as though they were now strangers.

He extinguished his torch and then turned to face Isa. His eyes burned and she knew he struggled to maintain his composure. She didn't know whether to speak, ask a question, or wait to be addressed.

Isa decided it would be safer to wait, so she adjusted her stance, placed her arms behind her back, and met his gaze levelly. She might have been afraid, but she hated giving anyone the satisfaction of seeing that. Even Sapora.

Minutes passed by, dragging slowly. She had plenty of patience, though, and wouldn't rush this. If she messed up this conversation, she doubted she'd live past the end of the day.

Eventually, Sapora spoke, 'I'll not protect you from Tacio a second time.'

Isa winced, the reaction so instinctive that she couldn't stop it. 'I made a mistake.'

'Yes. You did.'

The coldness of his voice caused goosebumps to rise on her flesh. Was this how it felt to be prey cornered by the snake? She didn't *want* to apologise. In truth, her mistake had been getting caught.

When it became obvious she wasn't going to say anything else, Sapora said, 'Roke said you needed to speak with me about something urgent. You now have my full attention.'

Isa looked away, unable to hold his gaze any longer. She had no idea how Sapora so quickly and easily could spin a conversation to put someone at a disadvantage. She'd seen him do it a number of times with Koraki, Tacio, and even some of the Cerastes. He'd never done it to her before, though, and hated how trapped and alone she felt.

The original reason she'd sought him out had been due to the Varkain in the city. And although they were still a problem, she thought she'd tackle the biggest issue she had while Sapora was listening. 'You need to deal with Tacio.'

'You deal with him,' he replied.

Isa blinked. 'But he's a bully! He's throwing his weight around, and insults me and the other Ittallan! The only one he listens to is you.'

Sapora's eyes narrowed. 'I'm not your babysitter. You will have to deal with him like the rest of us.'

'You could send him away. Back to Sereth? He always moans how he misses his tunnels.'

'No. He is here because I need him. He is ruthless when it comes to winning. He's a capable fighter, reasonably competent, and having lived in Sereth all his life, he knows the Varkain in ways I do not. And you are here because I need you. I need both of you, and I need your loyalty. Especially with Summercourt approaching.' His cold tone hadn't shifted, and he spoke more slowly than normal, an air of condescension seeping into his voice. He continued to watch her with an almost unblinking stare.

That stare alone unnerved her more than his admission that he needed her. 'You treat me like a child,' she said. 'You tell me nothing of your plans, you execute people without

232

warning, you disappear without letting me know!' Fear had pitched her voice higher than usual, and she struggled to keep from hysterics. 'You say you need me, you told me you trusted me as an advisor, but you haven't done anything of the sort!'

'I was not aware I needed to divulge my every movement to you. I care nothing of yours.'

Isa exhaled through her nose, her own anger rising. 'I just wish you'd tell me what you're doing!'

'What I'm doing?' He asked, almost amused. 'I am investigating the allegations of Aciel's powers within the city. I am researching the Arks and having any of their potential locations put forward. I need to consult with the Valendrin on what can be done with my prisoners so they can be put to use when I release the first Ark. I am hunting down the Ittallan spreading dissention in the city, the ones who say I am responsible for Taban Yul's sickness. I need more rebels found—Tacio's methods aren't bringing up anything. I need a team to fly to Corhaven and look for Morgen, who appears to have disappeared from Linaria. And before all that, I am overseeing preparations for Summercourt before our dear father and his retinue arrive and claim our worthlessness.'

Isa swallowed. She needed to regain her composure. 'You hid the Arks from me until I discovered you were hunting them. Now you have half the mercenaries in the world out looking for them. You put a bounty on Palom. He's an ally. A great fighter without whom we would not have defeated Aciel.'

Sapora shrugged. 'He killed my Varkain. Murdered them in cold blood. And then killed Mateli. I cannot let every transgression pass otherwise no-one will believe my word means anything.'

'I wish you'd drop the bounty. There are plenty of people

who've killed Varkain! Why make an example of the one who has given the Ittallan so much hope?'

He closed his eyes and exhaled in what appeared to be frustration. 'Is that enough information for you? Anything else you'd like to question? Any other orders you'd like to undermine before I continue?'

Isa bit her thumbnail as she often did when nervous. 'The Arks....'

'What about them?'

'Why the Arks? You already have a Sevastos at your control. Isn't the god enough?' She remembered trying to have this conversation with him once before, in the palace gardens. The sudden arrival of a fleet of warships attacking the palace had put things on hold. And after that, everything had just descended into chaos. She loved her brother. They'd grown up together, looked after one another, promised to make things better for the Ittallan and Varkain both. Many citizens of Taban Yul believed him to be *emonos*, to be a dark omen. And she'd known it would never have been easy to heal the rift between their two races, not after centuries of war and hatred. She wanted to badly to stand with him and help him achieve his goals, but he'd hovered on the edge of no return.

Now, she didn't even know whose side she was on anymore.

Sapora shook his head. 'I told you already that the Sevastos is not a god. It is a dragon. A beast. It can be tamed and killed as easily as any other.'

She tried another approach, 'But everyone in Taban Yul respects you with that dragon flying around. Why instill more fear with the Arks? Isn't that overkill?'

'Overkill?' He almost laughed at that. 'Why do you *think* I'm after the Arks?'

'How should I know? You never tell me your plans!' It

was a petty, childish response, and she knew it. But she didn't care.

'A Sevastos sealed Aciel and Moroda in crystal. Yet Aciel's power of compulsion, his will, is seeping out, turning those in the city against each other, or forcing them to commit suicide.'

She nodded, still scowling.

'A Sevastos is not invulnerable. If I can have one obey me and Aciel's will can break free of another, then what happens? What if Aciel's power is great enough to not just seep out of the crystal, but to eventually break completely free of it? We have an Arillian in the middle of our city. Everyone within ten leagues would be under his command in a matter of hours.'

The thought of Aciel breaking free terrified her. 'Then burn him with your Sevastos.'

'Like I burned the traitors who attacked me? Dragonfire is wild and unmanageable. Sevastos fire even more so. I lost a fifth of my city defending the palace. I'd lose all of Taban Yul just to kill one Arillian!'

She folded her arms.

'The Arks are *immortal*. In the entire war, they've never been defeated. Not by anyone,' he said.

'Until your Sevastos.'

'Until my Sevastos,' he repeated. 'Which is why I need the Valendrin. I bring back the Arks and they stop Aciel in his tracks. They remove him as a threat to Linaria. And they put a stop to the damned dragons who are killing the rest of us after what that stupid Arillian did.' Sapora's voice trembled.

Isa shook her head and walked away from him, pacing along the cellar as she tried to think. Even if Sapora was after the Arks with good intentions, it didn't detract from the fact they were weapons of war. They'd been responsible for the deaths of countless Ittallan when they had been used against them.

No Ittallan would ever trust him nor truly accept him as king. How did Sapora hope to control such ancient powers? What was to stop them bringing destruction to the whole world if they—or the Sevastos—decided they wouldn't listen to him anymore? Then what would happen? 'You'll destroy us all.'

'I'm *saving* us all. There's a difference.'

Isa dragged her hands over her face. 'The Arks were the end of the Ittallan! If they hadn't disappeared, there'd be no Ittallan left!'

Sapora shrugged. 'They were good at what they did.'

'Don't you understand?' She marched back to him. 'If they'd wiped out the Ittallan race, you and I would never exist! This city wouldn't exist! The Varkain would have taken over and the whole country would be underground! There'd be no palace. No gold. No resources! Nothing!'

'What will happen when Aciel wakes up and no-one can stop him?' Sapora's voice pitched almost to a scream. 'He will enslave every. Single. Person. What then, Isa? The Arks were so powerful they were sealed away. If anything has a chance of destroying Aciel once and for all, it's them.'

Isa's blinked away panicked tears.

'Dragons all over Linaria are now burning indiscriminately. What can put a stop to them? The Arks! It all comes back to the Arks! And if I have them under my control, there is no risk.'

Isa scoffed. 'Oh, really? The ancient weapons of the Varkain under the orders of a king less than half a year into his rule? And one who is half-Ittallan? I think not.'

His lip twitched as though he held back a snarl. 'I am a Varkain as much as any of them.'

'Exactly. You aren't an Ittallan. You aren't one of us.' She swallowed and immediately regretted her words. She and Sapora had always been outcasts together, not quite Ittallan, not quite Varkain. It had always been them against everyone who ever looked down on them.

'I am an Ittallan as much as you,' Sapora said.

'No, you're not! You're a snake! You've always been a snake! You're a snake just like Tacio! And you're bringing back the Ittallan's greatest enemies to kill us all!' Tears welled in the corners of her eyes, and she lashed out with her right hand.

Sapora's claws gripped her forearm tightly, their tips pressed painfully into her flesh, as he stopped her blow. 'You were about to strike the king.' His voice was still, and it chilled her to the bone. He snapped a moment later. Like a flame, venomous rage burst from him. 'You think I wanted this? If I did not claim my birthright and face the trials, we would be under King Tacio. He'd keep us in our tunnels, hiding from the world's threats, or let us submit to Aciel.' He pointed angrily through the door of the cellar with his other hand. 'Live the rest of my life under his smug grin? His condescending boredom? To be *his* thrall? Or rise up and bring the Varkain back into the light. To make our mark on Linaria as more than maggots in the dirt.'

Isa swallowed and pulled away, but Sapora's vice-like grip did not relent.

'I am *not* going to sit by as Aciel poisons my city and tries to destroy my world. I will fight him with every fibre of my being, call upon every power, even the Valendrin...even the Arks. If that's what it takes to keep Linaria from desolation.'

Sapora's grip relaxed slightly, and Isa yanked herself away. She leapt backwards and clutched her arm where he'd held her.

Sapora spoke quietly, as if hoping only she heard him, 'The Valendrin is key. I've visited Malashash's tomb twice

237

and failed to revive him both times. And *when* I do bring him back,' he paused as though daring her to object, 'I need to understand what to expect. How to control him and the others. I need to prepare for what happens when they breathe again.'

She looked to his muddied clothes and then back to his face. Realisation dawned on her. 'That's where you were just now, wasn't it? Malashash? His tomb?' Saying the Ark's name made it somehow more real. Like the fairy stories were slowly coming true.

He nodded. 'And to come back to my palace after being unable to resurrect him, only to find you had released one of my royal prisoners and Tacio was about to have your head....' Sapora left the sentence unfinished. 'I have no idea what you're playing at, Isa. But it stops now. I have too many other problems to worry about without you scuttling around the palace stirring up trouble.'

Isa bit her thumbnail again. For all her anger and disgust at what he was attempting to do, he was still her brother. Still her king.

She still loved him, and betraying his wishes ate at her very soul.

'I will bring you to my next council meeting. But know that Tacio will be present, and I'm not going to stop him every time he says something...*mean.*' Sapora walked to the large table and leaned his palms on it. 'He is a spoiled child who's always had what he wanted. He's an excellent fighter. Has a healthy dose of suspicion. And he's a better an ally than an enemy. You must remember that.'

Isa paced again, her loyalties torn.

Sapora wasn't going around and collecting weapons because he was power-hungry or deluded, as some of Lathri's followers would say, he was doing it to save them. To save all of Linaria.

But she still didn't agree with his methods.

Sapora continued, 'Much like the Ittallan of Taban Yul, come to think of it.'

'What do you mean?'

'They've grown lazy and soft here, in their rich city. Surrounded by all their gold and marble. Now they're having to share with the Varkain who have moved here to make a better life for themselves, the Varkain who—without me—would not have such an opportunity. Some Ittallan have had to give up some of their things and they don't know how to cope. Such a spoiled people.' He shook his head. 'Never told no. Never told to share. And when it happens, suddenly I'm the end of the world.'

Isa couldn't say anything to that. She knew much of the nobility were the same—all fawning over one another and trying to get into each other's good books. It had been half the reason she'd supported Sapora so much and for so long.

They'd spent fifteen years growing up together in the palace. Bastards were frowned upon in Ittallan culture, but the Varkain often had many children with different partners and there was no such concept as a bastard. The contrast in how they were treated had always put Isa on edge.

When Sapora had turned sixteen and shown he could transform into a *naja*, the royal cobra snake, Vasil had collected him and he'd moved to Sereth. Isa had desperately wished for the next year to pass quickly so she could catch up and transform herself. When Sapora left, she'd been alone in the palace beside Goldstones who despised her for what she was, and she no longer had his protection.

So when her own *meraki* had appeared and she'd finally been able to transform, she thought it would be her ticket to the life of a proper royal in Sereth with her brother. But she hadn't been a *naja*. She hadn't even been a snake. She was a wild cat, and that meant she'd never be permitted to enter Sereth.

She'd never be able to see her brother again.

Of course, Sapora had left on errantry two years later in preparation to take the throne on his twenty-first birthday. He hadn't left with an entourage, hadn't left with any gold. He'd only taken two of his father's scimitars and the clothes on his back.

Unlike most Varkain, who kept to their tunnels and never fraternised with anyone from outside—unless they were thralls, of course—Sapora had opened his eyes to everything Linaria had to offer. He'd gladly crossed into other countries and learned from different people, all to be a greater ruler than Vasil.

All to bring his people into the light.

All for this.

He'd visited her three times during his errantry, where he'd told her about his travels, about what he'd seen and the people he'd met. He'd purposely kept away from other Varkain so as not to be influenced by them.

When they'd been younger, they'd planned what they'd do when Sapora took the jade crown from Vasil, and became king. How they'd right the wrongs in their lives, how they'd get revenge on those who belittled them. How they'd make everything better.

True to their planning, Sapora had killed almost every Ittallan on the old council, along with influential Gold-stones who'd spoken against him or against the Varkain. That had been their first step, and Isa had known there would be no going back from that.

And although Sapora had fought for and earned his right to rule in blood, things had been very different when he became king. Aciel had thrown a small spanner in the

240

works, of course. But it was only after Sapora had moved to Taban Yul that things seemed to fall apart.

Instead of giving Isa the power and acceptance she'd craved all her life, he had become obsessed with some hidden Varkain treasure—which she now realised had been the Arks. He'd brought a Sevastos to the city—something she hadn't even *known* about, despite being a princess.

Tacio had arrived, too, and immediately set to undermining and insulting her at every chance he had. Sapora seemed to act on impulse and did things that would drive a bigger rift between the three of them and the Ittallan.

Then she'd met Lathri, she'd been saved by her rebels.

Everything had been messed up. Everything.

She'd betrayed Sapora twice—once when she'd begged Morgen to attack the palace and remove her brothers from power, and again when she'd freed Kylos. And still she planned to free Lathri.

She'd betrayed Lathri twice—once when Lathri had led the rebel attack, where she'd refused to fight her brothers alongside the rebels and fled to the palace to hide, and again when she'd delivered her to Tacio when they'd been caught by him and his Cerastes.

She betrayed those who looked to her for support and loyalty, and she felt sick for what she had done. Perhaps she would have been better off in Tacio's cell, under his torture.

The same tears that had welled up in her anger now threatened again as emotion overwhelmed her. She turned away from Sapora and paced, running her hands through her hair and wiping away loose strands.

'Change is never easy,' Sapora said. His tone seemed somewhat gentler. 'Once I rid the world of Aciel, they'll see that.'

Isa nodded, but didn't reply. She didn't trust her voice not to break if she tried to speak.

A hesitant knock on the stone wall carried from some-where above them.

Sapora darted to the foot of the stairwell before Isa could even blink. She watched as he raced up the stairs three at a time, and hurriedly wiped her eyes dry.

She used one of the mirrors to double-check her reflec-tion. The whites of her eyes were red raw, and her skin was blotchy. Even though she hadn't burst into tears, her height-ened emotion was clear to see on her face. There wasn't a lot she could do about it, but she wiped her face with her sleeve and smoothed her hair down as much as she could.

She'd been about to turn back to the stairs when a flicker of movement in the mirror caused her to stop. Isa took a step closer and peered into it.

Her reflection looked back at her, but there was some-thing else in the glass, too. She blinked several times and wiped her eyes. Had she been imagining it?

The mirror was a tall oval held in a heavy iron frame with ornate details running along the edges. Small snakes intertwined with each other like rope, and Isa brushed them with her hand to feel the twisted metal. When she looked back into the mirror, she saw a dark tunnel. Blue flames burned from a pair of torches in the wall, but she couldn't make out any more detail.

She'd been in the mines of Feoras Sol as a child, and this looked similar to that—although it seemed much better kept. The walls curved slightly and the floor was meticu-lously clean.

'Isa.'

She spun around to find Sapora watching her from the foot of the stairs, evidently having returned down them too quietly for her to have noticed. 'What's wrong?' Isa asked.

'The first guests for Summercourt are here.'

She nodded and looked back to the mirror, intrigued by the blue flames burning brightly in the tunnel.

'What did you say these were, again?'

Sapora approached and reached out a hand. He grasped the top of the mirror and turned it to face the wall. 'Varkain communication.'

The realisation hit her immediately. 'That was Sereth?'

'Part of it, yes.'

Isa grabbed the mirror to look at it again. 'I've never seen Sereth...'

Sapora kept his hand tight on the mirror and refused to let her see it again. 'Another time, I'll show you. There isn't anything there for you. Right now, you need to be presentable for Summercourt. Can I trust you to do that?'

Isa could tell he was taking great care to speak politely to her. If he had been Tacio, there'd be no kindness, only threats.

Guilt plagued her. She hadn't been looking forward to the event as it was, much less now she was on her final chance with Sapora. Any other slip ups and she'd be gone.

Of course, the idea of simply leaving Lathri to Tacio and ignoring the rest of her rebels also appealed. It would be an end to her double life. And it would ensure that neither Sapora nor Tacio ever suspected her of traitorous behaviour again.

Betraying Lathri and her rebels certainly had less severe consequences for her than betraying her brothers. Again.

First and foremost, she had to survive. If that meant taking it one day at a time and choosing the best course of action when she was presented with a decision, then that was what she would do.

If she ever were to rule as queen, the idea that her rise to glory had been shadowed in treachery and reason didn't sit well with her. But she supposed there were very few rulers who weren't corrupt in some way.

At least, that's how she justified her actions.

She was on her last strike with both groups, and although she'd been lucky up until this point, it wasn't going to last forever.

Isa nodded and allowed the smallest smile to lift her lips. 'I'll be ready.'

17

K ohl couldn't rid himself of the sight of his brothers and sisters plummeting to their deaths. He'd heard the "drowning pits" mentioned since arriving in Estoria; he knew he was surrounded by thieves and criminals, and he knew of the high bounty on Arillians thanks to Traego's warning, but he'd never thought he'd see his own people murdered for gold.

He now understood why Amarah had been so keen to pull him away. Carav, too, come to think of it. They *had* tried to spare him that horror.

It sickened him.

Better he face the terrors with eyes wide open than remain blind and ignorant.

He'd never felt more out of place than he did in Estoria. Despite the laid back facade of the islands and people, the danger was palpable. Everyone seemed ready to kill everyone else at a moment's notice, and he blamed the brewing, violent atmosphere for driving him to snap at Amarah before he'd seen the drowning pits.

If he had, then he doubted Amarah—or anyone nearby —would have survived.

He stared at his own hands, remembered the power that ran through his fingers. His Frost-touch. Violence was never the way. He'd spent countless decades trying to teach that fact to Jato.

But what was the point, if your power only killed and destroyed? What was the point if people looked at you and felt only terror? What about joy? What about love?

No. If he fought back, if he gave into the destructive nature most of Linaria believed he and all Arillians were slaves to, then it would only make everything worse.

And yet, Amarah's words against Moroda and Jato were hard for him to listen to without reaction. After everything he'd done for her in Oren and beyond, he'd hoped that Amarah was more than just a treasure-hungry sky pirate. Perhaps he'd been wrong to think there was actually more to her than that.

She'd seemed so set on freeing Moroda that he'd ignored her despicable, selfish nature, and offered to help her find a Sevastos—if one truly was the key to saving Moroda.

Although he realised it was difficult for Amarah to continue on her journey while grounded, her barbaric nature and aggression made it hard to truly believe she acted for someone else. Or at least planned to.

He half-expected her to turn against him at the last minute and laugh at him for believing that she'd ever try and help someone else. From her words about allies, rather than friends, everyone really did seem out for themselves and only for themselves. While he was useful, she kept him around. While he could offer something that she wanted—providing her with his dragon-hunting capabilities—she tolerated him. But as soon as he fulfilled his purpose, he imagined she'd fly off into the sunset, and he'd never hear or see her again.

But Amarah had redeemed herself somewhat by showing concern for him and trying to stop him from seeing the deaths of the captured Arillians.

He still saw their terrified faces when he closed his eyes, heard their screams echoing down into the abyss, *felt* them plummet into the seawater as though he'd leaped into it himself. He'd been too stunned to react, and it had all happened so quickly. He didn't know if he'd even have been able to fly down to grab them and escape before the metal lid of the pit closed to trap them forever. If he'd managed to save only one of them, would that have been worse? Knowing he'd have had to choose one to save and let the others die?

Or was letting them all die together, while he stood and watched, the better option?

He replayed the scene over and over in his mind, wishing he could have stopped it. Wishing he could have done something, said something, anything, that would have made a difference. But if he had, and revealed himself as another Arillian, he'd have been bound like the others and met with a similar fate.

And he couldn't do that. Not while he'd pledged himself to Amarah's journey.

So while Amarah and Carav had returned with Traego to the thief's lodge after the public execution, he'd excused himself. There was no chance he'd let slip what he was to anyone outside Traego's crew. Not after seeing his people suffer that terrible fate. Amarah had believed him—at least, she hadn't tried to stop him when he said he wanted some time alone.

Kohl made his way back to the beach where he'd met up with Amarah and strolled along the sand, keeping to himself. While the fishing boats had long since finished their morning's work, the beaches were full of Estorians and

Goldstones; tourists and beggars, thieves and pirates. This was their home, and they played in the sea, lounged in the sunshine, and were perfectly at peace with the murders happening on their doorsteps. As long as their pockets were filled with gold. He walked along the beach, getting further away from the bustling activity on the shore.

The fewer people he saw, the better.

Guilt riddled him, even though he couldn't have changed the outcome, even if he had revealed himself. All his life, over two hundred years, he'd tried to do what he thought was best, to look after his people and his family, and ensure they had a future. And he'd failed them all. There was never one right way. There were always conflicting actions, conflicting emotions, that meant every decision worked for some and never others. He could never make everyone happy all at the same time.

And Jato seemed unhappiest of all, whatever he did or suggested.

Now the closest person he had to a friend was set on hunting her down, and he couldn't do anything to stop her.

Kohl followed the beach as it curved around the island's edge, paying little attention to those around him. Few took much notice of him, anyway—they were too engrossed in their own fun. When he reached a relatively bare section of sand, which had combined with soil to darken the land, thus keeping the tourists away—they seemed to prefer the more pristine beaches—he finally stopped.

A single figure stood alone some way off, arms folded as they stared out across the sea. The man wore a robe of what appeared to be grey roughspun cotton, and Kohl saw his dark, curly hair blowing slightly in the breeze. The man seemed preoccupied, so Kohl picked a spot beside a large palm tree and sat down at its base, his back and wings still covered by his cloak pressed against the trunk, grateful at last to have some quiet. From here, he could see the man quite clearly and make a quick exit if he came over.

He tried not to think of the drowning pits, but that decision of course had the opposite effect, and no matter how hard he tried, he couldn't escape the vivid memories. And although the shade from the palm tree brought some relief, the insufferable heat of the place did nothing to ease his fraying temper. He felt utterly at a loss. Forced to remain on the edge of society and converse with thieves and criminals while his people were hunted down like vermin. For profit!

For all his immense power, he was powerless. What good was it being able to wield the Frost-touch of his ancestors if he couldn't use it to help his people? The Ice Golems hadn't responded to him when he'd been in Oren—although he'd only been there for a few days before Amarah had ruined everything with her impatience—and he was at a loss as to what to do next. If he kept his promise to aid Amarah, it wouldn't be long before they'd encounter Jato again. As Amarah had fought her once before, he doubted the sky pirate would be defeated. She didn't seem like she lost very often.

If Jato killed her, then he'd lose his only ally. If Amarah killed her, he'd lose his only daughter. Again.

He had no kin, save Jato, and any friends he'd had, any true friends, had been lost to Aciel or were back on Oren, trying to rebuild morale and give the Arillians something to live for. Perhaps he'd return there one day, when he'd fixed all the messes he'd created but right now, he could do nothing.

Helplessness settled over him like a blanket that held him down. Grief and anger warred in his chest at the injustice of how his people were treated. Aciel had been the cause of the war, not any of them. And if they *had* been involved, it was through Aciel's compulsion. No Arillian in their right mind would fight against the people of Linaria.

Not after they'd been decimated in the Great War and banished from Linaria's mainland.

Kohl picked up a shell and rubbed a thumb over its smooth surface. The waves crashed gently against the beach and brought with it the smell of salt. Estoria could be very beautiful if it wasn't for all the corruption.

He glanced up as the man on the beach suddenly turned towards him and began walking. Kohl sighed, readying himself to stand and get away, when he noticed something familiar about the man's walk. He had a very slight limp, as though his left knee pained him.

Kohl squinted and stood, brushing sand off his cloak. He didn't want to hurry away too quickly—that might draw even more attention to him—but he needed to make sure the man was actually coming to him before he left the spot, which gave him the peace to consider what had happened to the Arillians here.

Just as the man drew within speaking distance, he stumbled in the sand and braced his fall with an outstretched arm.

'Are you okay?' Kohl asked reflexively. He stepped towards him.

The man straightened and squeezed his bad knee. As he opened his mouth to reply, he paused, then his eyes widened. They brimmed with tears. 'My lord. What are you doing in Estoria?'

Kohl stiffened. Only an Arillian would ever call him "my lord," and this man couldn't be....'General Fogu?'

'Please forgive me, my lord.' Fogu immediately dropped to his knees and bowed low, his nose pressed into the sand. Words tumbled from him like an overflowing bucket. 'I could do nothing against Aciel. I tried, truly, but...but he was overwhelming. My actions and words were not my own. I swear on the ice itself. I tried to push him from my thoughts, I tried so very hard. I tried every day, but he...he....'

'Stand up, Fogu,' Kohl said as gently as he could. He glanced around in case anyone had wandered to their part of the beach, but thankfully they were still alone. 'It's okay.'

Fogu ignored his request and remained on his knees, tears streaming freely down his cheeks. 'I couldn't.'

'General! Stand up!' Kohl grabbed the man by the front of his robe and lifted him to his feet.

Only when Fogu was manhandled did he get hold of himself and stand under his own strength. 'Please, my lord. I would never have acted so, never have spoken so, if it hadn't been for Aciel's compulsion.'

Kohl shook his head. 'I'm well aware of what Aciel did to you. He did it to a thousand others.'

Fogu trembled. 'I belittled you. Threatened your companions...my lord...I *attacked* you. If you wish for me to pay the penalty then I shall accept your word. But please know that it was not my intention, I did—.'

'Don't be ridiculous. You said yourself that you weren't in control. I know it to be true. You've nothing to apologise for.'

Fogu looked away, unable to maintain eye-contact. 'I am ashamed, lord. I should have fought him harder.'

Kohl placed a hand on Fogu's shoulder. 'He over-whelmed you, as he did to all the others. You cannot blame yourself for what he made you do, old friend. I don't.'

At the mention of "friend," Fogu turned to face Kohl. He trembled but did not cry again, and then grabbed Kohl's arm with his own. 'You forgive me, my lord? I have exiled myself from our people—'

'There's nothing to forgive.' Kohl squeezed Fogu's arm and smiled as much as he could allow himself to. The surprise at seeing the general on the beach had passed, only to be replaced with grief for the Arillians they'd both lost through Aciel's war and now the Estorian bounty hunters. 'There is no penalty for what you were forced to do. Nor any of the others.'

Fogu's shoulders dropped, and he struggled to keep from weeping again.

Considering there were Arillians in Estoria, Kohl shouldn't have been surprised to bump into one. He'd just not expected it to be Fogu of all people. And he hadn't even recognised him until he'd been almost upon him. Kohl frowned and looked Fogu up and down twice, just to be sure. 'But, where are your wings?'

Fogu adjusted his robe and pulled at the fabric around his neck. 'I'd be drowned by now, if the Estorians could see them. My body would probably be on a ship bound for Val Sharis. If I'd stayed wearing a heavy cloak like yours, I'd have melted in the heat.'

The bluntness made Kohl wince. 'True enough. So how have you hidden them? I can't tell you're an Arillian at all!'

The tiniest smile pulled at Fogu's lips, and it warmed Kohl's heart to see. 'They call it a *Thief's Shroud*. These sky pirates might be callous but they have some very good tricks up their sleeves. I was able to procure one to hide my wings to the eye. If you look closely enough, you'll see them. But to most, they can't be seen.'

Kohl gasped and leaned forward for a closer look. He'd encountered two *Thief's Shrouds*—one in the Karoun Mountains of Corhaven, where Veynothi's tomb had been hidden, and the second in Tum Metsa, where Amarah had hidden an old thief's haunt while they'd waited to be picked up by Traego. He'd therefore assumed that a *Thief's Shroud* could only be used to hide something very large. He hadn't realised one could hide something on a person.

And even after Fogu had mentioned it, he still struggled

to see even the hazy shimmer that gave away the presence of the shroud.

'You must have paid dearly for it,' Kohl said.

'I stole it.' Fogu looked at the ground in shame. 'After...after what happened in Val Sharis, I threw off my armour and bundled myself up in the robe of a larger man who'd perished. His blood was still damp on the cloth. But it was chaos. People running everywhere. I overheard a group say they were escaping to Estoria. I'd never heard of the place before, but it had never come up in Aciel's campaign, so I thought it would be somewhere inconspicuous to lie low for a while. My head was still fuzzy, I could barely walk, let alone fly. I had no idea how to hide what I was, but when I reached the airship I saw some pirates removing a shroud to reveal their stash of goods. When they'd gone, I took it.'

Kohl nodded, amazed. If their positions had been reversed, he imagined he'd have panicked and been slain for gold. 'But why come here to lie low? Why not return to Oren? Many have.'

Fogu's enthusiasm diminished and he turned away again. 'How could I go back there after what I'd done? I'm ashamed of what I am. Arillians have only brought destruction to Linaria. I was too weak to fly, to move, really. The airship journey gave me time to recover. By the time I arrived in Estoria, the bounties on Arillians were already on the rise. So, I'm hiding here, among thieves and criminals.'

Kohl frowned. 'You aren't ashamed. You're *surviving*. If that means hiding what you are to avoid being...drowned, then that's what you must do. There's no shame in that, friend.'

Fogu's pained look told Kohl that he, too, knew of the drowning pits. 'Please, my lord. I must make amends for what I've done. The people I enslaved and killed because of Aciel.'

'You were at *war*. You were acting against your will. You cannot hold yourself accountable for what happened. I promise you that I do not.' Kohl took a breath and shook his head, trying to keep an eye on their surroundings in case any Estorians wandered nearby. He tried another approach, 'I did not believe myself worthy of returning to Oren, but I was permitted.'

Fogu's eyebrows shot up. 'The Golems...?'

'Permitted me.'

Fogu seemed to take a while to absorb the information. Several conflicting emotions danced across his face, and Kohl stepped back to give him a minute to process the gravity of what he'd just said.

Kohl knew they both sought forgiveness for things that were out of their control. While he struggled to face it himself, somehow it was easier to help someone else through their own turmoil. It was not unlike giving advice— it always seemed easier to offer it out than to accept it yourself, no matter how much sense it made.

Eventually, Fogu spoke, 'I didn't think they'd permit anyone back.'

'I thought the same. But they did. Jato had returned, too, but she's gone now.'

'Gone?' Concern laced Fogu's voice.

Kohl nodded. 'I returned with a friend, an ally. Her name is Amarah. She sought the Ice Golems counsel, but we left before she could. Jato and her fought.'

Fogu raised his eyebrows. 'Then...this Amarah is alive, still?'

'I intervened.'

Fogu nodded gravely, requiring no further explanation. He said, 'If they permitted you back home. They might...do you think...'

'Why not? I was exiled. You may travel freely as you wish.'

They fell into companionable silence, both simply enjoying being in one another's presence. Someone who knew who and what they were and didn't care. Someone that represented home and friendship.

'I can't stay here forever,' Fogu said. 'With the pirates hunting us down every day, I can't bear to see the Arillians they catch.'

Kohl dipped his head in agreement. Seeing it once was bad enough. If Fogu had been here since the end of the war, he dreaded to think how many Arillians he'd seen killed.

'My lord, we ought to return to Oren. To rebuild what we can. To bring in a new wave of peace. Our people need a leader. If Jato's gone, then why not you again? I would follow you, and so would many of the others, I'm sure.'

'If only I could.' Kohl watched as a particularly mangy dog hobbled along the beach, its nose to the sand as it sought out scraps of food. 'I am pledged to help Amarah. Once that's done...perhaps I'll return.'

'What pledge do you have? You're the leader of Oren, of our people. Your place is with them, especially now Aciel's gone.'

Kohl closed his eyes and walked away, leaving the dog to explore the beach by itself. 'I wish that I could. I've let her down too many times, caused too much trouble.'

Fogu stumbled after him. 'She'll be fine, I'm sure. She'll have enough money.'

'Money?'

'Only Goldstones here, correct? They have fortunes in gold and silver.'

Kohl swallowed. 'She...isn't a Goldstone.'

Fogu stopped short. Kohl didn't bother to look at him, he

could take a fairly well-educated guess at what his fellow Arillian thought of that. 'My lord, don't tell me…'

'Indeed, she is a thief. Jato destroyed her ship in the fight.'

'I see.'

Kohl led them along a narrow path that led further inland. Saying it out loud sounded ridiculous. He'd let Amarah down. He could fly. Why not just leave her and live his own life? She'd have no hope of ever returning to Oren without an Arillian guide—the Ice Golems wouldn't let her.

She'd be out of his hair, and he'd have no further dealings with the criminals who polluted Estoria. He could focus on his own home, his own people. And she'd probably be happier, too.

'If I returned to Oren,' Fogu said, 'would that I returned with you. I would assist you in whatever efforts you wished to take in rebuilding. I am done with war, with fighting, with death.'

Kohl considered. Returning home with one of his closest friends—now free of Aciel's compulsion—would make a statement. Fogu had always been well respected, and his battle prowess nigh unmatched. If any still loyal to Jato remained in Oren, they'd soon do as he said with Fogu standing for him, too.

If only things were simpler.

He could ask Amarah, he supposed. He doubted very much she'd like the idea—she'd made it perfectly clear that he was in her debt, and his own sense of duty and loyalty wouldn't permit him to flee from her. Even if there was no possible way she could ever catch up to him again.

But staying here, in this place, with Arillians dying, hiding who he was, while he waited for Amarah to get enough money to buy a new ship? He wasn't sure how long he could last.

It had been less than a day, and he already wanted to escape.

Kohl looked out into the open sky above. How easy it would be to lift his cloak, open his wings and soar into the clouds. To wheel high and far, away from pirates and corruption, from the politics and scheming of Linaria's mainland. To return to his people's exile in Oren and remain on the floating islands until the end of his days.

'My lord?'

Kohl sighed. 'It's a good offer. I'll consider it.' And he would. He just needed to figure out how to ask Amarah to release him from his promise. And if she said no, what his backup plan would be. 'Meet me at the same beach in three days' time. I'll have an answer by then.'

Fogu clasped Kohl's forearm and smiled, a true smile. 'Returning home with you will be less daunting than if I crawled back with my tail between my legs having succumbed to Aciel's will.'

'Never, Fogu. Most of them were the same as you.'

The mangy dog loped up to them, red tongue hanging out of the side of its open jaws.

Kohl leapt to one side as it sniffed at the bottom of his cloak, hackles raised. 'In three days, old friend.'

BY THE TIME the sun had set and the third moon had risen, Kohl still hadn't worked up the courage to return to Traego's lodge. Nor did he know what he was going to say to Amarah, or Traego, or any of them, depending on who he encountered first.

He felt more of an outcast than ever, especially after seeing Fogu, and yet he could not give himself permission to leave. Amarah would enact her revenge against Jato, of that he was certain. It was unlikely his daughter would return to Oren unless she could free Aciel anyway, so if he left, he wouldn't have to endure seeing his daughter slain.

All logic pointed him to leave, and yet by his own stupid loyalty, he couldn't. Not unless Amarah herself freed him from his promise. And there was about as much chance of that happening as Arillians losing their wings.

He huffed and cooled himself against the muggy night air with a shield of freezing wind. In Berel, the nights brought cool relief from the burning sun. In Estoria, the night was humid, with a thousand insects chirping and biting for his blood.

Veynothi: the Ark. Ancient powers and Varkain blood magic; stealing from a tomb. He didn't want to get himself mixed up in it all, but felt he was already too deep into the mess of Linaria that there was no way he could ever return.

This was a darkness that he wanted nothing to do with. And yet, if he returned to Oren, it was still a life of exile. What kind of life was it when you were banished to barren rocks in the northern wastes? When all of Linaria could be yours to fly in and explore and live, yet scrounging on the edge of a tundra was all you could offer your children and grandchildren?

He sighed and picked absentmindedly at his fraying hat. In the distance, the waves lapped at the beach. Conversations drifted through the palm trees as they had done all day. Estoria was a place that never slept, it seemed. There were always several pairs of eyes on watch, either guarding some treasure or on the prowl, looking for a fight. Perhaps it was paradise only if you could pay to keep everyone out. Traego had spoken of everyone being an equal here, something missing in the rest of the world, where you were judged on your class and wealth, yet Kohl saw small hierarchies and rules here that everyone lived by.

It unnerved him.

And although Amarah had every intention of leaving, she couldn't without a ship of her own. Traego was her best chance of getting the gold she needed for said ship. He allowed his mind to wander, and for once, his thoughts didn't settle on the memories of the drowning pits, but on Jato. Where was she? Was she safe? Was she surrounded by allies or enemies?

Was she causing utter devastation wherever she went or had she calmed down after fighting Amarah? Would he ever be able to accept that she'd gone? That there was no salvaging the relationship? He'd tried to come to terms with it, but saying something and believing it were two different things.

He glanced to his left where a wide estuary ran into the sea. Movement on the water had caught his attention, but even in the moonlight he couldn't see details clearly. He caught sight of a fin protruding from the water, its barbed tip glistening in the light, as it made its way inland. And then it was gone.

Kohl sighed. Cold filled his body and he let it seep into the air around him. A thin sheet of frost formed on the grass where he sat and crept up the length of the tree trunks around him.

The Ice Golems continued to watch and wait. Forever observing.

There was something of them in Veynothi. Or perhaps there was something of Veynothi in them?

The Varkain were the oldest race in Linaria, already millennia old by the time the Ittallan sprang up from their outcasts. Whatever deep magic the Arks boasted, he didn't know if the golems could match it.

How would the Ice Golems react to foreign invaders

looking to steal something of theirs? What would they do to the thieves if they were actually successful?

His skin crawled at the thought.

There was a real battle still to come, he was sure of that. Aciel had merely kicked the gears into motion. Now all of Linaria suffered for his greed.

Kohl wished beyond wishing that Aciel had not been an Arillian, that his actions hadn't sealed the fate of their people, but he doubted Linaria would forgive them a third time.

18

The acrid smell of death had a distinct way of permeating everything. Hair. Clothes. Even the air itself. Palom wrinkled his nose at the stench. If it wasn't his fellow Ittallan burning in their beds from the dragon attack, it was the two Arillians slain by Jato's own hand. They bled into the snow, and he shuddered.

Odi, Jek, and half a dozen others caught up with him and stopped, aghast, at the death and devastation in front of their eyes. 'Burn them,' Odi said. There was no hesitation in his command.

With great difficulty, Palom looked up from where he lay in the snow to see the elder pointing at the dead Arillians.

'Bring torches, dig a small pit, and burn them. Then we leave.'

The few Ittallan who'd come with him leapt into action, some moving the bodies, others heading back to camp to grab tools and materials.

Palom's vision wavered. Snow fell heavily, but he didn't need to see to know what was there. The dragonfire raged over the hamlet, melting metal and earth, both. He tried to stand, to help his companions, and immediately toppled to the ground.

~

WHEN HE AWOKE, he was back in his wagon, bundled up in a bed, with healers fussing over him. He tried to shoo them away, to say that he didn't need their help, but their gentle hands pushed him back into the sheets, and he didn't have the strength to resist.

Palom vomited several times and slipped in and out of sleep as the hours blurred together.

In between the healers' visits through the night, Odi came to see him. Palom also saw *Leillu*'s blue scales, which reassured him more than any healer could. Memories of the dragon attack and the Arillians fleeing flooded his mind after a while. In a way, the dragon had saved him. He'd been no match for Jato—not without his *Valta Forinja*, anyway—and he'd been running for his life when the dragon had attacked and turned the Arillians' attention away from himself and *Leillu*.

But the look the dragon had given him was utterly filled with hate, if such an emotion could be seen in a beast.

Palom hadn't even the time to pray to Rhea for his life and the lives of his comrades.

Perhaps the Goddess had been kind, as the dragon had grown tired of the devastation and flown away, leaving them to deal with the death it had created.

When dawn finally came, the dragon's fires still raged, and the hamlet had been burned from existence. Smoke plumed into the sky, thick and heavy, and the stench of burned flesh and singed wood choked the air.

He'd done his job well, Odi had told him. He'd protected the caravan from threats—be they Jato or rampaging dragons—but the Arillian's powers had been too great. Seven Ittallan had perished under her lightning attacks. More had been injured, but Odi had explained that Arillian attacks usually left no survivors. Palom would be paid well for his efforts, Odi assured him.

The caravan had moved on that very same day, even though Palom didn't feel up to another battle if they encountered more enemies. But they needed to bury their dead in the mausoleum at Taban Yul, and the elders needed to reach the capital in time for Summercourt. It held cultural significance for the Ittallan more than anything else, but there were politics at play, too.

Although Palom understood that, he didn't care too much for it. As far as he was concerned, going up against the snake and his Arks—whenever Sapora brought them back —was suicide. But he'd spent so long running that he had to stand and fight sooner or later. He might as well stand with Lathri and her allies and try to do some good.

Aetos had flown off at first light to report back to Taban Yul—he was a messenger after all—and the palace would need to know about another dragon attack so close to their walls. Palom had bade him tell Lathri's allies that he was coming to aid them in whatever way he could.

They'd travelled quickly that day. Most wanted to put the smoking hamlet far behind them, and in the next two days, they'd passed through the rest of the Rio Neva forest and would soon be able to spot Taban Yul on the horizon.

The capital city lay just south of the Feor River, a commanding presence in the wide valley, as though it dared any to approach and attack it. Although protected by twin marble walls, Taban Yul displayed wealth rather than fortification. With Sapora's Sevastos now flying guard, Palom supposed it didn't really need anything else to keep the inhabitants safe.

Now the trees fell away to reveal the valley below, the road broadened to accommodate larger wagons and heavier traffic, which meant their final push to the capital would be much quicker than the snail's pace through the forest had been. Even the snow didn't fall as heavily here, and the road only iced over in small patches that they could easily navigate around.

Outposts dotted the road on the approach to Taban Yul. Usually these were manned by only a handful of Imperial Guard, but it seemed Sapora had put many of his snakes to work, and dozens of them now stood guard. Even from this distance, Palom could see their red and gold armour glistening in the low sun as they milled about the outposts or stood at attention, awaiting orders.

And beyond the outposts, almost at the gates of the city itself, the crystal pillar lay gleaming. It shimmered between turquoise and blue, a marker for the end of Aciel's campaign, the death of the tyrant, and the one who'd sealed him away: Moroda.

Seeing it now brought back sudden, vivid memories of the battle in the sky against Arillians. Everything had been chaos and confusion, with thunder bringing everyone to their knees, and bolts of lightning searing through the sky. Until Moroda had ended the fighting.

They'd made camp on the edge of the forest, in plain sight of the outposts and the glittering city of Taban Yul beyond. Odi had not wanted to push the pace too much and have them arrive exhausted in the capital. From their position, they had less than half a day's travel to reach Taban Yul, and Palom was secretly pleased to spend one more night outside the city.

To return meant facing those he'd left—abandoned, really—and after seeing the destruction of both the Arillians and the full grown dragon, he wasn't sure he was ready to jump back into whatever war brewed within the city's gates.

Palom poked at the roaring fire while Leillu curled around the burning logs, her bright blue scales grey where she pressed her body to the ash, and slept soundly. The caravan's healers had done a decent job of patching him up. Mostly, he was exhausted. The wounds and burns he'd gained from the fight against Jato and her Arillians would heal within a week or two. But he couldn't rid himself of the memory of the dragon's utter devastation.

As he continued to fuss over the fire, Karvou came up to him. His bottom lip quivered but his eyes were defiant.

Palom sighed. He'd been neglecting his duty to take on the lad as an apprentice. While he could claim to be busy guarding the caravan as it travelled through the day, there was no excuse for ignoring him so much when they stopped to rest. He considered how to apologise and what he would suggest now they were on the cusp of reaching Taban Yul..

Karvou took a deep breath and said, 'See? I told you they were near! You should have listened to *pali*!'

Palom almost smiled. He'd forgotten how worked up Karvou and the other Ittallan of Tum Metsa had been when Arillians had first been sighted nearby. They'd descended into chaos, expecting to be attacked at any moment. Although Palom knew they were vicious, it was clear that Jato and her retinue were only interested in slaying dragons. 'Maybe....'

'You should *always* listen to what *pali* says!'

Palom smiled, then. He remembered being so young and believing with all his heart in everything his father ever told him. Perhaps when the war against Sapora was finished, he'd return to Feoras Sol and stay with his family. Considering his father was now an Archigo of the village, he wouldn't be surprised if he was already in Taban Yul for Summercourt—or at least on his way there now.

Jek approached and sat down on Palom's other side. *Leillu* opened one eye to watch him for a moment before settling back into a light doze.

'That were close, back there.' Jek also grabbed a stick and poked at the fire, mirroring Palom's actions.

'I know.' Palom's shoulder and waist had been bandaged, and he still winced every time he twisted too far. At least Jek had waited until he was out of bed before talking to him about it.

'Did they try and control yeh?'

Palom shook his head. 'That was just Aciel. These are...remnants...of his followers. She was after dragons. I do not know what it means, but I know it will be bad for Val Sharis if it continues.'

He'd tried to escape the war, but Jato's presence proved it was still right behind him, a shadow that grew every day, and one that he could not ignore. If Jato was flying around Val Sharis hunting down whatever dragons she could find, he wondered if she'd be bold enough to attack Taban Yul and Sapora's Sevastos. Perhaps the snake king would do his job for him by getting rid of her.

But after seeing Jato flee from the adult dragon in the forest, he somehow doubted she'd be that stupid.

Having to cross open fields to reach Taban Yul made him nervous. At least when they travelled in the forest, they had thick cover all around them. Waltzing down the main trade path to the capital left them exposed and vulnerable—especially to attacks above, if Jato decided to try her luck again at slaying *Leillu* on their final approach to the city. They wouldn't have another dragon swoop in to "rescue" them, this time.

He'd run from Taban Yul a hero of the Ittallan, having

played a key role in defeating Aciel and forging the legendary *Valta Forinja*—weapons created with the power of a Sevastos crystal. Around him, as those in the caravan sat around their own fires and ate their supper, he heard more songs of his recent heroism. This time he'd defeated an entire squadron of Arillians, seen off a fully grown dragon, and protected them all from their attacks.

He'd never enjoyed the attention and tried not to bring it upon himself. But it seemed once again his reputation had swollen without his realisation, and he wouldn't be surprised if young bards and minstrels up and down the country were singing of his exploits in every tavern in by the end of the year.

Palom scratched his chin where a scab had formed over one of his recent cuts as he considered just how far he'd come. There was no hiding what he was: a blacksmith by trade, the son of a poor mining family. Now, a hero throughout Val Sharis, if not all of Linaria. And all because of the dragons.

He looked at *Leillu* again, but she didn't so much as open her eyes. He poked the fire, sent up sparks, and stared into the flames.

To the south, in Taban Yul, people gathered. His people. Varkain lingered among them, drawn by Sapora's power, to the Sevastos, and rage simmered within him at the thought of the Arks joining them. He had never cared about who ruled so long as he could live and work in peace. Now, though? Sapora had enslaved Lathri, probably tortured her, too.

'Dragons.' He shook his head, then sat in silence beside Jek, while Karvou chewed on his bottom lip as though he wanted to say more but couldn't quite work up the courage to do so. Odi came close to the fire, the edges of his robes wet from where they had been dragged through snow all day. He sat down with a deep sigh and lifted his hands to the warmth of the flames. Without preamble, he said, 'In the battle against Aciel, you had a weapon of great power. The *Valta Forinja*, am I right? But you don't carry it anymore?'

Palom sighed. He had no interest in opening that dark corner of his heart again. 'It is danger. It is lost to me, now.'

Odi nodded but didn't ask anything more about his sword. After a moment, he said, 'Some of the Imperial Guard are on their way to inspect us.'

Palom looked up at that, and indeed saw a handful of uniformed and armoured Varkain heading up the wide road towards them. Overhead, several ships loomed near the city. One had the red and gold colouration of the Imperial Guard, but other ships flew in more neutral colours. It had been a long time since he'd seen so many ships in the sky— since before Aciel's campaign. Despite the growing dragon threat, the air seemed far busier than it had been in months. Almost like how things used to be.

Yfaila and several other Ittallan emerged from their wagons to join their comrades by the fires or to stand and watch the Imperial Guard approach. Palom would prefer to remain seated, but he couldn't shake years of respect driven into him by his father, so he, too, stood. He clapped to *Leillu* who immediately hurried after him. Palom pointed up at his wagon, and *Leillu* half-leaped, half-flew up into it. Palom gently stroked her nose with the back of his hand, and then drew the canopy over to hide her from view.

If the Imperial Guard were to thoroughly inspect their wagons, they'd discover her. But he hoped Odi would see them off with a few words, and they'd be welcomed—probably escorted—to Taban Yul in the morning. There was nothing wrong with having a dragon with him, but considering the problems they'd been causing, he thought it best to keep her out of sight for the moment.

He hurried back to stand beside Odi as four members of the Imperial Guard approached.

'Welcome, sirs.' Odi opened his arms wide as if to embrace them. 'I am Odi, son of the Gal Etra Archigo, and have come to Taban Yul to represent her at Summercourt. Travelling with me are friends and families from the northern towns of Val Sharis.'

Palom watched the Imperial Guard carefully. Three were Varkain, and one was Ittallan, yet he watched the snakes more closely. One of them nodded to his comrades and stepped forward to address Odi. 'I am Captain Renaud, charged by His Majesty to protect the city's North Gate and the crystal pillar, and I welcome you to Taban Yul.'

The Varkain's friendly words surprised Palom, but he said nothing to draw their attention. He felt the weight of his sword at his hip and knew he could draw it swiftly if he needed to.

Odi bowed, exaggerating the respectful gesture and keeping his eyes low all the while. 'Thank you for your most gracious welcome, captain. But my travelling companions and I are tired, and would not burden you with our needs this evening. With your leave, we will rest here tonight and enter the city in the morning when we are refreshed and ready to meet Summercourt.'

Captain Renaud nodded. 'Of course. We would be happy to escort you. The roads are getting heavier with those arriving for Summercourt, but I must advise you the North Gate has been sealed since Aciel's siege on the city. The East Gate is also undergoing some repairs, so I can only direct you around to the South or West Gates.'

Palom frowned. Renaud behaved exactly as any other member of the Imperial Guard would. There were no threats, no hissing, no sarcasm or snide remarks. He was polite, gracious, and spoke with all the formality of any Ittallan captain he'd ever dealt with.

Palom looked to the other soldiers, who had begun some small talk with those Ittallan nearby. He even saw one of the Varkain smile and laugh.

Odi was too busy talking with the captain to notice his glances, so Palom moved away from the two and towards the other Varkain. 'How fares Taban Yul?' He asked as casually as he could. 'We encountered Arillians on way here. They attacked us.' He pointed to the canopies of a few wagons, which had been singed by the Arillian's lightning.

'This is why King Sapora has called Summercourt earlier than is customary,' the Varkain replied. 'With the elders of the villages and a voice for every person in Val Sharis, we can understand the extent of the problem and put in a plan to stop them.' She seemed younger than anyone else he'd encountered in the Imperial Guard, but spoke confidently. 'King Sapora wishes only for the land to flourish. That cannot happen with enemies such as these Arillians given free reign. He has already placed a bounty on any captured and delivered to his palace—dead or alive.'

Palom hadn't known that. Neither had Odi, otherwise surely they would have brought the bodies with them for gold, instead of burning them. That, and Palom had been so caught up in what Sapora wanted with the Arks that he'd not realised the other moves the snake was making.

'How long have you been at the outpost?' One Ittallan asked her.

She shifted her weight, her armour clinking, 'I've been here almost a moon, now. I'd never have been an elite, a Cerastes. But King Sapora gave me the opportunity to protect the city gates and make a difference. Feeling the sun on my skin every morning is worlds away from the tunnels of Sereth.'

Palom scratched at his chin again. This woman didn't act anything like the Varkain he knew.

'What is Sereth like? I'll bet it's all dark and muddy!' An Ittallan child giggled.

The Varkain didn't seem to take any offence. 'Not at all, young one. Our tunnels are immaculate. They're wide, too. You could easily fit all your wagons down the main parts of Timin Rah. They're bright, too. We have special fire that lights our tunnels but won't burn us...'

She continued to describe Sereth and Palom walked away. The Varkain appeared gentle. Kind, even. It conflicted so greatly with his experience and thoughts of them that he felt sure he would vomit again.

He wandered over to the other two members of the Imperial Guard. The third Varkain was likewise in conversation with the travellers, while the Ittallan soldier scribbled something down on a bit of parchment with a rather ragged-looking quill. Even with Varkain as...kind...as these three, he wondered how it was for the Ittallan to work with them every day.

As Palom approached, the Ittallan looked up and lifted his quill from the parchment. 'Palom! I hadn't known you were returning to Taban Yul!'

Palom squinted as he tried to place the young Ittallan. Freckles covered his nose, and his bright blue eyes were in contrast with his dark hair. 'I am...Summercourt....' Palom muttered as he hastily attempted to come up with an excuse for his return. Summercourt was the obvious choice, and even though he was no Archigo, many Ittallan flooded to the capital for Summercourt—the new Council and laws would influence them, and being present was always of great benefit to traders and merchants. But he could not place the young soldier.

Almost as if he sensed Palom's confusion, the Ittallan

soldier said, 'I celebrated with you after Aciel's defeat. Stood beside you for the funeral. You probably see your fans all the time, so I'm not surprised you don't remember me. I'm Garinus.' He clasped a hand to his chest and inclined his head as a mark of respect.

'Thank you.' It was all Palom could say. 'How are Varkain?' He added, with a brief glance to the other soldiers.

Garinus frowned. 'They're...well?'

'I mean. How are they to work with. I worked with falcon Ittallan for years and we fought often because of our differences.'

'Oh. Just the same as any other member of the guard.'

Palom didn't know what to say to that. He supposed Garinus was being professional and would not disrespect his comrades—certainly not in public, anyway. But unless he looked at them, he could not tell these soldiers were Varkain. They seemed too...nice.

It had to be some sort of trick.

He watched as Jek threw himself into conversation with Captain Renaud, utterly at ease with the strangeness of Ittallan and Varkain mingling as they were, now. He supposed Jek had traded often with Varkain and was used to them, but Palom bore a deeply-rooted hatred for them, as did most of those from his village. He'd been attacked by too many Varkain to count, and had killed half as many in self-defense.

Even Yfaila approached them and spoke as graciously as she seemed capable of.

Perhaps all the horrible ones were still in the palace, surrounding Sapora.

Palom took his seat again by the fire. Clearly he wasn't needed. There would be no threats to meet, no fighting that would break out. They were welcomed into the city with open arms, and he wondered whether these soldiers even suspected treachery.

The captain and his comrades didn't seem to have much to do that evening, for they all joined Odi's caravan and ate with them. The Varkain regaled the Ittallan with stories of their homeland, and caught them up on many things that had been happening within Taban Yul over the past year.

Palom only listened with half an ear. They had done nothing to arouse his suspicions, but he knew the real reason Odi led his people to Taban Yul, and didn't trust the Imperial Guard—who worked for Sapora—not to try anything when their guards were down.

He'd been almost ready to relax enough to eat when more movement along the darkening road caught his attention. On his feet in an instant, he darted to where Odi chatted and put a hand on his shoulder. 'Someone is coming.'

Both Odi and Captain Renaud got to their feet just as two more armoured Varkain appeared. These were not in the glistening red and gold livery of the Imperial Guard, but in a dark blueish-black scaled armour, and they carried spears with wicked-looking edges.

'Cerastes!' Garinus whispered somewhere to Palom's left.

'Captain.' The first one barked.

Renaud hurried over and stood at attention before the Cerastes.

'What are you doing?' The Cerastes asked, eyeing Renaud with suspicion. 'You are not at your post and have not been for an hour. Is there an issue here?'

Renaud trembled slightly but shook his head. 'No issue, sir. The road is quiet, and they offered to share their supper, and—'

The Varkain backhanded him. 'Get back to your stations.

All of you. Prince Tacio will hear you've abandoned your posts.'

The other Imperial Guard were on their feet, and hurried down the road to the outpost before the shock of the brutality faded. Palom gripped his sword and stood firm, watching the two new Varkain. The Cerastes were clearly of a different caste to those who'd eaten with them. They were bigger, leaner, and looked like their only jobs were to hunt and kill.

They were far more like the Varkain he was used to than those Sapora had placed in the Imperial Guard.

The Cerastes who had dismissed Renaud and the others looked over the gathered Ittallan with barely masked disgust. 'Who is in charge here?' He waved his spear at the gathered travellers.

'I am.' Odi lifted his chin in defiance, all his earlier mirth gone.

The Cerastes stepped towards him. 'Do you have an Ittallan in your company called Yfaila?'

Palom's stomach turned. What did the Varkain want with Yfaila?

It seemed Odi wasn't about to give up one of his travellers so easily, either. 'I have already been through the checks of your Imperial Guard colleagues. I need not give you any further information.'

The Cerastes narrowed his eyes and tightened the grip on his spear. 'This is beyond the Imperial Guard. I am under direct orders from Prince Tacio himself.'

'And the Imperial Guard reports to King Sapora, unless I am mistaken.' Odi stood firm. 'Has she done some wrong? There's no need for a spectacle.'

The Cerastes huffed. 'There is no need for your insolence.'

The pleasant conversation that had been going on

274

around them slowly drew to silence as everyone turned their attention to the Cerastes challenging Odi. Palom knew they had the numbers to overwhelm them, if it came to it, but then they'd announce themselves as traitors. Killing two of Tacio's elite soldiers would stir up more trouble than he was willing to take on just yet. Surely Odi wanted a stealthier approach that wouldn't give away their true objective?

'There's no need for any of it. I am Yfaila.' The old Ittallan made her way slowly through the gathered crowd, limping slightly, she used her stick.

At her arrival, the Cerastes straightened and smiled, several fangs poking over his lip. 'Excellent. We received your message some days ago. The swiftest notice all the way from...Gal Etra, isn't it?'

Dragons above, what had Yfaila contacted the Varkain for? And the Cerastes, of all Varkain?

Yfaila stopped a few steps before the Cerastes, and stood in front of Odi. 'Yes, that's correct. I'm pleased you took my message seriously. I expect my first payment now, before I reveal anything else.'

At the mention of money, the Cerastes untied the pouch at his belt and threw it at her. She caught it with both hands, dropping her stick in the process, and unfastened it to peer inside. Palom saw the yellow gold reflected in her eyes, and his skin crawled. What had she sold to them?

Odi's rouse? The fact they were joining rebels?

Nervous talk rippled through the Ittallan, but Odi continued to keep his gaze fixed on the two Cerastes, his face unreadable.

Palom glanced to his wagon, but Leillu remained hidden inside, thank Rhea.

Once Yfaila was satisfied with her payment, the Cerastes said, 'You'll find the Varkain royalty to be *most* generous with their gold. Especially during these tumultuous times.'

'I should hope so,' Yfaila snapped. 'What good is royalty if it doesn't keep its word? I need to rest. My old bones aren't what they used to be, and it has been a long, arduous journey. Take me to the palace and I'll speak with Tacio himself.'

The Cerastes shared a look. The second one spoke for the first time, 'That won't be possible, Ittallan. We speak for him. Anything you wish to say to him, you can tell us.' He shifted his stance and waved his spear.

The look she shot him was withering. 'If you think I'm telling a pair of snakes where one of the Arks is, you're mistaken. I'll speak to Tacio or not at all. Or you can kill me, as you seem so desperate to, and none of you will ever know. Now, what's your decision?'

Palom watched, stunned, as the Cerastes escorted Yfaila away from camp and down the road towards Taban Yul without so much as another word to Odi or any of the others. He'd never considered she knew where one of the Arks was, much less would sell that information to the snakes. Had she no knowledge of the destruction the Arks had wrought to the Ittallan?

Was she happy to pay for a comfortable life in snake gold dripping with blood?

Why had she turned on her people?

Palom, Odi, Jek, and the others stood as night blanketed the valley and it began to snow.

19

Amarah had always loved the night. There was something about the energy in the dark sky that made her feel alive, like the trials of the day were meaningless as long as the moons were up.

Most of the other sky pirates seemed to agree with her. Airship races, especially on Estoria, were held at night more often than not, accompanied by gambling, drinking, and usually a good deal of fighting.

Tonight was no different.

She, Carav, and Traego had been joined by the captain's remaining four crew members—other than Antar and Oris, of course—making up his full complement. She'd been surprised to discover that he had a Samolen in his ranks. It wasn't unheard of them to travel the world, but considering Ranski's peaceful laws, it seemed bizarre to see a jewelled Samolen fraternising with thieves and criminals who often had to resort to brute force in order to get what they wanted.

The Samolen, Malot, said she never got her hands bloody, and so was not breaking any rule of her birth country. Amarah simply took it to mean that she knew others who would do the work for her. Malot had black hair that grew perfectly straight and reached her waist, though she'd braided it several times to keep it out of the way. She'd also swapped her desert robes for more practical garb—plenty of boiled leather and belts to hold her various pouches and bottles—flat, open-toed boots and a loose cotton shirt to stave off the Estorian sun. Her left cheek boasted a small oval jewel which glimmered in wine red and flashed when her emotions ran high, and she'd also adorned her ears, nose, and braids with silver rings and jewelled studs in all manner of designs and colours. It was a peculiar contrast to her soft brown eyes and olive skin which had darkened in the sun.

Malot was also the main reason Traego had access to so much Samolen magic.

While the bottled magic of Ranski was readily available on the black market—so long as you knew where to look and who to ask—it still had to be produced to order, or you had to make do with whatever stock happened to be around at the time.

Malot could produce everything Traego wanted almost instantly. Her red jewel marked her as a conjurer, a Kalosuk, if Amarah remembered rightly, and while she could produce most of what Traego wanted, her real talent lay in *Thief's Shrouds*. Traego had more than half his fortune squirreled away in various hideouts throughout Linaria, and he trusted in Malot's expertise to keep them safe. It had, in fact, been one of Malot's shrouds that Antar had used to mask Veynothi's cave—Amarah refused to refer to it as a tomb any longer in the hopes it would prevent any curses from following her—which was testament to the woman's skill in conjuration magic.

The rest of Traego's crew were quite unremarkable. The other two Estorians were brawlers for the most part. Amarah guessed they did more of the breaking than entering, and lacked the finesse of Antar, both in looks and fighting expertise. Both were stocky and muscular, with broad shoulders and bigger chests. One fought with a short sword, the other a mace, and they had introduced themselves as cousins. The mace-fighter, Ernold, had broken his nose at some point during his youth, which meant it sat crooked on his face and gave his grin a rather lopsided look. His cousin, Farlan, had finer features, high cheekbones, a gold lip-ring, and seemed to think of himself as something of a prankster. His black hair curled, and he spent most of his time flicking it out of his eyes. From what Amarah understood, they owed Traego a large debt, and were serving him until it was paid, on pain of death.

It wasn't as good as those who worked with you through loyalty, but considering Traego had marked them with his *Thief's Ink*, there was nowhere in Linaria they could run where Traego couldn't track them down.

The final man was clearly from one of Corhaven's backwater towns—with grey-blond, lifeless hair, pale skin that appeared to burn easily, bushy eyebrows and a bit of a belly. Before Aciel's war, he'd flown transport ships around the country. Too much money for too little work, it seemed. While he hadn't been part of Aciel's compulsion, his employer had, and Judd's comfortable life had suddenly disappeared from under his feet. Traego had picked him up from a small harbour town in the north of Corhaven, claiming a need for competent airship pilots, and whisked him away on *Otella*. Judd therefore worked as a backup pilot, mostly, and had a nervous disposition which meant Amarah didn't think he'd last long in Estoria.

However, his knowledge of airships rivalled anyone Amarah had ever known, and after being introduced, she began picking his brains on what her next ship should be. Given his experience in flying with both Traego and Malot,

Amarah hoped Judd could also make recommendations on any Samolen magic that could be used to give her ship the edge when it came to flight or combat situations.

Especially against lightning storms.

The six of them made their way into town, where the taverns and beachfront bars were almost overflowing with sky pirates and Estorians both, enjoying their night's revelry. The most popular spots on the island tended to be where the rivers met the sea, as there were fewer trees and more space on the sand to drink, dance, and brawl.

A trio of fiddlers played rather bawdy tunes which kept the energy on the seafront high, and ale, wine, and rum flowed freely.

Despite being desperate to hunt down Jato and seek out a way to free Moroda, Amarah guiltily enjoyed being "back to normal" for a bit. The sounds and smells of the Estorian night, with her fellow sky pirates and pilots all around her, the great ships swooping overhead in a never-ending contest to see who had the fastest or most maneuverable vessel, all the while the waves crashing in the distance, was her paradise. It was what she loved.

With Traego's monopoly on Samolen magic, there were few ships which could rival *Otella*. His ship wasn't built for speed, but he could hold his own against almost anyone. Amarah remembered with relish the time she'd beaten *Otella* in a breakneck race against *Khanna* and bought her freedom from his troupe. She supposed that was why he'd enlisted Malot's services to give him an unfair advantage ever since.

'So, you've got your five main classes of airship,' Judd said. They'd found an empty table close to the seafront and taken their seats.

Amarah nodded and took the offered tankard of ale.

'*Khanna* was a class four, mid-size. I don't wanna go no bigger than that. Too easily seen.'

'Yours had a class five engine, though, didn't it? That's why she was so damn fast, right?'

Amarah scowled at Traego, for only he knew what modifications she'd done to her ship, but nodded, grudgingly.

'*Otella's* a class one warship, and that's definitely not on your agenda. But I flew class three cargo ships, and you might think "why would I want one of those" but they have a lot of room for...improvement.'

'I'll take the heavy artillery from a class one.' Amarah shrugged. 'I'm going after some big things and I'll need some firepower if I can't fly away.'

'You're not gonna fit any of the big guns on another class four like *Khanna*. But a class three? Maybe you've got some more wiggle room there.'

'Price goes up with a bigger ship. I've got gold coming, but I need to get in the air as soon as possible. It has to be class four. Same size as what *Khanna* was.' Amarah took another sip and watched as a pair of single-seater class fives sped overhead. Although both had dark wood to make them harder to pick out at night, one decided to fan out silver and white sails. It could be seen for leagues away, surely.

The noise from their propellers had hardly died down when a pang of longing struck Amarah square in the chest. She wanted to be up there, a deck under her feet, a wheel under her hand.

Amarah took another sip of ale, though she'd suddenly lost the taste for it, and put the tankard back on the table. Along the sand, merchants and traders continued to sell to the gathered crowds. When they had a bit of drink in them, most were more free with their gold, and the traders tended to find more success overnight than they did through the day. At the far end of the beach, where the crowds had thinned, a Gold-stone stood by his fleet of ships. Most were commissioned and then built in Corhaven before being transported to Estoria, or to wherever the buyer wanted their new ship delivered.

Amarah scratched her head. Even if she had the gold for something bespoke, it would take weeks to build.

No. She needed something now.

She ran a hand through her hair and tried not to sigh like a spoiled child who wasn't getting their own way. Judd carried on talking, oblivious, and she drowned him out. It wasn't as though she could pick and choose what ship she bought. She didn't have the time—or the gold—for that. She'd simply have to discover what was available and pick the best from that. Malot seemed competent enough to provide her with additional Samolen magic. Considering she was currently working for Traego, she didn't see why she couldn't tap into the vast resources he had at his disposal, anyway.

Besides, until Sapora paid out in full, she was part of his troupe. She might as well take whatever she could get while she had the chance to.

'Why the long face, Amarah? Ya looked happy a minute ago.'

It was Traego, of course.

She shrugged and sipped at her ale in an attempt to mask her self-pity. Turning the conversation away from her, she looked back to the other pilot. 'Judd, are you racing tonight?'

Judd stopped mid-sentence and shook his head. 'Me? Oh no. I'm a transport pilot. I'm all about comfortable, safe flying. Not these daring maneuvers and cornering. Can't risk a tear in one of my sails.'

Amarah snorted. 'That's no fun.'

'Flying is practical. It's not supposed to be fun.'

Amarah lost her interest in the man at that point and rested her chin in her hand.

Ernold and Farlan kept glancing off to the side, and Amarah looked over her shoulder to see what they were so interested in. Another pirate troupe lingered nearby, their knives drawn, though they made no attempt to approach.

'Traeg—'

'I see 'em. I think Cyd owed 'em money.' Traego shrugged. 'They won't do anything.'

Amarah doubted that. She'd seen that look on people before. It was a look of hunger, of desperation, and it rarely ended well. She had brought her scythe with her, of course, and was confident in its power if she needed to use it.

They continued to watch the races and carry on their conversations, but Amarah couldn't help but check over her shoulder as more and more people joined the group who watched them. Almost an hour passed before she reached the end of her patience. Amarah grabbed her scythe and was about to stand up when the other pirates moved towards their table en masse. In several swift steps, they had the table surrounded.

'We want a word with you, Traeg.' One of them said. He was particularly tall and lanky, with greasy hair.

'Ya've been wanting a word all night. Finally got the guts ta actually come speak ta me?' Traego said. He kept his gaze overhead on the current race, where several class four ships careened around the island, their propellers sending blasts of wind their way.

'Two ships were meant to come in today. They were carrying fifty barrels of tea leaves. I had a deal with a Goldstone in Val Sharis to buy 'em. And now those ships ain't come in, I ain't got my deal with the Goldstone.'

Traego suppressed a laugh. 'Ships are late all the time. Bad weather out there.'

283

'Yeah. Bad weather. Like *Otella* bad weather. You and that damned witch of yours.' He threw a filthy look to Malot.

Traego replied, 'I don't see how it's my problem if ya made a bad deal.'

Amarah held her scythe tight, and the blade sent out a crackle of blue energy. The pirates surrounding them leapt back at the sudden light and roared in defiance.

Traego ignored it and continued. 'It's a busy night for deals. I suggest ya spend the rest o' this one tryin' ta salvage what ya fucked up. Like I said, it ain't my problem if ya struck a bad deal.'

The pirates grumbled more loudly. Clearly Traego wasn't going to talk himself out of this one.

'My deal was with Cyd. He had both his ships full for *me*. I lost my twenty-five crown deposit, and the way I see it, *you* lost it. So *you* can pay me back.' He lunged forward, dagger drawn, and slammed it into Traego's palm on the table.

Amarah leapt up and swung her scythe at the nearest pirate, vivid blue light arcing from the blade, and threw him a full ten feet away where he landed in a heap in the sand. She whirled around to help Traego, only to see the pirate's dagger embedded in the table, and Traego's hand perfectly okay—she hadn't realised he'd moved out of the way so quickly.

Traego had the pirate by the throat, both his hands wrapped around his neck. 'Ya can take ya twenty-five crowns and give 'em ta me as a deposit for not killin' ya right here and now.'

The other pirates rushed forward at their leader's predicament, and the sudden eruption of brawling almost caught Amarah off guard. She'd been expecting it, but hadn't realised it would be so swift and so sudden.

Malot leaped onto the centre of the table to avoid the fighting, but Amarah, Carav, and even Judd rushed into the fray to defend Traego and their troupe. Amarah hardly had time to think, she blocked blows and returned them as quickly as she could. And even though there were more aggressors, she and the others were more experienced when it came to brawling, it seemed. That, and her *Valta Forinja* gave her a massive advantage.

She felt the weapon's power surge through her fingers, and she had to hold herself back to save killing any of them. She wanted to defend herself and teach them a lesson, nothing more. Besides, Traego hadn't told them of any other troupe fighting nor suggested they were to go out murdering people tonight.

It was a simple scrap where everyone needed to live to tell the tale.

As she whirled around to smack the bottom of her scythe against the temple of a burly man who attempted to rush her, the fighting died away. The others drew back, clutching bleeding arms and faces, and Amarah was certain she heard the distinct sound of a nose breaking from somewhere behind her.

When she looked to Traego, he still had the man by the throat. After a few moments more of struggling, Traego released him, and he crumpled to the ground like a sack of potatoes. 'My deposit?' Traego asked.

The pirate shakily got to his feet and paid Traego the gold.

Traego patted him on the cheek as though he were a dog, then shooed him away with a gesture.

Only when they'd slunk off did Amarah lower her scythe.

'Ya know that ain't gonna be the last of it,' Traego said, pocketing the coins.

'I know. Welcome to Estorian life.' Amarah couldn't keep the sarcasm from her voice. 'It's the part of this place I don't miss. No rules except for who can bite first, or who can bite back harder.'

'Glad ta see ya ain't forgotten.' Traego took his seat again and picked up his tankard, which hadn't been knocked over in the skirmish.

'You don't have to get involved,' Marlot said. She gingerly stepped down from the table and brushed her clothing clean of sand and dust that had been kicked up during the spat.

Amarah couldn't face sitting again and disagreed with Malot that she actually had a choice in any of this. Estoria was the closest place she had to home, and even it wasn't safe. She supposed nowhere in Linaria was truly safe. Not anymore. 'I can't wait for the next time.' She rolled her eye. 'The sooner I get outta here the better. I was never one for fighting all the time. I miss having a damned ship!' She wanted to smack the bottom of her scythe on the ground, but as they were on sand, it wouldn't have the desired "crack" that she was after.

Traego watched her carefully, considering.

'What?' Amarah asked, when she saw him staring. She hoped he didn't want to send her after the others and wipe them out.

'Maybe I've been unfair. Maybe I should cut ya some slack after what ya did.'

She raised an eyebrow. 'What I did?'

'Jumping overboard for me. For that little treasure.'

Amarah blinked. She hadn't thought he cared about it— he certainly hadn't given her any praise or mentioned it since they had arrived in Estoria.

'How's this. I have twenty-five crowns in my pocket that I wasn't expecting. Before I do something silly with it, I'll loan some of it ta ya. So ya got enough that ya can stop whining and get on with things.'

Amarah couldn't believe it. Maybe Rhea did exist after all and had knocked some sense into Traego. Before she could say anything in reply, Traego fished out the freshly given coins, pulled her over to him, and dumped them in her hand. 'Ya don't wanna be flying off inta the sunset quite yet. Ya have my ink on ya arm, remember.'

She knew it was as real a threat as was his offer of the gold. She looked down and saw ten crowns gleaming in the moonlight. Ten crowns would be enough to buy and outfit a new ship exactly the way she wanted. More than enough to.

'Stick on this job like I asked, and I'll take it back outta ya pay. Plus some interest o' course.'

'Of course,' Amarah echoed quietly.

Ideas and opportunities swirled around in her mind as she considered how best to use the money.

Traego grabbed her attention again. 'Wanna finish ya drink now before ya go shopping?'

With a grin that she couldn't hide, Amarah sat back down with the others, and they each picked up their mugs and tankards. Amarah nodded to Traego in thanks for giving her wings back, and promised herself that she'd pay him back double.

KOHL OPENED his eyes with a start. Moonlight shone down upon him, and he could hardly believe he'd fallen asleep out in the open. Background chatter of drunk Estorians faded in and out of his awareness as he roused himself from his groggy sleep.

A sudden intake of breath from somewhere far below him brought his attention entirely to the present, and he looked down to where a pair of people were huddled together in the shadows of the cliff he'd fallen asleep on.

Kohl was beginning to grow used to the pirates' exaggerated gestures and boastful conversations, but this seemed more discreet than usual. He leaned forward and pushed himself up into a crouch, ears straining to catch their words.

'...told yer not to go there! Sea dragons, mermaids, and Rhea knows what else!'

'Nah, the cove were empty. Just rocks and water. But...but...'

'Sshh. Keep yer voice down! Don't wanna bring the whole island down here, do yer?'

Narrowing his eyes, Kohl tilted his head. He slipped slowly down the cliff to get closer.

'I knows. I knows. But...what if it's...'

'Yer can't tell a shell from a pebble, Reg. Show me what yer saw an' I'll tell yer what is is.'

The two of them—shadows among shadows—turned and walked up the beach, the sound of their footsteps soon lost to chirping insects and the waves.

Kohl extended his wings to follow. He kept high above them so as not to tip them off to his location by the cool air which accompanied him when he flew.

From their fevered whispers, it seemed the pair were more interested in discussing whatever was in the sea cove that "Reg" had found to keep much of a decent lookout. To be fair to them, this part of the beach was nigh deserted, though he could hear the music, singing, laughter, and fighting from further down the beach. Kohl's heart pounded at the thought of potentially finding more Arillians tied up in some damp sea cave. They seemed to have the highest bounty at the moment, and if these two had some trapped, he wasn't sure if he could hold back his wrath.

He took a breath to calm himself. He didn't need to think of that right now.

Kohl struggled to keep track of them, as their shadows

slipped within the rocks and large boulders that lined this part of the coast, which grew in both size and number at the bottom of the large cliff. It was too dark to make out what they were heading towards, but Kohl suspected it could be one of any number of large caves and sea coves that littered the cliffs where it touched the water. Vast rock pools gathered here, and one of the many estuaries from inland split into tiny rivulets as they re-joined the sea.

With a quick flap of his wings, Kohl veered to one side, keeping out of sight as the two slowed their approach.

'It were this one.'

'Sure 'bout that?'

'Er...' The first one, Reg, scratched his head and glanced around stupidly. 'Or this one? Damn, these bastard caves all look the same at night!'

'Didn't yer leave no marker nowhere? Reg, yer an idiot!'

'Trust me. Ya can see the gold from the entrance. All square-shaped it were. But a long square. Like a sheet o' parchment. But a sheet o' gold. I mean, it were a bit *darker* than normal gold, mind, but it were still shiny. On the cave wall. Clear as anything. Dunno how nobody didn't saw it before.'

Kohl chuckled despite himself, and settled on a large, flat boulder. He was far back enough so he had a good vantage point, but well hidden in the shadow of the cliff as it rose some sixty feet above. He heard the slur of Reg's voice and wondered if perhaps it was the drink talking more than he'd actually found something of value. He supposed the caves and tunnels of Estoria's beaches had been looted by the first sky pirates who'd arrived here and set up a base, however many generations ago that was. It was highly unlikely that a drunkard would discover something new. If anything, he'd probably stumbled upon the stash of another pirate, and the blood that had threatened to spill all day would finally colour the beach.

Deciding his paranoia and worry for his people had got the better of him, and feeling rather foolish for following the words of a drunken pirate, Kohl stood, ready to fly back to Traego's lodge and call it a night. He crouched, wings lifting, when a sudden cry froze him in place.

The shriek tore through the air like a knife. Half of Estoria would have heard that, surely. And the low hiss which followed the shriek sent shivers up his spine. The echo of the noise told Kohl there was something in the cave. Something *big*. And it was angry.

Throwing caution to the wind, he leaped into the air and stretched out his hands, sending a blast of freezing wind into the two pirates, knocking them out of the way before the creature emerged onto the sand.

Kohl had never seen anything like it before. Part-eel, part-squid, part-reptile, and covered in scales, the creature dwarfed the pirates and lashed out at them with the barbs on the end of its webbed feet. Surrounded by rock pools and sand, the pirates stumbled over themselves in their haste to move. Even in the dark, it was hard to see exactly what was happening, and Kohl could only distinguish the monster itself by its large bulk.

It made enough noise, however, stomping heavily through the sand as it lumbered along on ungainly legs. The pirates threw themselves out of the way, arms over their heads to avoid the sting of the creature's attacks as it swatted at them.

Kohl hovered before the monster, moving slowly and trying to catch its attention. Its round face seemed out of place on land, and its eyes were half-open as though in a trance. It flexed its fins and spines, twisting as it pulled itself completely out of the cave. With a low growl, it swiped at

Kohl. It wasn't a full roar of aggression, but Kohl flew backwards in case it lashed out again.

'*Move.*'

The monster's voice echoed in his mind and Kohl almost fled there and then. The ferocity with which it spoke the command struck Kohl, and he slowly flew to the side to allow the creature to pass.

It took a step along the beach, its feet sinking into the sand, and it growled again—in frustration, this time. Clearly it was a creature of the water, with its fins and long tail, but it also had six limbs on which it dragged its squat body along the sand.

'*Veynothi...*'

Kohl shivered at the word. The monster's voice grated in his mind, hardly more than a snarl as it pulled itself along the beach to where the Estorian revellers enjoyed the night. But the word it had spoken...Veynothi?

Did this monster have something to do with the sword Traego had stolen from Veynothi's tomb? It seemed like far too much of a coincidence, otherwise. And he'd warned them!

He'd warned them not to enter that ancient place, much less take something from Veynothi.

Had this creature been sent to reclaim the sword? Would it slaughter any who got in its way?

A deep terror settled over Kohl, and he knew he had to warn Amarah, Traego, and the others about the monster.

'Ey! You're the Arillian what came 'ere wiv Traeg! One of the pirates yelled from the water, his confidence returning now the monster's attention was no longer on him.

Kohl looked down at him, but didn't reply. A short way ahead, the monster continued to pull itself along the beach, tail lashing wildly from side to side, its barbs leaving deep gouges in the sand.

'Oi! You 'ear me? I said you came in wiv Traeg, dincha?'

Kohl glanced back at the pirate, now shouting at him with both hands cupped around his lips, clearly unfazed by the forty foot long monster that had just emerged from the cave. He'd also appeared to have lost his shoes in fright—or through his drinking antics earlier in the night—and stood barefoot on the shore as if their conversation were the most natural thing in the world.

Kohl ignored him. Warning the others took precedence over replying to a drunkard, and Kohl flew off, chasing the monster.

'Oi! I wasn't done talking wiv you!' The pirate called out, but Kohl had no time.

He beat his wings, swooping past the monster as it struggled to progress through the sand and rocks. He powered towards Traego's lodge, and hoped they knew just what manner of creature this was, and how to deal with it.

20

Morgen's shield, a barrier of complete *Ra* magic, had progressed from something rather flimsy to an actual wall which truly did its job and protected him.

Andel, though firm, had pushed him to exceed when he thought he was too tired to do any more, and Topeko's kind, gentle approach had taught him much of the lore and theory behind *Ra* magic.

While Morgen's ability to produce and maintain a shield of magic proved his understanding of the manipulation of *Ra*, he wanted to learn more. He wanted to learn the reverse: how to *unmake* a shield. How to break something hidden.

From the reading he'd been able to cram in between his heavy training sessions, Morgen had discovered breaking things and destroying whatever magic was already there fell under *He*. But he knew there were ways of achieving similar goals through *Ra*—specifically through the branch that pertained to conjuring: to become a Kalosuk. Whenever he reached a high enough level of competence to begin learning that branch, of course.

He was still on the basics of the basics. Not even a Kalosai.

Topeko had been honest when he'd said not everyone could learn every branch of *Ra*. Only the Arch-Kalos could really claim mastery over all arts of *Ra*. And Morgen wasn't yet ready to attempt learning *Ra* as it pertained to the Kalosuk.

While he could understand that, it still frustrated him. He wanted to jump ahead and throw himself in the deep end, just to see what would happen. When he'd broached the subject as delicately as he could with Andel, the Kalosai had warned him that putting his body through too much strain could kill him. It was why the university existed. If anyone could just pick up the more advanced levels of *Ra*, then everyone would be doing it.

It required understanding, respect, and patience above all else.

'Why do you want to break something, anyway? You've been learning how to create a shield,' Andel said.

Morgen shrugged. 'I could break a sword or a lance. Something an enemy is trying to use against me.' Or break someone's hold on something...like Sapora's hold on his Sevastos. That would ruin the king's plans. The balance of power in Linaria had tipped when Aciel had come onto the scene. Now Sapora was taking the leftover power and using it for his own gain.

It was always the dragons.

Sapora controlling one, especially a Sevastos, would not be doing Linaria any favours. They'd received news from Val Sharis that many wild dragons had begun attacking villages and small towns. Morgen had been well aware of those doing the same in Corhaven, and it seemed the rampaging dragons were spreading. Sapora had to realise that forcing a Sevastos to obey him surely wouldn't help the dragon threat.

But there was no way Sapora would simply relinquish that power because a few towns burned. Why would he? Morgen thought something like that was bound in blood, anyway. Moroda lost her life in exchange for using the Sevastos's power. Now she resided in that pillar, sealed away in crystal beside Aciel.

What would happen to Sapora once he fulfilled the goal he'd set out to achieve with his Sevastos?

What *was* the goal?

Andel folded his arms. 'I suppose you could break a sword. But that's leaning into *He*. You must focus on *Ra*. That's what we're teaching you. *That's* the power that Rhea gifted us with. Besides, you're supposed to avoid fighting wherever possible. Isn't that why you said you left the Imperial Guard?'

Morgen scratched the back of his neck. 'Partly. But even after I left, there are still people out there who want to fight. To hurt and kill us. I'll need more than shield magic to stand against them.'

The two of them were sat in one of the bigger rooms in Topeko's house. Bookcases lined the walls and tapestries of great Samolen historians, cartographers, and jewellers hung in between them. Morgen spent most of his time here, if he wasn't training, for Topeko had set him an uncountable number of heavy tomes he needed to read. Never a great reader at the best of times—he was the seventh son of a farmer from a tiny village called Kebbe—Morgen struggled with the theory more than anything else, and frequently found himself chatting to Andel instead of studying the books. Especially when he came to a difficult or dull passage.

Despite Andel's ferocity when it came to physical training, he seemed to have endless patience with him when Morgen wanted to talk instead of read.

'What about breaking the crystal seal? The one in Val Sharis?' Morgen asked.

Andel looked up from the scroll he read, though he marked his place with his index finger. 'What crystal?'

'Like the ones here, at the university. The one that Moroda's sealed in.'

Andel's forehead creased as he thought about it. 'Even if you could, wouldn't breaking the seal on that crystal free Aciel as well as Moroda? No. I don't think that would be a good idea. I don't even know if it'd be possible.' He went back to his scroll, a clear message that he didn't like the turn the conversation had taken.

Morgen sighed quietly. The point of coming to Ranski, to learn *Ra* and what it was capable of, was to ultimately take out Sapora and pay him back for the terror he'd instilled in Eryn and so many others when he'd slaughtered those at the ball.

He wanted, desperately wanted, to do the right thing.

If that meant learning what *He* could do, if that was the only way he could stop Sapora's path of conquest, then it was a path he was willing to take. Otherwise how was Sapora any different to Aciel? Both used dragons as a vessel for their own power, and Linaria suffered under both of them.

Aciel acted as he did out of a love for his people and hatred at the world for what it had done to them. Sapora was much the same.

Someone had to do something about that.

And then perhaps, when the world was free of tyranny, he could break the seal and resurrect Moroda. Yes, there was a chance Aciel could come back, but how was it fair that the most peaceable person was the one who had lost her life?

If he knew enough of *Ra*, he could beat Aciel and avenge Eryn.

He would be able to restore the balance of power to Linaria.

He wanted to free Moroda. Wanted to resurrect Eryn. But bringing back those who had passed on would be impossible, surely. Varkain Blood Magic might have been a possibility, but the only experience he'd had with that were the few conversations through mirrors with Sapora. Even that had made him feel unwell, so he had no interest in diving into that type of darkness. And even then, Eryn had been dead a while.

No. His only chance was to take out Sapora and release Moroda. If he succeeded, he was sure he'd be strong enough to bring down Aciel—for good, this time. If Sapora wanted more power with his "Varkain treasures," as he'd called them, then he was down a path of destruction from where there would be no return. If anything, he was worse than Aciel. Sapora was too deeply rooted in Linaria, and no-one seemed able to stop him. Sapora used his own power to the detriment of the people, and even in Corhaven, Morgen had feared him so much that he'd fled and effectively gone into hiding.

Breaking the bond with the Sevastos would level the playing field, and to do that, he needed full mastery of *Ra*.

If *Ra* could not break anything, then he needed to learn *He*.

That's all there was to it.

Sapora flouted the laws of the land, and all Linaria suffered for it. Morgen vowed to put a stop to that—just as soon as he was able.

'Why are you actually here, Morgen?'

Andel's question caught him off guard, and he looked at him.

'I understand you wish to learn *Ra*, but you showed little interest when you were here before. I know the world has changed a great deal since then, but...you must have had plenty to do in the Imperial Guard. Kalos Topeko won't ask, but I'd like to know your motivation. Your true motivations. I'm training with you, after all.'

Morgen hadn't expected Andel's brutal honesty and wasn't sure how to reply. Honestly in return, he supposed. Morgen opened his mouth, then thought better of it. He didn't want to offend or lie, nor did he want to be kicked out of Berel. He'd paid Topeko in advance to prevent just that, but he supposed the scholar would refund his money if he refused to teach him any more.

'There's always work to be done in the Imperial Guard. Now, more than ever,' Morgen said. 'But I don't want a life following orders I don't believe in. Orders that are wrong. I want to make a difference, a real difference. I want to right the wrongs.'

'Right the wrongs? What wrongs?'

'Sapora.'

Andel carefully rolled his scroll and re-secured it with red twine.

'Persecution isn't the answer. We're all allowed to live freely in Linaria. Sometimes unfairness is part of that.'

Morgen stood up, his tome long forgotten. 'I *know* how the world works, but this has been taken to the extreme. In all Linaria's history, how many times have Sevastos been slaves to people?'

'Never.'

'Exactly. Aciel and Sapora are using stolen power. I guess that's what I'm doing, too. But this is a power freely given, not forcibly taken. I don't want to wipe out all Arillians or Varkain or any other race of people. Just a few individuals.'

'And what gives you that right?' Topeko asked.

Morgen whirled around to see the Kalos in the doorway, a tall glass of iced water in one hand.

'No-one...' Morgen knew it was a foolish reply, but it was the truth. 'But if no-one steps up, then this will go on too far. Didn't you warn us about the balance of power tipping? Didn't you say that dragons would destroy us all if this was allowed to continue?'

Topeko entered the room slowly. 'That may be the given fate of Liaria. It cannot be changed, but nor do I want us to hurtle towards it more quickly. Say you kill these individuals. And then what? When does it end? Dragons are killing people, would you kill those, too? To prevent our fate?'

Morgen stammered. 'Well, only the ones who are killing...'

'But if you slay them, then others will rise up and kill again. It is a vicious, endless cycle. An inevitable end. This is why peace is the answer. You kill everyone who is a problem and you end up the only one left.'

Morgen lowered his eyes.

Topeko sat down beside Morgen and spoke gently. 'We cannot get involved in Linaria's wars and struggles. We're here to protect the knowledge and history of the world, and to preserve Rhea's breath—teaching it to those who are capable and willing.'

'No!' Morgen flung his hands up in exasperation. 'You can't sit and hide forever! Sapora's too strong. His sights are set too high. What will you do if he marches on your gates? Sit back and let him take whatever he wants?'

'Why are you so afraid of him?' Andel asked.

Morgen pointed a finger. 'You're an idiot if you aren't. Sapora's a king, and he has a *god* working for him.' He couldn't stand their cowardly pacifism. He'd come here to learn a way to overcome his own weaknesses and fear, and do something good in the world.

He didn't want a lecture on how he was wrong.

Morgen slammed the book shut, which sent a plume of thick dust into the air, and stormed out of the room.

Andel rose to follow, but Topeko held him back.

Morgen wasn't so childish as to slam the door shut behind him, but he needed to get away. His frustration with his slow progress in learning *Ra*, the heavy books that he never seemed to get through, the limitations of the magic. It was all just too much.

He angrily ran a hand through his hair—already growing back—and took a steadying breath.

'...angry because, for all his learning, swords, and magic, he is powerless. Powerless to change anything at all.' Topeko's voice drifted down the corridor, and that infuriated him even more.

Morgen ran down the hall. He needed a break. He'd been working solidly for weeks, and he needed some fresh air and fewer pressures placed on his head.

He'd already resolved to do the impossible. Learn *He*. Slay the Sevastos, or at least break Sapora's bond with it. If he couldn't bring Moroda, Eryn, and Anahrik back—along with the countless others who'd perished in the wake of Aciel's wrath—he'd do *something* to make Linaria a better place. Even if Topeko disagreed.

As he ran out of the building and into the bright, sun-drenched streets, he stopped to squint. Isa's mocking voice echoed in his head from when he was in Taban Yul, waiting for Aciel.

'The whole world is a pit of fucking snakes.'

MORGEN PEERED over the edge of the bridge which connected Berel new and old towns, and stared into the vast lake that divided the two. *Rhea's breath*, they called it. Pure magic. The very lifeblood of Linaria.

The jewelled Samolen had a small piece of it embedded in their cheeks as a mark of mastery of understanding the art and as a way to boost their own innate powers. Now he'd had a little education on the differences, Morgen found it interesting to see how many of each type there were.

Of course, given his proximity to the university, there were many younger Samolen with blue cheek jewels which marked them as Kalosai, and a fair number of teachers, Kalos, with purple jewels.

Of white, yellow, green, or red, he saw far fewer. In fact he'd only seen one healer despite spending almost two hours on the bridge. Topeko had said it was a rare and difficult art to master, so he supposed that was to be expected.

Most common were yellow jewels, with a fair number of greens thrown in, too. But the red Kalosuk? Morgen only counted three, and there must have been two hundred people crossing the bridge in the time he'd been there.

He wondered whether the Kalosuk were originally responsible for creating the legendary *Valta Forinja*. While it was manipulation of energy that existed already, in the Sevastos crystals, it was turning them into something never before seen. That had to fall under the Kalosuk, surely.

The *Valta Forinja* could throw out beams of pure energy to attack and defend. Energy that didn't come from within. It was created as the weapon was wielded. Though Morgen knew little and less of blacksmithing than he did of *Ra*, the logic made sense to him. Palom and Anahrik were no Samolen, and yet they had been able to harness the power of the Kalosuk in the forging of those five weapons; his short sword, Palom's greatsword, Amarah's scythe, and Anahrik's twin daggers.

Morgen hadn't yet had a complete tour of the university,

but he knew the original *Valta Forinja* lay within the university walls. How many had been forged originally, he didn't know. One? Two? Twenty?

They were ancient treasures and he had no doubt they would have retained their formidable powers, even all these years after their forging.

Perhaps if Topeko ever accepted him back, he'd ask about that. Palom wouldn't know, and he'd *made* them. No, their power came from Samolen magic, and only a Samolen could understand and explain how it worked. Considering their love of peace, Morgen found it ironic that their powers could create something so utterly devastating. It was this knowledge that drove him to learn more about magic and what he could do with it.

He sighed.

Somehow, without his usual sword at his hip, he felt vulnerable. While he knew people in Ranski were not permitted to carry any kind of weapon, he still felt naked, somehow. Of course, he probably hadn't been away too long —there was every possibility he could return to Corhaven and speak to the Imperial Guard at any one of the outposts to re-join. He could just say he'd been away on a campaign from King Sapora. He doubted any of them would have the guts to question him if he said that.

But did he want to return?

Just so he could hold a sword again?

No. That was why he'd been studying *Ra*. So he wouldn't have to rely on any weapon again, *Valta Forinja* or not.

Morgen knew he'd snapped at Topeko out of foolishness and irritation. So much for all the self-control he had supposedly improved on since arriving in Berel. He hoped Topeko and Andel would forgive him, but even if they did, he knew they'd be keeping a much closer eye on him.

Perhaps even lump him in with other inexperienced Kalosai, so Morgen didn't impede on Andel's own training.

He huffed aloud, annoyed at the damn heat. He wished for a little cloud cover, even rain, to cool his fraying temper.

'Morgen.'

He didn't even need to look to recognise Andel's voice.

'Are you okay?' Andel asked, patting Morgen on the back gently. The gesture almost made Morgen laugh. 'You've been gone a while. You'll miss supper if you stay out.'

'I'm sorry, Andel.' Morgen knew he had to apologise. 'I just...the heat got to me and—.'

Andel held up a hand. 'You don't need to explain yourself. You're forcing yourself through an intense training scheme. You've taken shortcuts, skipped steps. It's not surprising your body is feeling the strain of it all.'

'And my mind.' Morgen ran a hand down his face. 'Will Kalos Topeko let me back?'

Andel's shocked expression was answer enough for Morgen. 'We'd have no students left if we booted everyone who had a small meltdown. Come on. Food helps. Let's put this behind us.'

Morgen followed the other student back to the new town, and wondered whether Andel was secretly older than he was. For one so young, he certainly acted and spoke like someone far more mature. Perhaps it was all the training he'd done up until now which kept his emotions so well checked. He didn't think he'd ever heard Andel so much as raise his voice, even when he struggled with a particular exercise or when he was starving hungry.

All at once, Morgen felt even more foolish than before.

But at least he'd managed to release some of his pent up emotions, and he was sure he could keep himself in better control from now on. 'I am really sorry, Andel.'

'It's okay. You don't need to keep apologising!'

303

Morgen bit his tongue and continued on. Now the rage had passed, shame and embarrassment set in. He kept replaying their conversations over in his mind, and thought about what he should have said differently instead. And Topeko's last words echoed most of all: that he was powerless. For all he wanted to do, the changes he wanted to bring to Linaria—all of it meant nothing in the grand scheme of things.

He couldn't do anything.

Earlier, that had angered him. Now, it saddened him.

Something large passed overhead, and Morgen exhaled in relief at the shade. He smiled and looked up, hoping to see several clouds and some respite from the burning desert sun.

Andel said, 'I don't think—'

A roar echoed through the sky and stopped Morgen in his tracks. He'd never forget that noise.

'Hmmm, dragon?' Andel looked quizzically at the sky. 'They don't often fly so close.'

'Get down! It's going to attack!' Morgen yelled, grabbing Andel by the sleeve of his robe and diving for the floor. They collapsed in a sandy heap, and the Samolen who passed looked down at them with some confusion.

'Morgen! Morgen, please!' Andel coughed, shoving him off and getting to his feet. 'Dragons are commonplace here, surely you remember that?'

Morgen had thrown up his shield and covered himself with *Ra* magic. Using magic instead of fleeing or grabbing for a sword had been instinctual, and he was grateful that his defensive reflexes were so sharp.

'Relax. It's okay.' Andel got to his feet and extended a hand to pull Morgen up. 'Sometimes they're curious, the young ones, especially, and they can—'

Morgen never heard the rest of what Andel was going to

say. A plume of fire enveloped the rooftop canopies as a bronze-scaled dragon swooped overhead. The fabric rooftops caught alight at once, and went up with a *whoomf*. Screaming followed immediately after, and then feet kicking up sand and dust as people scattered, thundering up the street and away from the dragon.

Morgen glanced up but didn't relinquish his shield. There were other dragons—six more, he counted. 'Andel, get away!' He leaped to his feet and darted past the shocked Kalosai. 'Andel! Come on!'

His instincts had been right. Ever since the dragon had attacked Rosecastle in Niversai, he'd always remember the sound of wingbeats and a dragon's roar. The noise was enough to instil terror in anyone, and the Samolen seemed unable to fathom the attack.

'Run, Andel!' Morgen screamed, racing down the street and towards Topeko's home. If he could just get to his *Valta Forinja*, he'd be able to see them off.

Two more dragons flew low overhead and unleashed their flames to devastating effect. They circled above and peeled off, one by one, to breathe more and more fire on the sandy-coloured buildings of Ranski's capital. The fabric canopies were burned first, as Morgen expected. But the stone buildings, too, began to sweat under the intensity of the heat. Even stone could crack and melt, if the fire was hot enough. Rosecastle was proof of that.

Morgen risked a glance behind him, but Andel remained in the middle of the street, gawking up at the dragons as they attacked one by one. He didn't even have a shield up. 'Andel!'

The Kalosai lowered his gaze slowly and shook his head. His movements were slow and unhurried, as though he were dazed or half-asleep. He watched as the attacking dragons drew nearer, fanning the flames with their wings and sending thick smoke into the air.

'Get inside, Morgen. They do not seem to be attacking indiscriminately. They are moving towards the university.'

It was Topeko. Morgen had been so focussed on getting Andel out of the way that he hadn't even realised Topeko's approach. 'Kalos, Andel is—'

'I'll keep him safe. Get inside, now.'

Morgen had never seen Topeko so stern, not even when he'd been reprimanding him. He waited only a moment longer before realising he couldn't keep his shield up forever. 'Yes, sir. Be careful, there are lots of them.'

'I can deal with it.' Topeko's voice was eerily calm, and Morgen didn't need telling again. With a final glance at Andel, he raced away from Topeko and joined the crowd of fleeing Samolen.

It didn't take him long to reach Topeko's home, and he didn't waste any time. He hurried along the hallway to his room and shoved open the door. He kept most of his belongings in a solid wooden trunk at the foot of his bed, and he wrenched open the lid and pulled out clothes and bundles haphazardly. With Topeko and Andel both out of the building, and both about to see what he was about to do anyway, he threw caution to the wind. He could tidy up the room afterwards—if they made it.

When he found the bound package at the bottom of the trunk, he breathed a small sigh of relief. He could still hear the screaming from outside as well as the dragons' roaring, and knew he didn't have much time left. They'd melt Berel back into the desert if they weren't stopped immediately.

Unwrapping his bundle as carefully and quickly as he could, he let the thick linen fall to the floor to reveal his *Valta Forinja*. Once an ordinary short sword, now a weapon of legend, the blade glimmered blue and hummed in Morgen's grip.

He spoke aloud, 'Now I'll make a difference.' Morgen tightened his hold on the sword and exhaled slowly to control his breathing and steady his nerves. He'd never *actually* fought a dragon before. The one which had attacked Niversai had been more interested in chasing after Amarah on her airship than taking on the Imperial Guard who'd gathered to defend the castle and city.

He wished he still had his armour with him as he marched out of the building to face his adversaries. A torrent of people rushed past him, and Morgen struggled to keep his balance as he hurried through them, towards the old town. He half-thought learning some kind of offensive magic might help the Samolen here, but he supposed they'd been peaceful for millennia and had never suffered an attack of any sort. They were completely out of their depth.

Morgen saw the dragons circling above the university in the distance, their roars load even from here, and he ran back through the new town towards the connecting bridge. He leaped down stairs and tore around corners as he tried to get to the dragons as quickly as possible.

When he reached the rapidly emptying bridge, he staggered to a halt. Topeko and half a dozen other Kalos stood on the bridge, their arms outstretched above their heads. One dragon had landed on the domed roof of the university and proceeded to incinerate the rafters. As the fire licked at stone, a wave of silvery-blue light leaped up from the building against it, forcing the dragon up and back into the air.

It let out a snarl of defiance and dove towards the Kalos on the bridge. It opened its jaw and sucked in a breath. Morgen covered his face with one arm and crouched down, bracing himself for the blast of heat.

307

But it didn't come.

Peeking over his forearm, Morgen watched in amazement as the Kalos' efforts created a shield of silver-light above them. It pressed gently upwards and out, joining the one already protecting the university and gradually extending, until the entirety of Berel Old Town and the bridge were covered.

Above, the dragons circled, angrily swooping down to blast the university with fire, only to have their flames rebuffed from the magic. They dove again and again, slamming into the shield with claws and tail, but they could do nothing to get past the strength of *Ra*.

Morgen couldn't believe it. The shield magic that he'd struggled to produce for himself was now being used to protect the entire island of the old town. All the relics and books, ornaments and artefacts. All the people who were still inside. Everything was safe.

The dragons seemed confused. Morgen didn't blame them. How often were they thwarted?

One dragon, a little larger than the others, and sporting scales of forest-green and ochre broke away from the others. It circled high, fanning its wings out wide to gain altitude quickly. Morgen kept his eye on it, and squinted against the sunlight when it was almost too high to see anymore.

He blinked several times, light spots dancing across his vision and blurring everything. He closed his eyes and shook his head to properly clear his vision. When he opened them again, the dragon was almost upon him, soaring down like a stone. Morgen lifted his sword instinctively, the energy from the blade arcing up and onto the dragon's snout. He hadn't even realised what had happened until he felt the beast's hot blood on his face as it swooped overhead.

The dragon roared in pain, crash-landing on the street

behind him. Morgen wiped the blood off his forehead and whirled around to face it. The creature had to be twenty feet long, nose to tail tip. Significantly smaller than the one who had attacked Rosecastle, but still a threat. 'Leave, now!' Morgen bellowed at it, putting as much force into his voice as he could.

In retaliation, the dragon bared its teeth and lowered its head, its smooth, black horns glinting in the sun. Smoke rose gently from between its fangs, and Morgen saw the white-hot, orange light flicker in its mouth.

With a furious roar, Morgen slashed his sword, pre-empting the dragon-fire, and watched as a wave of energy careened from its edge and slammed into the dragon—engulfing it in blue light and drowning its groan of pain.

The resulting explosion threw up a great cloud of dust, obscuring the dragon from view.

Morgen braced himself for another attack, but felt only sudden wind as the dragon took off, unwilling to challenge such a powerful adversary. It beat its wings frantically, trying to get into the sky and away from Morgen as quickly as possible.

Morgen panted as he watched it leave, and then turned to see the other dragons fly after it—their own attacks on the university fruitless after the Kalos had created the shield.

Relieved beyond measure, Morgen collapsed onto the ground and sprawled out. Warm sand pressed against his fingers, and he smiled, pleased to feel the sun on his face and not the shadow of dragons.

21

D awn appeared like any other, but Isa had been awake since before the first birds began to sing.

Today, Summercourt would begin.

Today, the future of her country would be written—certainly in blood if Tacio had anything to do with it.

She could only hope that Sapora would remain firm with what he said he would do, but she'd always seen him jump to Vasil's orders, and their father would be present today. Whether that trend would continue despite the fact Sapora was now king, she couldn't say. Her nerves had been on edge all night, and now they threatened to break as sunlight slowly crept up over the horizon and made real the day she'd dreaded since Sapora had mentioned it.

She'd gone into the city early that morning for a final scout before Summercourt kicked off with the arrival of various members of the Goldstone nobility or Varkain royalty. Isa mostly avoided the north of Taban Yul, and went nowhere near the sealed north gate. It was the closest point to the crystal pillar on the edge of the city, which held both Moroda and Aciel—a constant reminder of that battle and how close they'd come to being decimated by the Arillian conqueror.

Whatever insidious magic Aciel had managed to seep through the crystal and into the city had taken over many vulnerable people—the elderly or infirm, mostly—many of whom were committing suicide in a number of spine-chilling ways. Those who had been unlucky enough to touch them had succumbed to Aciel's compulsive voice and had also injured or killed themselves. She'd been unfortunate enough to touch one such woman for only an instant, but even that was enough to understand how powerful Aciel's abilities were.

While Isa knew it was Aciel, and Sapora believed the same, they'd not made any announcements to Taban Yul or wider Val Sharis. Those who lived in the capital simply believed some unknown, unidentified sickness coursed through the streets. They'd been told the king was looking into matters, but many believed Sapora himself was responsible for it. They were all too wrapped up in Palom slaying Aciel and saving them to even consider the Arillian might somehow still be alive.

It annoyed her, but she saw the wisdom in withholding the information from the Ittallan in this instance. Tell them Aciel still lived—somehow—and it would cause a mass panic. Besides, even if she believed it was Aciel, she had no idea how he *actually* controlled anyone. And she'd actually felt his powers directly. None of them knew enough about Arillian magic to explain it, so they kept silent, watched and waited until they were in a position to either say more or do more.

However, several restless citizens had sprang up, claiming to understand what this sickness was caused by, and how to cure it.

311

It was Sapora's fault.

Of course.

The acceptance of a Varkain as their ruler had always been fraught with difficulty. When Vasil had conquered Val Sharis and brought an end to the Ittallan-Varkain war, he'd returned to Sereth after barely a month in Taban Yul. He'd left in his stead a ruling council of hand-picked, influential Ittallan and left Val Sharis to look after itself while he reaped the rewards of the rich country with homages throughout the year.

Sapora, on the other hand, had made himself quite at home in the palace. And it was his presence, this dark omen which loomed overhead, that had caused such strife throughout Taban Yul. Not to mention all the Varkain who had pushed their way in following Sapora's ascension to the throne.

Early in the mornings, the fanatics would gather Ittallan near the north gate—as close as they dared get, lest they, too, succumbed to the compulsive powers—and would spout nonsense about Sapora's darkness and how if he remained in the city, he'd doom them all. How it would only be a matter of time before the sickness spread across Val Sharis and the Ittallan race was lost forever.

Tacio's Cerastes moved them on as soon as they spotted them, but many of these Ittallan were birds and could quickly fly out of range of the Cerastes' blades or fangs.

Isa just wondered how long it would be before they'd turn their attention to her, and *she'd* be the next target for their cause. Princess Isa: responsible for death and destruction within Taban Yul. Sapora was nigh untouchable. But she was vulnerable.

Isa wondered if stirring up enough Ittallan would cause a new civil war. Lathri couldn't possibly work with every rebel in the city, and other factions were bound to be equally unhappy with Sapora on the throne as they were. But a civil war would result in more deaths, and that was something Isa didn't want. So she was more than happy for these rebels to be chased away.

She'd wanted to see Aetos again, or Solvi, before everything kicked off. She'd wanted to make sure Kylos had made it back to them safely and was recovering. But after getting caught by Tacio and pardoned by Sapora—with a stern warning—she didn't want to risk it. So she simply made her usual rounds in Taban Yul, well aware of the Cerastes who followed her.

It was too early for businesses to be open, but Isa made her way along the main thoroughfares to ensure no-one had killed themselves overnight and lay in the middle of the streets, ignored and forgotten. The thought of discovering more bodies made her feel quite ill, but as a princess, she had a duty to be aware of what happened in the capital, even if Sapora or Tacio seemed to care little about it. She was still responsible for her people, especially considering her part in how Sapora had come into so much power so quickly.

By the time the sun had risen properly, and the streets began to fill with traders, customers, and beggars, she knew it was time to face Summercourt. The event would begin early, and she didn't want to face Sapora's wrath if she arrived late.

Visitors had been turning up in Taban Yul over the past few days, most of whom were vetted by the Imperial Guard, but those who wished to enter the palace had to go through Tacio and his Cerastes. After the attack on the palace, and escapes from the dungeons, he was taking no further risks. It made sense, and was something she'd do if their roles were reversed. Sapora himself seemed more relaxed about the whole thing, but Tacio was paranoid and suspicious of everyone. Even other Varkain didn't warrant free entry into the palace, and his Cerastes detained anyone who didn't pass the prince's stringent entry requirements.

If they weren't absolutely necessary, they weren't coming in.

While it made everything take far longer than normal, it did mean that the palace wasn't full of every noble's entourage as it usually would be. Tacio permitted only two people to accompany every Archigo instead of their full fifty-strong retinue, which Isa was more than happy with.

She made her way to the grand ballroom where servants finalised the finishing touches for Summercourt. A long dining table had been laid out and set up for a banquet. Sapora had ordered in a plethora of plants and flowers to decorate the room and table, both. Bright red petals brought colour to the table, and long hanging baskets of blue lavender trailed down the walls in between the tapestries. Isa suspected they'd been brought in to mask the smell of blood, for any Varkain or Ittallan with a keen nose would be able to detect it even now, rather than to enhance the look of the room.

Sapora was there, too, overseeing the final arrangements and making slight adjustments to furnishings where he thought it necessary. As she moved past the bustling staff, Isa was pleased Tacio was nowhere in sight. 'Are you ready, brother?' Where she could, she tried to reinforce their connection to keep his attention off her.

'Not really. But things must be as they are.'

Isa narrowed her eyes slightly. Sapora looked...tired. 'I'm looking forward to some peace and quiet once this is all over.'

'Me, too. Hopefully this farce will prove useful. It'll be a colossal waste of time, otherwise.'

His sudden sharpness stung. 'I'm sure it will be. The people will be pleased by a new council, especially if there are Ittallan speaking with their voice, instead of all Varkain.'

'Your Majesty.'

Isa and Sapora turned to the door where Koraki entered, his black robes cleaned and pressed, billowing about him as he strode towards them. 'I would not interrupt on such a day, otherwise...but you have a visitor from Estoria. He says he brings you news of...of one of the Arks.'

If Sapora had been annoyed at the interruption, it was swiftly gone. 'Bring him in, now. And if you see Tacio anywhere nearby, send him in, too.'

'At once.' Koraki bowed quickly and turned on his heel.

Isa's stomach tightened into knots. All she had thought about was Summercourt. Now the Arks, too? She helped Sapora clear the ballroom of maids and servants and joined him at the head of the long dining table. The silver plates and settings had been laid out ready to receive the feast being prepared by the kitchens. Isa deliberately sat to Sapora's right, claiming that seat as her own. When Tacio slunk in a few minutes later, accompanied by two of his Cerastes, he had to sit beside her, further away from Sapora—for Vasil would be sat at Sapora's other side.

She smiled sweetly at her other brother as he took his seat, and didn't bother to offer him a glass of the chilled white wine she had poured for herself and Sapora.

Koraki returned to the ballroom not long after, followed by two grubby-looking men. She leaned forward to get a better look—one was tall, dark, muscular, with several knives attached to a strap across his chest. She wondered why he hadn't rescinded his weapons, but supposed Koraki's haste to get him in front of Sapora was preferable to the argument with the man, who was clearly a criminal. The other man was little more than a boy; shorter, thin, and pale.

He looked around the ballroom with wide eyes, as though he'd never seen gold before.

The first man had a commanding presence, his stance wide and arms behind his back, and Isa kept her focus on him. Whatever he said, she'd need to remember throughout Summercourt until she could pass the news onto Aetos and the others. He didn't look like a messenger, and was surely aware of the dangers of walking into the heart of the snake pit, even with a claim of what the king snake wanted.

'Your Majesty, this man...this Estorian...is Antar. He would not tell me anything more, only that he wishes to see you.' Koraki gave Antar a dark look but said nothing further.

'As I should hope, with information as important as this,' Sapora said. He held his glass of wine casually in one hand but didn't drink. 'Speak freely, Antar.'

The man met Sapora's gaze levelly. Either he was very bold or very foolish. Then he said, 'I have nothing to say to you. But I have this to give.' He produced a folded sheet of parchment and held it up between two fingers. It was stained with travel and beginning to fall apart.

Isa wondered what the conditions for flying were like if a simple parchment was so weather-beaten. She knew dragons had been seen attacking towns and wondered whether Antar and his young companion had been caught up in something like that on their way from Estoria.

'Read it aloud, then,' Sapora said. His voice had tightened. He was losing his patience.

Guests for Summercourt were no doubt milling around in the palace reception rooms, waiting to be admitted for their breakfast and the informal beginning of their discussions. Isa shivered a little as she picked up on Sapora's irritation. If he grew too annoyed and killed them, there wouldn't be enough flowers in all of Linaria to cover up the fresh blood on the marble floor.

316

Antar shook his head. 'Can't read. You'll have to.' He stepped forward to give him the message, and Tacio's Cerastes leaped into action, barring his path with crossed spears and low growls. 'I ain't gonna hurt you. I want your gold. You kind of have to be alive to give it to me.' Antar laughed, showing white teeth and not a hint of fear.

Tacio let out a low hiss at the blatant disrespect, but Sapora took the man's confidence in his stride and set his glass down gently. 'Isa. Would you be so kind?'

Isa didn't fear this man. Her reflexes were faster than a thief—clearly that's what Antar was—and she got up from her seat and walked towards him, her steps echoing on the marble. She held his gaze as she took the parchment from him, and Antar had the gall to wink at her.

She wasn't sure she masked her distaste as well as Sapora had, but she unfolded the parchment where she stood and skim-read it once before she did anything else.

'Well?' Tacio said, his own impatience in full view.

Isa exhaled through her nose, looked to Sapora, across to Antar, then back to the parchment. She read, 'Sapora, King of Sereth and Val Sharis, forger of the Imperial Alliance with Corhaven, I have found the tomb of an Ark—Veynothi. I know you desperately seek this relic, and so I am prepared to sell you the location for no less than your full offered bounty: five hundred crowns, as well as safe passage of my ships in the lands you rule in perpetuity. Send payment of at least half this amount, and we shall meet. I will provide you with the exact location at this time. Captain Traego of *Otella*.'

Isa smiled. She knew the name.

Traego had been a notorious thorn in the side of the Imperial Guard of Val Sharis for years, smuggling and trading under their noses and somehow slipping away every time he was cornered. No wonder Antar was so bold.

He was no common thief, used to burglary. He was a sky pirate.

And Traego was based in Estoria, which made sense considering that was Antar's country. Out of range of Sapora and the Imperial Guard.

She folded the parchment slowly and walked back to her seat. She very much doubted Sapora would give him any money to sail back with, much less the requested two hundred and fifty crowns. But Traego's reputation was what it was, and she doubted he'd bluff.

Sapora laced his fingers together and studied Antar. 'Koraki. What do you know of this...Traego?'

The steward straightened his robes somewhat aggressively. 'He's a sky pirate. He's been known to us for many years. Been in half a dozen dungeons from Val Sharis to Corhaven. He's a crook and utterly despicable.'

'We don't want anything to do with him,' Tacio said. 'We've no need to lower ourselves to—'

Sapora cut him off. 'Koraki, when have you last seen him?'

'In a dungeon? Not for a decade or so.'

'Hmm. A good crook, then. Utterly despicable, and beneath us, but good?'

Koraki flushed. 'Well, I suppose, yes, your Majesty.'

'Sister. You know these lands better than I. Do you agree?'

Isa nodded. She sipped her wine and tried to still her beating heart.

'So. He's a true sky pirate. Infamous, even. I'll agree it is within the realm of possibility that what you say is true. *Such* a positive start to what would have otherwise been a trying day of talking to self-obsessed nobles.' Sapora ran the tip of one claw along the rim of his wine glass, sending a

318

shrill tone echoing through the room. He sat quietly for several minutes as he calculated what he was going to say next, and Isa's anxiety grew every minute that passed without him speaking. Eventually, Sapora said, 'I'll give you one hundred crowns.'

Koraki's mouth dropped open, and Antar's smile broadened.

'See to it now,' Sapora said.

Koraki stammered for a moment before bowing his head. 'At once, your Majesty.'

Antar nodded to the lad with him, who hurried after Koraki, then he looked back to the three gathered royals. 'And the rest?'

'The rest will be paid, gladly paid, on receiving proof of this claim. Even for a king, it's a lot of money. I can't pay every thief who turns up at my door claiming to know where my Arks are.'

Antar laughed at that.

'Isa, would you be so kind as to escort Antar and his companion out? Summercourt should be over in three days or so. That should be plenty of time to fly to Estoria and back if you take one of my sister's ships. They're small, but very fast, you understand. If you return with proof, you get paid. If you disappear with my gold, I'll send Tacio and his Cerastes after you. Estoria may be out of my jurisdiction, but the Cerastes are a law unto themselves. Do I make myself clear?'

Isa didn't like the idea of Sapora loaning out her personal ships to sky pirates, but the fact he had done so showed her just how keen he was to find out more. All year, Tacio and his Cerastes had been searching for information. She and he had both advised against Sapora putting a public bounty out, but it seemed to have proved fruitful.

Who else would you send to find a treasure than a treasure hunter?

After all, they made a living out of hunting down rare and valuable treasures, breaking in to grab them and...breaking out before anyone noticed.

Her heart picked up, excitement growing before she'd really even figured out her thoughts. 'Of course. I'll return shortly, in time for Summercourt.' Her voice shook, she knew it. She only hoped Sapora thought it was her own excitement for the Arks.

She tapped Antar lightly on the elbow as she walked past him, and he followed her across the ballroom and into the passageway. The Goldstones and Archigos milled near a bronze statue depicting the construction of an Imperial Warship to her far left, but Isa kept her gaze fixed straight ahead. She dared not glance to the sides or behind her for fear anyone who saw would see her newest scheme would become clear.

Isa almost marched along, leading him through the lower corridors of the palace, into the airship hangar and along the line of docked ships. Only when they were in front of one of hers, in a quiet section of the hangar, did she turn around to look at Antar. 'Sapora always remains true to his word. There'll be riches for you and Traego if what you say about Veynothi is true.'

'Oh, it's true all right. I was there.' His grin hadn't left his face.

Isa glanced back along the corridor to ensure they were alone. 'Good. My ship is fast. It'll be much quicker than anything you flew in on. But...I must ask. Is there a sky pirate called Amarah in your crew?'

Antar shrugged. 'I ain't no sky pirate. And I ain't in a crew. But I know her.'

Isa smiled at Antar's vague answer. 'She's travelling with an Arillian, right? Kohl?'

Antar narrowed his eyes.

'So you *do* know her?' Isa winked, and his grin faded.

Antar's jovial mood had dampened somewhat as he picked up on her serious tone. 'She's a friend of Traeg's. Why?'

'You know, if you wanted to be a better pirate—and have any chance of surviving the coming years in Linaria—you ought to be more selective with the information you reveal, and to whom you choose to reveal it. And mask your emotions on your face, for Rhea's sake. I can read you like a book, you don't need to say a word.'

Antar straightened, his brows turning down.

'Just because a pretty lady winks at you, doesn't mean you're safe.'

'What do you want with Amarah?'

Isa gave another quick glance around, then reached into her pocket and pulled out several gold coins. Koraki, and Antar's companion, would be back any minute. 'Here's ten crowns. Just for you. I need you to get a message to Amarah. Tell her to come here, to Taban Yul, immediately.'

Antar looked at the coins and for half a moment, Isa thought he was going to bite down on it to check it was real. 'What for?'

'If she can't talk to me, she'll need to speak with an Ittallan in Little Yomal called Aetos, he's a black eagle.'

She heard footsteps coming down the hangar and knew she was out of time. With nothing else to do, she leaned up on her tip toes and kissed him lightly on the cheek. 'Just tell her I asked for her. It's *very* urgent.'

Antar put a hand to his cheek and smiled crookedly at her. She could tell he was confused but not altogether displeased, and she put the coins in his own pocket just as

Koraki rounded the corner. 'You got our payment, Oris?' Antar asked, his earlier confidence surging back.

The young lad nodded, his eyes wide and wearing a smile bigger than Antar's had been.

Isa stood back to make room for him to walk past. 'Safe and speedy flight, Antar. Treat my ship well.'

As Koraki spoke to the two before they left, Isa raced away. She had no idea whether or not Antar would deliver her message—desperate plea more like—but she was out of options and time. Who better to break something—or someone—out than a sky pirate who did it for a living?

She'd been beaten down by poor luck, by Tacio, his Cerastes, and even by Sapora. But she wasn't defeated, not yet. This was her opportunity. She was going to seize it and run with it, otherwise she'd never be able to get out of her brothers' shadows.

Voices carried through the hall as she made her way back to the ballroom. Most were somewhat disgruntled and raised in impatience. Goldstones, of course. She didn't blame them. She was always a little grouchy when her breakfast was late, or she missed it entirely. Sapora didn't care, that much was clear. But if he wanted a smooth Summercourt, he needed to keep his guests well fed, well drunk, and as comfortable as was possible.

By the time she made it back to the ballroom, the other servants had opened the doors to welcome the guests in. She saw Varkain and Ittallan both, and hoped the event wouldn't result in a blood bath like the winter ball. Of course, she and Sapora had orchestrated that, and her brother had definitely not spoken of any killings that were to take place this time.

She slipped past those who dawdled in the hall and hurried along the main table without really paying attention to where she was going—only enough so that she didn't accidentally barge into someone who would make Summer-court even more difficult for her.

When she reached Sapora's side, she stopped.

Tacio had moved into her seat.

His two Cerastes stood guard behind the high-backed chair, and beside Tacio sat the Valendrin.

The blood mage's skin was thin and papery. It had lost most of its grey tinge and appeared almost transparent. He no longer had lips, and his fangs and black gums protruded out in full display.

The shock of having her seat stolen from her, and seeing the Valendrin up close without expecting it, made her squeak in surprise. All the nearby Varkain looked up at her with varying looks of scorn.

Sapora ignored her.

On Sapora's other side, Vasil stood, greeting his son cordially. Savra, his current wife, and Tacio's mother, sat in the chair beside him and poured herself a large glass of wine. Her full retinue had been allowed in—there was no way Tacio would insult his own mother by subjecting her to his checks—and Isa had no intention of sitting beside her.

The other Archigo drifted in, their talk less irritated now they'd been placated with wine, regardless of the early hour, and slowly took their seats. The oldest, highest-ranking Archigo sat closer to Sapora, and their entourage filled the lower half of the table. The few servants who had come with them sat at a small table at the back of the room, furthest away from Sapora and the other important figures at the main table's head. As Tacio had culled most of them before they'd even come into the palace, most of these chairs were empty.

Isa licked her lips and headed towards that table. The insult stung deeply. It shoved her back into her childhood, when she'd been picked on and bullied at worst, and ignored at best. Being beneath the notice of her peers, of her *family*, made her want to run away and hide. She could see the tapestry on her left, behind which was her secret hiding spot—the abandoned passage that ended up at the back of the dungeons. She'd used to hide in there, lock herself away from the pompous Goldstones and royalty who looked down their noses at her like she was a worthless piece of dirt.

Now, she wanted to make them pay.

Her eyes prickled as tears of rage threatened, but she refused to let them fall.

They knew what they'd done. They knew they'd shoved her to one side and put her with the servants as though she was worth less than them. She didn't want to give them the satisfaction of seeing how upset it made her.

Sapora seemed too engrossed in conversation with Vasil to even notice her. She knew he'd said he wouldn't stand up for her, wouldn't fight her battles. That she needed to do that on her own. But what was she supposed to do? Cause a scene and ruin the chance of a peaceful Summercourt before it had even begun?

No.

She'd do as she was told—even passively—and sit quietly at the back, out of the way, and pretend not to be there. If the Varkain didn't see her, or forgot she was there, they were less likely to call her out.

She'd always known Vasil only had time for his more Varkain-like children, and Tacio most of all. He'd never been there for her, never done anything for her except imprison her in this palace and claim she was spoiled and should be more grateful for having the run of the palace and the city.

She couldn't leave because of her high birth, but neither was she accepted because of what she was: a cat, and not a snake.

Isa had even wished she was a non-royal snake. She didn't have to be a *naja* to be accepted in Sereth, and she was sure there were plenty of half-breeds in those tunnels. They just *looked* better.

Anything was better than being sneered at and looked down upon, surely?

She sat in one of the empty chairs on the far side of the servants' table, closest to the wall and the windows where she could peer out at Taban Yul below. If she had any doubts about siding with Lathri over her family, they were squashed now. Why ally herself with Sapora if he wouldn't stand with her? Why help the Varkain-Ittallan alliance when no-one wanted it?

Lathri was right. She'd always been right.

Sapora and his ilk were no good for the Ittallan. If Sapora had a Valendrin at his disposal, and Antar, Traego, and Amarah had truly discovered one of the Arks, it would be the beginning of the end for them.

Getting Lathri and her allies out of the dungeons was the first step. She'd stand with Lathri and lead them against the Varkain. Drive the Varkain back out of the city and into the tunnels they seemed to love so much. Even now, she heard bits of conversation, Varkain complaining about the sun, the weather, the uncouthness of Val Sharis.

She wanted to yell, to scream at them to go away and get back to Sereth if they missed it so badly. Why did they want to come here and take her home from her?

Composing herself, Isa took a glass and filled it with the water on the table—no wine for the servants, of course—and sipped. She had a plan.

She was optimistic that Antar would deliver her message to Amarah, and she'd be able to put her idea into motion. Princess Isa watched and waited, listening to the conversation and observing those in the room, just as she had done as a child.

This time, it wasn't just to survive.

This time, it was to plan their downfall and take the power she. She was ready to act now, blood be damned.

The chug of propellers careening through the sky echoed across Estoria, their high-pitched whines and low rumbles working in tandem to tell everyone in the vicinity that airships were racing.

For Amarah, it was what she lived for.

And now that she had enough gold in her pocket to get herself a new set of wings, she watched the racing with renewed interest, eager to get back in the air. Judd, too, enjoyed the spectacle, and added a new layer of technical proficiency and knowledge with his commentary that Amarah found quite fascinating.

Traego, being Traego, remained seated, his feet up and crossed over one another—ever the epitome of ease. Malot sat beside him, and they spoke in hushed tones, drinking rum straight from the bottle and grinning broadly. Carav, Ernold, and Farlan alternated between watching the races, getting more food and drink, and keeping an eye out for any other rival troupes. Traego still wore Veynothi's blade at his hip, and Amarah didn't blame him. There was no way *she'd* leave something that valuable unguarded at the lodge, where any pirate desperate enough could force their way in and take it.

Of course it meant they received some strange stares. Traego's jacket mostly covered it, but the tip of the blade could still be seen below the fabric, and a stone sword definitely stood out against the usual steel or iron.

Amarah had always known Traego was notorious among sky pirates. You weren't that successful for that long without attracting some attention. But the other pirates seemed to *despise* Traego. To begin with, she'd chalked it down to jealousy. After all, who didn't feel just a *little* envious at seeing your competitors fly back with holds bursting with loot and gold? Having avoided the Imperial Guard for what must have been the thousandth time?

But considering Cyd's aggression on their way here, and the looks Traego received from the other pirates, not to mention having to move base every time he returned...it all put Amarah on edge, and she wondered just what he'd done to upset so many people.

At this rate, he wouldn't be able to stay in Estoria for too much longer.

She wanted to ask him what was going on. Or perhaps Judd or Malot would give a more truthful answer, if she asked one of them instead. But it could wait. Right now, gold coins weighed down her pockets, and she needed to put them to work and buy herself some new wings.

It made sense to browse the ship merchant's wares. After all, he was selling the latest models, so checking over his stock would be a good starting point for her hunt.

She picked up her scythe and stood up. 'I'm going for a wander.'

'Have fun.'

She looked back and saw Traego grinning at her like a foolish child. 'Give it a rest, Traeg.'

'Where are you going?' Judd asked, half getting to his feet.

Amarah pointed to the merchant at the end of the beach with her scythe. 'Gonna see what he's got for sale.'

'Can I come, too?'

Amarah frowned. 'You don't need to ask permission. Do what you want.' She headed towards the shoreline, past the fiddlers, and towards where people had gathered by the various traders. She picked her way through the crowd and drew close to the merchant she was after.

She didn't know his name, had never bought anything from someone like him, but he was already engrossed in conversation with a Goldstone couple, and she was happy to eavesdrop as he explained the features of one particular model to his wealthy clientele. They seemed unhappy with the amount of storage the class four ship came with and were concerned with how many people it could comfortably hold.

'We have twelve staff, you see.' The woman had golden-blonde hair that she wore loose. It partially covered her jewelled ears, but not quite.

Amarah had the sudden almost irresistible urge to pull them from her ears.

She went on, 'We summer in Iryl or Lavonn every year. Is it suitable to fly from the capital there with the whole family *and* our house staff? I'm not paying for them to fly separately on a transport ship.'

The merchant took her questions in his stride, clearly more interested in nabbing a sale than being honest. 'Well you could modify the ship's hold into staff quarters if they aren't bothered by the amount of space they have.'

'In addition to six bedrooms for all of us?' Her partner asked doubtfully. 'It's quite an important family affair. We take the trip every year. The ship must be practical.'

'Of course, of course. A class four is far bigger inside than you would think.'

Amarah snorted. *Khanna* had eight rooms in total. Once you allocated space for supplies, food, and weapons, there wasn't much left for anything else. Claiming there would be six big rooms for the Goldstones and twelve servants? It was utter horse shit.

She sighed. She wasn't going to learn anything from someone who was more interested in taking money from gullible Goldstones than selling a product of quality.

Judd caught up with her and stood by her side, listening to the conversation for a minute. He and Amarah shared a knowing look. 'Dodgy traders everywhere these days.'

Amarah's lip lifted in a half-grin at his words. 'I know. I suppose you can sell anything to someone's got more gold than sense.'

The Goldstones and merchant's conversation stopped suddenly as the three of them stared at the two pirates. Amarah continued, 'Shall we see if we can find a trader who *actually* knows the prow from the stern?'

Although Amarah had thought Judd soft and weak, the man had a sense of humour and played along well. 'Sure. There has to be someone on this damned island who's an honest trader.'

The two grinned as they walked off down the beach.

She was about to ask Judd if he actually knew of any other ship merchants in Estoria—reliable ones—when a gust of freezing air stopped her in her tracks.

There was only one thing that could cause a chill breeze like that. 'Kohl?' What was he doing flying around out in the open? Had he forgotten about the bounty on Arillians? He'd seen a group of them shoved into the drowning pits only that morning!

It didn't take others on the beach long to notice the

disturbance. The music slowed and the cheering, laughter, and talking faded as people stopped what they were doing and looked up for the source of the cold.

'Amarah!'

She looked up to see the Arillian's outline silhouetted against one of the moons. Stunned, Amarah didn't know what to say. Did she acknowledge him? Tell him to get away? Ask him what in Rhea's name was he doing?

'Amarah! There's something coming! Some kind of creature! It's following the sword, I'm sure!'

All around her, sky pirates pointed up at him, and ripples of conversation grew. Some had already drawn their weapons. All they could see was the gold Kohl would be worth to them if they captured him.

She balled her fists. 'Fly away, Kohl! They'll kill you!'

He didn't seem to pay any attention to her warning. 'Get the sword away now! It's here!'

Amarah didn't have time to ask what he meant. She didn't know what "it" was, but her question was answered quickly enough.

The palm trees which dotted the edges of the beach, where revellers hadn't quite reached, swayed suddenly. Kohl hovered above her, and Amarah realised the swaying was not from the Arillian's powers. She grasped her scythe, energy crackling around her wrist as she readied herself against whatever threat Kohl had deigned destructive enough to reveal himself to the pirates of Estoria.

One tree groaned as it slowly tipped to one side. Abruptly, its trunk snapped with an ear-shattering crash, and the monster from the sea lumbered into view. In the darkness, its green-blue scales seemed almost black, and its pointed teeth seemed to glow. The barbed tips of its fins and webbed feet glistened in the moonlight, and Amarah's *Valta Forinja* crackled in her hand.

331

The creature shouldered away the fallen tree and stepped onto the open beach. She'd never forget the sight of it. Not as long as she lived. 'Dragons above.' Her words came out in a whisper.

Beside her, Judd drew a long dagger and widened his stance. 'What is that?'

'A monster. From the sea. I think Kohl's right...I think...I think it's after the blade.' The words spilled out of her, hesitant and fast all at the same time. 'Get to Traego!'

In a heartbeat, the pair of them whirled around and raced back across the beach. The monster's heavy footsteps vibrated in her chest as it rushed forward, teeth snapping at anyone who didn't move out of the way quickly enough. She felt, rather than heard, the bones crunching of those people the monster fed upon as it entered the beach, and then all around them was chaos.

Screams filled the air and people ran about, carelessly fleeing and shoving into one another, pushing people over and trampling on them in their haste to escape. Their panic caught, and Amarah's heart pounded in terror. She still held her *Valta Forinja*, yet had no desire to attack the creature. It had been terrifying enough in the sea, and now that it was on land, she just wanted to get away from it. 'Traeg! Run!'

Traego and his sky pirates were already on their feet at the monster's sudden arrival, but all of them seemed shocked into stillness.

'Amarah. This thing...This creature...' Malot began, seemingly unable to form words. The light of her red cheek jewel glimmered.

'It's too strong to fight. It attacked me in the sea. We have to get away!' Amarah yelled.

'You've seen this thing before?' Traego gazed up at the monster, his mouth smiling, his eyes wide. 'I dunno what it is, but think o' the gold from its hide...'

332

'Don't be an idiot!' Malot snapped at him. 'Not everything is made of gold!'

As if on cue, the monster let out a ground-trembling roar, the deep bass notes of its voice rattling in Amarah's chest.

'Fight it if you want. I'm gone.' Amarah raced off, kicking up sand as she powered through the escaping crowd to get away. She didn't care if the others thought she was weak or a coward. She knew when she was outclassed. She didn't want to die on some beach in Estoria because she was too proud or stupid to know when to quit.

And she *knew* it was her own fault the thing was after them. She should never have agreed to come on Traego's Ark hunt. She should have asked more questions before signing up. Should have known they faced.

'*Veynothi...*'

The creature's voice was so loud that Amarah stumbled over. She braced her fall with her hands and dropped her scythe in the process.

It had spoken to her. Again.

'What do ya want with Veynothi?' She heard Traego yell across to the creature.

Amarah looked up, sand spilling from her face and hair. Had Traego heard it, too?

'*Veynothi...*' The monster repeated. It had eaten all those around it and dragged itself towards Traego and the others, leaving bloody trails behind it.

Amarah watched in horror as it drew closer to Traego, Malot and the others, and raised one barbed foot to strike. She screamed, 'Move!'

Traego dove to the right as the monster swiped at where he'd stood, the sharp tips of its barbs slashing into thin air and missing him by a fraction. It let out another growl and twisted its body to face Traego.

'*Veynothi...*'

'Veynothi ain't here!' Traego yelled, spitting out sand as he got back to his feet. 'Ya on the wrong island! It's just us here and ya ain't welcome!'

'*I...smell...Veynothi...*' The monster replied in a deep, grating voice. It raised its head to look upon Traego with greater interest, pupils contracting and fins twitching as it considered.

'The sword!' Kohl yelled, swooping overhead and blasting the monster back with a wall of ice. 'I warned you it was evil! I warned you it was an ancient power and not to be touched!'

Angered, the monster lunged back from the ice, its feet scrambling to gain purchase in the sand. With another roar, it attacked those nearby. Ernold and Farlan split as the tip of the barb lashed at them, and Farlan lifted his hand to cover the streak of blood streaming from his cheek.

Amarah got back to her feet, picked up her scythe with both hands, and held it defensively across her body. Kohl *had* warned them. Dragons above, *she'd* warned them. She'd told Traego that it was wrong to be there, in Veynothi's cave. In Veynothi's tomb. Told them that the ancient Varkain was deep magic, blood magic, and they ought to have nothing to do with her.

She'd wanted to leave. Begged, almost.

And they'd carried on anyway. The bounty had been too great.

But this wasn't worth all the gold in Linaria.

She watched, frozen in fear, as the creature struck again and again, fast for its bulk, and Traego, Malot, and the others avoided its attacks or bled when they were too slow to move.

She sucked in a shuddering breath, and hated how it trembled, but could do nothing to stop it. With one eye gone, she wasn't half the fighter she used to be. Perhaps she wouldn't even be half the pilot she'd used to be, either.

Amarah took a step back and held her scythe close to her body. It let out another ripple of blue energy, the light arcing all around her. 'No...'

Her fingers trembled and struggled to keep their grip on the scythe's smooth surface.

The monster dwarfed them all by at least fifteen feet, and she couldn't see its tail, it was so long. The dark beach, the shadows, Kohl's freezing air, and the monster's voice rattling around in her head was too much. She'd been cursed for thieving from Veynothi. The creature had been sent to kill them all and take back the sword.

Even if they survived the monster and Sapora paid up, it would be cursed money.

They'd be dooming themselves by taking it, surely.

This was more than any treasure hunt she'd been on. More than she'd ever wanted to take on.

Goosebumps rose on her arms, and it had nothing to do with Kohl's powers.

Dimly, Amarah felt her legs cave under her. She thumped down to the beach, still clutching her *Valta Forinja*, desperately praying that its light didn't fade. Not only did she struggle to see in the darkness without it, but while she held it, she still had a chance of surviving.

'Amarah!'

Her ears rang, a low buzzing that filled her head and muted other sounds. Even the monster's enormous roar was hardly more than a murmur. She swallowed thickly and turned her head, but she couldn't see. Fog clouded her vision and hearing, and her chest tightened. She tried to breathe and found she couldn't.

Glancing down, she saw the vivid blue light from her *Valta Forinja* encasing her chest and body like a serpent. The light flickered and sparked like fire, crackling and sputtering. It twisted and coiled around her, arcing out into the darkness.

She tried to breathe again and managed the tiniest gasp.

Her heart continued to pound, and she was sure it would burst from her chest.

'Amarah!'

Someone called to her. She couldn't tell who. Couldn't tell where they were.

Granules of sand dug into her knees through the thin cotton fabric. She could almost feel every individual grain against her skin. Thousands of them. Hundreds of thousands.

Her cheeks stung in the cold wind that blew around her, buffeting her hair, and masking her already dark vision even more. Dumbly, she lifted one hand to touch it. Her arm passed through the light cast by her *Valta Forinja*, and she saw snakes wrapping themselves around her wrist.

Panic and fear consumed her.

It had been a mistake. A terrible, terrible mistake. The snakes would kill her now. If the monster didn't, the snakes would come for her.

Sapora would find her and kill her. Or his Arks would, with their blood magic and dark powers.

The snakes' cold scales pressed into her skin and squeezed her chest, tightening their grip with every tiny breath she managed. Their forked tongues licked her face. Their venom dripped from their fangs and burned her flesh.

She touched her face and brought her hand back, fully expecting to see blood, or perhaps venom. Instead, tears covered her fingers.

'AMARAH!'

A kick from a heavy boot sent her scythe careening off

into the distance, blue light streaking off it in a hundred directions as it span away from her.

Rough hands grasped her by her shoulder and waist, pulling her to her feet and holding her steady.

She blinked, her vision coming back dot by dot. 'T...Traego?'

'Come back to us, Amarah!' The sky pirate shook her almost violently, which cleared the rest of her vision and brought her back to the present.

Tears streamed down her cheeks, and her throat burned. She'd been hyperventilating, trembling, collapsed in a heap in the sand, unable to see, hear, or think.

She looked down to see her chest clear. There were no snakes, nothing constricting her.

'That damned scythe o' yours got ya worked up over nothin' there,' Traego said. He nodded to her left, where the scythe lay almost in the sea, its light flickering as it died. 'Here.' He shoved Veynothi's blade into her hands.

When Amarah realised what it was, some of her breath came back. 'No. No, I don't want it. It's evil! Don't give it to me.'

Traego looked over his shoulder where the rest of his crew kept the monster at bay. 'Run, Amarah. Get ta *Otella*. Bring my ship overhead and blast it with everything she has!'

Amarah blinked. She heard his words, but needed a few seconds longer than usual to process them. 'Get *Otella*?' Another blast of freezing air sent shivers up her spine. Small sheets of ice formed over her clothes.

'Go. Now!' Traego turned away from her to rejoin the fight, screaming at the monster and keeping its attention on him.

Amarah stood dumbly and stared down at the stone sword. Her heart still pounded as though she'd run fifty leagues. But she realised the monster needed to be driven back. Realised her scythe had done something to her.

Had been doing something to her.

She didn't have time to figure it out. Trying to steady her breathing, Amarah secured Veynothi's blade at her hip and ran back to Traego's lodge.

～

By THE TIME Amarah had lifted off in *Otella*, she felt somewhat closer to herself again.

There was something so primal in flying an airship. It was such an integral part of her that she could do it in her sleep. Which was probably why Traego had sent her off to get his ship.

She was in no fit state to fight, not without her scythe, anyway. Flying *Otella* would be the quickest way of bringing her out of her panic.

She had no idea what had happened. She'd never felt anything like it before, like she couldn't breathe. Like she was dying.

By the time she brought *Otella* around to the beach, other sky pirates had re-joined the fray in their own ships. They weren't all class one warships with *Otella*'s fire power, but even a couple of smaller class ones or twos could do a great deal of damage. Especially when they had clear shots.

Considering the size of the creature and the relative openness of the beach, they were doing a decent job of holding it back.

Amarah spotted Kohl in the air, too. He blasted the creature with attack after attack, and created dagger-like icicles that he hurled at its thick hide. If the creature still spoke, Amarah couldn't hear it over the propellers of *Otella* and the other ships in the air, and she thanked Rhea for that respite.

Swivelling *Otella* to hover in place, she raced beneath deck to the weapon's bay. She'd only ever been in here a handful of times—she'd never been much of a gunner—but found Traego's cannons pre-loaded with more *dragon's breath*.

She grabbed the small bottle of Samolen magic she always kept on her—her fire—and poured a tiny drop into the two nearest cannons. It would take a moment or two to catch, so she stepped back, held her breath, and braced herself.

The ricochet from the cannon fire a moment later almost sent her sprawling to the floor, but she held her balance.

From the depths of *Otella*, Amarah heard first the fire-dragon's roar, and then the monster's bellow of pain. Even from her position, the stench of *dragon's breath* hung thick in the air in the wake of the attack. She raced along to another two cannons and fired those just for good measure, hurrying back up to the deck before they'd even hit their target.

When she got back to the wheel, plumes of thick, black smoke obscured her vision. The other airborne ships had also ceased their attacks in the low visibility, and Amarah held her breath. Echoes of the monster's groans and roars still carried, but they seemed more distant now.

Gently, she moved *Otella* forward and to the side, around the pillar of black smoke, to where she had a better view. For a moment, everything seemed too dark to make out any detail. Then she heard a mighty splash and looked to the sea. She managed the ghost of a smile. The monster pulled itself into the water, the waves lapping at it as it half-dragged itself into the ocean.

Several ships followed it out, shooting at it with their cannons and screaming insults from on deck, but the monster was far faster in the water, and the pirates' weapons hardly touched it as it fled.

Sudden déjà vu hit Amarah, and she remembered fleeing the dragon in Niversai back when she had *Khanna*. How long ago that seemed.

When she was certain the monster wouldn't be returning for another charge, she settled *Otella* down on the beach. Given the ship's size, part of it touched the sea, but there was little Amarah could do about that. Ships rarely landed on the beach and it wasn't particularly wide.

She stumbled away from the wheel and used all her strength to remain standing.

Kohl reached her first, landing on deck beside her. He trembled, but from what, Amarah couldn't tell. He'd been flying above the battle and hadn't been in any danger. Shame and guilt coursed through her, and she couldn't bring herself to meet his eyes. In the end, she muttered, 'Thanks for the warning. And helping us fend it off.'

Traego and the others clambered up the steps and onto the deck before their conversation could continue, and Amarah was relieved at that.

'Never seen anything like that before!' Ernold said, his eyes bright and his blood high.

His cousin Farlan ran a hand tenderly over his forearm, where he'd been caught by another of the creature's barbs. 'You're telling me. Dragons above, that thing'd be worth a fortune if we killed it. I say we get a pack of us together and track it down.'

Kohl turned on them. 'Go after it? After all the damage it did? Your kin have been slain! Eaten!'

Farlan grinned and shrugged. 'Call it revenge, then. We don't get many bounties around here. Look how everyone is over your lot. Why not go after that monster. Be doing the world some good, wouldn't we?'

'No-one's hunting anything.' Traego put a stop to the idea before it had a chance to grow. 'Amarah. Ya alright?'

She nodded, her throat still tight, and her voice weak. 'I never thought...my scythe would have...bad side effects.'

'All great power has its drawbacks. Even those dragon-forged weapons,' Kohl said.

Amarah nodded again. She thought to her battle against Jato. She'd been able to hold her own because of her *Valta Forinja*. If she didn't use it when they fought again...she'd end up like *Khanna*.

In pieces.

She hadn't even realised the weapon's influence until it was too late. Had Traego not kicked it away and snapped her out of it, she was certain she'd have died there.

Flying *Otella*, even briefly, made her want to get back into the air again, back on her own terms.

Conversation broke off around her as the troupe congratulated each other on a battle well fought and showed off their wounds to one another. They didn't seem at all bothered by the slaughter left on the beach, nor did they wonder where the monster came from or why it attacked. Her mind fogged again, but this time it was the groggy fog of exhaustion, rather than some dark magic affecting her.

She wanted to lie down and sleep for perhaps a week.

'Oh, that's a nice one!'

Judd's excited, pitched voice caught Amarah's attention. The other pirate ships had either landed on the beach beside *Otella*, or had returned to their docks. But Judd looked out to sea at a small ship approaching at speed.

Amarah blinked several times and stumbled to the side rail, where she peered over to get a better look. In the night sky, ships were hard enough to spot. This one didn't make it any easier with its dark copper colouration and grey sails.

She could tell it was a tiny class five. Something that

barely carried three people. The high whir of the propellers almost squealed as the ship flew at them at what must have been top speed, and created deep ripples in the sea as it passed overhead.

When the ship reached the beach, the nose pulled up abruptly, and the ship whirled around as it fanned out its side sails to brake and land. The power of the ship sent up clouds of dust and sand, and fanned away the remaining *dragon's breath* smoke.

Coughing, Amarah crossed the deck and scrambled down onto the beach. She wanted to get a better look at whoever had just waltzed in on fifty crown's worth of pure speed.

'Damn. Was hoping to get back in time for the races!' Antar's loud voice boomed over the smoke. 'Looks like I missed it all.'

Traego clambered down and rushed past Amarah to meet his second-in-command. 'I swear ya left Estoria on a bigger ship than this?' The two clasped each other's hands in greeting.

Antar's smile could have lit the world. 'Got ya a hundred crowns, didn't I?'

'Well done. I didn't think the snake'd part with ten! Not for a pirate!' Traego replied. He clasped Oris's hand in a similar manner and walked the two back to the others.

Antar rolled his shoulders. 'The princess vouched for you a bit. Think that helped.' He fished out his purse and handed the whole thing to Traego. Traego took out a handful, pocketed them, then gave the mostly-full purse back to Antar.

'Dragon's above, that *is* a nice ship.' Judd whistled as he walked around the vessel, its engines still whirring as they died down and cooled off. 'Who'd you steal that from? The king himself?'

Antar laughed. 'Close enough. That was the princess, too. Loaned it to me. Sapora wants his proof in three days or he sends his snakes on us.'

'That's Princess Isa's ship?' Kohl asked, eyebrows raised.

'Yep. I can have a couple hours' kip then fly back?' Antar suggested.

Traego licked his lips as he thought. 'Veynothi's sword has given us a tonne o' trouble. Trust me. It's a good thing ya didn't get here an hour ago. Probably for the best that Sapora gets it.'

Amarah snorted. It was the truest thing Traego had said in a while. The sooner he got rid of that sword, and the sooner she had a ship of her own, the better. Her discarded *Valta Forinja* lay halfway along the beach, waves lapping gently at it as the tide came in. She'd relied on it so much since Aciel's attack that the thought of being without it scared her. And yet she was in no hurry to retrieve it.

'Oh, Amarah? Princess Isa had a message for you,' Antar said.

Amarah looked up. What on earth could the princess want with her?

'She asked you to go there. Now. Said it was urgent. Said you had to talk to her or some Ittallan called Aetos. She seemed pretty desperate.'

'What..what for?' Amarah asked.

Antar shrugged. 'That's all she said. I just passed the message on.'

Amarah shook her head. It was all too much. She'd only just come to terms with the fact there was a monster out there hunting down her, Traego, and the others on account of Veynothi's blade. Her greatest weapon now appeared to be her greatest threat. And the Princess of the Ittallan wanted a personal meeting with her.

Before she slept, Amarah wanted a bottle of rum.

23

D awn broke over the valley, and Palom rose to meet the sun.

He, Odi, and the others had talked long into the night, about Yfaila's betrayal, about the Arks, and about what they were going to do once they entered Taban Yul.

Palom wanted to visit the mausoleum in South Galeo first and foremost. Anahrik and Eryn had been laid to rest there, and he wanted to pay his respects to them before he did anything else. Walking down the path of war once again somehow didn't seem right if he hadn't fully closed the door to his past.

When he'd taken part in the funeral procession, he'd been overwhelmed by grief—enhanced tenfold by the influence of his *Valta Forinja*—and he'd left too quickly.

This time, he could pay his respects, make peace, and say his farewells.

Through Aetos, Odi and the majority of his travellers had a link to Lathri and the rebel movement she'd been growing in the city since the end of Aciel's siege. Palom hadn't realised quite how unpopular the snake was until he began speaking to Odi and listening to the other Ittallan travelling with them.

Varkain were disliked, that was a universal truth. But with the Arks, the Sevastos, moving Varkain into the Ittallan city, and everything else Sapora schemed, the Ittallan of Val Sharis had had enough.

Odi was going to join Summercourt, as was his right. It was his last attempt at securing some influence and power for the Ittallan on the ruling council. If he and enough of the Ittallan Archigo were accepted, then perhaps it didn't need to come to a civil war.

But if Sapora kept to his Varkain and dismissed the Ittallan, then bloodshed was inevitable.

Odi explained it as if Sapora was a ship's captain who made poor decisions, and led the crew into danger after danger. Eventually, the crew would mutiny and choose someone better suited for the task.

Just because Sapora was a king and not a captain didn't change the fact the people of Val Sharis were unhappy, at a disadvantage, and didn't trust him.

Palom could understand that.

He'd also run away from so many problems that it was now time to turn and face them like the tiger everyone knew him to be. What good was it having all his strength if he didn't use it to defend his friends and family?

But then there was the issue of Karvou. The young lad had travelled all the way down to the capital with him just for the chance to become a smith's apprentice. Palom supposed when the war ended and if he still lived, he might return to his smithing trade. But the chances of either happening were slim, and he couldn't let Karvou continue to follow him around in the hope that he would one day have time to teach him how to make a sword.

No. The boy had to stay in Taban Yul. There would be

plenty of other smiths, or other trades, if Karvou changed his mind. Palom couldn't in his right mind lead Karvou into a war where he might die. Especially since Palom was going to join the rebel movement and stand by its leader.

He looked back over the camp as the Ittallan roused themselves. Jek might want some company, and he and Karvou did get on well. Learning how to buy and sell, how to negotiate and bargain. Those were useful skills.

Yes. It made sense to ask Jek if he'd take the lad on. It would be the safest thing for him. He'd get to travel Val Sharis with the merchant, see all the sights and cities, and make himself a small fortune if he was adept at it.

And it wasn't as if Karvou had had any time to bond with Palom during their journey south. It would be for the best.

'Good morning, Palom,' Odi said. The Ittallan looked even older, somehow.

'Odi.' Palom dipped his head in greeting. 'Do you go into city today?'

Odi looked down at the road leading to the capital, the Imperial Guard standing by the outposts and outside the city's gates. 'I do. Summercourt is underway and I must be there if I'm to have any say in what Sapora does. Maybe we'll be able to avoid bloodshed.'

'You think he will listen to Ittallan?' Palom raised an eyebrow. Overhead, Leillu flew in widening circles, her wings spread wide to catch the morning sunlight.

Odi shrugged. 'Who knows. He might listen to reason. But I doubt it.'

As Odi made to leave, Palom said quickly, 'Karvou. Palin's son. I was thinking of letting Jek take him on. To apprentice under merchant.'

'I thought he was going to be your apprentice?' Odi asked.

Palom shook his head. 'If I am fighting against Sapora, I

346

have no time to smith. No time to teach him. It will be dangerous.'

Odi considered for a few moments. 'It's up to the boy. See what he thinks. I'll try and make the caravan's passage into Taban Yul easy. At least the Imperial Guard we dealt with yesterday were accommodating.' He patted Palom on the shoulder, smiled once, then walked off.

Palom watched as the elder made his way along the road in his slow, unhurried way. He could tell Yfaila's betrayal still pained him, and Palom wondered what would become of her once Tacio had seen her.

He doubted that Tacio would be kind to an Ittallan, but if what she spoke was the truth, then the snakes were one step closer to bringing back an Ark.

Leillu came in to land, her wings fluttering to slow her descent. She touched the ground gracefully, rear feet first, and then her front, and folded in her wings carefully against her body. Palom ran a finger along her snout, and she nuzzled him. He could have sworn her colouration had faded somewhat overnight. Instead of the rich blue scales she usually donned, they seemed greyer and lighter somehow. Believing it to simply be the pale morning sunlight, Palom returned to the camp where Ittallan finished their breakfasts and were securing their supplies ready for the last bit of travel into the capital.

Several of the wagons were empty after their occupants had met with Jato. Palom still didn't forgive himself for that. He'd heard the warnings, he should have known an Arillian attack was a possibility. Odi had praised him and said that without him, more would have died. Palom didn't doubt that, but he still blamed himself for their deaths.

They had been in his care, after all.

'Odi's gone,' Palom said as he approached his wagon.

Jek was sat on the ground, his back pressed up against

347

the wheel, as he tied up the laces on his boots. 'Hopefully he'll be able teh make a difference at Summercourt. I don't want no fighting in Val Sharis. It's bad fer business.'

'I hope there is no fighting, too. But if there is, it will be over quickly.' Palom wasn't sure if he was trying to convince Jek or himself. 'I do not think the capital will be safe for long. Are you moving on again soon?'

Jek finished with one boot and shifted his attention to the other. He grasped it and pulled it snug before tying the lace. 'A few days. See some of my suppliers. Then I'll be off. Heading further south. Antir Yul, first. Then Tannon Sona, then all the way down to Gur Bano. Might cross the Feor Mountains east, might not. Gur Bano is such a busy trading port I could stay there all summer. Depends what the state of Val Sharis is like, then, I guess.'

It was quite a journey and would take him months on foot. But it would take him well away from the capital and all the strife that came with it. 'Sounds good. Why don't you take Karvou with you?'

Boots done, Jek stood up and dusted himself down before reaching inside the wagon to grab his cloak. 'The young lad? Why?'

'He would be safer with you, I think. Away from war. Fighting.'

'I suppose. I thought he was teh be yeh apprentice?'

'Better ask what he wants to do. If you are okay to take him.'

'Take me where?' Karvou came around the side of the wagon carrying a large bucket of water. He doused the small campfires from the morning's breakfast and looked up at both men.

Palom glanced to Jek before looking back at Karvou. 'These are...dangerous times, Karvou. We are on brink of war. There will be more fighting. More death to come.'

348

The boy put his bucket on the ground, his bottom lip quivering.

'Is not easy. I know. And I know you and your *pali* wanted you to be smith. Apprenticed to me. But I will be fighting in this war. I cannot teach you. You would be safer if you went with Jek. He travels south, away from fighting. Away from death. Will you go?'

'So you're just giving me away?' Karvou asked, his voice louder than Palom had expected. 'Keep me around while we travel and now I'll get in the way, you want me to go? Get rid of me?'

'It isn't like that.' Jek jumped in. 'We want what's best for yeh, and that ain't sticking around in a city that's being attacked. Jato is nearby, dragons are on the loose, and we have Sapora teh think of, too. Your *pali* wants you safe.'

'Your *pali* wants you to have future. Bright future,' Palom added in what he hoped was a sincere vice. He'd never been good with children.

Tears formed at the corners of Karvou's eyes. 'I want to be a smith...'

'There are smiths in Taban Yul. Jek could take you to one—'

'But I want to fight back, too. After losing my friends to Jato...' He struggled to keep his voice from breaking with emotion. 'And Sapora not wanting to protect us like a king should...I want to stay with you. With the rebels. I want to fight back. I know I'm still young. Too young. I don't have my *meraki* yet...'

Palom frowned. Karvou spoke like he had done, before he'd had his *meraki* come through. When he'd wanted desperately to save his brother, to have the strength he'd lacked as a child. That desperation had led him to joining Mateli, and all the horrors that had followed.

He didn't want to be responsible for leading Karvou

349

down a similar path of destruction. And given his father, Palom believed Karvou would also be a hunter Ittallan when his *meraki* came. 'How old are you, Karvou?'

'Fourteen.' He hurriedly wiped away the tears that dribbled down his cheek and sniffed loudly.

Another two years, at least, before his meraki. But there was nothing to say he couldn't learn to fight before then. 'Your *pali* would be angry with me if I led you into war.'

'My *pali* has never left Tum Metsa!' Karvou shouted. 'I don't want to run away and hide when people like you...heroes of the Ittallan...are fighting. I can help you. Give me the chance. Please?'

Palom couldn't see that he had a choice.

If he took him on, not as a blacksmith's apprentice, but just as a student, one that he could teach how to fight, it might keep him safe. For a while, at least.

If Sapora won, war would spread through to the farthest reaches of Val Sharis anyway, and then they'd all be dead.

At least this way, Karvou could go down fighting, if that's what it came to.

It's what he would want, if he had the chance to relive his youth.

Palom looked to Jek, who gave no indication of his thoughts, and then nodded. 'Okay. You stay with me. But you will do as I say, when I say. Understand?'

Karvou brightened immediately. 'Yes, sir!'

'Then it is settled. Get everything packed. Odi has gone already and we cannot be too far behind.' Now that Karvou had joined him officially, there was no need to keep him in the dark about their plans, either. 'I will visit mausoleum when we arrive. I have lost many friends. We are then meeting with Aetos in city. You will stay with me until we have decided on next steps.'

Karvou ran forward, jumped, and hugged Palom full around the belly.

Almost frightened, Palom froze, before returning the boy's hug. 'Enough. Get ready. We leave now.'

Jek laughed as Karvou raced off. 'I didnae know yeh had a soft spot for the lad!'

'I don't.' Palom's mood had soured a little. He never wanted to protect anyone else, not after failing his brother, Lathri, Anahrik, Eryn, and Moroda. But somehow he always found himself looking after those around him, willingly or not.

At least this time he'd made the decision himself, for whatever consequences that would have.

IT WAS afternoon by the time Karvou and the other Ittallan travellers had everything in order and they could finally press on the city.

Palom was almost itching to fight someone by the time they finally got moving.

As they made their way down the winding road to Taban Yul, Palom noticed how many airships hovered overhead. Taban Yul had always been a bustle of activity, both on the ground and in the air, but there seemed more airships than most here, very few of which moved.

Thunder rumbled in the far distance. Spring storms were not uncommon, but every time he heard thunder, he assumed the worst - Jato, or one of her Arillians. Palom looked east, to the Feor Mountains on the horizon. Black clouds grew near the peaks, and he saw a few tiny flashes of sheet lightning.

From this distance, there was no way to tell whether it was a normal storm or one created by Jato and her Arillians.

It was close enough to be Jato, he supposed, if she'd flown to the mountains to take refuge there and gather more of her allies.

But he also didn't want to be paranoid. Linaria's weather was more extreme near the mountains, and swift changes in temperature frequently created storms. Every bolt of lightning didn't have to come from an Arillian's hand...and yet he couldn't be too careful.

'Keep moving. We must be inside city gates quickly.' He paused to let a couple of the wagons trundle past down the road. He waved them along, hurrying people. 'Keep moving, keep moving.'

A few Ittallan had also heard the thunder and glanced back to the gathering clouds. Between that sight and Palom's motivation, they increased their pace and the whole caravan sped up. The storm had to be three days travel away, at least. But the sheer scale of it made it seem as though it loomed much closer.

Whether a natural storm or an Arillian one, he would be safer in the city. With the airship defensive guard, the Sevastos, and all of Sapora's Varkain, the city would be safe from any attack. In fact, Jato would have to be stupid—or mad— to launch an attack against Taban Yul given the city's defenses.

Twin walls protected the capital from would be invaders, and the Imperial Guard's ranks had clearly been bolstered by the influx of Varkain. And there were the Cerastes to consider, as well. If the two that had come to camp the previous day were anything to go by, Prince Tacio's elite fighters would be problematic.

Palom only wondered how easy it would be to leave the city, if they needed to.

The same walls and defenses which kept Jato out and the citizens safe would also be in his way if he and the rebels decided to go for Sapora. Palom hoped that Lathri, Aetos, Odi, and the other rebels had a better plan in mind than simply storming the palace.

A fleet of warships had fallen when it had attacked the palace. Even they could not stand up to the Sevastos. There surely would be no way they'd all march on the palace walls. That would be suicide.

Palom chewed on the inside of his lip as they progressed closer to Taban Yul. They soon began to pass heavily manned and armoured outposts. Most of the Imperial Guard here were Varkain, like the group that had come to visit them, and the caravan halted when they reached the outpost led by Captain Renaud.

'Odi passed through earlier this morning,' the Varkain captain said, addressing Palom and the others at the front of the caravan. 'Allow me and my comrades to escort you the rest of the way.'

Palom was grateful that Renaud remained as polite as before, and was pleased there were no signs of the captain's Cerastes superiors.

Eight armoured members of the Imperial Guard stepped away from their post, leaving another dozen still there, and surrounded the caravan at intervals. Their swords gleamed at their hips, and they were as friendly and professional as could be expected. Palom still didn't quite know how to react to them.

Captain Renaud joined Palom and *Leillu* at the head of the caravan, and they fell into step with one another. Despite his earlier reservations, he seemed to have little to fear from Renaud, and so felt comfortable allowing him to see the young dragon.

'I've not seen a dragon so close, before.'

Palom shrugged. '*Leillu* is different. She hatched with me. She has followed me since.'

'That's quite astounding,' Renaud said. He watched her with clear fascination, sometimes slowing his pace so much that he had to suddenly jog to catch up. 'I suppose it's like King Sapora's Sevastos. You have a bond with her.'

'He cannot bond with Sevastos,' Palom snapped. 'It is god of this world. There is dark magic at work.'

'Magic? King Sapora is simply too great, too powerful. The Sevastos obeys him as your dragon obeys you. There's nothing dark about it.'

Palom glowered but said nothing. He didn't understand why Leillu followed him, nor did he understand why the Sevastos followed Sapora. But a young, defenceless hatchling following someone who looked after it made more sense than one of Linaria's gods bowing to a snake. No matter what the Varkain thought of him.

Captain Renaud took no offence at Palom's brusque words. 'You will be safe in Taban Yul. We have King Sapora's protection, and that of his Sevastos. We've sighted no Arillians anywhere near—not within striking distance, anyway. King Sapora will drive away any aggressors.'

Palom rolled his eyes and turned his head away. He didn't want to listen to the Varkain's sickening devotion to Sapora, nor did he want to hear about being kept "safe" while in the Varkain's city. He had no doubt that Sapora was capable of driving off Jato should she attack, but that said nothing about the rest of the country that burned under dragon-fire or was wiped out by her storms.

What kind of king let his people die while he basked in the safety and luxury of the palace?

Captain Renaud's voice droned on and reminded Palom of Jek. In fact, Palom preferred the Ittallan trader's non-stop yapping over the sickening love Renaud had for Sapora. He didn't even seem bothered that the Cerastes had called him out on his lax behaviour and struck him for it.

354

When the twin city walls of Taban Yul towered above them, and Palom could see the detail of the golden statues atop them—instead of vague shapes—getting inside and away from the Varkain couldn't come soon enough. A shiver ran through him as Captain Renaud led them down to the south gate, where they joined a high-traffic road. Many Ittallan, mostly on foot, lingered near the gates as the Imperial Guard went through their paperwork and decided whether or not they would be permitted entry.

Fewer Ittallan were leaving the city than trying to get into it, Palom noticed. Suddenly he was pleased they had an escort. It would hopefully make their entry into the city much faster.

'Captain Renaud.' One man at the gate said. He wore his helm, unlike the Varkain soldiers, and its three spikes and gold sash across his chest marked him as a captain himself.

The two soldiers nodded to one another. 'Odi told me to expect you today. Didn't think you'd be quite so late.' The captain looked Palom over before removing his helm to reveal his face. 'Palom!'

'Captain Chyro?' Palom blinked in astonishment.

'Welcome back, friend,' Chyro said. 'And you still have your dragon with you? Wow.'

Clearly his surprise and delight at seeing Leillu made him lose all professionalism.

Renaud cleared his throat somewhat awkwardly. 'Do you have everything you need, captain?'

Chyro returned his attention to his comrade. 'Yes, yes of course. Thank you. You may return to your post, now.'

Palom saw Renaud's smile fade a little. The two soldiers clasped a fist to their chests. 'Farewell, Palom. Fortune find you.' The Varkain inclined his head and then dismissed his comrades, and the group made their way back along the road to their outpost.

355

'There's space for the whole caravan in South Galeo,' Chryo said. His voice had dropped to just above a whisper. 'Aetos has managed to secure a tavern for you all, *The Last Grape*. There's room for you all to stay.'

Palom realised with horror that Chyro was in on the ploy against Sapora, too. No wonder he had got rid of Renaud as soon as he could. 'I have heard of this tavern.'

'Good. Aetos will meet you there later. Just get settled in for now. Food and lodgings have been paid for. Odi will join you when he's done with Summercourt.'

Palom was surprised at that. *The Last Grape* was a particularly large tavern that ranged over three stories and took up almost an entire side of one street. South Galeo, too was one of the more expensive parts of the city. Unless Lathri had inherited a fortune, he didn't understand how she, Aetos, or any of the others could pay for such accommodation for so many people, but he didn't question it.

'Are you going to be there, too?' Palom asked.

Chyro shook his head and began waving the caravan in, lest the wagons blocked up the road for too long. 'Later, perhaps. I'm serving as my king commands until it's time. The city is in chaos at the moment with Summercourt underway. Too many people, lots of big crowds.'

Palom thought the young captain was trying to tell him something, but he wasn't sure.

'Everything okay, Palom?' Karvou asked as he hurried along the line of wagons to catch up to him.

'There is no turning back now,' Palom said. 'You are sure this is what you want? I can take you to Trader's Alley and find smith or tanner or weaver or—'

'I'm sure,' Karvou said.

Despite his age, the young Ittallan had a real fire in his eyes, and Palom felt bad that he'd not spent enough time with him on their journey to the capital.

Leillu chirped and fluttered her wings.

'You can keep the dragon under control, right? It'd cost a small country to repair *The Last Grape* if she sets fire to the roof.' Chyro said, watching the dragon with a wary eye.

Palom scowled. 'Of course she is not going to burn down building. You just keep Varkain off our tails. I do not want to be trapped in a tavern at mercy of the snakes.'

Chyro grinned despite the seriousness of their conversation. 'I'm doing my duty. That means looking after the citizens.'

There wasn't much point in arguing with Chyro, and the wagons had almost all entered the city now. 'Ready, Karvou?'

The lad nodded and hurried on to catch up with the others.

With a final look back to the growing thunderstorm on the horizon, Palom took a breath, stroked *Leillu*, and entered Taban Yul.

24

W hen Amarah woke some hours later, cold sweats wracked her body.

When she moved, she was sure she would vomit.

She'd slept out of exhaustion rather than a desire to rest, and nightmares had plagued her through the small hours of the morning. Snakes had somehow managed to track her down in Estoria, had bitten her, poisoned her, and her mind's pain of the imagined attack had finally woken her.

It took several seconds for Amarah to remember where she was and what had happened the night before. And it took even longer for her to realise that her nightmares had just been the terrors of sleep—there weren't any real snakes in her room, nor were there any Varkain looming over her, ready to strike her down. Amarah clutched the butcher knife she'd taken to bed, and realised she still had the purse of gold coins stuffed inside her pillow.

She spent a few minutes taking control of her breathing. She'd shoved away all thoughts of the previous night, but they now poured into her mind: the intense fear she'd felt in Veynothi's tomb and Kohl's warnings about it; the monster in the sea, and again in Estoria; the weapon that had helped her survive against Aciel's onslaught, against Jato one-on-one, and every battle she'd fought since. The *Valta Forinja* had almost held her hostage under its power, and she couldn't do a thing against it.

The scythe still lay on the beach somewhere, unless another sky pirate had picked it up and claimed it as their own.

She didn't care.

Let it curse them instead.

And now Princess Isa wanted her, had *pleaded* for her. Right when Amarah had the gold to buy herself a new ship to finally hunt down Jato and get her revenge.

Amarah rolled over, pulled the sheets over her shoulder, and buried her head in the pillow. She knew she wouldn't fall asleep again, not now she was awake, but she could hold onto the comforting warmth of a real bed while it lasted.

At least today she could get her new eyepatch, get a new ship, and then she'd feel ready to take on whatever challenges Linaria threw at her.

Through the thin, wooden walls of the lodge, she heard the other members of Traego's troupe bustling about. Amarah discerned two sets of feet as they walked along the creaking wooden floorboards. Not everyone was up so early.

Bright sunlight streamed through the small, single window, already carrying a fair amount of heat. Warmth crept up her skin and made it itch where she started to sweat, and at that point, Amarah knew she had to get up.

She couldn't hide in bed all day and hope her problems disappeared.

Without her *Valta Forinja*, she felt empty somehow, as though she'd lost a vital limb. Shoving the thought to one side, Amarah got out of bed and ran a hand through her hair. She filled the small copper tub at the end of the room and enjoyed a cool bath, washing the remnants of the night's plagues from her.

When she left her room and wandered into the main hall, she wasn't surprised to see two others there already: Malot and Farlan.

The Samolen stopped bandaging Farlan's right arm and looked up. 'How are you feeling?'

Amarah shrugged, indifferent. 'I'm fine. You?'

Farlan smiled as he turned his head to show her the grim slash across his left cheek. 'Got me a war wound from that monster last night. I'll wear it proudly till the end of my days.'

Amarah pursed her lips. She didn't feel like celebrating anything. She just wanted to get rid of last night's memories and move on.

'I've got a jug of cold peppermint tea just made. Want a cup?' Malot offered, almost as though she had read Amarah's mind.

Amarah gratefully accepted it, walking to the side table and pouring herself a large mug of the stuff. It would wake her up as much as anything else would, and the peppermint in it would help settle her mind—she hoped.

Malot stepped back from Farlan and inspected the bandages she'd put on him with narrowed eyes and furrowed brows. 'Just keep it clean. I'm no Kalosin, so don't make it worse by picking at it, okay?'

'Thanks, Malot. That's brilliant.' The big Estorian patted his arm gently. 'Should heal just fine.'

Amarah sipped her tea. 'Where's Traeg?'

'He went out to get the news. We used to get deliveries every morning, just before dawn. But since all the shit that's kicked off in Val Sharis, it don't come that often anymore.' Malot stretched her arms above her head and flicked her braids out of her eyes. She spoke with the lightest of accents, and Amarah guessed she'd been out of the country for several years.

'Hmm.' Amarah supposed the downside to being in such a remote corner of the world was the lack of information about the more important parts of Linaria. Staying near a bigger town had more benefits than just the numerous Goldstones waiting to be robbed. 'And Kohl?'

'Not seen him. With good reason. If he has any sense, he'll make himself scarce.'

Amarah saw the sense in that. Kohl had put himself at risk by returning to the beach to warn them about the monster. Any of the sky pirates could have started hurling rocks at him or loosed bolts from a crossbow. Most of them were armed all the time, so it wouldn't have been a surprise. She drank the rest of her tea as quickly as she could. She had lots to do and not an awful lot of time to get it done.

Just as she finished her mug, Judd entered the room, barefoot, yawning wide and rubbing sleep from his eyes. He still wore his nightshirt—somewhat dishevelled—and a pair of loose brown trousers. 'Oh! Amarah! I didn't think you'd be up...' He turned a pale shade of pink and smoothed down the front of his shirt..

'I'm heading out.' She put the empty mug on the side and made for the door.

'Still looking for a new ship?' He called out after her. 'I remembered when I went to bed that there's a guy here, in Estoria. I normally get parts off him, but he gets a couple of ships in every now and then, and sells 'em on quickly. Wanna see if he has anything worth getting?'

Amarah's heart fluttered at the sudden excitement and anticipation of potentially getting her hands on a new ship. 'Sounds good. I need to pick up something from town first. Is your guy far?'

'Two beaches away,' Judd replied.

'Good. Let's go.'

~

THE SEAMSTER WAS EXACTLY the same as Amarah remembered her, down to the same red dress, and equally as brusque.

'I have patch for ye,' she'd said, when Amarah had entered the shop. Then, she'd promptly disappeared into the back, leaving Amarah and Judd among the racks of clothing and reams of fabrics.

'Rude woman,' Judd commented.

'She's efficient. If she has something for my eye, I don't care how she speaks to me.'

Judd had hastily grabbed a clean shirt and hurried after Amarah. She didn't know why he insisted on following her around like a shadow, but he seemed harmless enough, so she didn't mind too much.

She idly wondered if Traego had sent him to keep a close eye on her to make sure she didn't flee in the middle of a job. It wouldn't be the first time she'd been followed, and she doubted it would be the last.

But considering Traego had given her gold to get a ship, he'd effectively given her leave to do as she wished while he didn't need her talents. And now that Princess Isa had effectively summoned her, Amarah wondered whether her goals and Traego's were coming to align.

She'd been thinking about the princess's message all morning. Isa sounded desperate. She had to be, if she'd passed on a message to a sky pirate she'd never met before.

Perhaps the Isa wanted to hang up her royal duties and sail the skies as a pirate. Amarah knew Isa managed the fleet at Taban Yul and clearly had exceptional quality ships of her own. Maybe they weren't so different after all.

But what could she *want*?

And how did she know it had nothing to do with Sapora?

Just the thought of the Varkain sent shivers along her spine.

The gold Princess Isa had given her as a reward for fighting against Aciel had funded her for a while, but that money had been lost when Jato destroyed *Khanna*. Perhaps returning wouldn't be such a bad idea after all.

Amarah thought about the quickest route to Taban Yul. She'd need to speak with Antar, for sure. He'd just made a return trip to the Val Sharis capital and would have the most recent knowledge of conditions.

She was in the middle of mulling it over when the seamster returned from the back, clutching a piece of fabric to her chest. 'This is for ye.' The seamster grabbed Amarah's hands and shoved the patch into it. 'Ye with Traego, aren't ye? There's no charge.'

Amarah blinked and looked down at her hand. This wasn't a patch made from an off-cut she had lying around. This was a patch that she'd actually made for her. The fabric was soft, softer than anything Amarah had felt before, and she couldn't place it. Some kind of ultra-light cotton? It had been dyed a dark grey, and in the centre, a golden dragon's head had been embroidered.

She carefully ran a thumb over it, feeling every stitch. Nothing in life came free. 'I have gold?'

The seamster vigorously shook her head. 'Ye have what ye want? Good. Out with ye. I have other customers need serving!'

Amarah shuffled back out, dimly aware it was empty and she had no idea what "other customers" the woman was talking about.

'Very nice,' Judd commented.

363

Amarah lifted it to her socket and tied the patch into place, securing it with a tight knot. She smiled at the cool relief it provided. She took a moment to adjust the fit and nodded when she was satisfied.

'Better?'

'Much. Now, where's your seller?'

~

AMARAH HAD to admit that perhaps not everyone in Estoria hated Traego. It seemed he had a few merchants under his protection, which explained the seamster's free service.

Had it not been for Carav leading her to the shop, she'd never have known.

She needed to be a little kinder to the young thief in future.

Judd led her further inland, past the two beaches as he'd promised, and into a square patch of land that looked like it had been dug up a hundred times over. The thick Estorian jungle pressed against the edges and threatened to encroach into the wide, open space. Piles of sand, soil, and rock were heaped haphazardly across the sandy ground, scattered amongst piles upon piles of airship parts—most of which seemed in no fit state to ever be used again.

Propellers and sails jutted out from the ground, and Amarah wondered if perhaps this had been a crash site not too long ago, and Judd's trader had claimed the spot first.

They stopped at the edge of the sand piles and peered around.

'Venin? You about?' Judd yelled.

Amarah didn't know this trader nor Judd very well, and wasn't sure of the formalities. Many pirates and traders had their own processes of how they wanted things to run, and she was content to keep quiet and follow Judd's lead. She was the one with the gold, and she'd be the one to decide if it was spent.

After a moment, a tall man appeared from the trees at the back of the area. Even from this distance, Amarah saw his scowl. She sighed. She didn't want this to be a fight.

'Who's that?' The man—Venin—yelled back.

'It's me, Judd!'

Venin's scowl deepened, but he made no move to come closer for a better look.

Judd waved a hand and then approached, and Amarah followed a few steps after.

When they were only a couple of feet away, Venin's scowl broke and he embraced Judd with wide arms. As they hugged, Amarah saw that Venin no longer had his right hand - the sleeve of his shirt had been tied loosely over the stump.

'Who's this?' Venin asked, stepping back from Judd to get a better look at Amarah.

'I'm the one with gold. Judd said you get ships in from time to time. Got anything worth looking at?'

Venin tilted his head from side to side, his long, wispy hair waving around his face. 'Depends on what you're after.'

Judd opened his mouth to speak, but Amarah interrupted. 'Class four. Twin engined, or bigger. Class five engines, preferably. Needs to be fast.'

Venin narrowed his eyes. 'Pretty exact.'

'You have anything or am I wasting time?'

Venin looked to Judd, who gave a half-shrug in what Amarah presumed was an apology for her brusqueness. 'Come through and have a look.'

Confident in her assertive approach, Amarah followed Venin into the trees without so much as a glance back at Judd.

Based on the messy front, Amarah expected to see felled

trees, plants growing over rusted and forgotten parts, maybe even birds nesting in whatever they could find. But she gasped when she reached Venin on the other side.

Hidden from the main street by the enormous trees, a veritable fleet of ships sat in a line as though awaiting orders.

Amarah swallowed, her gaze darting from one ship to the next then the next. They didn't seem to be in any order, massive warships sat beside tiny single-seater class fives, with everything in between. 'Only a few ships from time to time?' She said, partly to Judd and partly to Venin.

Judd shrugged. 'I never had to buy a ship. But I remembered Venin said he sometimes had some for sale.' He didn't sound at all apologetic, but Amarah didn't care.

This was paradise.

'Let's see, class four, class four...' Venin mumbled to himself, walking along the line of ships, his left hand on his chin as he thought. 'Ah, here we go. There's a couple this way. Might need a bit of patching up, mind you.'

Amarah all but ran after him, staring at the ships with every step.

The two he mentioned looked like they'd been salvaged from a battlefield somewhere. Both were missing sails and one had a catastrophic hole in the side, enabling her to see right through it. They were unvarnished wood, both fairly light.

Amarah rushed past Venin and onto the ladder carved into the side of the undamaged ship. She pulled herself up and onto the deck, and the immediate familiarity of a class four ship. It was very much like *Khanna*, but without the modifications and little touches she'd added to her own ship over the years.

'What's the firepower like?' She called as she slowly crossed the deck, running her hand along the sides.

'Ain't got no cannons left. So...uh...none?' Venin replied.

'That's no good.'

'I get all sorts of ships. Sometimes they need some love to bring 'em back.'

Amarah rolled her eyes. She needed something that could fly *now*.

'Well how much you got to spend? A five crown ship ain't half as good as a ten crown.'

'You don't say...' Amarah muttered under her breath. 'Show me the best you got, and I'll see if it's worth my time.'

'Knows what she wants, don't she?' Venin said to Judd.

As Amarah scrambled off the ship, her heart pounded. This was really happening. She was going to find herself a new ship and get back into the air on her own terms.

Finally she'd be able to get her revenge on Jato.

She and Judd spent the better part of an hour going over all the ships Venin had, most of which were in varying states of disrepair, which explained why he sold so many parts. Twice she'd found a great ship, but Venin had been unwilling to drop the price for her, no matter how hard she negotiated.

Judd had suggested trying a class three, which was a notion that Amarah refused to entertain.

Finally, when Amarah threatened to pass out under the burning heat of the midday sun, she saw a class four tucked away in the shade of several palm trees. The ship was larger than *Khanna* had been, and wasn't much smaller than the class three cargo ships Judd kept on about. Like all the others in Venin's yard, the ship didn't have any sails, and wasn't without war wounds of its own. It had only one engine attached, though the propellers needed replacing, and had more than its fair share of scuffs and scrapes.

But it was a double-masted, triple-decked, sleek beauty in mahogany, with cannons ready and a large hold.

An imperfect ship that was perfect to her.

'This one.'

'It's a non-flyer,' Venin said.

'You sure?' Judd asked, casting a skeptical gaze over it.

Amarah didn't care. It didn't need much work to get back into the sky. 'How soon can you get it ready?' Amarah asked, ignoring Judd's hesitation. 'She'll need two more engines, and I want class fives. And...navy blue sails. Dark as you can get them.'

Venin huffed and tilted his head to one side again, which Amarah put down being to a nervous tic. 'I have the parts here, so...three or four days?'

Amarah shook her head. 'How quick can you do it if you don't do anything else?'

'Well that rush fee will cost you extra.'

Amarah pulled out the coins from her purse, careful not to show Venin how much she had, and held them out to him. 'Six crowns. Five for the ship, one for the rush. I want her ready tomorrow at the latest.'

Venin licked his lips and glanced to Judd.

'I'll be sure to let Traego know you helped out one of his crew,' Amarah said. 'Or that you couldn't. Choice is yours.'

Venin didn't take long to decide. He snatched the coins from her and shoved them in his own pocket. 'Okay. Done. You drive a hard bargain.'

Amarah grinned. It was no bargain at all. Traego's name was enough for him to take her gold.

Venin said, 'She'll be ready to fly tomorrow. What name shall I paint on the side?'

～

BY THE TIME Amarah and Judd returned to Traego's lodge, it was late afternoon.

368

She'd struggled to mask her growing excitement in case Judd thought her childish or silly, and she doubted very much she'd be able to sleep that night.

Carav hurried out to meet them as they approached. 'Was just 'bout to look for you two!'

'We're back now,' Judd replied.

'I can see that.' Carav sniffed then looked back at Amarah. 'Hey! You got your patch!'

'Thanks for sorting that, Carav,' Amarah said.

Carav beamed at her words then raced back to the lodge. Amarah shook her head. Small things.

'...biggest damn thundercloud you've ever seen!'

As Amarah and Judd entered the lodge, she looked up to see Oris with his hands held far apart as he gesticulated to Traego. 'Honest I thought it was the whole sky!'

Amarah made her way over to where Malot sat at one of the tables with Farlan and joined them, helping herself to another mug of peppermint tea as she got comfortable.

Traego sat on another table, his leg resting on a chair, and spoke to Antar, Ernold, and Oris. His gaze lingered on her for a few seconds before he continued the conversation he'd evidently been in the middle of. 'Gonna make flyin' a bit o' a problem, then?' His brows were furrowed as he puzzled out something in his head. 'Did ya see the dragon? The Sevastos?'

Amarah's head shot up. They were talking about Taban Yul.

Antar said, 'From a distance. It wasn't near the palace. Thing is enormous. And Sapora's pretty damn desperate. Pure desire, that one.'

'What about Jato? You see any Arillians?' Amarah asked, unable to help herself. She'd have a ship within the day. If she knew where Jato was...

'That's what Oris was sayin',' Traego said. 'Giant thunderstorm building near Taban Yul. It's Jato alright.'

'If Princess Isa's ship wasn't so fast, we'd have been caught up in her storm. Had to leave my cousin's ship at the palace,' Antar said.

Amarah bit her lip.

'I cannot believe what Jato's doing.'

It was Kohl.

Amarah hadn't even seen him—but the Arillian had been standing in the corner, listening to the sky pirate's talk with folded arms.

'If Jato is...truly is continuing Aciel's work and slaying dragons, then we have to act,' Kohl said.

'We don't have ta do anything,' Traego replied shortly.

Kohl carried on as though the sky pirate hadn't spoken. 'Amarah. I've been thinking about your scythe. Your *Valta Forinja*. Palom forged it using dragon ore, right? From a Sevastos? You told me how Palom behaved oddly, and now look at what it's done to you. I fear these weapons are doing more harm than good. Yes, they're formidable in battle, but at what cost?'

Amarah snorted. 'The university in Berel has the originals. They've had 'em for years. Nothing's ever happened to Berel or anyone there.'

'Maybe it's when they're used? Perhaps that is the issue.'

Amarah swallowed. The memory of the light, the snakes, the hallucinations, the fear. It was all still fresh. She wished she could talk to Palom about it, and knew that she'd had some kind of connection to him through the weapons. But with her scythe gone, she'd lost that.

When she'd last spoken to him, he'd been on his way to Tum Metsa. She'd wanted to wait for him, but Traego's Ark hunt couldn't wait. She was annoyed at herself for that. Even if he was still in Tum Metsa and not in Rhea knew where, the town was miles away. It would help anything. And Isa needed her *now*.

She realised why Kohl had steered the conversation to the weapons. He still defended his daughter. 'Well I don't have the scythe now and I ain't gonna pick it back up anytime soon,' Amarah said. 'But if Jato's just outside Taban Yul...Stopping her is more than revenge for me. I'd be doin' a service to Linaria itself. The weapons might be affecting the dragons. They might not. But Jato *definitely* is. Get rid of her and maybe the dragons'll settle again.'

Kohl bristled, his wings trembling, but he didn't say anything more about it.

'Amarah, you thought about the princess's message?' Antar asked, turning his dark eyes on her.

She scratched her chin. 'Well, I just bought me a ship— thanks again, Traeg—so there's nothing stopping me from flying to Taban Yul and seeing what she wants.' It wasn't a decision so much as a statement. She *could* go there, if she wanted to.

'Going to your princess would be the right thing to do,' Kohl said.

Amarah shrugged. Killing Jato was what she *wanted* to do.

'Dragons. Magic. Ancient weapons. Monsters from the sea. I wonder where the Arks'll fit into all this,' Traego said. 'Either way, there's more at stake than just gold. Amarah, ya're part o' my crew. But I can't stop ya from leaving if ya have ta answer the summons of royalty.'

'Isa can handle herself, I'm sure. She wouldn't ask for help unless she was absolutely desperate,' Amarah said.

'She *was* desperate,' Antar said.

Oris folded his arms. 'What I wanna know is why the princess is enlisting the help of a sky pirate? She didn't say anything to *me*, and I was there!'

'She probably needs something stolen?' Malot said, her red cheek jewel flashing.

Farlan said, 'Could be a trap. The Imperial Guard don't need no reason to pick any of us up.' He'd spent most of the conversation picking at the bandage on his arm, but looked up now things had quietened. 'You'd be flying right into their arms if you went.'

'Not to mention Jato's thunderstorm! Flying anywhere near Taban Yul will be risky,' Malot added. 'This isn't a friend inviting you for tea, this is a don't-fly-zone, now.'

The thought of being near Sapora made Amarah's stomach turn, especially after her nightmares and hallucinations. But she wondered what the chances were she'd actually see him—especially if she met Isa in town instead of the palace.

Antar added, 'Thing is, Isa's a princess. She has plenty of gold.'

Amarah came to a decision. 'For Isa's sake, and the promise of more gold, I'll risk going.'

Traego turned his head away as he scratched his ear.

Amarah continued, 'I have a warship at the palace, too, don't forget. It's under Isa's control, she commissioned it for me. Could add it to your little fleet, Traeg? Another ship, same size as *Otella* would be a boost, right?'

Judd muttered an agreement that rippled through the other sky pirates.

Traego scratched his nose. 'And what about our bounty with Sapora? He wants proof, and the only proof he'll accept is Veynothi's blade. Ya'd think if he was so desperate for it, he'd pay more.'

Amarah laughed at that.

Antar and Traego shared a look, and Amarah couldn't quite tell what passed between them. Then Antar said, 'If

Isa's in Taban Yul, why don't you take Veynothi's blade there?'

Amarah nodded. It made sense. And she'd get to try out her new wings.

'Take *Otella*,' Traego said, cutting off her train of thought. 'Sapora's expecting my crew, and he knows *Otella*. It'd send the right message. Ya're going there to see him. But then ya can see Isa and figure out what she needs. We stick with our plan ta take Sapora's gold, then move onta the next job, just like always.'

Amarah didn't like the idea of not even getting to fly her new ship, but she saw the sense in his suggestion. Not to mention the fact she'd be flying back to Sapora. She tried not to groan. 'And Jato?' *Otella* would surely have the fire-power to sort out one Arillian.

'Jato changes nothin'. Ya wanna help Isa, so go see what she wants. And ya get the gold from Sapora. Win, win.'

Considering the monster following them was after Veynothi's blade, it made sense to get rid of it. Have that awful creature go after Sapora instead of them.

'Be good to get my warship back as well. But I can't fly two ships at the same time,' Amarah said.

'I'll fly with you,' Judd offered.

'Me too. I have to return Isa's ship anyway, and they're expecting me,' Antar said.

'Time's o' the essence,' Traego said. 'Amarah, ya fly *Otella* to Taban Yul, and take Judd with ya. Oris, ya go with Antar, and follow in Isa's ship. Sapora's expecting ta see ya. Might as well play along. Amarah, ya can take Veynothi's blade as proof. If it all goes well, ya leave Taban Yul with two warships and a purse full o' the king's gold.'

Amarah half-expected Sapora to kill her on the spot, but she nodded anyway. And Malot was right. Jato could wait. The Arillian wasn't going anywhere. Isa's cry for help could lead to things of more value—if not gold, then information, or power.

It made sense.

'And what if it's a trap?' Malot asked. 'We'd have no way of knowing you're in trouble until it was too late?'

In response, Traego got up from the table and walked over to Amarah. 'Where'd ya get ya new ship from? Venin?'

Amarah nodded, her mind already racing at what was to happen. What she'd do if she saw Jato or Sapora. 'Ship'll be ready tomorrow.'

'I'll mind ya new ship for ya and follow on with everyone else, in case King Snake don't keep ta his word or ya get trapped by Isa. Can't be losing half my crew and all my pilots!'

The fact that Traego and the others would be following on her ship gave Amarah some comfort.

'I'll see Venin in the morning. What's the ship called?'

Amarah smiled and didn't reply.

374

25

S ilence greeted the setting sun but for the sound of shovels and pickaxes as they worked the stone streets.

Music did not fill the city of Berel as it did every evening and morning. Tonight, there was no magic to ease away the day's aches.

Tonight was sorrow. Grief. Shame.

Morgen, along with the other Samolen, helped move debris from the dragons' attack, clearing streets and sweeping roads, and doing what he could to restore order and balance to the mage city.

Topeko hadn't said a single word to him, nor had Andel, and he hadn't seen either of them for the past hour or so. Whenever he said or did the wrong thing, Morgen had been able to rely on Andel to soften the blow and show him where he went wrong.

But today, he knew perfectly well where he'd gone wrong: he'd wielded a weapon.

Having an unsheathed sword in Berel was bad enough. But his sword was a *Valta Forinja*.

If the Samolen weren't so peaceful, he'd have worried about being beheaded for his transgression.

He lifted stone and shovelled rubble beside the Samolen of Ranski in an effort to help them and show he wasn't evil. Mostly they ignored him. A few brave souls watched him from the corners of their eyes, but quickly glanced away when Morgen looked up to check.

They didn't seem to care that he'd acted on their behalf, that he'd struck the dragon to protect them and their city. They held a cold fury which seeped towards him.

Even with the little *Ra* he'd learned, he could feel their energy pushing at him, turning him away.

Although he understood their laws, he didn't understand *why*.

What did it matter *how* he fended off the dragon, so long as no-one was hurt, or worse?

As dusk fell over Berel, Morgen realised how monumental both the dragons' attack and his actions had been. He'd learned that the music of Berel played every morning and evening, and had done so for generations.

The fact that they all shovelled dirt in silence proved what he'd done was unlike anything the Samolen had ever experienced.

He should have been terrified. Mostly, Morgen was defiant. He dared any Kalos to tell him he'd acted improperly. Yes, they'd defended the university with their shield magic, but the dragons had shown no signs of retreating until he'd stepped forward and attacked.

Yes, they were sacred creatures, but they were on the warpath.

He'd made a choice to drive them away and protect the Samolen in the city.

What was he supposed to do? Sit and do nothing while

the dragons turned their attention from the university to the people? Burned and ate them?

Fury rose in his chest. Fury just as hot as the Samolen around him.

He would not be reprimanded for his actions. He wouldn't!

He wanted to *help*. To make Linaria a better place. If that meant ignoring a few of their teachings, then that was a price he was willing to pay.

'Kalosai Morgen.'

Morgen jumped at the sudden address and whirled around. Though he wasn't a true Kalosai—he didn't have a blue cheek jewel like Andel and the other students—the title was a familiar one. He studied under Topeko, after all.

Two tall Samolen stood before him, their long purple robes richly embroidered and skimming the sand. They both had two cheek jewels - one purple, one white. Masters of the healing arts and teachers of it, no doubt.

'Aye?' Morgen said, straightening and dusting off his shirt.

'Kalos Topeko has summoned you. You'll follow us to him now.'

'Can't he get me himself? Or send Andel?' Morgen asked. As soon as the words were out of his mouth, he knew how childish he sounded, but it was too late to snatch them back, now.

The first Kalos glowered. 'You are facing *severe* punishment for the desecration of our laws. Do not address Kalos Topeko or Kalosai Andel without their proper titles. And some advice: remain silent unless asked a direct question. Is that clear?'

Morgen shuffled his feet. 'Yes.'

'Excuse me?' The second Kalos said, rounding on him.

'Yes...Kalos.'

'Better. Come with us. Kalos Topeko is in the university.'

Morgen wanted to ask about his work in restoring Berel, about his tools, his belongings, where Andel was, where the music was, whether the dragons had been seen returning. A thousand and one questions rolled around his mind like a torrent, but he held his tongue as directed and followed them.

Years of obedience in the Imperial Guard meant he could follow orders, but he seemed to have a penchant for disobeying the ones he didn't agree with.

Everything had started when he'd looked for a medic in Rosecastle to help Amarah's shoulder wound after he'd brought her in. He'd arrested her, as ordered. He'd arrested Moroda, as ordered.

But he'd tried to help them, too. And if he'd been ordered to execute them—well, Moroda—he was certain he'd have balked at the command.

Perhaps being traitorous was simply in his blood.

He hadn't stayed at home with his family and brothers to be a farmer, either. It had been expected of him that he'd stay and work the land, maybe marry someone in his village or one nearby. His children would live their lives in the same way, and so would their children after them.

But Morgen had always held lofty ideals about making the world better, about doing the right thing. Staying home and farming wasn't part of that.

And now, what was it all for?

To be punished for trying to help because of another stupid rule?

Morgen pursed his lips and tried to keep the maelstrom of emotion from showing on his face. But he supposed if the Samolen were so in tune with the energy of the world—*Ra* —they'd probably be able to tell how aggravated he was, and then it wouldn't matter how well he masked his thoughts.

He kept his eyes low as he followed the two Samolen, and mostly focussed on the bottom of their feet and robes, watching how the granules of sand were flicked up by the wind of their passing. The ground changed underfoot as they moved from the rough streets to the smooth bridge connecting the old and new towns, and then finally to the flat stones of the university courtyard.

Morgen had never been to the old town at night before. Without the usual music that accompanied darkness, it was particularly eerie.

He glanced up to see a row of robed Kalos along the university wall, all of them facing him with their hoods up and their eyes covered.

Their silent disapproval was deafening.

He thought of Amarah, and her spending her youth here, with these people. Trying to please them but being unable to do so.

In that moment, Morgen knew why Amarah had run away. He'd have done the same, if not for his desperate need to learn magic to the fullest of his ability.

The two Kalos' pace didn't relent as they entered the university—the first time Morgen had been inside—and he jogged to keep up. Their strides seemed to cover more ground than was possible, and he struggled trying to keep track of where he was going and keep up.

They led him through halls and corridors, their footsteps echoing all around them. The university appeared to be deserted, and Morgen idly wondered where the original *Valta Forinja* were kept. Perhaps they'd moved them, following his actions today. It wouldn't surprise him if they had. Better to keep those weapons locked up securely so no-one could ever access their power again.

Just as his legs began to ache, they stopped. Morgen took several deep breaths to regain his composure as he looked around. They were in another hall not too dissimilar from the ones they'd passed through, though this one had diamond-shaped floor tiles cut from what appeared to be marble, as it reflected the candle light and torches vividly.

'Thank you for bringing Kalosai Morgen.' Topeko's voice echoed from across the hall.

Other than the candles flickering along the walls, the room was in darkness. The unsteady light threw shadows all around him, and reminded Morgen of Sapora's mirror conversations.

That memory alone was enough to steel his nerves. He knew what he'd come here for. What he needed to do. He'd face whatever punishment Topeko thought necessary. He'd survived lashings, starvation, and marching for days on end in the Imperial Guard. He'd survived worse as a boy by his father's hand.

He would face whatever Topeko threw at him, too.

Morgen looked in the direction of Topeko's voice and saw him standing with a candelabra in one hand, a thick book in another. No other Kalos or Samolen stood near him, but plenty filled the hall behind Morgen, blocking the doorway to witness Topeko's judgement.

Morgen had half-expected to see Andel beside Topeko, but aside from himself, the only other people in the hall appeared to be other Kalos.

Following the advice of the two who'd brought him here, Morgen kept silent, his head slightly bowed. There was no point in making the situation worse for himself by saying the wrong thing, so he held his tongue and waited for his punishment.

'Kalosai Morgen,' Topeko said. 'Although you have not

yet earned your jewel, you are studying under me, and I will refer to you by the formal title.'

'Thank you, sir.'

'I'm sure you don't need to be told why you're here. If this were some minor issue, I'd deal with it myself. But you've breached the sacred laws of the Samolen and—'

'I was protecting you!' Morgen blurted out, before he could think better of it. 'You kept the university safe, and I protected the people!'

'—drew a *Valta Forinja* in Berel, then used it to attack a dragon. We have reason to believe you were intent on slaying it.' Topeko continued as though Morgen hadn't interrupted him. 'Would you have?'

'Would I have what?'

Topeko paused and looked pointedly at him. 'Would you have slain the dragon?'

'No. It flew off.'

'But if it hadn't? If it had stayed and attacked you?'

Morgen glanced around at the other Samolen present. Clearly they wanted a yes or no answer, but it was impossible. Of course he'd fight for his own life. He didn't want to die! But neither would he run after the dragon and hunt it down like Aciel had done.

Their wordless accusations fuelled his anger. 'I'm not going to die needlessly. If the dragon wanted to kill me, then I'm going to defend myself. Am I interested in slaughtering them? Of course not.'

The Kalos muttered among themselves at his words and the fury with which he spoke them.

Morgen's heart raced and his breathing increased as he became more and more worked up with the injustice of it all. He clenched his fists tight and bit his tongue.

'He is no Aciel.' Topeko's voice cut through the murmurs. 'I told you he wasn't. I would not take on a student with such a darkness. But you must understand, his background in the Imperial Guard...his instinct in a crisis is to draw a sword and protect those who cannot protect themselves.'

Morgen swallowed. Was Topeko *defending* him?

'The laws of Ranski cannot be broken!' One Kalos yelled. 'A sword. A *Valta Forinja*. Attacking a dragon. Ignoring the Kalos. One act on its own, perhaps. But all of these cannot go unpunished.'

Now it made sense. It was the other Kalos that wanted him gone, and Topeko stood against them. Spoke *for* him. Morgen didn't understand it. He'd gone against Topeko again and again, challenged him, talked back, and even stormed off in a huff.

Why was Topeko still fighting his corner, after everything he'd done?

'And speaking of the Imperial Guard.' Another Kalos—a woman—stepped forward to speak, 'We received notice from Niversai requesting word on Captain Morgen's whereabouts. If he has passed away, the news must be sent to his family. You would have us lie to the allied force that protects Corhaven and Val Sharis? For this traitor?'

Morgen almost replied.

Topeko beat him to it. 'He is no traitor. He is not a child.'

'I haven't asked anyone to lie for me, or speak for me.' Morgen glanced at Topeko. 'I have done nothing wrong by leaving. There is no law which states I must tell my superiors where I move to, or what I do. I paid my fee. Kalos Topeko accepted me as his Kalosai. And today, I protected all of you. The dragons raged against us. Probably because of King Sapora and his Sevastos. Perhaps because of Jato and the destruction she brings to Val Sharis. I'm working with you to learn, to understand. So I can leave with knowledge and act. To prevent more death and destruction. I may not be able to save Linaria on my own. I may not even be able to make a difference. But dragons above, I'm going to try. If the esteemed Kalos Topeko can give me a chance, then why won't you?'

He stared at the shocked faces. Of course he stood out. He was no Samolen child brought up in their culture. He wasn't the son of a rich Goldstone looking for the best education in Linaria.

He was a soldier.

One who'd left his comrades to face the horrors of Sapora's wrath while he looked for another way forward. He would always protect those around him—even when he failed.

If Sapora hadn't taken so much power, Linaria would never have found itself in this situation.

If Moroda had killed Aciel instead of sealing him, perhaps Jato would have stayed away and grieved.

But everyone seemed after revenge on everyone else, even him.

And he wanted to put a stop to it.

Surely if peace was his ultimate goal, the Samolen would be able to forgive him?

'Kalosai Morgen. We do not take part in Linaria's wars.' Topeko spoke gently, almost apologetically. 'It is the first of our tenets. The reason why the Sevastos dragons of old saw fit to bestow upon us their crystals. We use their power for peace and protection. Going against this most ancient of laws is not something that can be overlooked. Even if your intentions weren't malicious.'

Morgen's throat tightened as he listened. The death sentence surely wasn't something they could carry out, was it? Would he be dismissed? Exiled? Branded a traitor wherever he went?

'But you *did* save lives today. You even spared the dragon

383

that attacked you.' Topeko's voice echoed all around the hall, and the candle light flickered. The Kalos turned to his book and opened it at a pre-marked section. 'We do not often encounter someone like you. Ranski is a nation away from all others and our laws are not broken. Does the intention forgive the action? I do not know. Does anyone here know?'

The other Kalos went quiet.

Topeko peered at the open pages of his book. 'Nothing here is written, either. So there is no process to follow, no punishment we can justly provide.'

'He cannot act without consequence!' The woman snapped, her yellow jewel blazing gold.

'But it is not for us to say.'

Morgen's nose itched, but he kept his arms firmly at his side. Would he claim the Goddess Rhea had to be the one to judge him? Would there be some test to check his resolve? If not they, the Kalos of Ranski, then who?

Topeko held the room in silence for several long moments. His gaze lingered on every man and woman present, and rested longest of all on Morgen himself. 'It is a matter for the Arch-Kalos.'

The room exploded into noise as the Kalos' spoke all at once, over one another.

Morgen had no idea what it meant, who the Arch-Kalos was, or what they would say about his actions. He tried to listen and only caught snatches of conversation—the din was too much for him to properly grasp what was being said. He assumed the Arch-Kalos was a big deal, perhaps parallel to a king?

'What's to be done with him in the meanwhile?' One Kalos asked. 'He's your charge.'

Topeko nodded. 'He is. And he will remain with me. He'll not enter the city unescorted and certainly never at night. Not until the Arch-Kalos arrives and passes sentence.

Until then, I shall continue with his studies, with a particular focus on the laws of Ranski.'

The Kalos didn't seem happy. When Morgen stole a quick glance at the others, most shared a similar look of disgust.

Morgen had the good sense to keep a grin off his face, but he knew it was simply delaying the inevitable. If he'd be bound to Topeko's home, he could at least speak with him or Andel to find out about the Arch-Kalos. In fact, there'd probably be a book on the topic, knowing the scholar.

He kept his mouth shut as the other Kalos' discussed Topeko's decision among themselves. But it was clear there was nothing to be done tonight, no matter how much they grumbled about it.

Topeko allowed them to have their unhappy chatter for several minutes before he cleared his throat, 'Well, my fellow teachers. If there is nothing more to be said, then I would retire with Kalosai Morgen.'

Eventually, they nodded, their hoods once again covering most of the eyes in the hall.

'Good. Kalosai Morgen, come with me.' Topeko's voice had remained calm and measured throughout the entire affair, but that somehow made Morgen feel worse than if he'd bellowed his anger.

Topeko handed both the candelabra and the book of laws to the two nearest Samolen, then strode from the hall, his robe billowing out behind him.

MUCH AS MORGEN EXPECTED, there was no detour on the walk back to Berel New Town and Topeko's home. The music was still absent, and the hairs on Morgen's arms raised in the quiet gloom.

Andel met them at the doorway, his face as impassive as Topeko's.

Morgen held his gaze, and although Andel held it for a long while, he eventually blinked and looked away.

There was no point in challenging his dismissal. Andel's stare had been more than he'd received from any of the Samolen in town, and he'd been working alongside them to clear the damage.

Morgen wondered if he'd have to spend the next few days in silence, or at least until the Arch-Kalos arrived.

When Morgen thought neither of them would say a word to him, Topeko spoke. 'Get some rest, Morgen. A good night's sleep and a full breakfast in the morning. We'll speak about it then.'

Morgen's eyes widened at the courtesy. Any prisoners in Niversai would be thrown in a cell and given stale bread if they were lucky. The fact that Topeko still wanted him fed and looked after spoke volumes.

He'd been about to agree and hurry off to his room, when he stopped. 'Why?'

'Why what?' Topeko had taken a seat at the dining table where Andel had a small bowl of stewed vegetables waiting for the Kalos.

'Why help me? Defend me? Invite me back to your home and comforts?' Morgen's words came out in a blur, and he tried to hold himself back so as not to overwhelm Topeko.

'We'll speak in the morning.' Topeko repeated the words as he lifted his spoon.

Morgen walked back to the table. 'I need to know.'

The Kalos sighed and looked up. Morgen saw the whites of his eyes were tinged red with tears. 'Must you be so defiant?'

Morgen rolled his shoulders. 'I just want to know. I'm sorry.'

Topeko shook his head. 'Amarah. You remind me too much of her, sometimes.'

Morgen frowned. 'You helped me because I'm like her?'

'She transgressed often. Usually it wasn't her fault. She tried. She wasn't evil, like many of the Kalos said. And...and I don't believe you are, either. Your bloody past isn't easy to erase.'

That cut. Morgen spent a moment dwelling on the meaning of those words. 'Thank you, Topeko. I'm going to rest.'

He didn't know what else to say. What else he *could* say. With a final nod to both Topeko and Andel, Morgen left the room and walked down the corridor to his own chamber.

When he finally reached the sanctuary of his room, he sighed. On the cabinet to his right, there were indeed more books that hadn't been there before. Three of them were thick tomes with dust obscuring the titles on their spines, and the other half dozen or so were smaller but still looked dense.

Morgen ran a hand through his hair as he took in the state of the room. His belongings had been thrown haphazardly across the floor. Clothes, shoes, books, trinkets scattered to each corner. He remembered how much haste he'd been in when he'd looked for his *Valta Forinja*.

His heart pounded.

Where was the sword?

He struggled to think. Things had been chaotic with the dragons attacking and people running for their lives. He'd challenged the dragon, struck it, and it had flown off.

Then what had happened?

He sat down on the edge of his bed and thought. He remembered the dragon flying away, that was quite vivid. And then...?

And then he'd collapsed.

When he'd woken up, evening had fallen, and he'd begun to help the other Samolen clear the streets and repair the damage.

Morgen scratched his head, trying to think, trying to recall some detail.

But it was blank.

Had...had something happened? Had some of the Samolen magic affected him? His memories?

Morgen stood and leaped to the door. But when he grasped the handle and pulled, the door had been locked.

He trembled slightly. He'd known he'd done wrong, known he was effectively a prisoner until the Arch-Kalos arrived. But this?

'Topeko!' Morgen called out. 'Kalos Topeko! I need to speak to you!'

He rattled the door handle, gently at first, then more vigorously. He pounded on the wooden door with his fist. 'Kalos Topeko! What happened? Is my sword with you?'

Panicking, Morgen ran to the window and peeled away the drapes, only to find the window had been sealed in. A wall of stone sat in its place, as though there had never been a window to begin with.

Morgen swallowed. 'Andel? Topeko? Please! What's happening? What's going on?'

He went through the rest of his belongings, going so far as to pick up the trunk and shake it in case they'd missed the small dagger he'd also brought with him.

But he found nothing.

Every weapon had gone, his trunk stripped of all but his necessities, his memories taken. His room had become his prison.

26

Nerves coiled in Amarah's stomach like writhing snakes, and the notion wasn't altogether out of place. She was, after all, about to fly directly into the snake pit of her own free will.

She, Traego, Antar, and Malot had discussed the journey for another couple of hours before Traego had been happy to let his pilots go.

Antar was clearly Traego's second-in-command, but Malot's opinion was also greatly valued. And there was no denying the way Traego looked at her.

By the time they had their route planned and had eaten a good meal, it was almost time to head off. The sooner they flew, the sooner they'd get to Taban Yul—and hopefully avoid Jato's growing thunderstorm. There was no way to know how difficult it would make their flight as Antar had only seen it in the distance when he and Oris had left the city.

Amarah pinned a lot of her nerves down to the thought of encountering Sapora again. She'd never really been afraid of the snake—she just found him disgusting—but he'd been aboard *her* ship, and she'd been in control. Now, he was a king. Now, he had real power.

There was nothing to stop him arresting them on sight. But if she brought him Veynothi's blade, it might be enough to keep them alive. And despite Traego's optimism that they'd all leave the city with their ships and gold, Amarah wasn't so sure. She'd always been highly suspicious, and a healthy amount of caution had kept her out of real trouble for most of her life. So she prepared for the worst—being arrested.

She had helped herself to the various lockpicks of Traego's stash and raided his tools for anything that might be useful if she ended up being trapped in the palace.

And if she needed to fight, she no longer had an ace up her sleeve. She'd abandoned her *Valta Forinja* on the beach when the sea monster had attacked, and had no intention of going back for it. As formidable a weapon as it was, she needed all her wits about her.

She couldn't afford to break down again, not against Sapora and all his Varkain.

No. She needed to go back to basics and re-arm herself with a normal weapon created with steel and nothing else. No magic. No powers. No added flair.

She'd fled Ranski because she couldn't read nor perform magic that was supposed to be innate—especially because of her blood. She'd cut out her cheek jewel and forged a new life for herself in Corhaven.

The thought of having another magical weapon that had the power to curse her made her skin crawl.

Once the finer details of their plan had been confirmed, Amarah slipped away to get her hands on another scythe. Kohl's sour face hadn't been lost on her, and she'd purposely avoided talking to him about Jato any more than was necessary.

And while she didn't like the idea of not being able to fly her own ship—typical that it was snatched away before she had the chance to use it—she wouldn't trust anyone else with her wings than Traego. She'd piloted *Otella* several times while she'd been working with him, and she had let him fly *Khanna* once. So it made sense that she could entrust her ship to him.

That, and it was Traego's way of ensuring she came back to him after she grabbed as much of Sapora's gold as she could. Of course.

Ally, not a friend, Amarah reminded herself.

By the time they all met up again on the beach, the sun had already begun its descent to the horizon. Antar had said if the route was clear, they'd reach Taban Yul by dawn the next morning—the third day since he'd been there with Oris.

Amarah disliked night flying at the best of times, and considering she hadn't flown a ship properly since losing her eye, she was more apprehensive about the flight than she normally would be. But Judd would be with her on board *Otella*, and Antar would lead the way on Princess Isa's class five.

'I'll be picking up ya new ship about the time ya get ta Taban Yul,' Traego said. 'So we'll be a day behind ya at most.'

Amarah nodded. The new scythe she'd picked out wasn't anything close to the quality that Palom had made, but it would have to do. After all, she wasn't planning on taking on Jato. This was a mission to get to Isa, get the gold, and get back.

Her scythe was more to have something to hold. The weapon gave her a sense of security that she couldn't put into words. Once they'd navigated the pirate-strewn air around Estoria, they had to cross the Sea of Nami with

Veynothi's blade on board. The sea monster couldn't fly, but the thought of it in the water below, following her, made her want to vomit. They had to navigate the Feor Mountain range to reach the valley on the other side, where Taban Yul sat, and avoid the thunderstorm and Arillians who were moving in slowly. And, of course, hope the Sevastos didn't attack them.

That said nothing of the Varkain that Sapora had in the palace, and whether or not the king would order their deaths once he had what he wanted: Veynothi's blade as proof, and information on where it came from. If Sapora was a sky pirate, she'd put money on that happening.

But Sapora was a Varkain, and she had no idea what he would do in this situation.

Amarah had to hope that he was so desperate for news on the Ark that he'd let them leave with the promised gold instead of arresting them as sky pirates.

'A day behind us. Right.' Amarah nodded, trying to keep her focus. Although she had a scythe, it wasn't her *Valta Forinja*. She hated herself for having relied on the dragon-forged weapon for so long.

She never relied on anyone. But this time, the weapon had used her as much as she had used it. Damned cursed thing.

Once all this mess had been sorted out, she was going to track down Palom and make him forge her a whole set of scythes. That would keep her going until the end of her days.

'I've reloaded *Otella*'s cannons with *dragon's breath*, so they're ready if you need them,' Malot said. 'There are also a couple of shrouds, too. If I'd had more time, I would have loaded the ship properly.' She looked down for a moment.

Amarah shook her head. 'What you've done is fine. If Traeg's right, there won't be no fighting anyway.'

'I hope. But we're dealing with kings and ancient powers. Who knows what'll happen.'

Amarah couldn't argue with that. She respected the fact that Malot was blunt and practical. She could see why Traego valued her so much. 'Why don't you come with? You know *Otella* as well as Judd or Traego. Be useful to have you.'

The woman thought about it for a moment.

'Go if ya want,' Traego said. 'If anything, ya can be a go between. We won't be far behind.'

'Fine. I'll come along for the ride,' Malot said.

Amarah smiled. 'Appreciate it.'

Judd shuffled forward, kicking sand up in great plumes with every step. He shouldered a large sack and gestured to it with his head. 'Supplies. We should be there within a day, but better to have extras in case we're thrown off course by the storm. Flying blind is never fun.'

'Good,' Amarah replied. Malot and Judd walked past her and clambered up the steps on *Otella*'s side and to the deck.

'Traeg, I got a bad feeling.' Amarah said, once Judd was out of sight. 'You never met Sapora, you don't know what he's like.'

Traego shrugged. 'I've met plenty of Varkain. They ain't so different from us. They want what they want. They'll fight ta get it.' He unhooked the sword sheathed at his hip and held it out to her. 'The proof for the king.'

Amarah swallowed. This was the reason for the monster. The curse.

With a huff, she grabbed it from him, ensuring she only touched the leather sheath and not the stone blade itself. They'd only just seen off the monster, and she had no desire to draw it to them again so quickly.

She resorted to an aggressive defense to cover her nerves. 'You treat my ship nice, Traeg. It's been through a lot and I ain't even been in the air on her once.'

Traego chuckled. 'Who d'ya think I am? O' course I'll treat her nice. We'll be followin' ya. Malot's gonna load her up with her magic so we can fend off any Arillians who come try their luck.'

Amarah couldn't say anything to that.

A short way ahead, Antar and Oris were already on board Isa's ship, the propellers whirring happily.

She glanced around to the others. Traego and Malot, Ernold and Farlan, Carav and Kohl.

She couldn't put it off any longer. 'I'll see you in a day, then. If King Snake don't kill us all, first.'

'He won't,' Traego said. Amarah almost believed the confidence in his voice. 'He'll be too busy after his own treasure ta care. Ya know how some o' us can get. He'll be the same. He wants the Ark about as much as *we* want his gold.'

Amarah wasn't sure about that at all, but she didn't have a choice.

She had a royal summons from Princess Isa, and the proof of the Ark for King Sapora. Waiting around on Estoria while she tried to overcome her nerves wouldn't help matters, and time was quickly slipping away from them.

'Amarah.'

It was Kohl.

She lifted her chin to look him in the eyes but kept her lips pressed tightly shut.

'I do not know what Jato's plans are. I fear she seeks revenge against Linaria for what happened to Aciel. If our Ice Golems are capable of resurrecting Moroda, they will be capable of bringing Aciel back, too. I do not know enough about the powers of a Sevastos to know if our Golems can counter them.'

Amarah nodded slowly and wondered what he wanted.

Kohl continued, 'I would like to investigate this. Use my

394

experience as a dragon hunter to track them down and find out what I can about the destruction they've wrought. Perhaps I can stop Jato, too.'

'Good luck with that.' It was all Amarah could think to say. 'I still want revenge against her for what she did, y'know. What she took from me. That ain't stopping. But I need to reply to Isa. So Jato's on hold for now.'

'And I appreciate that,' Kohl replied. 'I cannot come with you. I'd...I'd only slow you down.'

Amarah sighed. In all the discussions and planning, Kohl hadn't been factored in. She'd just assumed he'd fly with them as he always did. But now he actually seemed to have the guts to speak his mind to her.

Before she could say anything in response, Kohl said, 'I can do more good by investigating the dragons. You...what you're doing now? This is what you've always done. You don't need me for that. And considering King Sapora created the bounty on Arillians, flying near my kin and into his city seems an unwise choice.'

Amarah couldn't argue with that. She could see how dejected he was, and she softened. 'Where you gonna go?'

Kohl looked out to sea, the breeze ruffling his hair and wings as he stared into the distance. 'I'll follow the dragons to wherever I need to go. Beyond that, it's hard to say.'

Amarah thought about it, rolling her tongue against her cheek as she did so. 'You still owe me, you know? I got myself a ship because I can't sit around and wait when I have an opportunity dropped in front of me. But I'll be coming to collect once I've sorted out Isa and Jato. I'll fly back to Oren if I have to, even with your Ice Golems there. They let me in before, they might again.'

A ghost of a smile flickered across Kohl's scarred face, but he didn't say anything against her flying back to the floating islands. 'Then I shall leave you with your comrades?'

It was almost as if Kohl was asking permission. 'And I'll see you when it's over. Come back to Estoria when you're done and fill me in. Otherwise I'll hunt you down in Oren.'

Kohl smiled then. 'Thank you, Amarah. Safe travels and speedy flights.' He leaned forward and grasped her forearm.

Amarah grabbed his arm in return and felt the chill of his Frost-touch even through their clothes. She wondered what power Kohl really had, if he wasn't so cowardly and afraid to use it. 'You too.'

'Amarah. We good to go?' Judd yelled from the deck of *Otella*. The sudden chug of propellers sent sand flying as Traego's ship rose about a foot off the beach.

She waved at Judd and hurried to the ship. With a short jump, she clambered onto and then up the steps to join the other pilot on *Otella*'s deck. Antar and Oris were already in the air and hovered a short way out to sea, waiting for them.

'Sorry, had to sort some things out.' Amarah swiftly apologised to Judd. She looked over the side to where Traego and the others gathered, and then to Kohl. The Arillian watched her for a long moment before stretching his wings and leaping into the air.

Within a few powerful beats, Kohl had risen and then turned to fly back deeper into Estoria.

'No time to waste,' Amarah said. She strode to the wheel of *Otella* and gripped the spokes firmly.

'Sky's clear. Sun's still up. We should get a good way over the sea before nightfall,' Judd called. He took a position near the prow of the boat, near the yellowed boar's head carved into the ship's front.

Amarah grinned. 'Then let's get our gold.'

~

TEARS THREATENED, but Kohl ignored them. He had thought saying goodbye to Amarah would be easy. After all, they'd come to actual blows and had argued almost constantly since they began travelling together. Being away from her would be relief more than anything else. He would no longer have to listen to or see her criminal ways, ignore her anger and aggression, and pretend to accept what she did.

But seeing her on that great warship, about to cross the sea and into the snake pit? Something about that had caused a lump in his throat.

He hoped her thirst for gold was stronger than her thirst for revenge. After all, she'd be flying within spitting distance of Jato and her followers. If she had a warship at her finger-tips, there was nothing that could stop her from blasting them all out of the sky.

He just had to hope that Jato didn't attack first.

Amarah would defend herself from any aggressor, of that he was certain. If Jato watched but didn't approach, then perhaps there wouldn't be any more bloodshed. Both women were foolish enough to fight to the death, and he doubted anyone nearby would be willing—or able—to stop them if they fought.

Kohl flew higher than he would have liked, but the bounty on Arillians was still a real threat, and keeping himself out of view while he flew was the safest thing. When on ground, his enormous cloak covered his wings, and he could pass for an Ittallan as long as no-one looked at him too closely.

The idea of finally leaving Estoria brightened his spirits somewhat. He'd find Fogu and the two of them would leave immediately. While he knew Fogu wished to return to Oren, Kohl needed to investigate the dragons, first. That hadn't been a lie, and he intended to keep his word.

Although quite what he'd learn—much less how to implement it—he wasn't sure, but by the Ice Golems, he'd try.

Kohl hovered and tried to get his bearings. All the beaches in Estoria looked much the same, and he couldn't recall which one he'd been on when he'd bumped into Fogu. He supposed he could land on each of them one by one, until he recognised where he was, but that would take time, and Fogu had probably been waiting for most of the day already.

He squinted down through the thin clouds as he tried to pick out landmarks or trees that might jog his memory. The heat of the sun in this part of the world seemed to cause a constant haze in the air that distorted his view of the other side, which didn't help matters at all.

Deciding to risk flying lower for a better view, Kohl gently dropped in altitude, his wings fanning out to slow and control his descent. The haze below him grew thicker, and he masked his eyes with his hands against the flickering air.

And then he saw the airship's mast.

'NOW!' A voice roared from his left.

Kohl whirled around in time to see a heavy net hurled towards him. He twisted to the side to avoid the net, but another fell on him from behind, ensnaring his wings.

He dropped like a stone, falling through the haze of the *Thief's Shroud*, and his eyes widened as the airship materialised in front of his eyes.

Another net fell on him from above as panic tore through him, and then he landed with a sickening crunch on the deck of a ship a little smaller than *Otella*.

'Tie his wrists!' The same loud voice as before ordered.

He'd landed hard on his knees, the ricochet of the impact jarring his entire body.

People swarmed him like ants. Too many to count.

Their arms grasped at him, rope crossed his arms and legs, and their drawn knives cut into his flesh and drew blood from a dozen different points. Pain laced his body, and white spots filled his vision.

'Thank Rhea we got one!' Another sky pirate yelled, tightening the knot at Kohl's wrists. He shoved a bundled rag that stank of seawater into Kohl's mouth and then tied another rope around his face to keep it in place.

These sky pirates were taking no chances.

The shock and pain of his sudden capture stopped Kohl from struggling, from saying anything. He'd been mistreated before, but never man-handled to this degree.

His wrists were bound behind him, pressed uncomfortably against his wings. Other pirates had tied his legs together at the knees and ankles, and Kohl toppled over onto his side like a sack of grain. As he lay prone and vulnerable, the solid kicks of heavy boots pummelled him over and over.

Kohl could do nothing but whimper meekly as they had their fun.

'Okay, okay, enough. I said enough, lads.'

From the deck floor, Kohl could only see the soles of the man's feet as he shooed his crew away. Kohl assumed he was the captain, or at least in charge of the others.

'Let's get turned around! Need this one locked in ASAP!' He boomed.

Kohl trembled involuntarily in response to the pain.

'I told yeh!' A new voice said, hurrying over and shaking the deck with every step. 'I told yeh this was the one what was with Traeg and Amarah!'

'Good lad, Reg,' the first man said. 'Hear that, ya silly bird? Traeg don't want ya no more so ya don't got no protection. I get my bounty and these lads get ta fill their pockets with the king's gold.'

Kohl shuddered. Blood from a cut across his right eyebrow trickled slowly down his face and into his eye. He blinked rapidly to clear it, but he couldn't so much as turn his head. He recognised the voice as the drunk sky pirate from the beach the night the monster attacked.

He should have known better than to fly in the open with every pirate in Estoria looking for Arillians to capture.

He'd seen his kin killed right in front of his eyes.

How could he have been so stupid?

Kohl struggled against the ropes binding him, but the pirates knew their knots and at most he could wiggle his fingertips. He forced his eyes closed and concentrated, trying to summon up his Frost-touch. The ropes binding his wrist tightened as they grew brittle in the sudden cold, and he grunted with the effort of using his power while bound.

'Don't you be trying none of that!' The captain said, walking to the side and stamping on Kohl's bound wrists.

The pain of bones fracturing tore through Kohl with more force than anything he'd ever felt before. He lost his grasp on his Frost-touch and the ropes slackened slightly.

'You try anything like that again...' The captain trailed off, his boot still pressed firmly on Kohl's wrists. '...and your death'll be slow and painful.' He put his full weight onto Kohl's left wrist, and Kohl heard his little finger pop as the bone cracked under the boot.

Kohl screamed around the gag, the noise coming out as a muffled gurgle.

The captain didn't relent, shifting his weight slightly, and breaking Kohl's fourth finger next. 'I can break all the others one by one. That'll be just the start, ya understand?'

Kohl understood but couldn't say anything. The pain was too much.

'I need ya ta say ya understand.' He increased the pressure again, on Kohl's middle finger this time.

The most Kohl could do was let out a squeak as his head lolled forward.

Another voice called out, 'Captain, the pits are ahead. Want us to dump him in now?'

Tears fell, stained with pink from the bleeding on his face, and Kohl squeezed one eye open to see them drip onto the deck. He couldn't move, couldn't speak, couldn't do anything.

'This one ain't got no more fight in him anymore. They care too much about their fingers.' The captain let out a deep belly laugh that shook the deck of the ship. 'Might as well get him off here and start looking for the next one.'

'Aye, sir.'

Kohl swallowed thickly, his vision tinged black as consciousness threatened to leave him.

The captain kicked him again, shoving him across the deck. Kohl rolled several times and saw the bloody smears on the wood from his wounds. He tried to keep his head forward so as not to choke on the rag shoved into his mouth, but knew it wouldn't matter soon.

Estoria wasn't a large place, and the drowning pits were a centre of entertainment for the pirates and Estorians both.

Why would these pirates wait to claim their reward?

'Pell, ya got our banner?'

'Aye, just coming.' A woman replied to the captain's question.

From his side, Kohl watched the young pirate hurry over, a strip of brightly coloured fabric trailing in her wake.

'Good lass. We'll have something ta eat and then collect the body.' He took the fabric from her and approached Kohl.

When the captain knelt down to tie the strip around his neck, Kohl smelled unwashed clothes, stale sweat, and pipe-smoke. If these weren't his last breaths, Kohl would have pushed away. But the suddenness and pain of the attack and his broken fingers had rendered him meek as a lamb awaiting slaughter.

'Lower the rail,' the captain barked, as three other pirates hurried forward. They unhinged a small section of the side and kicked it flat.

The scent of salt filled Kohl's nose as the captain rolled him toward the opening with the toe of his boot. It cleansed away the stench of the pirate somewhat and Kohl took a few deep breaths through his nose.

'Even if ya can swim, ya won't last. Most of ya are dead within an hour.'

Bile rose in Kohl's throat at the captain's sickening words and the fear of what awaited him.

Finally, his head lolled over the edge of the ship, and Kohl saw with his own eyes what fate had claimed the other Arillians captured in Estoria. The drop had to be a good fifty feet, and the abyss below beckoned like the mouth of a hungry creature. Even from this height, Kohl heard the sea water sloshing against the square pit dug into the island. The wind caught him, blowing his hair into his face and masking his view.

'Lower us a tad, will ya?' The captain called out, and the ship groaned as it struggled against the wind to approach the pit.

When the drop had lessened to twenty feet, the captain decided it was close enough. He knelt down again to double-check his flag was secure. 'I should thank ya for filling my belly and pockets. Great bounty on these birds, this is.'

He leaned in close so Kohl could see the man's face clearly. He had a thick black beard, small, beady eyes, and far too much gold jewellery around his neck.

The captain didn't hesitate. He grabbed Kohl by the scruff of his cloak, then pushed him overboard and into the drowning pit below.

403

27

I sa watched Summercourt unfold from her seat at the servant's table. She knew most of the Archigo by name —after all, she'd grown up in the palace and had been present when many of the Ittallan leaders had visited—but Sapora, Tacio, and the other Varkain certainly didn't seem to have done their research.

Many of the Ittallan had to introduce themselves two or three times, and Sapora appeared almost irritated by the conversation. Their blatant disrespect made her so uncomfortable, she kept her head down and focussed on her drink to distance herself from her half-brothers.

Tacio just seemed bored. The prince played with his food, shut down conversation, and drank far too much wine. At least if she'd been able to keep her original seat by Sapora's side, she could guide the king with the introductions.

But Sapora seemed to care more about speaking with his father, the Valendrin, and the other Varkain than managing the Ittallan.

Today marked the second day of Summercourt—the traditional event where new council members were selected and laws were written—and Isa knew Sapora simply used it as something to keep himself busy while he waited for proof of Veynothi. It was stupid that Sapora was more interested in whether Traego was telling the truth than running the country he claimed to rule. It annoyed her that they were squandering the best chance to unite the Varkain and Ittallan by behaving like petulant children.

Summercourt had been a traditional event held when the country needed new blood in its leadership, and Archigo had the chance to influence all of Val Sharis, instead of only their own town or village. Ittallan from all around the country would flock to the capital to be present for the announcements and to meet the esteemed leaders of their country.

She'd counseled Sapora to take on at least three or four of the Archigo—many of whom would support him and help change the public's perception of the new king. Tacio, of course, wanted only Varkain on the council. If Sapora's goal truly was to unite the two races, then he'd need to integrate instead of push out.

So far, all Sapora had done was bring more Varkain into the country and expect the Ittallan to accept them without question.

Summercourt had taken much the same route, and she felt foolish for having thought Sapora would give her advice consideration.

Ever present, Roke remained by Sapora's side throughout, as did Tacio's Cerastes. The Cerastes still watched her, even when they ignored her. When she excused herself for some air, more Cerastes followed. When she retired to her chambers at the end of the day, other Cerastes guarded her doors.

She half expected to have a personal guard thrust upon her who could keep a closer watch than anyone else. And

Isa didn't dare leave the palace to update Aetos and the others. Not before Summercourt ended, anyway.

Even the servants mostly ignored her. Of those who did realise she was the princess, and thusly nodded to her in greeting—she'd never warrant a full bow with Sapora and Tacio in the room—many were polite, if frosty. Those who didn't know treated her as though she were invisible. Many took cues from the Varkain present and as the snakes saw her as beneath their notice, the servants followed suit.

So she remained quiet, kept herself presentable, and tried to listen to as much conversation as she could. She'd need to report to the others just as soon as she could get away.

Perhaps if Sapora, at least, had taken her more seriously, it would never have come to betrayal. She'd backed him because of their childhood. She'd agreed to help him when he took the jade crown because he'd promised a better future for all of them—one where they weren't insulted or looked down upon. One where they had the power of their birthright. One where everyone was equal, instead of a select few with the right blood in their veins.

Isa sipped her water as a new Archigo entered the room near the end of the day. She recognised his features but didn't know him by name. From his stature and colouration, Isa could tell he was from the north, perhaps as far as Gal Etra, and definitely a hunter. At least they commanded a little more respect from the Varkain than fodder.

But Sapora seemed to dislike his lateness, despite his long journey to the capital, and she sank back in her seat as her brother brushed over the interruption and continued his conversation with Vasil.

Her confidence in her brother had vanished. He'd ignored the pressing threats of the city, focussed on his Ark hunt, and ended up burning half of Taban Yul to the ground with a Sevastos—one she hadn't even known he had.

It wasn't the two of them against the world.

It was just him.

As the day drew on and the afternoon sun streamed through the floor-to-ceiling windows, Sapora finally called the day's discussions to an end. He'd heard all he needed from the Archigos for that day, and would reconvene in the morning.

Isa raised her eyebrows when Koraki made the announcement, and then the grumbles and muttering followed from the gathered Archigo as they were again shoved to one side. They stood in respect and watched as Sapora pushed his chair back to stand. 'We shall continue at breakfast. I'm sure you'll enjoy the city and palace while you rest.'

He spoke to the Valendrin, but with chairs scraping against the floor and chatter breaking out among the gathered Ittallan and Varkain, Isa couldn't make out the words.

Isa watched them speak with narrowed eyes, and then stood as they made their way along the table and past where she waited.

'Sister. I do hope you have not grown too weary following all these discussions?' Sapora asked, pausing a few steps away from her.

She blinked at his passive aggression and held back a growl of annoyance. 'Not at all.'

'Good. Please come with me.'

Sapora continued on, with Roke hot on his heels, Tacio and the Valendrin following close behind.

Isa had no idea what her brother was playing at, but it seemed he had invited her to a private discussion with the most important Varkain. She simply nodded and followed quietly, careful not to draw any unwanted attention to herself.

She'd regressed to how she'd behaved as a child. Head down. Avoiding eye contact. Speaking only when spoken to. It had always been the way she'd survived, especially when there were Varkain in the palace. Isa hated being so weak, but she knew it was only temporary. She just needed to get through the next few days, and hopefully Amarah would come to her aid. She'd paid the sky pirate enough gold after Aciel's defeat. That, if anything, would be enough to bring her back, Isa hoped.

Sapora led them through the palace hallways, Roke and the others only a few steps behind, while Isa trailed them all. She knew Tacio's Cerastes would follow at a distance, ever watching, but considering she was obeying Sapora's direct order, their presence didn't bother her for once.

Isa had a feeling she knew exactly where Sapora was taking them but furrowed her eyebrows when he led them away from his rooms and deeper into the palace.

The council tower, perhaps?

Her suspicions proved correct when they reached the bottom of the tower, and Sapora ordered Roke to stand guard while he and the others made their way to the top to discuss urgent matters. She followed them through the doors and hurried up the winding stone stairway, their foot-steps echoing all around them.

Dread rose in her chest, and the desire to run away along with it.

Only when they entered the council chamber and closed the door behind them did Sapora address them.

'I apologise that you have had to endure Summercourt. Some of this country's traditions...'

'Not a problem, my liege.' The Valendrin held up a hand, and Isa saw his claws were overgrown, curled, and black with dirt. His skin—part-scaled like most Varkain—was pale and papery and peeled back from his cuticles to leave a thin line of dark blood on every finger. Purple veins lined every inch of flesh, and Isa wondered how much power the blood magic actually gave him to reduce his body to such a hideous state.

Just the sight of his hand made Isa want to be sick, but she needed to keep her focus. She'd long suspected Sapora wanted to speak with the Valendrin about the Arks, and wondered if she was about to be proven correct.

Sapora strode towards the large table in the centre of the tower, upon which maps of varying ages had been left strewn haphazardly, and leaned on it. 'You will be aware of the problems caused by the Arillians in Val Sharis?' He addressed the three of them.

Tacio and the Valendrin nodded, and Isa knew the question was so obvious she didn't bother to react. She crossed the room to peer out of the tower window but kept most of her attention on the Varkain.

Sapora continued, 'I'm told they are being led by one Arillian. Jato. She worked with Aciel and may be trying to get to him.' He pointed at the illustration of Taban Yul on the map, and then drew a claw over to the Feor Mountains nearby. 'The large thunderstorm gathering over the Feor Mountains is gathering strength. It appears to be growing every day and now stretches towards the city, which is preventing many of our airships from flying safely.'

Tacio made his way to the large cabinet at the head of the table and helped himself to another large goblet of red wine. 'Why should we concern ourselves with one Arillian? She's insignificant.'

'May I remind you of the devastation Aciel caused? He was only *one* Arillian,' Sapora replied coldly.

Tacio shrugged and took a large gulp of his drink. 'Didn't bother us in Sereth.'

The audacity of Tacio irritated Isa. 'Because you were hiding down there, in your tunnels!'

Tacio gave her a long look. 'We weren't *hiding* anywhere. We live there. For good reason.' He took another large swallow and said, 'We'll win. Nothing to worry about.'

'Oh? And what makes you so sure?' Sapora asked, turning to face Tacio.

Tacio simply grinned around his goblet as he drank. 'You aren't the only one with a trump card.'

Isa worried what on earth Tacio meant, but he didn't share.

The silence grew around them, punctuated only by Tacio's noisy gulps, when Sapora decided not to entertain Tacio, and turned his attention back to the Valendrin. 'I've been re-reading our history and speaking with Vasil. I know the Valendrin created four Arks over five thousand years ago. Karekis, Malashash, Veynothi, and Brahm. Accounts of their abilities are vague, but they are—and were—the most powerful force ever to live, as far as any of Linaria's histories can attest. Is this correct?'

Isa tried not to look at the blood mage directly in the eye, for she feared she'd somehow be sucked into his gaze and never return to her body again.

'You are correct, my liege. My brothers and sisters in blood magic are extremely long-lived, and yet none of them, nor I, created the Arks ourselves. Those who did are long dead. Why discuss this now?'

'Because I want to bring them back. If Jato is successful in freeing Aciel, we'll be thrown into the middle of a war. Even if she is unable to, Aciel's influence is seeping through the city like poison. His corruptive powers have caused dozens to kill themselves and turned even more Ittallan mad. It's a kettle about to boil and overflow, and I must be ready for when that happens. I can think of no better power against that than the Arks.'

Isa hadn't known Sapora to speak so candidly. Half the world knew of his bounty on the Arks, but she supposed half the world had no idea what the Arks actually *were*. As far as they were concerned, it was a simple hunt for ancient relics in exchange for gold.

Only the Varkain—and only really the Valendrin—knew just what those Arks were capable of.

Sapora added, 'The immortal protectors of the Varkain. There's no better time to bring them back.'

The Valendrin watched Sapora with deep suspicion and didn't seem moved.

Tacio continued to drink, taking a seat in one of the large, high-backed council chairs, and smirked has he watched his brother struggle to convince the blood mage.

Sapora licked his fangs. 'I know more than my father. He may have been a warrior-king, but I have travelled the length and breadth of Linaria. I know more than any of the Varkain royalty for several generations. The jade crown enables me to rule in Sereth. It also grants me access our greatest powers. Moroda's sacrifice stopped the war against Aciel by using the power of a Sevastos. It reminded me of my histories. If the dragons decide to burn all Linaria, there isn't much any of us can do to stop them...except, perhaps, the Arks. Bringing them back will safeguard us. But if they can be brought back, it shows that a Sevastos' power is not absolute. It means Aciel can come back too. If Aciel is able to break free before we are ready, I don't think even my Sevastos can stop him. But the Arks? It's a fail-safe plan to ensure Linaria survives. After all, I cannot rule a dead world. But what I don't know, despite my best efforts, is *how* to bring them back.'

He looked pointedly at the Valendrin, and even Tacio seemed disinterested in his wine.

The blood took in a deep breath, his thin body expanding with air as he steeled himself against the barrage of words and the question at the end of it. When he turned his head to think, Isa saw the bones of his skull pressing through his skin, and she quickly looked away.

Pressing his advantage, Sapora continued, 'I've been scouring the tomes in our libraries. Read books brought from Sereth, Corhaven, Ranski. I've been studying them, cross-referencing them, looking for things which crop up over and over, things that might glean some insight into how to break the seal. I know a Sevastos sealed them. I don't know why, or how.'

Eventually, the Valendrin spoke in a slow, lethargic tone, 'The immortals were created through the deepest use of our blood magic, twisting their forms and giving them exponential power. They devastated Val Sharis, killing and enslaving Ittallan for our royal family during the war. No-one was safe against their power.'

Isa sat on the windowsill and drew her knees up to her chest as she listened.

'When the Sevastos the Arks, it could not kill them. The savagery of the immortals was forever sealed away, and the Arks became nought but legends. A Sevastos demands death, you see. The ultimate sacrifice for the use of their power. Funny, they aren't so different from us.' The blood mage grinned wickedly, skin pulling up to reveal gums and layers of pointed teeth. 'The Arks could not be killed and so the Sevastos did not fulfil its promise—its power bound to the Varkain forever more. But I digress. The Arks were created with blood magic. It is again with blood magic that there is a chance they may be freed.'

'Wouldn't that reverse the bond with the Sevastos?' Isa

asked, her heart pounding. 'That...that it would no longer be under Sapora's control?'

'I think not,' Sapora said. 'The payment has been made. The debt is the debt. Its power is mine.'

Isa bit her thumb. That didn't seem right at all. Ideas rolled around in her mind like a hurricane, but there were too many for her to pin them down.

'I don't know what they are,' Tacio said. His voice slurred a little, but he did a good job of covering most of it. 'What are they? Old Guard? Something else?'

'You're a prince and don't even know that?' The Valendrin hissed, venom lacing every word.

Tacio shrugged. 'I doubt Vasil himself knows much about them. Why would we need to know about ancient fighters when Vasil conquered everything?'

Sapora didn't bother to hide his grin. 'The Old Guard were Varkain strengthened by blood magic. Bigger forms. Longer lives. More power. It's why defeating one is the only way to the jade crown.'

The Valendrin nodded in approval. 'Correct, my liege. Unfortunately, it made them...volatile. While they were unquestionably great defenders of Sereth, the Old Guard often went mad and turned on other Varkain, or even killed themselves, if they didn't have a proper focus, proper control. A double-edged sword, both one of the Valendrin's greatest successes and failures. We created the Arks to look after the Old Guard. They were the great commanders; immortal leaders cited to bring the Varkain into a new era. The blood magic needed to create them required enormous deaths. As such, we could only create four of them.'

'Prince Karekis was the first Ark,' Sapora said. Isa couldn't help but hear the reverence in his voice. It terrified her.

The Valendrin nodded his approval. 'He was the first. He

was the most powerful and led the Old Guard against the Ittallan during the war. They were unstoppable weapons, all of them. Malashash always defended Sereth. Brahm defended our borders from sea attacks with his monster, and Veynothi sapped our enemies' strength. We Varkain were the undisputed victors of the war!'

'Sounds great.' Tacio said, pouring himself another goblet and oblivious to his rudeness. 'Where's the Sevastos come to play in all this?'

The blood mage let out a low hiss. 'Our magic is more powerful than any other. But it is unstable. Flawed. The Arks acted on their own, ignoring the orders of other Varkain, including our King and Queen. They couldn't be fully controlled. Our...our greatest weapons became our greatest threat. Before they could destroy not just Sereth, but all of Linaria, our royals turned to a Sevastos. They pleaded with it to stop that which they'd created—and a Sevastos was the only power that could stand up to them.'

'But it couldn't kill them...' Isa said, almost numb. 'They were...they *are* immortal.'

'You are correct.' The Valendrin studied her a moment before turning back to Sapora. 'Having failed in its task, the Varkain commanded the Sevastos to sleep deep within the bowels of Sereth until such a time as it was called upon again to fulfil its oath.'

'And then we lost the war,' Tacio said.

Sapora echoed, 'And then we lost the war. Forced into our tunnels like rats.'

The Valendrin said, 'King Sapora. My liege. Having heard how close we came to losing our world to the Arks, how can you hope to bring them back? They may have enough power to protect us from our threats, but after? I must advise against this course of action.'

Sapora looked up sharply, his pupils contracting in

anger at being challenged. 'We lost the war. We were pushed back into our tunnels. Vasil may have re-conquered the Ittallan in one brutal, bloody night. He may have fathered myself and Isa with Ittallan women to bind our races. But we are loathed. Hated. Despised. Feared. I *will* be better than my father. With the Arks returned and a Sevastos to keep them under control, the Varkain will be the true power in Linaria. No more Arillians. No more Imperial Guard.'

Isa swallowed.

'I am here to show the world that we do not fear dragons. To prove that a Sevastos is a beast like any other—able to be tamed or killed. I admit their power is significant. I admit the magic from their existence should be respected. But it is *not* the only power in Linaria. The Varkain have been here since time began. We have been shunned and spat upon.' Sapora looked meaningfully at Tacio. 'Our pride may have let us adapt to this life in the dark. But I refuse. I refuse to fear the Arillians, the dragons, or their magic. That's why I need to bring back the Arks. I need them to save this wretched world from itself, and show all of Linaria that we are not to be ignored and pushed around. Not anymore. We do not bow to anyone.'

Her brother had spoken with such force, with such passion, that Isa had almost believed that what he had said was indeed the right thing. That she *ought* to stand by him in his quest to restore the Arks. That it was best for Linaria that he did so.

Almost.

The Valendrin stared at Sapora in stunned silence.

Tacio's glass lay half-full and forgotten in his hand as he watched Sapora through wide eyes.

Eventually, the blood mage said, 'I shall consult my ancestor's books, King Sapora. There may be a way to break these seals.'

At the Valendrin's words, Isa knew she'd lost her brother to blood magic. He'd wanted this power for so long, could practically taste it, and now the final lock would be opened. There was no going back now.

She watched, teary-eyed, as Sapora approached the Valendrin like a man possessed. Tacio, too, was transfixed by the knowledge, and Isa took her chance.

In a flash, she'd transformed, and slipped out of the council tower window.

～

ISA RACED THROUGH THE CITY, keeping to alleyways and side streets where she could, and leaping from rooftop to rooftop where she couldn't. Taban Yul had taken on several thousand more people in the days leading up to Summercourt, and Isa couldn't remember the last time it had been so busy. She made her way south—directly this time, there was no point to take any longer than necessary—heading straight for Little Yomal.

Isa pulled up short when she reached one of the small bridges leading to the residential district, where the couple had killed themselves not two days prior. Solvi sat on the bridge, legs dangling over the edge as she peered into the rushing waters below.

Isa quickly glanced around to check whether any Cerastes were nearby, and breathed a sigh of relief when she failed to spot any. 'Solvi!'

The young Ittallan looked up immediately and was back on her feet half a heartbeat later. 'Princess Isa! What are you doing? I thought Summercourt was—'

'There isn't time.' Isa interrupted her. 'The situation in Taban Yul is at breaking point with Aciel's power. The

Archigo have all reported dragon attacks, Arillian attacks, or both. And the worst is yet to come.'

'Worse? How could it possibly get worse?' Solvi sighed.

'Sapora's going to free the Arks.'

'Yes, we know this is his goal—'

'No, no. You don't understand. He's really going to do it. He's with one of our Valendrins right now, learning how to break the seal!'

'Valendrin?' Solvi asked, tilting her head to one side.

Isa had forgotten just how young the Ittallan was. 'They're blood mages. They're responsible for creating the Arks however many thousands of years ago. Sapora wanted them to come to the palace under the ruse of Summercourt so he could figure out how to break the seal and free the Arks. It's happening. It's happening now.'

Solvi's eyes widened as the enormity of the situation grasped her. 'But...then...what do we do? Aetos said my *kali* is coming to the city. He is bringing more Ittallan who believe you should be queen.'

Solvi's words threw Isa. 'Your *kali*? Palom? He's coming back?'

'Yes. Not everyone's happy, though. Aetos is trying to bring people around. But many think he's a coward. Or that he betrayed Lathri.'

'Of course he didn't betray her! Sapora sent Mateli to *kill* him!' Isa shouted.

Solvi nodded. 'Yes, *I* know this. I am pleased we have him back. He is the great tiger. I just want to see my *kali* again.'

'Me, too.' Isa gave Solvi a warm smile, as genuine as she could muster under the current circumstances. 'Solvi, listen. I have a plan to free Lathri and the other rebels. They'll be out of Sapora's clutches and safe.'

Solvi nodded slowly and gave her a hesitant smile that didn't reach her eyes.

'Don't worry. I'm getting outside help. A sky pirate will help us.'

'A sky pirate?' Solvi asked.

'I know it sounds silly. But I can't think of anyone better to break valuable treasures out of heavily guarded places. She's called Amarah. She'll be in the city soon, Rhea permitting. Tell Aetos she's working for me. Give her any aid you can.'

Solvi's grin broadened. 'Of course. Lathri helped me so much. We need her back. And everyone else Sapora and Tacio have captured.'

'I know. It won't be long. I'll take back my power. Blood be damned! So, you'll need to keep a look out for Amarah's ship. It's a—'

'Got you!' Tacio roared.

Isa and Solvi whirled around to see Tacio and a small army of Cerastes approaching from one side of the bridge. Isa spun around to escape, but more Cerastes had gathered on the bridge's other side.

They were trapped.

Her heart pounded again—but in terror rather than excitement. There was no way she could flee from this many. Their spears were already lowered towards her, and other Ittallan cleared the way for their approach.

Damn that Tacio. He must've followed her. She'd been too focussed on reporting back to check her surroundings well enough.

'Is this another conspirator that you've caught, sister?' Tacio asked, pushing his way to the front of the line of Cerastes.

Isa swallowed. Had they heard much of what she'd said?

Were they just acting on the assumption she was betraying them?

'You hear a few of our most deeply guarded cultural secrets and then run away from the palace. Now even you must admit that's suspicious...?' His sneer deepened. 'And Amarah? Who's she? Another rebel we need to take care of?'

Isa glared at him. He enjoyed this far too much.

She heard Solvi's panicked breathing beside her. Did she give her up, like she had done with Lathri?

'Well, Isa? Nothing to say?' Tacio goaded.

'I don't have to say anything to you,' Isa snapped.

Tacio's grin remained plastered on his face, fangs poking over his lips. 'Maybe not. It's respectful to, however. But you need to answer to the king. You and your little friend.'

When Tacio's eyes flicked to Solvi, Isa's breath caught.

She was too young, too innocent. She wouldn't last an hour under Tacio's torture.

'The Ittallan has nothing to do with this.'

'Oh?' Tacio said, his eyes still on Solvi. He took a step closer to the pair on the bridge.

Isa cursed herself. There was no way she could put Tacio off his prize, not when she was right in his claws. Twelve Cerastes stood behind him, and another twenty blocked off the bridge.

She couldn't flee, and she couldn't fight her way out of it. Handing Solvi over would buy her almost nothing, when Sapora was on the brink of releasing an Ark.

She had no choice. Sapora was gone, but Solvi, Aetos, Kylos, Lathri, and the others were still here. Were still counting on her. And Palom and Amarah, too.

She needed to step up and be the queen she claimed to be.

'You win, Tacio. You've caught me. I can't escape,' Isa said.

She lowered her hands and let them drop to her sides. 'The Arks are wrong. Evil. Even those who created them knew the mistake they'd made. Sapora cannot bring them back.'

'That isn't your decision to make. And hold your tongue in public!' Tacio said. 'Seize her!'

Isa turned very slightly to Solvi. 'Get away, now.'

Solvi trembled and then transformed, her snow leopard form taking up almost the entirety of the bridge. With a low growl, she leaped over the gathered Cerastes as they rushed forward to bind Princess Isa in chains, and raced deeper into the city.

28

Flying *Otella* had been easier than Amarah had thought it would be. Judd's competence as a co-pilot and the useful information he gave helped her maneuver Traego's warship efficiently.

By the time night fell, she'd regained the confidence lost through her missing eye, the *Valta Forinja*, and the two encounters with the sea monster.

'Storm clouds ahead. Looks about five leagues away,' Judd called.

'Jato.' Amarah's eyebrows furrowed at the thought of being so close to the damned Arillian. Jato had taken everything from her. 'Cannons are all loaded, right?'

'They are. You don't *want* to fight them, do you?' Judd approached Amarah by the wheel. 'Thought we were skirting round them.'

'We are.' Amarah grit her teeth. But if Jato decided to attack *Otella* or Isa's ship, she'd damn well regret it. 'We'll bear further south, try and cut across the mountains.'

'Aye.' Judd drew a longscope from his pocket and put it to his eye. 'It's too dark to see much detail. Looks to be clear on the other side of the mountains. Land's flat there, right? I think Jato's clouds are rolling around there.'

Amarah licked her lips. She simply had to imagine Jato and her Arillians were a fleet of Imperial ships that she needed to avoid. She didn't want to deviate too far south, or they'd arrive late to Taban Yul. But she needed to keep her ship far enough away that they didn't present themselves as an open target. 'Look out for their lightning.' Amarah was sure Judd didn't need the warning, but she felt more in control if she said something.

Without her *Valta Forinja*, she needed to rely on her skills as a sky pirate or in the firepower of *Otella* to keep them in one piece. Amarah was sure she heard thunder rumbling in the distance, but wondered if she was simply being paranoid.

Her stomach tightened again. She'd fought Jato one-on-one and had just about held her own against her. Just.She wondered if she could follow the Arillians back to wherever they had a base. Wondered if she could kill Jato in her sleep. It would probably the best chance she'd have at getting her own back.

But then Jato wouldn't know *she* had been the one to kill her.

Amarah would get her revenge, but Jato would never know. And that somehow took the meaning out of it. Amarah had never killed for fun, and avoided killing whenever she could.

But this was a personal vendetta.

No. She'd have to figure out some other way of beating the spoiled brat. Some other way where she'd have the advantage over the Arillian, and then Jato would *know* she'd fucked up when she'd stolen Amarah's eye and ship.

The whir of *Otella*'s propellers cut through the quiet, still night, and Amarah glanced to the left where Antar piloted

Isa's tiny ship. It was much faster than *Otella*, though he flew beside her for the most part. A clear convoy. Amarah supposed most of the Varkain in the palace and all of the Imperial Guard would know Isa's ship by sight. She was the princess, after all. Having that ship beside *Otella* surely would make them less likely to be stopped or attacked.

'You ever fought Arillians before?' Amarah asked Judd as they approached the dark clouds.

He shook his head. 'You mad? They'd drop me from the sky like a stone. When Aciel was rampaging around, I kept to the north of Corhaven. He never came near so I was safe. Heard about all the destruction his Arillians caused, though.'

'Destruction ain't the word.' Amarah remembered the battle outside Taban Yul. The sky had been thick with Arillians and ships, smoke hung in the air, and people died in droves. Their electrical attacks were something else, and caused utter devastation.

Taking on Jato again was one thing—so long as no-one else got involved. Taking on another army of them was not something she wanted to experience ever again.

She needed to ignore Jato and focus on getting to Isa.

Veynothi's blade weighed heavy on her hip, and Amarah had been sure not to accidentally brush it. She almost wondered how Sapora would react if that awful monster approached his doorstep.

Would he be afraid? Would he fight it? Or would he hide like any other coward?

That amusing thought settled her nerves a little, and she adjusted their course to avoid the bulk of Jato's storm. The wind picked up, buffeting the sails and pushing the ship slightly off course.

'You feel that?' Judd asked.

'Thunder? Yeah.'

Judd rubbed his forearms. 'But they're still leagues away!'

'That's what Arillians are like. Storms and devastation everywhere. You never wonder why the bounties on 'em are so damn high?'

'I just thought it was because they'd been with Aciel.'

Amarah cackled. 'You got a lot to learn, Judd. Let's hope they don't approach us, or you'll be feeling *a lot* more than just thunder.'

Judd swallowed visibly and sat down beside Malot, gripping onto the edge of his seat with white knuckles.

'I'll keep well clear of 'em. Don't worry,' Amarah said. She had no idea if her attempt to reassure Judd would work or not, and she didn't know if she really would avoid them or not. Having Jato right where she wanted her, at the mercy of a warship, was quite appealing. 'Anyway, you wanted to come to the palace where all the snakes are. If you're scared of some birds, how d'ya think you'd cope with Varkain?'

Judd shook his head. 'I'm a pilot. I'm here to fly ships, not fight anyone.'

'Then you shouldn't be a pilot for Traeg.' Amarah cackled again and scratched her chin. 'Fightin's part and parcel of working for him.'

The Feor Mountains loomed ahead, dark and gloomy, and wreathed in fog. Once they were past the peaks, they'd be able to see Taban Yul. Bright pinpricks of light flashed in the distance. Lightning.

Thunder rumbled ever louder as they approached, and Amarah tightened her grip on the wheel. Now she'd need to work hard. 'Keep eyes on Antar. Don't wanna lose him in the fog or their storm.'

Obedient, Judd got to his feet and walked to the side of *Otella* to peer over. Amarah wondered if he was also going to throw up over the side while he was there.

424

Wind screamed past as the pressure built. They had only just reached the edge of the Arillian storm and already *Otella*'s sails flapped about in the brutal winds. Another peal of thunder tore through the sky, rattling the ship's beams and sending loose objects flying.

Judd glanced back and gave her a thumbs up, his voice lost in the roaring wind.

This was it. Fly over the lower peaks and keep the Arillians at bay.

Then she'd be staring right into the entrance of the snake pit.

Amarah took several deep breaths to steady herself and keep her nerves quashed as she flew into the fog surrounding the mountain peaks. Only a fool wouldn't be worried about their task, and she had a healthy dose of fear to accompany her.

When her skin touched the fog, cold water droplets condensed, and goosebumps rose on her flesh.

Flying so high in such conditions was never a good idea, and *Otella* was too large and slow to quickly make the journey like *Khanna* or her new ship would. At least Traego would have an easier time crossing the mountains in that.

Amarah reached down and pulled at a line of switches on the control module, lighting the torches scattered across *Otella*'s deck and up each of the masts. They were Samolen fires, much like the one she carried, though far larger and brighter. Smokeless flames, they could be lit in almost any condition, and wouldn't extinguish unless plunged into water. The halo of light produced by the flames increased their visibility in the dense fog, and Amarah used them to navigate over the peaks. She didn't bring *Otella* too low in case she risked a breach from one of the wicked-looking rocks, but neither did she want to fly much higher.

Although nothing like the floating islands of Oren, they

were still high enough for the air to thin and the pressure to tighten her chest. She didn't want to risk either of them passing out, and balanced her altitude, speed, and direction to bring *Otella* safely across.

She glanced to Judd every so often, to ensure he still remained standing and hadn't collapsed in fear or cold, while also watching out for the dark storm clouds that rolled alongside them. The thunder was intense, now. It was so loud her ears rang constantly, and her vision danced through pained tears.

Otella creaked under the pressure and listed to the right. Amarah fought the wheel to keep the massive ship on course, and worried that Antar and Oris would fare worse in the smaller vessel.

Risking a lack of control to gain Judd's attention, Amarah lifted one hand from the wheel and waved to him. Her co-pilot saw the movement and hurried back over to her. He was drenched in a fine sheen of sweat, and had paled since the thunder had grown louder. 'Judd. Signal to Antar. Get them on *Otella*'s deck. It's too risky to fly solo now!' Although Judd couldn't have been more than two steps away, Amarah had to scream over the wind to be heard.

She pulled a small torch out from beside the wheel, a splash of colour painted on it to signify different instructions. Each torch had a match at its tip, which she flicked with her thumb as she handed it to him—igniting the torch in a vibrant purple flame.

Judd took the Samolen torch and hurried back to the side of *Otella*, waving it wildly to attract Antar's attention.

Amarah took a quick look at the other torches and their varied colours before slamming the drawer shut with her knee and grasping the wheel with both hands. *Otella* had a fantastic offense, first and foremost, but Malot had also installed a few rudimentary shields that would protect the ship's most vulnerable areas from attack. She'd explained that shields weren't her area of expertise, but something was better than nothing when you were being fired upon.

Amarah kept the switches for the shields in her peripheral vision at all times, bracing herself for attack by Arillian at any moment.

Several long minutes passed as they flew through the fog, the peaks of the Feor Mountains seeming to reach up from nothing to grasp at the hull of *Otella*. Amarah kept the ship out of danger and fought against the pressure from both the altitude and the Arillians' movements, and she breathed a sigh of relief when she saw Antar pilot Isa's small ship onto *Otella*'s deck.

The two sky pirates leaped off and strolled towards Amarah and Judd. Both of them were bleeding.

'What happened?' Malot asked, hurrying forward with rags to mop up the blood.

'Arillians,' Antar said. He took the offered rag and wiped his face. 'Can't see a damned thing in this fog, let alone their black clouds. Came at us from out of nowhere, their attacks sliced into us and then they were gone.'

Amarah narrowed her eyes. 'I guess they can't see too well in this, either. Good thing you saw us.'

'Those flames are brilliant. Dunno what we'd do without you, Malot.' Antar handed the rag back and stood beside Amarah. 'I can't even get our bearings in this.'

'Me neither,' Oris added. 'How d'ya know ya ain't flying along the mountains instead of over 'em? Or straight into the Arillians?'

Amarah glared at the youth. 'I have a good co-pilot.'

True to her words, Judd had resumed his position near the front of the ship, longscope in hand as he looked ahead, calculated distances, and fed back to Amarah, who adjusted

427

their course on his words and hand gestures when it was too loud to hear him.

'Won't be long till we're clear of the mountains. Then we'll be able to see again,' she said.

Antar folded his arms and looked ahead, his eyes dark with worry. Oris walked along deck to stand beside Judd, where they spoke together, their words lost to the wind.

Amarah ignored them both and focussed on her task.

Judd suddenly waved both hands at her, his mouth open but his voice drowned in the wind.

Amarah tensed, unsure what he'd seen, when a bolt of lightning careened into *Otella*'s side. The force of the strike split the wood and splinters filled the air in a bone-chilling explosion.

Otella groaned as Amarah twisted the wheel and pulled a lever to dip the sails, dropping the ship away in time to avoid the second lightning strike. 'Damned Arillians!'

'Fire back?' Antar screamed.

'At what? I ain't wasting our shots. Can't see a damned thing!'

'You might get lucky?'

'Not shooting into the dark, Antar.' Amarah snapped and plunged the ship further down, swallowed by the thick fog as they dropped closer to the mountains. 'They couldn't see you when you got attacked. I just need to get away. Damn, this ship is so slow!'

Flashes of lightning lit up the fog around them for several seconds, but Amarah's visibility didn't improve. The fog was too dense for even the lightning to show the way through, and she relied on her honed reactions and flying instinct to keep them safe. 'Sit down and hold on. This might get bumpy!'

Another bolt of lightning ripped through the ship's main sail, cracking the mast but not quite splitting it apart. The ship juddered underneath, the propellers coughed, and Amarah tightened her grip on the wheel. She dug her heels into the deck and braced herself.

'Why ain't you firing?' Oris yelled, rushing from the main deck to the control panel. Judd arrived a moment later, panting heavily.

'Because the smoke from *dragon's breath* is thicker than the fog. I ain't risking crashing into the mountainside!' Amarah yelled.

She pulled another lever and turned *Otella* hard to starboard as the face of the mountain materialised from the wall of fog. The tip of the wooden boar's head scraped along the rock as Amarah turned the ship, sending chips and dust flying. Amarah powered forward, pushing *Otella* up to a faster gear to put some distance between them and the Arillians who had attacked them. Heavy thunder echoed, throwing off Amarah's sense of direction even further, but she held on regardless, and drove *Otella* away.

She had no idea if it was Jato attacking her or if it was a few random Arillians who'd spotted them. Either way, she didn't want to engage in a fight. Even if *Otella* could blow them out of the sky with *dragon's breath*, it would be a waste. If she had to use the cannons, it'd be against Sapora and his Varkain in their escape.

'Get everything secured if you don't want it flying overboard!' Amarah said, pulling another lever to adjust her sails as *Otella's* speed increased. She hated being a target. Hated lacking the speed to get away from her enemies. Hated having to baby Traego's crew.

They ran at her command, although *Otella* had been lightly packed for the journey, and they didn't have a huge amount of things to tie down. Mostly they went to Isa's ship, prone on deck, and looped rope around it to keep it from rolling around in the sharp turns and acceleration.

'Amarah! We're almost at the edge of the mountains!' Judd yelled, scope in hand as he made his way back to her, one hand covering his head from the roaring wind. 'They drop away below us. Taban Yul will be in sight once we clear the storm clouds!'

She nodded slowly, too engrossed in keeping *Otella* from being blown away to reply to him properly. But at least they were still travelling due west and had crested the Feor Mountains. One step closer to—

Another bolt of lightning streaked overhead, the accompanying thunder so powerful it dropped everyone to their knees. Amarah lost her grip on the wheel, and the ship keeled to one side, tipping away from the barrage of wind.

Antar grabbed it as Amarah rolled away, gravity pulling both her and the ship down.

'I got it!' Antar called, though most of his shout was lost in the thunder accompanying the lightning.

Strips of wood peeled from Otella's deck as the ship fought the ferocious gale. Amarah pulled herself to her feet and fought her way back to the wheel, where she helped Antar steady the ship.

'We have to get away!' Antar yelled.

'What d'you think I'm trying to do!' Amarah screamed back, steadying herself.

The dark storm clouds and remnants of the mountain fog still surrounded the ship, and she couldn't see where the Arillians were. They'd certainly not shown themselves directly, and Amarah wondered if they were simply trying to ward off any who flew too near them.

She knew she should probably fire back, but she didn't want to draw the Arillians any closer or into combat. Clearly the Arillians couldn't see them well enough or they'd already have gone up in smoke.

'Just keep hold of Isa's ship! We can't lose that!' She

430

yelled. Antar frowned for a moment, then saw the sense in her words and ran back to hold onto the ropes, tying new knots in them to keep the ship tight to *Otella*. At least he trusted her to keep hold of the wheel while they flew through the thunderstorm.

Sheet lightning rippled overhead, turning the black clouds grey and showing Amarah the way into the valley. Thick forest lined the lower half of the mountains and much of the steep valley below, and she knew she was heading the right way. Taban Yul lay just beyond the trees.

Where Sapora waited.

Amarah suppressed a shudder as she fought with *Otella*, bringing the ship through the storm and towards their goal. If Jato made an appearance now, she didn't know what she'd do.

Fighting her went against her instincts as well as common sense. But she couldn't bear the thought of seeing that Arillian again and letting her live.

If she just turned north, she'd bring the ship closer to the heart of the storm, where she was sure the Arillians would be. She wondered if she'd even be able to tell them apart. Amarah was sure she'd recognise Jato's power again, if she saw it.

Judd made his way back to her to report. 'I spied several Arillians. They're flying around in circles to the north, just throwing lightning about in all directions. They don't seem to be following us.'

'Good. That's good.' Amarah chewed the inside of her lip.

It would be a sneak attack, then, if she brought *Otella* round to face them. They were so busy creating the storm, they weren't even aware of *Otella*. That's probably why they'd been able to avoid all their attacks. They were just offshoots from the storm they created.

Even if Jato wasn't there, killing some of her Arillians would be a good thing, wouldn't it? It would make their escape route easier? Even if word of their deaths travelled quickly, Amarah didn't think they'd be in the palace long enough before their reinforcements arrived.

Or Jato herself, if she wasn't part of the storm.

The idea rolled around in Amarah's mind as she brought *Otella* lower now they'd passed the mountain peaks. Just a slight adjustment to their path and they could be on top of the Arillians within minutes.

Perhaps Sapora would even thank her for getting rid of the Arillians here and clearing the airspace around the capital city.

She swallowed, scratched the skin beneath her missing eye, and adjusted her altitude again.

Start taking her revenge now, or ignore them and go straight to Princess Isa?

Antar, Malot, and Oris remained by Isa's ship, their hands on the rope to hold the ship secure. Judd remained half in the control cabin, half on deck with his scope.

She could send Oris down to man the cannons. Fire two or three and then get away before the Arillians had even realised what hit them.

It would be easy.

So very easy.

But Antar had explained Isa sounded desperate. Afraid, even. And it had been two, almost three days since speaking to her. Who knew what the damned snake had done to Isa in the meanwhile?

The princess had been desperate enough to beg help from a sky pirate. And she'd asked for her by name.

Amarah's fingers trembled where they clutched the spokes of the wheel. *Otella* was a warship. She had the firepower at her control.

At best, she'd destroy the Arillians in a couple of blasts and clear the skies. If Jato was there, then she'd be gone, too. If she wasn't, then it would draw the Arillian to her.

At worst, she'd miss, and the miniature army would be upon them in seconds. They'd never make it to the palace, they'd lose out on gold, and Isa wouldn't get the help she seemed so desperate for.

Isa was in the snake pit, surrounded by disgusting maggots who slept beneath the earth and surfaced only to instil terror and hatred in the eyes of those who met them.

Amarah remembered vividly when she'd been a youth, younger than Oris even, trapped in a dirty alley somewhere in Niversai surrounded by a group of Varkain. She still carried the scars on her legs from their fangs, and probably would have died in the dirt and muck had it not been for Traego.

Her heart thudded at the memory. The raw fear. The helplessness. The pain of their venom snaking through her body, leaving her completely at their mercy.

And the thought of anyone trapped by the snakes made her blood boil.

Dawn lit the edge of the horizon, burning away the little fog that remained and clearing her vision to Val Sharis below.

Amarah sighed. She'd spent too long with Moroda. She'd grown soft.

Cursing herself for her weakness, she pulled *Otella* further east and powered the ship on towards Taban Yul and the rising sun. She would answer her princess's call, not because Isa was a princess, but because Isa was an ally who needed help.

And Amarah would help her destroy the pit of snakes if it was the last thing she did.

29

The streets of Taban Yul had changed so much since Palom had last been there that he almost thought he was somewhere else. He'd heard about the Sevastos and how it had defended Sapora and the palace from a fleet of warships. He'd known parts of the city had burned in the ensuing fires. But even that knowledge hadn't prepared him for what he saw after passing through the city's gates.

Soldiers in red and gold livery, coloured sashes clasped at their chests and shoulders, stood at attention outside many buildings, swords at their hips and spears held aloft. Others marched along the streets in threes or fours, their presence clearly intimidating the locals who hurried out of their way. Only one out of every ten was an Ittallan—all the others were Varkain. Palom occasionally saw other Varkain in darker armour—black, blue and silver—and he recognised these as the elite caste that had taken Yfaila.

They were Cerastes.

He'd known about Cerastes, of course. Growing up in Feoras Sol on the border with Sereth meant he'd been introduced to the various castes of Varkain at a young age. But the Cerastes had never actually *left* Sereth.

They'd always been defenders, protecting Sereth from outsiders who weren't permitted entry. Palom wondered if this was the first time these Cerastes had actually seen sunlight.

And they all seemed to be watching him.

Leillu chirped suddenly, leaping forward to pounce at a butterfly that drifted past.

No. Perhaps the Cerastes were watching her.

The rest of the wagons trundled along Taban Yul's main streets, many having to slow to allow people walking the other way to get through. He'd known the capital would be full—it was Summercourt after all—but he hadn't realised how such a busy city could be so quiet.

Then the shadow passed overhead.

Palom, Karvou, and *Leillu* flinched and looked up in time to see the Sevastos fly over the streets, its massive wings spread wide, the white marble buildings darkening beneath its vast shadow.

Palom watched as the Sevastos soared, lazily flapping its wings every so often to keep itself aloft. The head of the massive creature had to be ten times the size of a wagon. It dwarfed even the fully grown dragon that had attacked the hamlet and burned it to the ground.

Its scales glittered in the sunlight, almost glowing red, as though its very body were on fire. Each claw, spine, and horn looked to be carved from the darkest, smoothest ebony. The underside of the dragon's body was a paler red, as though it were metal rusted over centuries. It scoured the city below with eyes of gold and let out an earth-shattering roar as it wheeled around for another pass.

Leillu ran back to Palom and looped around his legs, her wings folded tightly to her body.

435

'I see you have healthy fear of gods, *Leillu*,' Palom said.

Although *Leillu* was far larger now than she had been when she'd first hatched, she still barely measured up to a medium-sized dog. And she clearly knew when it was best to hide.

Palom wondered whether she'd learned to fear the bigger dragon because of their recent encounter, or whether she had an instinctual knowledge and understanding of the power of a Sevastos.

Either way, it went against nature that a dragon of that size obeyed a snake. Seeing the Sevastos in the flesh would have been astonishing. Now, it simply angered him.

'The inn isn't too far from here.' One of the Ittallan from the caravan approached Palom, apparently unfazed by the god flying overhead. 'You coming or you gonna go sight-seeing?'

Palom ignored his condescending tone. 'I will be going to mausoleum first.'

The man shrugged. 'Those of us who Jato killed'll be buried there, too. You don't need to guard 'em.'

'I am not guarding them. I am paying respects to my fallen friends.' Palom didn't understand why that was such a problem. 'Once I am done there I am coming to inn. Karvou, you will follow these Ittallan to *Last Grape*. I will meet you and Odi there later.'

The young lad, awe-struck by the Sevastos, nodded mutely. He struggled to tear his gaze away from the sky.

'Good. Go, then. And take *Leillu* with you. I do not think she will be liked much in mausoleum.' Palom shooed the young dragon towards Karvou, who reluctantly left Palom's side. *Leillu* looked back several times and called out to him —a low, keening noise that sounded more bird-like than dragon-like. Palom shook his head and stood firm. 'I will be back by tonight. Go rest.'

Again, Palom had no way to know whether *Leillu* under-stood his words or not, but she soon got the gist of what he wanted and followed Karvou down the street after a little gentle persuasion from the lad.

Once sure *Leillu* wouldn't follow him, Palom made his way across the city towards South Galeo, where the mausoleum stood as a constant reminder of his failures to protect those he loved.

~

THANKFULLY, the Ittallan who lived and worked in the mausoleum had not been replaced by Varkain, and a trio came out to greet him wearing their traditional long, grey robes. Pleased there were still some places that remained sacred in his homeland, Palom entered through the enor-mous double doors and braced himself for an onslaught of emotions.

But none came.

He supposed he'd had his *Valta Forinja* when he'd last been here, and the cursed weapon had manipulated his emotions to the point where he couldn't tell what was real and what wasn't.

Now, he was visiting his fallen allies and comrades with a clear head.

One of the shrine guardians asked if he needed an escort, her voice little more than a whisper.

Palom declined with a short shake of his head and made his way through the passageways and stairways of the build-ing, accompanied only by the scent of burning wood and incense. The mausoleum seemed ever peaceful and unchanging; a stone on a beach forever buffeted by the sea, but never moved by it.

It didn't take Palom long to reach the large chamber that

served as Eryn and Anahrik's final resting place. Runes had been carved into the doorway—prayers and well-wishes in the ancient Ittallan tongue to help guide them in the after-life and help them find lasting peace.

Palom entered the chamber slowly, trying to make as little noise as possible. Disturbing the dead was never a good thing. His heavy boots thudded loudly, no matter how lightly he tried to step, and in the end, Palom simply crossed the room as quickly as possible. There were six stone coffins here, all enjoying sunlight as they rested.

Palom knelt by Anahrik's coffin and placed a massive hand on the lid—where he'd sealed his business partner in, only a handful of months prior.

How much had changed since the funeral.

'Anahrik, you were never one to rest in daytime. Maybe now you can rest, now you are safe. Now you are at peace.' He bowed his head, not wanting to give words to his other thoughts and memories lest he cried. He didn't want to cry, not in front of the dead.

Anahrik had been ready to head north, back to his family, away from the destruction caused by Aciel and his Arillians. Palom had made him stay, made him help forge the *Valta Forinja*. And then Moroda, Eryn, and Morgen had been ambushed. If Kohl hadn't abandoned those three, if Kohl had stayed to fight, then they wouldn't have died.

Anahrik wouldn't have perished coming to their aid.

Kohl was a formidable fighter. He'd seen him take down a dragon single-handedly. But Kohl never used his powers. He fled instead of fought, hid instead of stood his ground.

And it was causing deaths. So many deaths.

How many lives could have been spared if Kohl had fought back?

'You don't blame him, do you?' Palom asked Anahrik's coffin, his voice echoing around the chamber. 'You always saw good in people. Positives. You forgave. Maybe not Varkain, but most others.' A little smile pulled at his lips. 'Now you can fly skies of Linaria as you want to. Faster than any dragon. Faster than any ship.'

Palom shifted position to ease the pain in his cramping knees. He wasn't getting any younger, and all the battles he'd been through didn't help. 'Look at me. I am old man. Knees ache. Back hurts. Heart is heavy all of time, now.' He laughed at himself and shook his head. 'I always had to run to keep up with you. Even when you were *not* falcon!'

He stood up and inspected the top of the coffin. Dust would normally accumulate here, but the shrine guardians had done a good job of keeping it clean. He couldn't even see cobwebs anywhere in the chamber. 'You are in good place here. It is clean. Bright. You can see sun and sky every day. I am sure you are happy. Will you forgive me for abandoning *Valta Forinja*? It was *emonos*, Anahrik. *Emonos*. I did not realise at time.'

Palom strode to the large window and looked out over the city. From this height, he could see all of South Galeo and the narrow brook that ran between many of Taban Yul's districts. In the distance, the palace loomed, its slender towers and golden statues showcasing the Ittallan wealth.

'There are others on way here now,' Palom said, though he had his back to the coffins. 'Allies of mine. Who were killed by Jato and Arillians. Just like you were. Wait here for them, will you? Show them way forward so they can rest as well. So they can be at peace.' Palom wondered what would happen to Yfaila, and whether her speaking with the Cerastes and Tacio would result in more bodies being brought to the mausoleum.

He paused, staring over Taban Yul as he weighed up whether or not to say anything more. In the end, he decided if he couldn't tell his best friend, then he was no true friend.

439

Even in death, Palom considered Anahrik a brother in all but blood.

He missed him more than he could put into words. And he didn't want to hide who he was or what he did any longer.

He spoke carefully in case any of the shrine guardians heard and reported to Sapora. 'I am going to be doing...some more things here. Dangerous things. In Taban Yul. But it is *right* thing to do. You would say it is right thing to do, I think. But...if it goes...badly, then please wait for me, too. I probably won't be long.'

～

PALOM LEFT the mausoleum feeling lighter than he'd thought he would.

There was one more thing he wanted to do in Taban Yul before joining the other rebels at *The Last Grape*.

He wanted to see Moroda.

Taban Yul was full of Ittallan and Varkain both, and Palom couldn't remember a time he'd ever seen so many Varkain in one place. But as he made his way further and further north, the crowds thinned. Shops had been boarded up or were abandoned and left in a state of disrepair with cracked stone, broken windows, and chipped paint.

While every city had richer and poorer districts, almost every street near the North Gate lay empty, and the only people he saw were those in the Imperial Guard. Although none tried to stop him, most looked at him curiously as he marched towards the city gate and the crystal pillar which lay beyond.

Only when he reached the gates themselves did Palom have to stop.

'North Gate is sealed.' One of the two Imperial Guard

stationed there barked at him. 'If you wanna leave, take the South or West Gate.'

'I want to see pillar,' Palom replied.

The guards shared a look. Then the second said, 'Are you mad? Why d'you wanna see it? You suicidal or something?'

Palom frowned. 'No. My friend is in pillar. Moroda. She stopped Aciel.'

'Yeah, we all know the story,' the first guard said quickly. 'The gate's still sealed.'

'Why? There are no Arillians there now.' Palom realised then that both of the two soldiers were Ittallan, and both were fodder. They'd need to be bulls or stags or something strong to make it into the Imperial Guard, but Palom wondered why Sapora hadn't placed his Varkain here if they guarded something so precious as access to the crystal pillar.

'Have you been living under a rock? This whole area isn't safe. That's why everyone with half a brain moved out of these districts.' Palom couldn't ignore the guard's patronising tone.

'Yeah, and the rest of 'em killed 'emselves.' The second guard laughed.

Palom didn't find any of it funny. 'This is why north of city is abandoned?'

'Sapora's a snake. A bad omen. Death comes in strange ways when you have a snake as king.'

Palom couldn't believe the soldier's words. A few months ago, he'd have punched him for his disrespect. But now he was on the cusp of joining the rebels, and didn't want to be a hypocrite. He still felt the guard was either foolish or ignorant for speaking his mind so openly, but decided not to challenge him. Standing guard all day in front of a locked gate had to be rather boring.

'You cannot open it quickly for me? I will be back in only couple of minutes.'

The second guard continued to laugh, an abrasive, high-pitched noise that made Palom seriously reconsider punching him.

But the first showed more sympathy. 'Look, I don't wanna die. I've got a baby daughter at home, and I'm trying to do my best to keep her fed and safe. The buildings down there,' he gestured with a thumb, 'are all empty. Maybe you could scale them and peek over the wall. But I'm warning you, bad things have happened to everyone who stayed within a league of the pillar.'

Palom considered his words and then nodded, grateful. 'Thank you, sir.'

As there was no-one else nearby, Ittallan or Varkain, Palom decided to risk taking the soldier's advice. He was sure he'd be quick enough that he could get back down before anyone else wandered into this part of Taban Yul, anyway.

So he hurried along the street nearest the enormous city wall that towered overhead. It didn't take him long to find a cluster of buildings that would work as something to climb —several were five or six storey high townhomes that had long been abandoned; the ivy trailing down their fronts was proof of that.

Palom pushed open the front door—barely hanging onto its hinges—and leaped up the stairs and into the loft of the building. The home still smelled of food and people, as though its inhabitants had just vanished a few hours ago.

Something about being inside another's home chilled him, and he hurried across the beams to where the roof sloped down. Many homes in Val Sharis had large windows in the roof to allow flying Ittallan to come and go more easily. Others would have balconies for the same job, but this particular townhouse had a window that had been left wide open.

Palom judged the distance, crouched, then jumped up. He grabbed onto the edge of the window with his fingertips and scrambled for a better purchase. Dust fell around him and he coughed, heaving himself up and through the window, and finding himself on a sloped roof of blue slate tiles. The city wall still rose above him, but he could now see the top. In his tiger form, he might just be able to make the jump.

Determined to see the crystal pillar and what remained of Moroda, Palom relaxed into his *meraki*. His body glowed briefly as his limbs changed form, fur pushed through his skin, and his teeth sharpened into fangs. Once in his true form, Palom assessed his jump again. Confident he could make it, he leaped as high as he could—a straight vertical that tested every muscle in his legs. His claws scrambled against the smooth marble wall, working with the momentum of his jump to grab another few feet of height, and he pulled himself onto the top of the inner wall.

He sat down, panting slightly from the exertion, and looked out into the wide valley. The Feor Mountains marked the edge of his vision, and the dark Rio Neva forest below seemed to sprawl endlessly. But the plains immediately surrounding the north of Taban Yul were what he looked at most closely.

No more than half a league away, surrounded by soldiers in heavy armour, a tall crystal jutted from the grass. Bright turquoise in colour, it matched any of the Sevastos stones he'd seen in Berel. It pulsed gently, sending out a wave of light every few seconds.

Aciel.

Palom let out a low growl, the only way he could really express his emotions while in his true form.

Inside that vessel of pure magic lay Moroda, the one who'd sacrificed everything to stop the fighting. And yet all around him, more fighting continued, while more still brewed. She'd been trapped beside Aciel, the one she'd wanted to destroy. She'd given her life's energy to a cause she believed in with all her heart.

And for what?

To pave the way for Sapora to take Aciel's place? For Jato to continue her destruction? For the dragons to turn against them all and burn Linaria from existence?

He bowed his head again, and the wind pressed against his body. He wished Moroda had finished it properly. She'd been able to enlist the aid of a Sevastos, had the power at her fingertips, and hadn't slain Aciel.

He understood it wasn't in her nature to kill. But it would have saved more trouble if she had.

'Kill them all....'

Palom looked up at the voice on the wind.

'Dirty. Poison. Death.'

He stood up and looked around. Other than the two members of the Imperial Guard by North Gate, there was no-one else close enough to hear.

'Must...must kill them...must kill them all....'

Palom snarled again as a cold chill descended and he smelled blood. He turned away from the crystal pillar and back to Taban Yul. He had an excellent view of most of the city from such a height, and looked back towards the palace. Having a snake on the throne had never sat well with him, but at least Vasil had kept to Sereth for the most part.

He heard steel boots marching on the cobblestones and looked towards the noise. Perhaps ten or eleven streets away, a miniature battalion of Cerastes marched towards the palace, their spear tips pointed up and glinting in the sun.

Even from this distance, Palom could tell who the prisoner was. He'd be able to pick out the princess from ten leagues away, if he needed to. Isa.

It didn't look like they were escorting her.

Grateful for the distraction from the disembodied voice, yet worried for his princess, Palom leaped down from the wall and back onto the roof of the townhouse. Jumping from building to building until he was back on the road, Palom raced along to catch up to Isa and the Cerastes, going by sound when he lost sight of them.

The crowds grew again as he left the north of the city further and further behind him. Within minutes, he'd caught up to the Cerastes' brisk march, and he transformed back, keeping himself hidden in narrow alleys running between buildings. Princess Isa's arms had been bound in thick chains, her head bowed in subservience.

The indignity of her treatment angered him, and the same notion of punching the soldiers came back tenfold.

He drew the sword at his hip and skirted back down the alley and across another. The Cerastes were heading towards the palace, that much was clear. And he knew Taban Yul well enough to find a road that intercepted theirs and make his move.

Keeping the Cerastes to his right, Palom made his way quickly through the streets, pushing past the citizens and tourists to stay ahead of them.

But the Ittallan and Varkain present were also interested in watching the princess and Cerastes, and huddled together in ever larger groups to peer out between the buildings to catch a glimpse of the unfolding drama.

'Move!' Palom growled, elbowing them aside as he forced his way closer to Princess Isa.

They didn't seem to care that they were in his way, even with his sword drawn, and huffed or tutted at him as they grudgingly stepped aside.

445

Palom shouldered his way through the thicker crowds as he approached one of the city's many squares. An enormous statue wrought in gold commanded the centre, depicting the union of Val Sharis and Corhaven with the creation of the Imperial Guard.

It was fitting. An ironic backdrop for his rescue of Princess Isa from the Cerastes' clutches.

He crouched behind a tall hedge, the statue directly ahead of him, as he waited for the Cerastes to reach the square from the street to his right. Palom flexed his fingers, testing his strength, before he gripped the hilt of his sword again in anticipation of the attack.

Every muscle tensed as he prepared his ambush.

He didn't need to kill any of them, just surprise them and push them back so Isa could run. That's all he needed to do. The shock of the attack would surely be enough to get the princess away.

'*Kali!*'

Palom whirled around at the word. 'Solvi?'

His niece almost pounced on him as she opened her arms for a hug.

Palom dropped his sword with a clatter and rose to meet her. He embraced Solvi with both arms as she buried her face in his shoulder. 'Solvi, you are still here?' He'd thought she would have returned home, to Feoras Sol. The thought that she'd stay in Taban Yul hadn't even occurred to him.

'Of course I am still here! I cannot believe *you* are here!' Solvi said, not letting go of him. 'Aetos told us you were coming back. I'd hoped and wished you were, and now you are!'

Her clear joy at his return almost brought a tear to his eye. Then the steel boots brought him back to the reason why he'd been crouched in a hedge. 'Solvi. Princess Isa is—'

'I know. She's been arrested. She was talking to me

446

and...and the Cerastes came and she let them take her so I could go free.' Solvi pressed her face into his shoulder again. 'Your sword is here. You weren't going to attack them?'

Palom exhaled slowly. The first line of Cerastes were approaching the statue, now. He had to strike now or his chance would be lost.

Perhaps the princess knew what she was doing if she allowed herself to be taken by the snakes.

'Solvi...' Palom said, hugging his niece and watching Isa walk past, metal chains clinking.

'Princess Isa has a plan. I was going back to tell Aetos and the others. A sky pirate is coming, Amarah, she—'

'Amarah?'

Solvi stepped away from him and watched the Cerastes. She then looked back to Palom. 'You know her. She's the one who fought with you?'

'She is.' Palom couldn't believe it. The Cerastes had marched across the square and were now on the road on the other side, making their way purposefully towards the palace.

He'd missed his opportunity to rescue Isa.

Solvi said, 'I trust Princess Isa. If she has a plan, then I believe in it.'

Palom wanted to tell her she was being silly and naive. Wanted to say that he could have freed the princess there and then, rescued her and they could have escaped the Varkain's claws.

But then what?

Other than getting her away from the Cerastes, he'd not the first idea of what to do next. Anahrik had always decided on their strategy. Palom had always carried it out.

Isa clearly thought more long-term than he, and though it killed him to watch her marched off like a common criminal, he needed to give her more credit. She knew what she was doing.

Or at least he hoped so.

'The others have gone to *Last Grape*. An inn. You know it?'

Solvi nodded. 'I am working there. We cannot always meet in Lathri's house, there are too many of us. It would be noticed too easily.'

It made sense, though he was surprised by the level of Solvi's involvement with Lathri's comrades. 'Let's go there. They will want to know of Princess Isa's arrest, and her plan.'

THE LAST GRAPE took up an entire street, dwarfing the buildings opposite, and claiming a level of privacy only afforded to Goldstones. Apparently Princess Isa had purchased the establishment some years ago, and while it served regular patrons and wealthy Ittallan, it could very quickly be emptied if Isa needed somewhere discreet.

Apparently Sapora cared little for his sister's actions, and she'd not used the inn since meeting Lathri, so Tacio and his Cerastes had no reason to suspect it, either.

It was a great base.

But Palom was sure it wouldn't last long.

When he and Solvi arrived a short while later, *The Last Grape* already heaved with Ittallan loyal to the princess. Wagons and oxen remained in the large courtyard to the rear of the building, attended to by young Ittallan who had not yet obtained their meraki.

Inside, steaming plates of food lined the tables where travel-weary Ittallan ate ferociously, spoke loudly, and thumped tables and floors as their emotions ran high.

Several aurochs roasted over the enormous fire that commanded *The Last Grape*'s far wall, and the spit of cooking meat almost made Palom salivate right there and then. Slices of potatoes had been boiled and then fried in duck fat, alongside caramelized brown and white onions, crisp, earthy mushrooms, and thick cabbage leaves that offered a dark green contrast on the plate. A rich, sticky sauce had been drizzled over the meat, and Palom could smell the honey in it with every breath.

A serving boy thrust a plate into Palom's hand almost as soon as he walked in, and another gave one to Solvi, who inclined her head in appreciation. They made their way to join the other Ittallan feasting and talking at one of the long tables.

For a group of people suffering under the rule of a tyrannical king, Palom thought they seemed awfully happy. But with Solvi sat beside him and the princess in chains, he didn't want to cause a scene.

'Palom! Here!' Karvou waved, looking up from his half-eaten plate. He'd found a quieter seat on the end of the table, close to the fireplace and the spit.

Palom gratefully wandered over to him, Solvi in tow. As he approached Karvou, he saw why he'd chosen this spot. *Leillu* lay almost in the flames, gnawing on blackened bones that she clasped between her pointed claws.

'Solvi, this is Karvou. Karvou, this is my niece.' Palom introduced them, and Solvi took a seat beside the youth. Palom sat opposite, and leaned down to gently scratch *Leillu*'s wings. He would have stroked her on the nose as he usually did, but she was too deep in the fire for him to touch her without getting burned. *Leillu* chirped happily, and continued to worry the bone with her growing fangs.

'Captain Chyro will be here soon,' Solvi said.

'And Odi,' Karvou added.

They both tucked into their meals as Palom listened to the talk, keeping one eye on *Leillu*. 'Good. Once they are here, I will tell them about Princess Isa. Odi needs to know.'

Karvou nodded. 'You might need to talk to some of the Ittallan about *Leillu*, too. She's a dragon. Dragons are turning against Linaria. Not everyone's happy...even if you are the great tiger.'

Palom tore off a hunk of meat and chewed. 'They have nothing to fear from her.'

As they ate, Palom heard the other Ittallan openly discuss what had become of their glorious city since Sapora had come to power. Of the Varkain moving in. Of the sickness, deaths, and suicides. Of the Sevastos and Summercourt. Of the dragons breathing fire at their doorstep.

Most knew the princess stood with them, but they didn't know how to get her in power without killing her brothers and reigniting the Ittallan-Varkain war. Many of them had given the snakes a chance, some had even employed Varkain who'd been looking for work. But it had all resulted in tears, bloodshed, or both.

Tacio patrolled the streets with his Cerastes almost nightly, using brutal methods to keep the citizens in line. The Varkain pushed Ittallan out of their jobs and their homes, and entire districts had been given over to the snakes. And of course, half the city had yet to recover from the dragon-fire when Sapora had unleashed his Sevastos.

The princess needed to put a stop to it and become a queen.

'I wish Amarah was here,' Solvi said. 'If Princess Isa asked her to come, she'll know what to do.'

Palom laughed. 'If gold is included, the sky pirate will come.' He wondered how it would be to finally see her again, having missed her in Tum Metsa.

He still didn't know if it had been poor timing on his part or she'd purposely left him there.

Palom ate another large mouthful of potatoes and considered how much he'd changed, grown, and moved on since meeting Moroda. Although he'd lost allies, he'd also met new ones. Though young, Karvou wanted to fight. *Leillu* was a creature unlike any he'd met before. He'd been reunited with his father, with his niece. Chyro, a captain of the Imperial Guard, was on their side, as was Odi, who spoke for the Archigo of Gal Etra.

He'd slain Mateli, his greatest rival.

And he'd join them all, he'd stand with them, for Princess Isa.

There was no more time to run. He'd do whatever it took to bring peace back to Linaria.

30

Kohl plummeted from the sky pirate's airship.

Their laughter and jeering followed him for several seconds, but it didn't mask the sheer terror that coursed through him. One moment he was in bright sunlight with the wind in his face, the next, he'd fallen into the drowning pit, darkness swallowed him, and the sea met him with open arms.

He plunged into the water, and the impact knocked the breath from his lungs.

Kohl tried to swim, but the rope around his ankles and knees had been too tightly knotted, and he couldn't move freely. He tried to calm himself, tried to keep his focus. He brought his knees up to his chest and kicked out, righted himself and pushed back towards the surface.

Kohl took a gasp of air and relaxed his body as much as he could.

Calm logic needed to win over blind terror. He could float, if he didn't panic.

He rolled over onto his back and took several deep breaths.

The pit had to be a good twenty feet square, but it was

full of sea water, and even in this confined space, waves lapped at him and off the sides, threatening to pull him under again.

Sunlight streamed in from high above, the bright light distorting his vision, further disorienting him. When he heard the heavy metal grate slam shut, and the light disappeared, he knew his chances of escape had disappeared.

Kohl was almost grateful that the bounty on his people was so high—at least the sky pirates would have collected the bodies of his kin. The thought of seeing dead Arillians floating in the water was almost too much to bear.

He shuddered. The shock of everything had masked the pain of his broken fingers, and now they screamed in agony. Perhaps Amarah was right. He was useless.

Now he'd die here, alone, like all the other Arillians caught in Estoria. His body would line the sky pirates' pockets with gold and encourage them to hunt down more of his people.

And he could do nothing about it.

He wasn't afraid of fighting. It was often necessary.

But he didn't want to kill.

His power was great enough that he could harm someone without meaning to. And he wanted to prove to Jato that no matter what happened, there were other ways to cope than violence and murder. He wanted to prove that they were better than what the rest of Linaria thought of them.

There was more to the Arillian race than destruction.

If he fought back. If he hurt people, killed people, he was reinforcing their hatred of Arillians.

Now his pacifism had led to his death, and he'd achieved nothing. Jato would continue on the warpath until Amarah or someone else found her and put a stop to it.

Tears threatened at the hopelessness of it all, but he wouldn't let them spill.

He bobbed and slipped under water for a moment, before relaxing again and floating back to the surface. He'd eventually tire and the sea would swallow him. Then the pirates would collect his bloated corpse when they were good and ready.

Fear raced through him, replaced quickly by numbness and a sense of acceptance. He'd messed up. In his two hundred and four years, he'd messed it all up. He had the Frost-touch, like the other two Arillian leaders. He had a daughter who became a General. He had friends he cared for.

And he'd ruined everything when he'd challenged Aciel.

Perhaps if he'd let the damned low class Arillian have his way, things would have worked out better. If he hadn't fought, he wouldn't have lost everything—respect, confidence, or Jato.

Exile had given him time to think and reminisce on his mistakes. But it hadn't given him a way to redeem himself.

Until Moroda.

By restoring her life, by unsealing her from the Sevastos's crystal, perhaps he could earn some sort of redemption. It wouldn't earn him true forgiveness for all his wrongdoings, but it would have been a start.

Amarah had believed in him, given him the chance to show what he could do. And he'd failed.

Amarah. Jato. Fogu. And himself. He'd failed them all.

Now, he'd drown in this pit and no-one would ever know.

No-one would care, and it was all his fault.

Tears spilled, then. He couldn't hold them back, and what was the point if he was going to die, anyway? A slow, cold, lonely death. How fitting.

He closed his eyes and waited for his strength to leave him.

~

THE SEA CHURNED around Kohl as a storm grew and an almighty crash echoed above, rousing him from the edge of consciousness.

He opened one eye, unsure if he was dead or hallucinating.

Wind lashed at him, splashing the water and sending spray into his eyes.

Blearily, Kohl opened his other eye and looked directly up from where he still floated on his back. The metal grate which had locked him into the pit had vanished.

He blinked.

No.

It had *shattered*.

Thousands of tiny metal fragments fell onto him and into the surrounding water, bubbles foaming on the surface where they splashed. He couldn't swim properly, couldn't paddle away, so he squeezed his eyes shut as more shards of metal fell onto his face.

'KOHL!'

He coughed and wriggled where he floated, trying to somehow push himself out of the way of the falling debris.

The wind continued to pick up, and then he wasn't writhing around in the sea, but in the air. He opened his eyes again and gasped. How was he floating?

'Kohl! Are you okay?'

He looked up at the sound of his name, his neck aching from the cold seawater, and saw the silhouette of an Arillian a short way above him. Had he died? Was this the one who would take him to the frozen lands of his ancestors in death?

'Kohl?'

Warm hands grasped him firmly by the shoulders. Kohl felt the wing beats of the Arillian, and he sank into their strength. 'How...' he muttered, coughing up water and metal fragments.

'I waited all day for you. I feared the worst. When I saw what they'd done to you...'

Realisation slowly dawned on Kohl. 'General Fogu...?'

'Yes, my lord. I'm here.'

Kohl fought to keep his eyes open as Fogu flew them up and out of the drowning pit, and landed gently on the hilltop.

Fogu balled his fists and then flicked his wrists, sharpening the air into a knife-like force and slashing through the rope that tied Kohl's wings, hands, knees, and ankles.

Kohl fell forward onto his hands and knees, unable to stand for the moment, coughing and trying to catch his breath. After several minutes, he looked up and gasped at the sight that greeted him. This part of town had been a bustle of activity earlier. Crowds of people gathered to watch events at the drowning pits, and ships and sky pirates had filled the area.

Now, everything had gone, replaced by a smoking mess.

Corpses lay strewn on the hilltop, some on the edges of the pits, some grouped together in heaps, as though an entire crowd of several dozen people had toppled over and died in the same instant. Blood stained the grass red, and somehow sapped colour from the air.

Kohl took a shuddering breath. 'Fogu, you didn't? You...did you...did you...'

'Kill them?' Fogu finished for him, his voice monotone. 'How else was I supposed to get to you?'

Kohl shook his head and struggled to his feet. He rested

456

one hand on Fogu's shoulder for support as he continued to take in the scene. 'The airships?'

Fogu pointed behind them, where several large ships had been reduced to splinters, half on the island, half in the sea. The tide sucked away more and more debris with each wave. Kohl could just make out a body clinging on to a piece of driftwood. He supposed it didn't matter if they were still alive, it was unlikely they'd remain that way for too much longer.

'There was a fleet of ships overhead, countless people by the pits.' Fogu steadied Kohl. 'What was I to do? Let you drown? Stand by and do nothing? Watch as my leader was murdered before me?'

Kohl took in a shuddering breath. He knew the power of the Arillian General, of course. But it had been a long time since he'd seen Arillian power working *for* him, instead of against.

He didn't have the strength to reply, so he remained where he was and took deep breaths to steady himself. Pain laced his right arm, his broken bones aching in protest. He tried to ignore the smell of burning wood and burned flesh. But he knew it wouldn't be long before others would be on their way. Certainly more sky pirates on their warships. Probably Goldstones, too, who wanted to protect their land and property. Who wanted to catch the murderers who'd taken their friends and family. 'More people...will come...'

'Yes, my lord. I shall kill them, too. Rest. I'll defend us.'

Kohl shook his head. 'No more. It's...it is done...'

Fogu pulled Kohl up straight by his shoulders. 'Do you know how many Arillians they drowned? How many of us, how many of *your* people, they have in chains?'

Kohl didn't know, and he didn't want to know. He turned away, but Fogu pulled him round again.

'Please, my lord. Don't pity them. Their lives are worth

less than nothing. They murder us, dozens of us, every day. Just for gold. Like we're some trophy.'

Kohl leaned away, wincing as his broken fingers pressed against his damp cloak. 'We are no better than them if we act in the same way.'

Fogu wouldn't let Kohl go, and held him fast. He stared into his eyes as though searching for some answer. 'What happened to you, my lord? Did Aciel hurt you that much?'

Kohl flinched, but couldn't look away. 'I...'

'You are the *greatest* of us. You command the Ice Golems. You have the Frost-touch! Why are you acting like...like...' He searched for the right words.

Kohl grit his teeth. 'Go on...say it. Call me a coward.'

Fogu closed his eyes. 'I would never insult you. But...You aren't the Kohl I know. Why didn't you fight back when they took you? You could have destroyed their ship, created a blizzard to halt their flight, anything!'

Kohl pushed away from Fogu and stumbled to the side. Already he could hear the chug of warships approaching from the south. He couldn't tell how many, but he'd bet any money in Linaria that it was a miniature fleet. They didn't have much time left. 'I lost everything, Fogu. Everything. Everyone I cared for. If I continue down that path, I...'

'I'm still here!' Fogu looped Kohl's arm over his shoulder to hold him steady. 'I know you long for peace. Who doesn't? But war is inevitable. There's no place for pacifism.'

Kohl disagreed, but he didn't have the strength to say so. He just shook his head and staggered further away from the gaping hole that Fogu had just pulled him from. Everywhere he looked, he saw death.

Fogu sent forth a sudden blast of wind so strong that it almost sent Kohl toppling over.

Kohl steadied himself against the General and glanced

back to see a large ship tip in mid-air, its crew struggling to hold it upright. 'We must go.'

'Can you fly?' Fogu asked, raising his free hand to summon a bolt of lightning to follow up his wind attack.

Kohl was grateful that Fogu didn't question him. He flexed his wings gently. The feathers were still sodden, and he doubted they'd dry off anytime soon. 'I don't think so.'

Fogu threw the bolt of lightning towards the incoming ships, the explosion sending wood and smoke high into the air. 'We're out of time. If you don't want me to kill anyone else, we have to leave. Brace yourself.'

Kohl nodded and took a deep breath. Arillians were masters of the sky. It was their dominion, and had been part of why Aciel was so against the dragons being in it. If they wanted something to fly, they'd make it happen. Fogu was no exception.

The General crouched slightly and raised his own wings, the feathers splayed wide to catch the air currents. He held his arm out and pulled the air towards him, whipping it up into a miniature gale around him, and lifted himself and Kohl off the ground.

Kohl relaxed into the pressure, as he had done when Fogu had rescued him from the pit, and allowed the General to lead them higher. It was a testament to Fogu's abilities that he could fly, keep Kohl airborne, defend them from the attacking ships, and send his own lightning bolts towards them to keep them at a distance.

Still exhausted from the drowning pit, Kohl slipped in and out of consciousness as Fogu flew them away from Estoria, and the sea opened up underneath them. He had no idea what direction they were going in, let alone what was going on, and simply trusted the General to keep the two of them safe as darkness clouded his vision.

WHEN KOHL finally opened his eyes again, it was fully night. A small fire crackled merrily to his left, and Fogu sat tending to it. He coughed as he sat up. 'Fogu?'

Unprompted, the General replied, 'We're in Val Sharis somewhere. I don't know the geography well enough to say where.' Fogu didn't look up from the fire. 'You've been asleep for two days.'

The enormity of that statement took a few seconds to sink in. Kohl looked around and realised they were in a cave, probably halfway up a mountain somewhere. The fire threw constantly shifting shadows on the walls, floor, and roof. But he was dry, and they seemed safe. 'Were...were we followed?'

'For a time.' Fogu poked the fire with a long stick.

Kohl didn't want to know the reason they'd stopped. It was naive to think the sky pirates had lost interest. If Amarah was any true representation of them, they'd follow a target to the end of the world and back again. And if that wasn't the case, he didn't want to know about Fogu killing anyone else.

They sat in silence for a long while, accompanied only by the crickets chirping and the occasional hooting of an owl outside.

Eventually, Fogu hesitantly asked, 'What now, my lord? Where do we go?'

Kohl adjusted his cloak, which had been thrown over him like a blanket. 'Oren, I think.'

Fogu nodded, a small smile on his face.

'But not just yet. I need to see the dragons, first. Need to learn what has become of them.'

At that, Fogu looked at him. 'According to the talk, they're on the warpath. Burning towns and villages until there's nothing left.'

'Jato. She's driving their anger.' Kohl sighed. He'd been foolish to think he could change her. She'd been too headstrong, too determined. Now she was grieving the loss of her lover, her father, her people. She'd been so sure in Aciel, in his campaign. She'd wanted every part of that for herself.

Unlike Fogu, who had been forced to act against his will, his powers used to devastating effect. He wondered what kind of ghosts the General lived with. He could hardly believe that Fogu had been so much and yet still fought so hard.

'There are others with her, too. Other Arillians,' Fogu said. 'Jato isn't alone. But even then, would their actions be causing the dragons to react so violently?'

Kohl sighed into his cloak. Fogu had reacted *violently* when he'd been thrown in the drowning pits. Jato needed to be stopped before she made a mistake and got herself killed. If he thought about it, Fogu might be strong enough to stop her. But he couldn't command the General to attack his own daughter. Not after everything he'd been through.

No, he had to do it himself.

Otherwise someone else—probably Amarah—would beat him to it. Amarah would show no mercy. And perhaps Jato didn't deserve mercy. But even after the atrocities she'd committed, the things she'd said to him, she was still his daughter.

He still wanted to save her from herself.

'There's also her thunderstorm to consider,' Fogu said.

'Thunderstorm?' Kohl sat up straighter, his back and wings aching in protest.

Fogu pointed with his stick towards the dark mountains in the distance. 'Hard to see at night, but it's all building there. Seems to be spreading across the centre of Val Sharis.'

Kohl squinted. Only when distant sheet lightning flashed could he actually make out the vastness of the building clouds. 'The centre of Val Sharis? I think Taban Yul is there, isn't it?'

Fogu nodded. 'Makes sense. Aciel's in the crystal just outside the city gates.'

'She's...do you think she's...'

'Preparing an attack on the city? Yes. Why else build the cloud?. She isn't going to be talking to anyone.'

Kohl thought. It could be both. Arillians had been talking to one another through their storms for generations. With a storm of that size, Jato could speak with every Arillian on the floating islands if she wanted.

But she was so single-minded that he somehow doubted that was the purpose of the storm. She was going against a city of Varkain and Ittallan, against a fleet of Imperial warships and a Sevastos. Jato was probably preparing herself to fight, or go out fighting.

'Maybe we should—' Kohl cut himself off before he could say what he'd immediately thought.

Fogu, ever respectful, didn't comment.

Kohl didn't want to drag his friend into the vendetta against his daughter, but neither did he wish to leave Jato vulnerable when she was surrounded by enemies.

He'd been slowly trying to accept the fact that he and Jato would never reconcile. Personally, he couldn't bear to be near Taban Yul and the crystal. There was too much death, too much power.

'Have you seen any dragons?' Kohl asked, trying a different angle.

'Not one. Too close to Jato.' Fogu reached to his side and pulled a pair of skinned rabbits onto the spit. He gently lay them over the fire and prodded them as he turned them.

'Perhaps. I wonder if they have some other purpose...' Kohl trailed off.

It was a puzzle. Dragons didn't attack without reason.

They were too intelligent for that. Even when they were enraged. But what was their target? According to the Estorians, there'd been dragon attacks all throughout Val Sharis, and even a few in Corhaven, too. They'd seemed random, and utterly devastating where they happened. Were they angry at all of Linaria for the death of their kin?

He wanted to find a dragon. An elder. One who was ancient enough to speak the common tongue and who might entertain his questions without eating him on sight. Of course, his Frost-touch would probably keep him safe against dragon-flame, but he didn't want to risk enraging one.

He'd saved an elder dragon before, though she had been uninterested in the affairs on Linaria. Perhaps he could try to find her again and speak with her.

He remembered kneeling on the battlefield in the aftermath of Aciel's attack. The dragon had spoken harshly to Palom. Had called him a thief of stolen power, and that he would understand sacrifice if he continued to use the *Valta Forinja*. That he was the same evil as Aciel. That he should be dead.'

Kohl had been too distraught at the time to pay much attention. Aciel had been sealed, they'd lost Moroda, but the fighting had stopped.

Now, having travelled with Amarah and seen what her *Valta Forinja* had done, he knew they were dangerous weapons that shouldn't be wielded.

If he could find that elder dragon again, perhaps she would explain more.

If Jato hadn't slaughtered her already.

'What is it, my lord?' Fogu watched him with a measured stare.

Kohl shrugged. 'I'm not sure. Palom, an ally of mine, used dragon-ore to forge several weapons. The *Valta Forinja*.

They're powerful and deadly, but cursed. A recreation of the weapons that almost destroyed us in the Great War.'

'I know them.' Fogu's voice was flat.

Kohl continued, 'Amarah, the sky pirate I travelled with, had one. She...the weapon seemed to control her in some way. Preyed on her fear. Trapped her. It's hard to explain.'

'They're despicable things.' Fogu turned back to the spit and turned the rabbits again.

'I wonder if the dragons agree. After all, they're created from their gods. Why wouldn't they hate them?'

'So what are you suggesting? The dragons are hunting them down? Why burn towns and villages, if that's the case?'

'I don't know. Perhaps they don't know where they are.' As soon as Kohl spoke, he felt foolish. It was a shot in the dark, based on guesses rather than fact.

Fogu scratched his chin. 'What about the others, then?'

'Others?'

'The originals. From the war. Where are they now?'

Kohl blinked. 'They're...at the university in Berel.' A sacred place, by all accounts. Even if he and the other Aril-lians didn't believe in Rhea, nor care for the teachings of the Goddess, he knew many who considered the city as a holy place. The source of magic, the home of Linaria's histories and knowledge.

If the *Valta Forinja* were truly as cursed as he'd seen, and the dragons really were after them, then the Samolen capital would become a target sooner or later. 'We should warn them.'

'Warn who? The Samolen?' Fogu almost laughed. When he saw Kohl's face, his mirth disappeared. 'My lord. These are not our battles to fight. The Samolen are a people of peace.'

'And they may well be sitting targets. Why not warn

464

them? Surely Jato's violence is making matters worse with the dragons.'

Fogu checked the spit one final time before standing up and brushing his robes down. 'My lord. I cannot stop you if you wish to help these people. But what of your own people? You told me they were suffering after Aciel. Let's return to Oren and do what we can for them. Linaria has always been in the middle of one war or the other. They're a barbaric people, for the most part. Look at Estoria. We're *above* them. We don't need to get involved.'

'For months, everyone has told me I need to do *something*. I need to stop being so cowardly,' Kohl said. 'Now I *want* to do something, I'm being told not to? You can't pick and choose when to get involved and when to ignore things.'

'Of course you can! Look after your people first. I will stand with you. We can rebuild what we've lost, regain our strength, and recover from Aciel's war.' Fogu almost pleaded.

'Aciel's war has only just begun. Jato acts on his behalf. Until Linaria is at peace, true peace, all this violence will continue. The dragons are a fundamental part of that balance of power. The ice will remain long after they have gone, but I'd rather live among the people of Linaria than live alone above them.'

Fogu sighed. It was clear he didn't agree, but he also didn't want to argue.

Kohl gave him time to think as he re-adjusted his cloak and shuffled his wings to get comfortable on the hard rock.

'So you want to go to Berel?' Fogu asked at last.

'Yes. As part of my investigation into the dragons.'

'And Jato?'

Kohl pursed his lips. 'I hope she won't do anything stupid. But...she is beyond me, now.' Admitting the truth hurt him more than he cared to say. But he couldn't let her slow him down anymore.

He'd tried so many times, and she'd stood firm in her decisions. Now, she was on her own.

If she changed her mind and returned home of her own accord, he would of course forgive her.

But there would be no persuading her now.

Fogu nodded, seeming to come to his own decision. 'And what of Oren and the Arillians there?'

Kohl considered for a long moment. He didn't want to abandon his people. If anything, Fogu putting himself in danger and incurring the wrath of Estoria just to save him had given him new hope, new motivation to live and make the most out of his second chance.

He needed to step up as a leader.

Jato was too busy after revenge for Aciel and didn't put her people first. If the Ice Golems accepted his return a second time, then he would not squander the chance to strengthen the Arillians and restore them to their former glory.

Kohl said, 'We'll return to Oren once we've done all we can to help in Berel. And then I'm going to visit Sirvat and Matsu. It's about time the three leaders were reunited.'

31

Antar's estimation that they'd arrive by dawn was almost perfectly accurate.

Amarah saw sunlight edge the horizon after clearing the Feor Mountains and fighting her way through the Arillian thunderstorm. By the time they approached Taban Yul, the sun had finally risen. She'd not realised how vast the Arillian storm would be—or could be—and worried that getting back through it would be nigh impossible if it kept growing. If anything, they'd have to detour far to the south to avoid it, even if it meant adding several hours —or days—to their journey back to Estoria.

Other than the battle against Aciel and his troops, Amarah hadn't really encountered Arillians before. They usually stayed on their strip of isolated land, and if they *did* venture into Linaria, it was in the northernmost towns of Val Sharis—which were equally isolated.

Now she could understand why there'd been a great war against them however many years ago. The Imperial Fleet had a purpose in keeping these damned birds out of the sky instead of harassing her and her ships.

She hoped Traego would fly her new ship safely, and

supposed he'd be picking it up about now. Or maybe a little while ago, since the sun rose in Estoria before it rose in Val Sharis. There was no-one else she trusted with her wings more than Traego, but she still didn't like the fact that he got to fly her before she had a chance to.

'Almost at the city. We'll get airborne again and fly with you,' Antar said. He patted Amarah on the shoulder and headed towards Isa's small ship, still secured to *Otella*'s deck with spans of rope.

'Better to stay here for a bit. We ain't going straight to the palace docks, mind. Trader's Alley has a dock and that'll be plenty busy. We can slip in easily and blend into the crowd. Avoid attention until we want it.'

'Why not go straight to the palace? Quicker to get our gold there, isn't it?' Judd asked, poking his head into the cabin where he'd evidently overheard their conversation.

'Because I ain't handing myself over to Sapora without talking to Isa first. The message said to talk to her or Aetos, right? Rhea knows what's been happening here since you left. I wanna get the lie of the land before I do anything. Aetos is my best bet to do that.'

Judd and Antar glanced at one another, but her logic seemed to win them over. 'Right. We'll stay close then. Head to the palace after.' Antar agreed.

Amarah didn't reply and braced herself to enter the city of snakes. She brought *Otella* slowly over the city walls, navigating towards Trader's Alley—one of the larger districts in Taban Yul, and easily identifiable from above with its blue-tiled roofs and hexagonal towers. The last time she'd flown into Taban Yul, they'd had an escort of Imperial ships to bring them in. This time, the skies were clear.

'Where's the dragon?' Oris piped up as Amarah lowered the ship. 'I thought there was a dragon?'

Amarah and the others scoured the skies, but aside from

the odd ship, they couldn't see the famed Sevastos anywhere near.

Antar shrugged. 'Maybe it's out for a fly.'

Amarah had no idea how a dragon like that was supposed to behave. But she couldn't see it, and as far as she was concerned, that was a bonus.

While the skies were clear, she brought *Otella* down and into the docks—which were full of grounded ships. If she was honest with herself, she'd probably hide in the city while a Sevastos, Arillians, and Rhea knew how many dragons flew above them. Amarah found room in a line of class one and two ships docked in the Traders' hangar. 'Reckon one of you should stay here? Keep an eye on the ship?'

Antar scoffed. 'What for? If anyone takes it, we'll see. Hardly anything in the air right now. They'd have to be pretty desperate to take an old warship. Most captains here'll probably know it's Traeg's, anyway.' He and Judd deployed a small *Thief's Shroud* over Isa's ship to cover it from view—it was the most valuable cargo they carried, after all—and then they all disembarked.

There was a thin crowd of pilots, crew, and regular Ittallan probably looking to barter passage away from Taban Yul. Amarah heard a fair amount of raised voices, cursing, and the occasional jingle of coin, and didn't blame them. The citizens wanted to get away with Jato and her Arillians on their doorstep, and the captains didn't want to risk their ships or crew.

'Amarah.'

She glanced up at a woman's voice confidently calling her name and spotted her near the hangar entrance. She wore soft leather breeches, a loose blouse, and a curved sword at her hip. Her long black hair had been tied back with gold clips, and she watched Amarah with orange-brown eyes. When they caught the sunlight, they seemed almost yellow. Definitely an Ittallan. Amarah approached her, but didn't say anything, ever suspicious of those who called her by name.

Sensing Amarah's hesitation, the woman said, 'I'm Kylos. I'm one of Princess Isa's allies. She told us to look for you. I was expecting another ship, though. A class four. *Khanna*?'

That didn't mean much.

Plenty of people knew her and knew of *Khanna*.

'You must have the wrong person in mind,' Amarah said. You could never be too careful. Besides, she'd been told to look for someone called Aetos, not Kylos. And Aetos was a male name.

Amarah and the others made their way past Kylos and out into the bustling street. Though never a fan of crowds, at least you could hide in one.

'Wait!' Kylos said. She jogged to keep up with them. 'We've all been waiting for yeh since the princess told us. She's been arrested now. We need yeh help.'

'Princess Isa's in prison?' Antar asked, his eyes wide.

Kylos nodded. 'Took us all by surprise, let me tell yeh. She was taken just yesterday. Anyway, there's plenty o' docks in the city. Aetos can't be everywhere, so he sent a few of us teh keep watch for yeh.'

At the mention of Aetos, Amarah relaxed a little.

Kylos went on, 'He's my brother. Our leader, Lathri, was arrested during the siege on the palace. He's been running things since then, but we aren't doing too well, to tell yeh the truth.'

'Clearly not if you're approaching everyone who turns up in Taban Yul.' Amarah scowled at her.

'Dragons above, you're a real piece of work, aren't yeh? How many ships d'yeh *think* have turned up in Taban Yul recently?' Kylos folded her arms. 'Not many are flying now.

470

Not with everything that's going on. And besides, I've dealt with sky pirates before. You all have the same look.'

The others muttered among themselves, indignant, but Amarah kept her gaze locked on Kylos.

Eventually, Kylos sighed and lowered her arms. 'Look. Princess Isa needs your help. We all do. Things haven't been going great since Sapora came teh power. We have a base nearby, it'll be better teh talk there—yeh never know who's listening. Come with me.' She headed off down the street, and Amarah turned to the others.

'Should we follow?' Oris asked bluntly.

'We don't have anything to lose,' Antar replied. 'And she said she's Aetos's brother.'

Amarah rolled the idea around in her mind. Every minute that passed in deliberation was another minute Isa might be closer to death. Who knew with Sapora. 'All right. We'll see what she's got to say.'

Amarah followed the Ittallan woman through the busy streets of Trader's Alley. She glanced back to the hangar once and stayed on high alert in case anyone tried to follow them, and saw Oris trailing behind as he kept watch. When she caught up to Kylos, she said, 'Anyone could have told you a snake in charge ain't a good thing. No wonder things ain't been going well for you.'

'But King Vasil was a Varkain,' Judd added. 'Didn't he rule Sereth and Val Sharis, too?'

'He did.' Kylos agreed, turning down a side street where there were fewer people. 'But Vasil stayed in Sereth and let us rule ourselves with a Council. Sapora put a stop to all that. And now the sickness in the city...' She trailed off as she navigated through side streets and alleyways, always avoiding the Imperial Guard on duty.

When Amarah realised what she was doing, she suddenly liked Kylos more.

'What sickness?' Antar asked. 'I don't hear no coughing or crying.' He looked pointedly at the Ittallan in the streets, who all seemed perfectly healthy.

Kylos shrugged. 'It's hard teh explain.' They reached a small bridge that joined Traders' Alley to another section of the city. Amarah peered over the edge at the small stream below, its waters flowing quickly.

'Amarah. Thief. How dare you steal from me. How dare you.'

Amarah stopped, struck by the thunderous voice in her mind.

'You don't deserve to live, do you? You traitor. Step off the bridge. Linaria is better off without you.'

She swallowed, turned to the side, and placed her hands on the bridge's rail. She peered over again.

'Good. Climb up and jump off. Now.'

The commanding voice rattled in her head, echoing over and over, drowning out the conversation around her. She couldn't even hear the rushing water below.

She shivered. She'd heard the voice before. Recognised the commanding tone.

It had taken control of her when she'd been on Jato's warship with Moroda and Sapora, when she'd been after the Ereven Sphere. Aciel had spoken to her, forced his will on her, and compelled her to listen.

She'd never forget that voice as long as she lived.

'...isn't that right, Amarah?' It was Judd.

'Huh?' Amarah half-glanced towards him, though a powerful, invisible force compelled her to keep her attention on the stream.

'Climb over. Jump.'

'I said there's all sorts of monsters in the world,' Judd repeated.

She remembered Veynothi's tomb, the blade, and the monster from the sea. The nightmarish visions from her

Valta Forinja filled her mind, and she shivered again. 'Need to get rid of 'em.'

Oris ran forward and shoved her to the side in his haste to get through. 'Got Imperial Guard marching up!' He warned.

The physical push distracted her enough for Aciel's voice to fade slightly. Shaking her head to clear it, Amarah grabbed onto Oris as he hurtled forward, and used his momentum to get away from the bridge. She and the others ran onwards, putting as much distance between themselves and the soldiers as they could.

If Aciel still lived, Sapora would be the least of their troubles.

～

THE LAST GRAPE was a Goldstone inn if ever Amarah had seen one.

Money practically oozed from the front.

She supposed it made sense—she was replying to Isa's call for help, and Isa *was* royalty.

Amarah hadn't shaken the chill from hearing Aciel's voice in her mind, *commanding* her. She had no idea how his powers worked and wondered whether she was simply having flashbacks after all the stress she'd been through, or if there was some way he'd overcome the Sevastos' seal and was able to influence people.

Either way, it didn't bode well, and she wanted to get out of Taban Yul as quickly as possible. She'd rather take on that awful sea monster again than be forced to act against her will by the damned Arillian. Aciel and Jato were just as bad as each other, it seemed.

Amarah had no idea what to expect inside the inn. Would there be half a dozen bedraggled citizens gearing

473

themselves up to fight Sapora? Would it be a small army? Or was the whole thing a trap, and Sapora himself would be waiting inside to chain them up?

Instinctively, she grasped the handle of her scythe. The familiar weapon in her clutches had always relaxed her somewhat. Antar was clearly a fighter too, and could hold his own. Amarah was less sure of Judd and Oris, but they'd spent some time in Estoria. They wouldn't have lasted if they couldn't at least swing a sword. And Malot, of course, was a Kalosuk.

She didn't want to glance at them or give them any reason to think she was afraid. She wasn't, of course. But she'd always been apprehensive about going into a new environment unprepared. If Isa was to be trusted, then there'd be nothing to fear.

Kylos nodded to a man stood guard in front of the door. 'Thanks, Chyro.'

He wore ringmail under his long-sleeved shirt and Amarah saw the hilt of a knife poking out from the top of his boot. His long jacket fell to his knees, potentially obscuring more weapons. He held himself confidently, feet wide apart and hands behind his back. If she didn't know any better, she'd have said he was in the Imperial Guard. Or certainly had been.

You could always tell the soldiers apart.

The Ittallan—Chyro—opened the door for them and Amarah followed Kylos into *The Last Grape*. She took a deep breath to steel her nerves, and tightened her grip on the handle of her scythe.

'Kylos!' A roar went up from the gathered Ittallan inside. There had to be at least fifty of them, many of whom were sat at one of three long tables, though others stood with mugs of ale or lounged by the fire pit. A few wore full armour, but most only had a few pieces—a breastplate, shoulder guards, a helm under an arm.

Amarah smelled the metal as she walked in. It was mixed with food, ale, and wine, and she was immediately transported back to Estoria. She relaxed the grip on her scythe, and the crowd's attention turned to her and the others.

Sudden movement caught her eye, and Amarah looked down in time to see a small dragon with vivid sea-blue scales launch itself across the room and bounded over to her.

'*Leillu!*'

'Palom?' Amarah gasped, incredulous.

The huge Ittallan leaped up to follow the young dragon, who skidded to a halt at his booming voice. 'Amarah is friend. We do not attack her.' He spoke down to the little creature like it was a toddler, his hands on his hips and a frown on his face.

The dragon tilted its head and then looked back to Amarah with quizzical, intelligent eyes. It flexed its wings and bobbed its head up and down several times, and then walked towards her at a more measured pace.

Anxious, she looked to Palom, who simply watched the dragon snuffle around her like a dog.

'Good. Are you happy now? Will you come back to fire?' Palom asked, after *Leillu* lost interest in the new arrivals.

Leillu chirped at him and returned to his side, tail lashing gently from side to side.

'Palom? Dragons above, what's going on?' Amarah asked, staring at him in bewilderment. To make her point perfectly clear, she pointed at *Leillu* with the tip of her scythe. No-one else in *The Last Grape* seemed surprised at the dragon's presence, so she assumed it wasn't anything new to them.

'Is...long story.'

'I can imagine.' Amarah didn't know what else to say. But considering she'd fought with a *Valta Forinja*, carried the blade of an Ark, and had arrived in a city patrolled by a Sevastos, there wasn't much that should surprise her anymore. She'd need to take it all in her stride, just like everything else.

'Take a seat. We need to get yeh up to speed,' Kylos said. She clasped Palom by the forearm in greeting before sitting down at the nearest table.

Amarah didn't disagree. It was a small army that had gathered inside the inn. Most were Ittallan but there were more than a few from Corhaven, too. Unsurprisingly, there weren't any other Samolen.

Malot was the first to sit at the table, positioning herself beside Kylos. Judd followed, and then Oris. Antar rolled his shoulders before approaching. He nodded to Palom and sat next to him.

Amarah kept her eyes on *Leillu*, then sat on Palom's other side.

The talk and laughter died down when Kylos cleared her throat. This was to be a full briefing, from the looks of things. 'Aetos'll be back soon. He and a couple o' others are at other docks waiting for yeh. Princess Isa trusts yeh, so we do, too.'

Two serving girls approached with flagons of ale. Amarah refused, but Antar and the others took the offered drink while they listened.

Kylos went on, 'Lathri's the daughter of a former member of the Council. Her mother, Drutia, was killed by Sapora. So were many of our friends and family. That's no way to start a new rule, is it? Lathri believes Isa should be Queen of Val Sharis, and we back her, too. Sapora can have Sereth. In retaliation to his slaughter, we attacked the palace at the end of winter. Isa managed to get some Imperial warships to fight for us, Rhea knows how. But Sapora pulled his trump card and we discovered his damned Sevastos too late.'

Amarah let her gaze wander to the others gathered in *The Last Grape*. Ittallan had an innate skill at arms. At least if she helped this lot, they'd be able to hold their own.

Kylos took a shuddering breath. 'Part of Taban Yul is still smouldering thanks to his dragon. And those of us he didn't kill, he imprisoned, including Lathri. Isa, me, and a few others tried to break her out, but I wound up getting caught.'

That surprised Amarah. Kylos looked too cunning to be caught by regular palace guards. She wondered what the security was actually like.

'But Isa managed to get me out. Since then, the snakes have kept a close eye on her. Yesterday, Isa reported that Sapora's now on the cusp of freeing an Ark. An ancient Varkain weapon used to kill thousands of Ittallan. When he gets that, the world is doomed. And I don't mean just Val Sharis. I mean all of Linaria is gonna be wiped out by these things.'

Amarah swallowed. Veynothi's blade suddenly weighed a tonne.

Kylos looked directly at Amarah. 'So we need yeh help. We need yeh to break Lathri out, and free Isa, too. We don't have much time left.'

'About the Ark...' Antar said, shifting in his seat. He'd put his flagon down on the table and scratched his cheek.

Amarah sighed. There was no point in keeping their knowledge of Veynothi from Kylos and the others. They'd all find out once they'd been to the palace, anyway. 'We have Veynothi's blade. One of the Arks.' She lightly patted her hip where the stone blade was secured in a thick sheath. 'We were asked to bring it to Sapora.'

Conversation exploded around them.

'Can't trust sky pirates!'

'Damned thieves!'

'Only interested in gold!'

'Kill them before they get to Sapora!'

'Traitors!'

Screams and shouting blurred into one another.

Amarah and the others were on their feet at the threats, weapons drawn in a heartbeat.

Palom and Kylos also stood, arms raised. 'Stand back!'

'It doesn't *matter* whether Sapora gets this blade or not!' Kylos snapped. 'He's already found the tomb of Malashash. He knows how to break the seal after talking to the Valendrin. It doesn't matter what Amarah and her pirates do!'

'We need Lathri,' Palom said. The enraged roars slowly settled. Clearly the Ittallan were unhappy, but lacked any other choice, and couldn't stand up to Palom. 'She is our leader. Sapora will do what he wants. Lathri cannot be freed without Amarah.' He stared down any who dared challenge him, and between Palom and Kylos, much of the excitement faded.

Pressing forward with practical planning in the lull, Amarah said, 'It's a hard thing to do. Breaking into *and* out of a palace.' She looked out the window to the deserted street, trying to work out the best approach. 'The palace is heavily guarded, right? Can't really scale the towers. No. Best thing is to get captured and then break everyone out.'

'What?' Antar snapped. 'What's the point of coming all this way if we're just going to let ourselves get arrested? We're here for gold, not to join some resistance movement.'

That caused more angry conversation.

'Don't worry. There's more gold in the palace than just in Sapora's pocket. We can have our pick of whatever we want on our way out. Good reward for the risk, don't you think?'

'We want Isa to be queen. We don't want you to rob her

home!' Kylos said, struggling to maintain her own composure.

'Well, I'd negotiate our fee with Isa directly but as she ain't here, we'll have to improvise,' Amarah said. 'We go to the palace as planned. Give Sapora this damned blade to get rid of it. We tell him where the tomb is and he'll go off to investigate.' She saw Kylos's horrified expression and grinned. 'We'll tell him to go somewhere else. Don't matter where we send him, as long as it's ages away. He has the blade as proof, he'll be so desperate that he'll fly anywhere. While he's gone, we break out and everyone's happy.'

A few Ittallan nodded. Amarah saw them as pirates in their own way, doing their own thing and going against the grain. But what they did wasn't for gold or glory. They were in real trouble. If they didn't put a stop to Sapora and these Arks, Linaria might never recover.

'You make it sound so easy,' Kylos said. 'Sapora will be annoyed when he realises you've sent him on a wild goose chase.'

'We do this for living.' Amarah cackled and allowed herself a grin.

Judd seemed unconvinced. 'How do we get away? Even if Sapora's gone, there'll still be Varkain in the palace, Imperial Guard in the city. Getting back to the ships with a bunch of prisoners won't be easy.'

'We don't put the ships in the docks. We land on one of the palace towers. Wherever's nearest the dungeons. Can you tell us that?' Amarah asked.

'They're on the east side. Below ground,' Kylos said.

'Then we land *Otella* on top of one of the east towers. A few of them have flat tops, I've seen.' Amarah replied. 'All we have to do is get to the top of the tower instead of crossing half the city. And Antar, you can get my warship. With *Otella* and my ship together, we'll have enough fire to cover our escape to Estoria.'

'Wait, you are going to Estoria? With Princess Isa?' Palom asked.

'You wanna stay in this city after what we plan to do?' Antar raised an eyebrow. 'Everyone knows you gotta lie low after a big job like this. Sapora'll be *pissed* when he gets back. I ain't staying anywhere near Val Sharis after I take his gold.'

Judd said to Kylos, 'You'll want to make yourself scarce.'

Kylos raised her arms and gestured to the Ittallan gathered in the room. 'We aren't abandoning our true queen. If we have to leave Taban Yul for a while and help her gain strength elsewhere, we'll do that.'

Amarah snorted. 'How exactly are you all planning on doing that?'

Kylos met her gaze. 'We fly with you. The ship you came here on is large. You talked about another warship in the palace. We can join you.'

Amarah wasn't sure how Traego would feel about ferrying all these Ittallan back to Estoria for free. From the looks of Antar and the others, they thought the same thing. But from the passion in Kylos's eyes, Amarah wasn't sure she could talk any of them out of it.

'There *would* be space,' Judd said, ever helpful. 'Amarah, if your warship is anything like *Otella*, there'll be plenty of capacity.'

Antar shook his head. 'This was meant to be a, "deliver something and take the gold," job. Nice and simple. Now we're taking all of you lot back with us?' He was incredulous. 'We ain't no transport company! What we came here to do with Sapora is risky enough. Now you want a palace jail-break, too?'

Amarah dragged both hands down her face.

'Do you want to help Princess Isa or do you only want gold?' Palom asked.

It was a stupid question. A year ago, she'd have answered gold without hesitation. But now?

She sighed, ignored Palom's question, and continued to plan. 'We'd need a ground team, then. And someone to manage all of you. Someone who makes sure you get to the ships on time. Someone who knows the city well. We ain't gonna have much time to stop, so if you're coming, you'd need to be ready.'

'I'll do that,' Kylos said.

'I will help, too,' Palom said.

The two looked at each other, then Kylos nodded. 'What else d'yeh need?'

Truthfully, Amarah wasn't sure. She, Antar, Judd, and Oris would be in the palace. Between them, she was sure her jailbreak could be instigated successfully. They'd help themselves to anything of value in the palace, make their way back to the ships, and fight off any defences Sapora left.

When they got to their ships, they'd need to rendezvous with the ground team and every one of Isa's followers who wanted to flee with their future queen. Traego would provide cover when he arrived, and they'd make their escape to Estoria.

In her head, she could see it all play out. 'You'll have to use this time to get your things. Whatever supplies you can carry. Food, weapons, gold, anything. Sapora's gonna leave immediately, so we need to get moving tonight.'

'There's another thing,' Oris said.

'What?' Amarah asked, irritated that he'd found a crack in her plan.

'Jato.'

The tension in the room increased at the mention of the Arillian's name and Amarah frowned. The damned thunderstorm wasn't going anywhere. They'd need to take the longer route out, which would make escape even harder.

'She killed few of us when we were on way here,' Palom said. 'Many are in mausoleum now.'

Amarah said, 'You're welcome to join the queue for revenge on Jato. We flew here. We'll fly out again. Damned bird ain't going nowhere. Let's focus on one thing at a time.'

Palom folded his arms but didn't argue.

'I don't plan on giving Jato up to no-one. You can say your friends are avenged after *I* kill her.'

'Was it Jato who...' Palom nodded to her eye patch.

'She took a lot from me. She won't get away with it,' Amarah snapped. 'I'm more than capable of fighting my own battles.'

'Where is Kohl?'

Amarah couldn't ignore the edge in Palom's voice as he spoke of the Arillian. 'He's gone off to investigate the dragons. He's a dragon hunter, right? He wants to find out what he can.'

Antar drained his flagon and stood up. 'Well, it's *lovely* catching up and everything, but we're on a tight deadline. Sapora's expecting his proof by the end of today.'

Amarah knew he was right. She'd always known she'd have to see and talk to Sapora. But the heist excited her more than her apprehension of seeing the Varkain again. She cackled. 'I'm used to breaking in, not breaking out. But it's pretty much the same thing, ain't it?'

'Let me help you.' It was a young woman, an Ittallan, who shared similar features as Palom.

'Solvi. Is dangerous. Stay with me on ground,' Palom replied quickly.

Solvi shook her head. 'I want to help Lathri. I want to help Princess Isa. They've done so much for me. I can fight.

My senses are better than these sky pirates. Amarah, please. Let me come with you.'

Palom looked pleadingly to Amarah.

Amarah shrugged. 'Can always say you're part of my crew, I suppose. Doubt Sapora will care who you are when he's just interested in the Arks.'

'I don't want you in danger,' Palom said. 'Going into palace with Sapora. He might kill you.'

'*Kali*,' Solvi said softly. 'I know you want me safe. But I've been here, in Taban Yul, since you left. I've been working with Aetos, Kylos, and everyone else. I wouldn't ask to help if I didn't think I could do this.'

Amarah smiled. She was definitely related to Palom. If she was half the fighter the tiger was, then she'd be an ace up their sleeve when it came to dealing with the guards.

Kylos said, 'Solvi's tough. She's kept up with us, no complaints, since she got here.'

Eventually Palom sighed. 'I do not like this, Solvi. But...I cannot stop you.'

'Wait for me, *kali*. I'll come to you with Lathri and Princess Isa. I promise.'

Malot stood up. 'I'll leave Taban Yul, see if I can meet Traego and the others. I'll let them know the plan and make sure they're ready to help. Amarah, if your new ship is fast, he'll be here soon.'

'Should be plenty fast so long as Venin kept his word,' Amarah said.

'He will. He knows his ships better than me,' Judd replied.

'Good luck, then,' Malot said. She nodded to the others and left *The Last Grape* as Amarah and the others went over the details of the biggest, most dangerous heist they'd ever carried out.

32

Morgen didn't bother to open his eyes when Andel knocked on his door.

He'd realised rather quickly that Andel only knocked to be polite. It wasn't an invitation for Morgen to approach the door, much less try and open it. It was simply a notification that Andel had brought a meal for him.

Whatever magic Topeko had done to him—and the door —Morgen didn't know. He supposed there was a chance it would be explained in one of the heavy books that had been left in his room, but he had no interest in reading any of them.

He just wanted to talk, face to face, instead of being confined to his room like a disobedient dog.

And he wanted to know what had happened to his memory. He'd lost hours of time, and had no idea what had happened, or why he'd been made to forget it.

Clearly his true punishment would come whenever the Arch-Kalos arrived. He had no weapon, no *Valta Forinja*. He was a rubbish student of magic. He was absolutely no threat to Andel or Topeko.

Yet every time he'd screamed these arguments through the sealed door, he was met with silence.

So when Andel came to deliver one of his meals, Morgen didn't bother to get up, didn't even open his eyes. He remained exactly where he was, curled up on top of the sheets, facing the windowless wall, his knees tucked up almost to his chin, and arms looped around his shins.

'...Morgen?'

His name was whispered.

He slowly unclenched his body and twisted to look over his shoulder.

Andel stood in the middle of his room, the door closed behind him, a plate of food held in one hand.

Morgen sat up immediately but was wary of further magic or trickery. He didn't dare say anything just yet in case Andel or Topeko imprisoned him further.

'It's okay. You can take your food.' Andel held the plate somewhat higher, as though tempting him closer. Still unsure, Morgen remained where he was.

Once Andel realised Morgen wasn't going to take the plate, he placed it on the side table, then smoothed down his robes. Morgen realised this was the first time he'd ever seen Andel look uncomfortable.

Andel ran a hand through his short hair. 'I'm...I'm sorry about...' He gestured vaguely to the room. 'All this.'

Morgen managed a pained smile and raised his shoulders in what he hoped passed for a shrug of nonchalance.

'It won't be for much longer. Arch-Kalos Dhabra is on his way to Berel.'

The name didn't mean anything to Morgen, but he nodded anyway.

'I'll be getting my new jewel before that, though. I'll be a Kalosin!' Andel beamed as he spoke, the epitome of pride.

Morgen couldn't bring himself to share in Andel's jubilation. Not after what he'd been through the past however many days. Without windows, he had no idea how to mark the passage of time. Stress gnawed at him, so he ate little and slept less. 'That's good.' His voice croaked.

Andel's smile slipped from his face. 'Yes. Thank you. It also means...'

'Judgement?' Morgen shrugged properly, then. He had no idea how Samolen punished their own. At best, he'd be kicked out. Maybe banished from Berel or even Ranski. At worst, he supposed he could have his mind completely wiped, and he'd forever walk Linaria a simpleton.

'Judgement,' Andel echoed. 'I don't know what'll happen. I've never seen Topeko like this.'

'Is he okay?' Morgen asked, though his throat hurt when he spoke.

'He'll be fine. I think he's at a loss. Even Amarah never did what you did. She just left.'

Morgen frowned. 'I'd leave if I could, but apparently I'm a prisoner here.'

'You don't want to study any longer?' Andel seemed aghast.

Morgen shrugged again. 'Well it's not like I'll be allowed to carry on, is it? I broke one of your most *sacred* laws, remember? I was only trying to protect you.' He couldn't keep the petulance from his voice. The fact he was being treated like a threat had wounded his pride and sense of duty.

Andel looked at the floor. 'I know you tried to help. You weren't malicious. Topeko knows that, too, you do realise that?'

'Then why does it feel like...like...' Morgen struggled for the right words. 'I murdered someone?'

Andel opened his mouth to reply but thought better of it. He ran another hand through his hair and glanced back

486

to the door. 'Because you *can't* do what you did. You *can't*. If we break our oaths of peace, it would doom us all.'

'What do you mean?' Suddenly, Morgen wished he'd read more. He'd never sworn an oath, had he? Not since arriving in Berel? But with his memory apparently something that could be manipulated and erased, now he wasn't so sure.

'You know the crystals at the university? The Sevastos crystals?'

'Yeah...'

'They power Ranski. The whole country, not just Berel. They give us heat, light, running water. Everything. This place would be a desert, otherwise. Instead, it's an oasis. A gift from Rhea's greatest children. And in return for this awesome power, we cannot and do not use it to harm anything else. No living thing may be attacked by our power, much less killed. It's why we can only learn *Ra*. Life. *He* is forbidden not just because of it's dangerous nature—there are plenty of Samolen who feel they are righteous enough to try it—but because that is *against* the power we have been given. Break the oath and the Sevastos crystals will lose their power.'

Morgen took a few seconds to let everything Andel had said sink in. Upholding peace, not getting involved in the conflicts across Linaria. It wasn't some arbitrary rule. It was the lifeblood of the Samolen. And he'd almost taken that away from them. 'But...but I'm not a Samolen. I'm from Corhaven.'

'Who knows if that matters or not? You harmed a dragon while standing in Berel. You used a magical weapon to do it. It's no wonder the Arch-Kalos has to come and assess the situation himself.'

Guilt and fear rose in Morgen's gut. 'But you were attacked first! It's not like I went out hunting for a battle!'

Andel didn't say anything.

Morgen pressed, 'The Sevastos crystals? They haven't changed, have they? Since I've been locked up? You can all still use your magic?'

'So far, no change. But again, who knows. Maybe we have days left. Maybe years. Maybe there'll be no change at all.'

Sweat beaded on Morgen's forehead at the thought of destroying an entire country by mistake. He wanted to learn what magic he could to *help* Linaria, not wipe one of its races from the face of the world. 'And...and my memories?'

'A precaution.'

Morgen understood that. It was no wonder Topeko was beside himself. If the Samolen lost access to their power because of him, Topeko would no doubt feel the brunt of his peers, too. Morgen sank to his knees as panic threatened to overwhelm him. Even though he'd been so sure in his actions, he'd never have dreamed it would cause the Samolen to lose their power. 'Oh Andel, I'm so sorry. I'm so, so, so, sorry. I didn't know! I didn't realise!'

Andel crouched beside him and rested a hand on his shoulder. 'I think it'll be okay. You can't be the first person to accidentally harm someone else in Berel. I'm sure hundreds of ants get stepped on every day!'

Morgen found little comfort in Andel's attempt at humour. 'It was a dragon...'

'It was.' Andel nodded gravely.

'I cut it. I felt its blood on my skin.'

Andel nodded again but didn't say anything. His humour had faded.

'Why...why are you telling me all this?' Morgen looked up at him, distraught.

'Because I'm going to get my cheek jewel. You won't see me for a few days. It's customary that when a Kalosai earns their jewel, they visit the other universities throughout Ranski. Berel isn't the only one, you know.'

Morgen didn't know. 'Of course.'

Andel pursed his lips together and patted Morgen gently on the back. 'I'll...I'll see you soon, Morgen.' He stood, straightened his robes again, and left the room.

Morgen watched him go, fear rising in his gut, utterly terrified that he'd be judged, gone and forgotten, by the time Andel returned

~

NIGHTMARES PLAGUED Morgen every time he closed his eyes.

If it wasn't Sapora and his snakes, it was an army of angry Kalos carrying spears and swords as well as their burning magic. The dread of not knowing exactly what was to come simply made the dreams worse.

He constantly woke in cold sweats and missed Andel's cheerful nature to calm him down or explain things to him. Though Andel couldn't have been more than thirteen or fourteen, he was the only companion Morgen had had since leaving the Imperial Guard. Morgen would go so far as to call him a friend.

And he'd thrown away that friendship with his stupid blunder.

When the dragons attacked, Topeko had told him to return to the house, Morgen remembered that quite clearly. If only he'd followed instructions and waited with Andel. He could see the Kalos' shield had protected the university from the rampaging dragons. Why had he felt it so necessary to get involved and try to help?

He picked at his fingernails, furious with himself.

He was always messing things up.

He'd messed up on his parents' farm constantly, and left

489

it to forge himself a new life in the Imperial Guard. He'd wanted to become a famous knight and earn sacks of gold. And that had also fallen by the wayside.

He'd tried to do the right thing when Moroda and Amarah had been locked up. He'd tried to find Amarah a medic, and while his back was turned, they'd all escaped.

He'd tried to track them down in the city, wasting half an afternoon searching through market stalls, and they'd got away.

He'd been relegated to watching over the castle armoury only to have the dragon attack the city, and when he'd tried to put a stop to it, he'd messed that up, too.

And he'd failed Eryn and Moroda.

Everywhere he looked in his past, he was met with failure. Right now, he'd threatened not just his own magical education, but the lives of however many millions of Samolen across Ranski. It wasn't as if they could just live without their magic, either. If what Andel said was true, there'd be no running water, no food, no resources. Everyone who lived in the country would have to move north into Corhaven, or cross the sea, or stay and perish.

Morgen sighed. It would be funny if it wasn't so damned terrible.

Perhaps he should have just stayed in Povmar. As a Captain of the Imperial Guard, he'd had certain perks. The money was manageable. Yes, it had been boring as anything, but he'd been safe. No-one had known where he was, and no-one travelled to that part of Corhaven.

His biggest worry had been the griffins.

Living in Povmar until the end of his days could have been a very real, very safe prospect.

And what was he doing now?

Even if he learned how to master *Ra*, even if by some miracle he could tap into *He* without destroying all of

Ranski, how was he truly going to make a difference? Sapora was a king. He had armies at his disposal. Elite soldiers. Warships. The strength of Val Sharis and Sereth. And a Sevastos.

Morgen had to accept the fact that he was simply the son of a farmer, with little gold to his name, and no chance of making a difference in anything.

He got up from his bed and walked to the door. Although he knew it was futile, Morgen tried the handle again. It was still locked, of course.

He sighed and leaned into the wood, feeling like the biggest fool in the world.

It was exactly as Andel had said; he wasn't malicious. Never had been. And he *did* want to protect others—it was a large factor in him joining the Imperial Guard rather than trying to find his fortune elsewhere. But what was the point of trying to be a good person when everything constantly crumbled or slipped through your fingers?

What was the point when you were punished for trying to help?

Balling his fists, Morgen pounded on the door again. 'Topeko! Please! Please let me out so we can talk! I'll obey everything you tell me, I swear to Rhea!'

He raised his arm to punch the door again when the lock clicked and it swung inwards, almost catching Morgen on the chin. He quickly stepped back and dropped his arm to his side lest he seem too aggressive, and tried to mask his surprise at having his request granted.

Topeko stood in the doorway. The Samolen was not old —he couldn't have been more than about forty-five—but he'd aged in the days Morgen had been locked up. His dark curly hair had somehow lost its shape, his cheek jewel had lost its lustre, and Topeko's eyes no longer danced.

'Kalos Topeko!' Morgen gasped. He didn't want to come

across as rude, not when Topeko had the power to keep him locked up again, so Morgen straightened his stance and waited for the Samolen to address him.

'Ah, Kalosai Morgen.' Topeko bowed in greeting.

Morgen didn't know why he sounded so surprised to see him. Surely Topeko knew it was his room? He was about to reply when Topeko took a step backwards to allow another man, a much older one, to approach the doorway.

Morgen stared at the man, his mouth slack. It had to be the Arch-Kalos. He'd never seen a Samolen with more than two cheek jewels, and this man had all four; red, yellow, green, and white.

His robe was more elaborate than the other Kalos' of the University, and he wore a headdress of trailing silks in a rainbow of colours. Under his loose sleeves, Morgen saw a ring of jewelled bracelets coiling up his wrinkled arms. Crows' feet grew around both eyes; one brown, one blue; and it was the blue eye that seemed to stare right through him.

Uncomfortable, Morgen dropped his gaze.

'So. This is your troublesome Kalosai, is it?' Arch-Kalos Dhabra said. His voice was sharper than Morgen had expected, somehow piercing, and did not match the old man's body.

Morgen kept his eyes fixed on a spot on the floor and listened intently.

'Yes it is, Arch-Kalos.' Topeko replied.

'Hmm.' His tone dripped with condescension. 'What have you done to secure things since the incident, Kalos Topeko?'

'The offending weapon is under the University's protection. It's in a sealed vault.'

'Good. Good.' The Arch-Kalos touched Morgen's chin

492

with the tip of one finger and lifted his face to stare at him again.

Morgen bit down the urge to flinch. Dhabra's skin burned where it touched him.

Topeko added, 'He's also been cleansed. It made sense at the time.'

'A pity. It always helps to get the story directly from the offenders.'

Morgen swallowed. He didn't much like being discussed like an object not worthy of his own name. But he knew Arch-Kalos Dhabra was the most powerful Samolen in Ranski. Offending him would *not* be in his best interest.

Suddenly, he wished Andel was here. He had a way of somehow diffusing tension and instilling confidence, both things Morgen needed right now.

He also assumed "cleansed" referred to his memories, and wondered if perhaps Topeko had done it as a precautionary measure to keep him safe from whatever magic Dhabra would inflict. He'd only met the man for a minute and was already terrified of him.

'Look at me, Kalosai.' Arch-Kalos Dhabra demanded, his voice hardening as he addressed Morgen.

Ever obedient, Morgen looked at the man directly and held his gaze.

The brown eye seemed normal at first glance, and the blue was certainly more striking. But with both eyes fixated on him, Morgen suddenly felt rooted to the floor as Dhabra's glare seemed to peel away his flesh, his soul, and look at his very essence.

Morgen was aware he trembled but could do nothing against it. He couldn't even breathe.

He was sure his heart had stopped beating, too.

How long he stood there, in the clutches of the Arch-Kalos, he didn't know. It could have been a lifetime.

When Dhabra deigned it, he released Morgen from his grip, and Morgen fell to the floor.

'Your cleansing was thorough,' Dhabra said. He sounded disappointed.

Topeko knelt down and helped Morgen back to his feet.

Morgen was grateful for Topeko's gentle warmth, and too shaky to do anything but lean on the Kalos and take shallow breaths.

Topeko said, 'I would not want one of my students to suffer unduly, Arch-Kalos. Wouldn't you agree?'

Dhabra had lost interest. He'd whirled around, robes skimming the floor, as he waved a hand dismissively. 'Yes, yes, of course. Get him back into training and keep the weapon locked away. Where is your other Kalosai?'

Topeko gently walked Morgen down the hallway after Dhabra.

Morgen was too dazed to protest. It felt like all their air had gone out of him, and he was struggling to work his body. His legs were slow and heavy, as though he walked through waist-deep mud.

'Kalosin Andel is visiting the other universities,' Topeko said.

'Already? That's young. He is adept, then?' Dhabra looked over his shoulder.

Morgen didn't dare look into Dhabra's eyes again and quickly dropped his gaze.

'Very. I am continually amazed and impressed by his skills.'

'Good. Good.' Dhabra was again dismissive.

Topeko led Morgen around the corner and into the large entrance hall where he and Andel usually took their meals.

'Have care, Kalos,' Dhabra said. He adjusted his headdress. 'The Arillian woman is causing chaos in Val Sharis.

I'd implore all Kalosai of the university to have a mastery of the shield immediately. It may be needed again.'

'Yes, Arch-Kalos,' Topeko bowed. He helped Morgen to sit at the bench beside the table, and then stood closer to Dhabra. 'I always look forward to receiving your wisdom. I'll ensure the students are well prepared.'

Dhabra stared at Topeko, but Morgen couldn't tell whether Topeko was affected or not.

'I need to be on my way. There's a Kalosai in Tarika who requires encouragement. I'm not surprised, considering he has not a drop of Samolen blood in him. But we must keep up appearances, mustn't we? And you always did have a soft spot for half-breeds and weaklings. What was that runt of a girl you had?'

Morgen could see Topeko's entire body pull away from the Arch-Kalos, but he didn't take a physical step away. Perhaps out of respect? Or fear? Or maybe Dhabra could control Topeko like he'd controlled him?

'Amarah,' Topeko said. Despite the not-so veiled insult, Topeko's tone remained polite.

Dhabra's face split into a wicked grin. 'Amarah. Yes. Your little dirt puppy. That's right. Well, he's much the same.' He waved a hand in Morgen's general direction. 'You ought to get rid of him. He'll bring you nothing but misery, just like Amarah. But I must be off. I'll return when he's ready—if he's ever ready—and we'll see what's become of him by then.'

Topeko bowed low and didn't look up until long after Dhabra had left his house.

'Um...Kalos...Topeko?' Morgen whispered, trying to control the tremors that rattled through his chest.

'Morgen?' Topeko straightened up.

'It's...I'm very cold...' The shivering rippled up and down

495

him, from his toes to his neck and back again. No matter how he tried to breathe, he couldn't relax.

Topeko exhaled through his nose. 'I'm sorry to have subjected you to that, Morgen. There was no other way.' He hurried over to the drawers beneath the bookcases which lined the walls and pulled a thick cotton blanket from one. 'Here. This should help. Believe me, your body isn't cold. Your mind just isn't used to being...interrogated. The chill will pass.'

Morgen gratefully took the heavy blanket and wrapped it around himself, sure to cover both arms. He held the fabric close to his face and waited for the shivers to stop. He felt as though he'd just spent a week solid doing drills. Exhausted, drained, overwhelmed. He couldn't give words to it.

Topeko sat opposite him. 'I hope you can forgive me.'

Morgen wasn't sure he'd heard correctly. 'Forgive you? What for?'

'For that.' He pointed to the blanket. 'I wish you hadn't done what you did. I wish I could turn back time and change what happened. I can help you through things when you're here, in my home. But when you're in public, in full view of everyone—including other Kalos—I can't cover it up. And Dhabra...' Topeko trailed off.

Morgen didn't want to think about Dhabra. But he thought a great deal about what Dhabra had said. He'd clearly insulted himself, Amarah, and Topeko, too. Andel he seemed rather impressed with, and Morgen wasn't sure that was any better for Andel.

Had Topeko sent him off to get his cheek jewel before he was ready so he wouldn't be here when Dhabra arrived?

'Kalos Topeko. I think...is it true you Samolen are all about peace? No conflict?'

Topeko nodded. 'You know that's true.'

'After seeing the Arch-Kalos, I have my doubts.'

Topeko rolled his eyes and rested his chin in his hands. 'The Arch-Kalos isn't like you or me. Or any of the other Kalos.'

'I didn't realise you could wipe my memory. I didn't realise it was possible to...to...*investigate* my mind?' Morgen tried to remember the phrasing Topeko had used.

The Kalos took one of Morgen's hands in his own.

The warmth from Topeko's fingers pushed away the cold instilled by the Arch-Kalos. Morgen stopped shivering. 'And here I thought it was just about lighting fires and moving them from one side of the room to another.'

Topeko smiled then. A genuine one. 'Andel will be back in a few days. Enjoy the rest of your break while you can.'

'So...I...I'm not going to be punished then?'

'No.' Topeko answered almost too quickly. Catching himself, the Kalos said, 'Not any time soon. You'll need to listen to me, Morgen. Really listen. Learn what I'm trying to teach you, and you'll be able to not only defend against powers like that of the Arch-Kalos, but I think you'll learn how to protect those you wish to save. Can you do that for me?'

Morgen nodded slowly. Whatever conversations he would have had with Topeko and Andel would be at risk when Dhabra arrived. That's why he'd needed to be locked away, his memories taken, and conversations forbidden.

He was relieved beyond measure that Topeko wasn't angry with him. That Topeko still believed in him. And terrified at what a Kalos was capable of.

Morgen knew his memories had been wiped because he couldn't give away anything if he didn't know it in the first place. He shuddered at the thought of Dhabra, of his eyes boring into his. Morgen asked, 'Didn't...didn't he say something about "that Arillian"?'

Topeko's frown deepened. 'Jato.'

Morgen tightened his grip on the blanket as pins and needles tore through his feet and calves. He winced in pain. 'I thought we'd be done with them. We have Arillians to contend with as well as dragons.'

It wasn't a question. It was a statement of fact.

Topeko said, 'If they should come here. Please do not think to attack them. It will be very difficult to convince the Kalos of your good nature if you flout our laws again.'

'Hah, no chance of that. I'll hide in here or go wherever you tell me to,' Morgen said.

'Good. I'll make sure Andel keeps a close eye on you, then.'

Morgen laughed aloud, some of his earlier tension dissipating.

The Arch-Kalos seemed very old. Possibly older than his grandparents. It was very likely he was still in charge when Amarah had been growing up here—he certainly seemed to be aware of her, after all. And with someone like that criticising you, it was no wonder Amarah had left.

Morgen promised himself that if he should ever see the sky pirate again, he'd ask about her childhood in Ranski, and whether Dhabra was part of her fleeing the country. Dhabra seemed to care little for anyone, and despised those who weren't of full Samolen descent. Morgen had never understood that kind of thinking. Who cared who your parents were? Surely what you did in life was more important than where you came from.

With that realisation, he knew he needed to cut himself some slack. He was a farmer's son, yes, but he'd broken the Samolen's most ancient laws, and survived. By the time he needed to face the Arch-Kalos' judgement, he'd be much further along in his training, and would be better prepared.

Dhabra had peered into his soul once. Morgen would not let him do it again.

And seeing Andel return with his new cheek jewel would fuel his desire to improve enough and earn his own. Topeko had warned him that he was no Samolen, that he may not be able to tap into his innate magic. He'd braced him for disappointment and been honest with him about his potential.

But he'd made a shield.

He understood the basics.

He had a goal of where he wanted to end up.

And that was all he needed. It was more than enough to drive him onwards. He wouldn't learn anything too complex too soon. And having seen the enormous capabilities of the Arch-Kalos, Morgen was more convinced than ever that he'd be able to sever Sapora's connection with the Sevastos, and avenge Eryn's death.

Sapora was the one meddling with powers that ought to be left alone. He didn't know how he could have a Sevastos obey him, but he did know that it was wrong. It was against Rhea herself.

The rest of the world might cower beneath the Varkain, and Morgen knew he'd even fled at the mere *idea* of Sapora finding him, but not anymore.

Linaria was changing, and Morgen needed to hurry up and prepare himself if he was to have any chance of surviving it.

33

Amarah flew *Otella* across Taban Yul and headed straight for the palace. Beside her, Antar, Oris, Judd, and Solvi watched their progress with differing levels of excitement and nerves.

Amarah had assumed Princess Isa needed help stealing something from a distant location. After all, why else would she enlist the help of a sky pirate? She'd never have thought Isa wanted her to break people out of the palace dungeons.

She also knew that landing *Otella* atop one of the palace towers was against normal proceedings, and would definitely cause quite a stir. 'Everyone know what they have to do?' Amarah asked.

'Nervous?' Antar grinned.

Amarah snorted. 'I'd be an idiot if I wasn't. Just making sure you don't get overexcited and mess something up.'

'*You're* the one getting us arrested,' Antar replied.

Amarah turned *Otella* slowly as she tried to line up the bottom of the ship with the top of the tower Kylos had said was closest to the palace dungeons. 'You never know. He might be so grateful he lets us go with a full pardon for being pirates.'

'Do you really think so?' Judd asked, hopeful.

Amarah didn't bother to reply. If he couldn't tell sarcasm from that, she didn't want to worry him any further. 'Brace yourselves, everyone!'

She cut the ship's engines and adjusted their position with *Otella*'s massive sails and rudder. Warships were not the most manoeuvrable ships, and she missed *Khanna* more than ever when it came to fiddly parking like this. With a heavier thud than she wanted, *Otella* finally landed on the tower.

This was it. Now, she'd face Sapora. The damned dirty snake who'd hidden his Sevastos from everyone. If he'd have been more open, perhaps Moroda wouldn't have had to die.

Then she wouldn't have needed to go on some dragon hunt to find a way to break the seal and bring her back. It was the whole reason she'd travelled to Oren, why she'd put up with Kohl's cowardice and indecisiveness.

It had cost her her eye and her ship. And if it weren't for Sapora, she'd never even have fought Jato.

Damned snakes.

She straightened her clothes, adjusted her eye patch, and stepped away from *Otella*'s wheel. This was it, now. No turning back.

'Is this *Otella*? Captain Traego's ship?' A thin, wiry voice called out from somewhere below.

As Amarah stepped onto the roof of the tower she looked for the voice. 'It's his ship, but I ain't Traego.'

'I've come back per Sapora's request. Where's the gold?' Antar asked, ever confident.

Amarah saw a balding, hunch-backed Ittallan shuffle forward. He wore dark robes and a black sash that trailed on the floor behind him. She remembered him from the palace ball. While she couldn't remember his name, she knew he was a palace servant.

'Ah, you again.' The steward did not look happy to see them, and he scowled up at *Otella*. 'Why didn't you land in the palace hanger? We've plenty of room and the moment. It's very secure.'

Amarah smiled as sweetly as she could. 'But then how could we make a quick getaway if our ship was secured in your hangar?'

Before the Ittallan could reply, several Cerastes flanked him, and behind them came half a dozen of the Imperial Guard. They marched towards them, swords drawn, spears pointed forward.

'Well, I cannot have notorious sky pirates like yourselves waltzing around the palace as you please. These fine soldiers shall escort you directly to King Sapora. He can tell you whether or not you'll receive any gold.'

Amarah disliked his smugness, but neither she nor any of the others resisted when the soldiers clasped their wrists in iron. One rounded up their weapons—including Veynothi's blade—but Amarah didn't care. At least she didn't have to carry it any longer. And so long as the soldiers stayed in sight, there wasn't any issue with one of them disappearing with it.

With a sigh, she followed the soldiers and the steward through the high tower door and down a winding stone staircase. Amarah committed the tower to memory. The palace had several of these, and she didn't want to return up the wrong one and end up wasting time when it came to their escape. She assumed Antar and Oris were doing the same, but made sure she knew exactly how to get back to the tower in case they let her down.

'MY LIEGE, the sky pirates you dismissed have returned. I

had hoped Traego himself might arrive, but alas he has sent his crew to speak for him.'

Amarah waited before the throne. Antar and Solvi stood to her left, Judd and Oris to her right. The steward bowed low, his back to the sky pirates, his attention locked on the Varkain before him.

Amarah had to admit it was an impressive sight—all iron armour and gold jewels. Sapora sat on a high-backed chair that seemed to have been carved from obsidian. A tall, scarred Varkain stood behind him, spear at the ready, eyes locked on her and the others. Another Varkain sat in a slightly smaller chair—though no less ornate—to Sapora's right, swirling a goblet of wine as he watched the proceedings.

A fourth Varkain claimed the chair on Sapora's left, but he was unlike any that Amarah had ever seen. Older by several decades than Sapora, his hair had thinned to strands, his skin showed every bone, and he didn't appear to have lips. He wheezed with every breath, and she could hardly pull her gaze away from his prominent, pointed fangs.

There was no sign of Princess Isa. She'd half-hoped Kylos had been mistaken about her arrest.

Dotted around the room at intervals every few feet were armoured Varkain. All carried spears in their hands and longswords on their backs. The soldier who carried their weaponry had taken a position against the wall of the room, awaiting his turn to be addressed.

'All this pomp and ceremony for us. I'm flattered, Sapora' Amarah said, when the steward had finished speaking. She'd never call him king as long as she lived.

Sapora looked directly at her then, and his right eye twitched. Recognition? Shock? Disbelief?

'You didn't need to take all our things from us. We'd never *dream* of hurting you,' she pressed.

Sapora drummed his fingers on the arm of his chair, the tips of his claws echoing off the marble across the vast room. 'I told you the next time you saw the palace would be from behind bars.'

Amarah stiffened. Her enjoyment at riling the snake disappeared immediately, replaced by a deep-set hatred.

'You know this riff-raff?' The Varkain beside Sapora said, before he took another large gulp.

'Amarah,' Sapora replied coldly. 'I flew on her ship prior to becoming king.'

The Varkain stroked his chin as he thought. 'Hmm, I know that name. Where do I know that name, from?'

Sapora blinked and turned to look at him. His lip curled in the beginnings of a snarl.

'Ah. Of course. Our dear sister mentioned her. Another conspirator, perhaps? Don't trust her.'

Sapora looked back at Amarah. 'Conspirator? Hardly. Sky pirate, definitely. The punishment for that particular crime is life imprisonment, but perhaps I should write in a new law that all sky pirates are to be put to death.'

'Shall I fetch a scroll, my liege?' The steward asked, almost excited at the prospect.

'Not necessary, Koraki.'

Amarah knew she walked the line of death with Sapora, but she continued to goad him anyway. She needed him to become agitated. 'If you kill us, you won't know anything about Veynothi.'

'I'm not so quick to kill as people might think,' Sapora replied. He sat back in his chair and exhaled slowly, as though calming himself down. 'So. What do you know about Veynothi that's so important? I told your friend beside you to get proof. I don't see any proof.'

Amarah took a step forward, but the guards around the room responded immediately, drawing their weapons and holding her at bay. She looked at them and laughed. 'Touchy, aren't we?'

'And with not much patience. I can have them kill your crew if it'll loosen your tongue.'

Solvi stiffened at the threat and Amarah swallowed. She caught Antar and Judd's eyes, who both gave away nothing, then she licked her lips. 'I don't have the proof because your guard took it from me.' She nodded to the Varkain in question.

Sapora leaned back to whisper something in the ear of the Varkain who stood at attention behind him. The guard then walked to the soldier with their weapons.

'Tell him which one,' Sapora said.

Amarah sighed. 'The odd one out. It's stone.'

When she said the word, tension shrouded the room. The two Varkain either side of Sapora whispered excitedly, and she even saw the whites of Sapora's eyes.

It didn't take the guard long to find it.

He drew the stone sword from its sheath and held it out for Sapora and the others to see. 'King Sapora. This...this is no weapon produced by a blacksmith.'

'Give it to me.' The old Varkain said, pushing up from his chair and hobbling over to the guard, his hands outstretched.

Amarah wanted to flee. The memory of Veynothi's golden eyes flickered in her mind.

The old Varkain claimed the weapon from the guard. He held it gently in his hands, almost delicately, as if it were a flower that might wilt at the lightest touch. He brought the edge close to his face to take a closer look, then shifted the handle from one hand to the other.

Amarah kept her eyes on Sapora, who was transfixed. He

looked almost hungry as he stared at the blade in the hands of the old Varkain.

'Well?' Sapora asked, but the other Varkain ignored him. He continued to test the balance of the blade, and even ran a claw along its tip. 'Valendrin! Answer me!' Sapora thundered.

Amarah couldn't ignore the raw anger and desperation in his voice.

At Sapora's roar, the old Varkain—the Valendrin—seemed to remember he was not alone in the room. He dropped his head. 'Forgive me, my liege. I have not...it has been so long that...'

Sapora half rose from his chair. 'It is real, then?'

In response, the Valendrin turned the blade on himself, deftly slicing into his forearm with it. Thick, black blood oozed from his flesh and onto the blade. It remained there for a few seconds before the stone appeared to absorb it, leaving not the smallest trace. 'My liege. This is truly one of Veynothi's blades.'

Sapora stood, then. He'd thrown formality away and rounded on Amarah and the others. 'Tell me where you got this. Now.'

Amarah had known Sapora was desperate. She hadn't realised how desperate. 'Our gold?'

'It's yours. Tell me Veynothi's location!'

She smiled. 'Southern tip of Ranski. Past a tiny village called Shay. There are some stony islands out to sea a short way past that. It was in among those.'

'Sapora...' the Varkain to Sapora's side breathed.

'Hush, Tacio. Do you think I'm so blind that I'd trust a thief's word?' Sapora approached the gathered pirates. Ignoring Amarah, he said to Antar, 'You agree with her location?'

Antar met his gaze levelly. 'Place is a fucking desert. But

that's where we got it from. So where's my two-hundred and fifty crowns? It's a dangerous flight, you know. You got Arillians right outside.'

Amarah could tell that Sapora wasn't entirely convinced, but he'd had the sword authenticated. He knew he was only one step away from bringing back the Arks he so desired. She desperately wished for him to go. If they were lucky, he'd give them the gold just to be rid of them.

'My liege, might I be of assistance?' The Valendrin asked. He still clutched Veynothi's blade tightly as he shuffled forward.

Amarah blinked. She didn't like the way he spoke, looked, or breathed.

'What do you propose?'

'A simple test. A little blood, that's all I need to verify the words.'

Sapora took a step back and folded his arms. 'Do what you need to.'

The Valendrin smiled wickedly, and then with speed unbefitting of a creature as old as he was, he grabbed hold of Amarah's upper arm.

She yelped in surprise more than pain, but with her wrists bound, she couldn't do anything in response.

'Get off her!' Judd yelled, but the soldiers in the room held him and the others back.

The Valendrin lifted the sword and pressed it against the soft flesh just below her shoulder.

'What the fuck? Stop it!' She screamed, but there was nothing she could do.

The tip of the blade pierced her skin and blood poured from the wound faster than she would have thought. It was as though the blade sucked it from her skin. A terrible cold crept into her arm, numbing it as the Varkain venom had done all those years ago when she'd been bitten. She twisted and writhed as she pulled back from the disgusting creature.

After a moment, he let go of her arm, and Amarah almost tumbled into Antar. 'I need a bandage!' She shouted, but neither Sapora, the Valendrin, or Tacio had any interest in seeing to her needs.

The Valendrin touched a claw to the blood on the blade and closed his eyes. 'She's lying. But I cannot get the truth from her. Perhaps this one?' He opened his eyes and stared at Antar.

Tremors coursed through her. Numbness spread down her arm and into her hand, but there was no pain. She glanced down and saw the wound was already closing. 'Antar...?'

Again the Valendrin lunged, and this time, Antar knew what to expect. He leaped back, hurtling into Judd and sending him flying. Three of the Cerastes charged forward, their spear-points keeping Antar where he was. If he tried to move again, he'd slice himself open on one of their weapons. 'You stay away from me you damned maggot!'

'Hush,' the Valendrin said, as though trying to soothe a crying baby. With Antar right where he wanted him, the Valendrin sliced into Antar's arm and drew fresh blood. The blade hissed this time, a thin line of smoke rising from where the blood touched the stone.

The Valendrin touched a claw to it and smiled. 'Ahh. Yes. He is the one who took Veynothi's blade.'

'Well?' Sapora asked. 'Is it in Ranski or not?'

Amarah watched as Antar's wound, like her own, healed itself. She had no idea what kind of dark magic this was, but she wanted absolutely no part in it. And if the Valendrin could obtain the truth through it, then it wouldn't bode well for them.

'It is not in Ranski.' The Valendrin opened his eyes as

Veynothi's blade absorbed Antar's blood, too. 'Veynothi is in Corhaven. In the distant north-west. Our griffins still watch over her resting place as they have done since she was sealed. I see them, now. They keep travellers away. They protect her as Brahm's monster protects the seas from invaders.'

Sapora didn't seem interested in the lecture. 'Koraki. Ready the largest, fastest ship we have on our fleet.'

'My liege, our fleet is still in disrepair after the attack, we have only a few that—'

'Get whatever you can spare together! Tacio,' Sapora rounded on the only Varkain still seated. 'Clear the dungeons. I want your best Cerastes, too. Have them escorted onto the ship. We sail for Corhaven now.'

'Sapora...Empty the dungeons? But what about—'

Sapora snarled in exasperation. 'They've been my prisoners for months. It's time they were put to good use. I'll need plenty of blood. Valendrin. Keep Veynothi's blade safe. You're coming as well.'

Too much happened for Amarah to take note of it. Her arm throbbed as the numbness faded, and the urge to vomit was almost overwhelming.

'And my liege. What about them?' Koraki asked, pointing to the chained prisoners.

Sapora narrowed his eyes. 'Amarah. I was in a good mood, earlier. I might have paid you your gold and let you go free. A token of my generosity. But now you've lied to me? I'm not so sure. Tacio. Before you round up your Cerastes, I want Amarah and her accomplices imprisoned. I'll deal with her when I return with Veynothi.'

Even if Amarah had wanted to say something back to him, any little jibe, to get the last laugh, she wasn't able to. Breathing was tricky for her after her brush with Varkain blood magic, and she shivered.

'Oh. Right. They're sky pirates,' Sapora said, as though he'd only just realised. 'Have them stripped and lock up their weapons.'

'Do it yourself. It'll be ages before the ship is ready to fly to Corhaven,' Tacio said. He'd clearly regained some of his composure after learning the truth about the blade.

Sapora smiled. 'Oh don't be silly. I'm not flying on the ship.'

Two Cerastes took Amarah by the arms and began to frog-march her across the hall. Others grabbed hold of Antar and dragged him forward—he'd clearly been more badly affected by the Valendrin's magic. But Amarah still listened to Sapora, and his next words chilled her.

'I'm going to have my Sevastos fly me there.'

~

TEN CERASTES HALF-MARCHED, half-dragged Amarah and her companions along—two to each of them. It was clear neither Sapora nor Tacio were taking any chances with their new prisoners.

They crossed a bridge linking one palace tower to the main building. Floor to ceiling windows gave Amarah an incredible view of Taban Yul in the late afternoon sun. She'd almost reached the other side when a dragon's roar split the air. It was a sound she'd never forget.

She didn't need to see the Sevastos to know it had been the one to make that deafening noise.

'King Sapora is flying that, you know.' One of the guards sneered. 'Even your "hero" Moroda couldn't do that. Her Sevastos killed her.'

Amarah bit back a rebuke. Reacting to his taunts wouldn't help her situation. She had to remain stoic.

She wouldn't show them her fear.

When Sapora's guards made good on the king's command, and Amarah was stripped to her underclothes, she didn't react. They unlocked a cell and threw both her and Solvi in it. It was cold and filthy, but Amarah wouldn't let that break her spirit.

She watched Antar, Judd, and Oris as they were shoved down the dark passageway and led further into the dungeon. A few minutes later, the Cerastes returned, carrying their bundled clothes, before disappearing up a flight of stairs. The door at the top slammed shut, cutting off most of the light and leaving Amarah and Solvi in semi-darkness.

The cell didn't have a window, and she shouldn't have been surprised at that. Kylos had said they were underground, which made sense.

'Amarah,' Solvi said. Her voice trembled a little, but she didn't whimper.

'I know. Bit of a set back,' Amarah said. She tried to hide her growing anxiety.

Solvi shivered. 'But you're a sky pirate. You break out of this type of thing all the time, right?'

'All the time,' Amarah said. She decided to change the subject and keep her mind focussed. 'Sapora's taken more than half the people from the palace with him. Aren't places like this normally full of people? Goldstones? Servants? Maids? That kind of thing?'

Solvi nodded.

'And how many people did you see from the throne room to here?'

Solvi thought about it for a moment. 'Not many.'

Amarah grinned, as though that explained everything. 'Sapora ain't best loved here, anyway. Wonder if he had to clear out the palace of...what he call us again?'

'Conspirators?' Solvi suggested.

'That's it. Conspirators. He had to clear 'em all out. If he's having trouble with his staff, that's in our favour. There's no guard in front of our cell, either. Just at the top of those stairs there.' She pointed to the stairway where the Cerastes had entered and left from. She couldn't know for certain, but with the skeleton staff in the palace, it was an educated guess. And she needed to keep Solvi's spirits up.

'Maybe.' Solvi didn't sound sure.

'Traego's gonna be here tonight. Or at least on the outskirts. He's on my new ship and that's much faster than *Otella*. Malot's never let him down. Don't worry.'

Solvi sank to her knees and wrapped her arms around herself. 'I don't like this.'

Amarah shrugged. 'Won't be for long.'

'And now Sapora is on his way to get the Ark.' Solvi almost welled up when she spoke. 'He'll release Veynothi, now. And then Malashash. That's two out of four!'

Amarah didn't know what to say to that. Even if she managed to escape, find Isa and Lathri and free them, and get them all safely to Estoria, it wouldn't change the fact that Sapora had his Arks. His super-weapons. With two of them *and* a Sevastos at his control, he'd be unstoppable.

He'd probably get rid of the dragons and Arillians in one swoop.

And then what?

He could conquer all of Linaria, if he wanted to.

But Amarah didn't know what his goals were. What he *actually* wanted.

She hoped Princess Isa would be able to shed some light on that, but she needed to get to her first—and then escape.

'Hey. I dunno how fast a Sevastos can fly, but he still needs to get across Val Sharis and the Sea of Nami, and get to the most distant place in Corhaven. *And* get back. We've got time. We'll get away.'

'Maybe. But then Val Sharis will face the Arks again.'

Amarah sighed. 'I can't whisk the whole country away on a handful of ships, Solvi. One step at a time. And two Arks isn't as bad as all four of the Arks.' She tried to find an angle that would help lift the young Ittallan's spirits.

'Actually, he will have three.' An old woman's voice reached them in the darkness.

'What?' Solvi gasped, on her feet.

Amarah narrowed her eye. 'Who's there?'

'Nobody, really. Just an old, foolish Ittallan.'

Solvi pressed her ear to the solid wall at the side of the cell. 'She's beside us,' she whispered to Amarah. Then she faced the wall and said loudly, 'Don't be silly. We'll get you out!

The old woman laughed, then coughed. 'No, young one. I'll stay here.'

Amarah grinned at Solvi. 'If you're worried about Sapora or Tacio, don't. I'm a professional. Everyone still in these dungeons is getting out tonight.'

'No. I've made too many mistakes,' the woman said. Amarah could tell she was crying. 'Because of me, Sapora will have three Arks.'

'What did you do?' Amarah asked.

'I told his brother, Prince Tacio, about one of them. It's in Val Sharis, you know. Near Tum Metsa. In the vast ice plains.'

Amarah gulped. 'Ain't nothing there but those damned snow wolves and trees. You give him a false location, too?'

'Oh, you're so naive. Those wolves are there to protect the Ark's location. Karekis is there. He was a Varkain prince too, once. Before the Valendrin changed him. He was blind, considered weak. The Valendrin made him into something else. Something more powerful than Linaria had ever seen. And I told Tacio. I betrayed my people for a bit of gold.' She was weeping now. The sound of her sobs carried through the stone and Amarah's stomach tightened.

She remembered those giant wolves. She and Kohl had rested on the edge of the forest on their way to Tum Metsa. She'd wondered why they'd been so keen to see them off, and now it made sense. And then she remembered what the Valendrin had said about griffins in Corhaven.

Dragons above, had the Varkain protected the Arks' locations with creatures? Predators that would stand guard and prevent any from discovering them? If that was true, then the monster from the sea, the one who had spoken Veynothi's name, had it been guarding another Ark? The fourth one?

Ideas and emotion churned in her stomach. She needed to talk to Isa about it.

'Gold? You didn't tell the Varkain about Karekis because of their bounty, did you?' Solvi asked.

'I am a foolish woman. I lost my two sons in Aciel's war. My husband, too. He plucked them from my home when he came south with his Arillians. They were taken from me, then slaughtered by my own Imperial Guard. When I sent letters to the capital, begging for news, I received a template response. A blanket message saying I ought to be grateful to Palom for saving the world. That anyone who died had died bravely.'

Amarah gasped at that. She supposed he had made the *Valta Forinja*, and the Ittallan would probably love him for that. She hadn't realised how far they'd taken it. No wonder Palom had wanted to get away.

'I'm old,' the woman repeated, still sobbing. 'I won't marry again. I won't bear children again. They destroyed my family. My grandmother and her grandmother lived in Tum Metsa. We keep the old legends going, even when most have forgotten. And when Sapora requested word of the Arks, I had nothing to lose. Aciel had taken everything from me. The Imperial Guard betrayed me. What did it matter if Val Sharis fell to the Varkain? I had nothing left.'

'What?' Amarah yelled. 'Just because *you've* lost things doesn't give you the right to doom everyone else!'

The woman couldn't speak for her tears. It took her a few seconds to recover herself. 'I was grieving. Tell me you've not done silly things when emotions ruled you? When you felt so certain that what you were doing was right?'

Amarah shook her head. 'So why are you in here then? Thought you got your gold?'

'Once a snake, always a snake. Tacio placed a bag of coins in my hand then sliced it clean off at the elbow. Had me thrown in here. Said I was a traitor, and I could rot in here for the king's pleasure.'

'I'm sorry,' Solvi said. There was genuine care in her voice. 'I'm Solvi. My *kali* is Palom.'

The old woman said nothing for a moment. And then, 'Your *kali* is a great man. *I'm* sorry I was so wrong.'

'You can tell him yourself! He is waiting for us. We're going to escape Sapora and this palace.'

'Palom is outside...?'

'Why d'you think they brought me in?' Amarah said. She'd shifted into her confident bravado to mask her terror at the thought of more Arks being released and what that would mean for Linaria. 'I'm Amarah. You are?'

Another pause.

'*Koma*?' Solvi asked, clearly using a word from the Ittallan language to refer to her.

The sobs began again. 'And Odi. I betrayed him, too. I betrayed so many people. Just because I was scared and alone.' Her voice was so utterly morose that Amarah could hardly stand to hear it.

'*Koma*, it's okay. If we work together, things will be okay.'

Amarah didn't agree—the world was never that fair—but she didn't say anything.

The woman sniffed. 'They took my stick, too. I can't walk well without it.'

'I'll help you. I promise,' Solvi said.

Eventually, with a final choked sob, the woman said her name, 'Yfaila.'

34

Sapora clutched onto the Sevastos' horns as the massive dragon flew through the cool night air. Trees, rivers, and mountains flashed by underneath in a matter of seconds. Sapora understood speed. He struck faster than anything in the world and could dash short distances in the blink of an eye. But here, on the back of a dragon, it was unlike anything he could have imagined.

He'd left Tacio in charge of an empty palace, save Amarah and her friends, and knew Roke and the ship of prisoners wouldn't be too far behind him.

The Valendrin sat beside him. He gripped Veynothi's blade as if his life depended on it.

'I told you I would change the world,' Sapora said. He had to raise his voice above the wind.

'You did, my liege. And you are. A Sevastos at your control. The Arks returned to Linaria. Your father would never have considered these things as truths.'

Sapora could hardly believe he knew where Veynothi was. Thanks to the Valendrin's blood magic, he'd sucked the truth from Antar, and the sky pirates would pay for their lies.

Veynothi was second only to Karekis and immensely powerful in her own right. If he had her, then the other Arks would fall in line as he brought them back.

Now, he was proving himself a better king than Vasil had been. Despite all the reservations of the Varkain and Ittallan both. Despite their distaste of his mixed blood. Despite all his perceived weaknesses and flaws, he'd shown them all.

Now, he was going to save the world from Aciel's tyranny. From the destructive dragons. From the Arillians who sought to kill everyone in their path.

He'd free them all.

Linaria would remember it was the *Varkain* who had stood up and ended the fighting. The Varkain who had saved the world from those who would see it burn.

And he would be remembered as the saviour.

But he didn't want to get too ahead of himself. He couldn't free Veynothi without the blood of his prisoners, and if he arrived too early, he'd end up waiting hours on a frigid mountainside.

Sapora leaned forward slightly and addressed the Sevastos. 'Slow down. Turn around. I want to see if my airship is following.' He spoke in his most commanding voice, even though he considered the dragon as just another thrall.

The Sevastos reacted to his commands, no matter how unwilling it was. Though capable of speech, it refused to respond verbally unless ordered to, but it obeyed and hovered in the air, turning slowly so Sapora and the Valendrin could look back over the Sea of Nami.

All three moons were still high, their light casting a silver-white glow upon the calm waves. He'd travelled in several airships before, but he didn't think he had a single vessel in the Imperial Fleet that could match the speed of his Sevastos.

It irritated him.

He'd been patient for so long, for so many years, that these final few hours were almost a form of torture. 'Do you see them?' Sapora asked, directing his question to both the blood mage and the dragon.

Neither replied.

His own night vision was fairly good, but even he couldn't see anything in the dark sky other than the moons and stars. Sapora swore under his breath, muttering curses while he waited for the ship to catch up. Koraki hadn't even selected the ship for the flight before Sapora had with the Sevastos.

He'd been too desperate. Too hasty.

And now his haste had made him wait.

'The ship approaches.' His Sevastos spoke in a low, deep voice that echoed through Sapora's body more than his ears. The dragon beat its wings powerfully, keeping them in roughly the same spot. He'd never known the dragon to tire, no matter how long it flew for. Sapora imagined it could fly around Linaria in its entirety without needing to rest.

Sapora wasn't sure exactly how many thralls and prisoners the ship carried. He'd taken a fair number off his father when he'd come to the palace for Summercourt. There had to be at least sixty or seventy. And they'd all serve their purpose. Their deaths would give life to Veynothi. Life that Linaria hadn't seen in five thousand years.

And then he could defend Taban Yul and the rest of the world from Aciel's compulsion. He saw no other way to stop the Arillian than with the power of the Arks.

At least the thralls' deaths would not be in vain—unlike when they died in Sereth for sport or the entertainment of other Varkain. Sapora would put a stop to that when he returned there, he decided. But it would be quite a while before he could return. He needed to save an entire world, first.

'I see it, too, my liege,' the Valendrin said. He raised a clawed finger and pointed at a spot in the distance.

Sapora followed his gesture but it took him almost a whole minute before he saw the ship in the darkness. 'Good. Let's continue, but keep the ship within sight.'

The dragon let out a snarl as it twisted in the air and powered on, beating its wings and gaining altitude as they continued onwards.

Corhaven appeared as a dark, shapeless mass underneath them. Although Sapora had spent the better part of a year in the country as part of his errantry, he couldn't quite work out where he was from their height. He knew Veynothi was located in the mountains to the far north-west, and it would still take a fair amount of time to get there, especially now he'd slowed their pace.

Sapora was almost upset that it was dark and most people would be asleep. How it would strengthen his rule for the common people of Corhaven to see him astride a dragon as he flew to reclaim one of his ancestors' lost treasures.

If he'd been a child, he would have found the sight inspiring.

It was still too late—or early, depending on which way you looked at it—for the fishermen and farmers to be awake. And if crickets sang, he was too high up to hear. The world slept, and he passed ahead on the back of the Sevastos like a silent dream.

Sapora glanced back periodically to ensure the ship still followed, and was pleased the Sevastos had regulated its speed to keep in sight of it. At least he could rely on Roke to maintain order on board. He supposed the soldier would have had to make up some story about their sudden departure from the dungeons and subsequent flight across the sea.

When he returned to Taban Yul, he'd be sure to give him a small bonus in appreciation of his continued, loyal service.

Sapora purposefully thought about Veynothi, the Valendrin, the Sevastos, or his other soldiers. It kept him from thinking about Isa.

But it had just the opposite effect.

Tacio had been almost giddy with glee when he'd brought her in, hands bound in thick metal chains. He'd caught her in the act of conspiracy, he'd said. She'd known the game was up and had turned herself over to him willingly. Tacio had told him over and over that she was traitorous, but Sapora hadn't believed it. Hadn't *wanted* to believe it.

His sister was still his sister. They'd grown up together. He couldn't ignore nearly eighteen years of friendship, of standing with each other against those who looked down upon them. Even though he and Tacio were physically more similar, Isa was the only one who'd shown him kindness as a child. He was the crown prince and had always commanded the servants as he pleased. But she'd treated him like anyone else. He wasn't special or scary. He was just her brother.

And together they saw the problems with the world.

Together they'd promised one another they would fix them—just as soon as Sapora became king.

He had no idea what games she was playing—if she was playing any at all—but he trusted her beyond anyone else. Whatever she did, she did for a reason. Tacio was simply jealous of their bond, that was all. There was no way that she would betray him.

Sapora wouldn't believe anything else of his sister.

He refused. She was a queen in her own right. The Goldstones who'd spat upon her were dead.

He was paving their new future. And blood sometimes

had to be spilled. They'd both come to terms with that. It was why she'd agreed to the slaughter at the ball.

Going back on that now simply wasn't an option.

The thoughts swirled in his mind and Sapora became even more determined to see through his plans of restoring the Arks. Linaria wasn't going to save itself. It needed ancient powers to restore balance and protect the people from Aciel.

Why else had he been given the power of a Sevastos if not to use it?

It wasn't far off first light when the mountains came into view. The Sevastos was forced to fly slow and low, following the natural valley as they closed in on Veynothi's location. Sapora and the Valendrin both peered over the side of the dragon's body, looking for anything that might mark where Veynothi rested.

Sapora saw checkpoints belonging to the Imperial Guard—none of which were manned—and ordered the Sevastos to keep flying. He would be sure to speak with whoever was the Captain at this location and make them aware of his displeasure.

Even in such a remote area, threats could be found. What was to stop Jato and her Arillians from attacking this place? Every Imperial Guard post needed to be fully manned and fully stocked, ready for any eventuality.

He wouldn't tolerate slacking.

Eventually they reached a section where the valley widened and the mountains were spaced farther apart from one another. 'This is it, my liege,' the Valendrin said. 'Antar saw this place when he claimed Veynothi's blade.'

Sapora frowned and peered below again. He couldn't see anything but mountains, tundra, and the occasional goat. 'We need to find it. And then somewhere for the ship to land. Sevastos, do you see anything? Sense anything?'

The dragon rumbled its disapproval at Sapora's address, but shook its head from side to side. 'I sense Varkain magic everywhere here. I cannot see it.'

At least the dragon concurred with the Valendrin, Sapora supposed.

'It would be easier to see if there weren't all these mountains in the way.'

'Shall I burn them?' Sapora suggested.

'No. You might damage Veynothi or more of her blades. Hmm. Let me think.'

Sapora didn't have *time* for the damned blood mage to think.

Screeches ripped through the air suddenly, and Sapora looked up to see several griffins wheeling around in the sky above them. The Sevastos snarled in response, hovered in place and watched them.

'The guardians are still here,' the Valendrin said. He smiled broadly. Without warning, he raised both hands to the sky, his palms flat, and chanted.

Sapora leaned backwards from him, unsure what the mage was doing.

A swirl of red tendrils engulfed the Valendrin, and he closed his eyes and twisted his arms in slow, sweeping motions. The tendrils of light arced from his palms and shot up towards the nearest griffins.

They screeched again as the light danced from one animal to the next, then the next, until the entire sky was lit with bright, swirling red.

'What is this?' Sapora hissed.

'Watch.'

Sapora did as he was told and saw the light swirl around each griffin several times before a thin tendril shot down into the mountains below.

'They are bound to guard Veynothi's resting place. My

forebears made it so with a ritual of sorts. I have simply revealed it.'

'Couldn't you have done that with the blade? It would have saved a lot of time if you'd used that to show us Veynothi's exact location.'

The Valendrin chuckled without mirth. 'My liege, you have much to learn about our ancient magic. It would not work with the blade. One needs something *living* to perform any kind of blood magic.'

Sapora understood and didn't question him further. 'Sevastos. Follow the light. Burn any mountain or rocks you see to flatten it. At least then the ship'll have somewhere to land.'

The blood mage had been about to protest when the Sevastos opened its massive jaws and unleashed a wave of white-hot fire. The few trees and bits of foliage that clung to life on the barren mountaintops were burned away in an instant. Rock cracked and melted under the heat, dribbling down the side of the mountain as the Sevastos used its fire to scour away the earth.

The dragon's scales heated up where Sapora touched them, and he tried to lift his hands to avoid them getting singed.

'My liege!' The Valendrin shouted, but Sapora didn't care.

This was the final step.

By the time the Sevastos had burned away half the mountainside, Sapora's ship had caught up with them. Both the dragon and the ship landed on the newly cleared land, and Sapora clambered down with as much grace as he could muster.

The Valendrin walked with him, and Roke led a trail of chained thralls and prisoners behind him.

The pale red light from the griffins above led to a path

almost hidden by rock and snow. Much of the snow had evaporated, leaving Sapora's way forward surprisingly clear and easy. He kept his mouth shut and his eyes on the path as he came closer to Veynothi's resting place.

Every so often, the Valendrin would tell him something about Veynothi herself, or the Arks, but Sapora had stopped listening after he'd shown him the way forward with the griffins. Now, he had only one goal in mind.

The route had been burned in a few places where the Sevastos had been somewhat overzealous with its flame, but Sapora was able to pick his way through it easily enough. It followed the mountain down and round, and Sapora wondered how long it had been since Varkain had walked upon it.

As it curved round to the left, a sheer drop fell away to his right, and Sapora wondered whether his Sevastos would catch him if he were to fall. Pushing the morbid thought out of his mind, he almost stepped off the edge of the path when it ended abruptly.

'My liege!' The Valendrin grabbed him by the elbow and pulled him back to the small ledge that appeared to be the path's end.

'I'm fine,' Sapora said. Loose rock fell away and he took a step backwards just to be safe.

'There's a door.'

Sapora turned slowly lest any more of the rock underfoot fell away, but his fears disappeared when he saw Veynothi's bronze plaque fixed to the rock. 'This is it.'

He took one final breath, then pushed the door carved into the mountain itself. It gave way easily, revealing a dark tunnel. 'I'll need light,' Sapora said as he stepped inside.

The Valendrin concurred and snapped his fingers, a thin dribble of blood trickling down his thumb where he'd cut it, and a bright red flame rose from the tip of his claw.

Sapora's heart pounded. He couldn't remember the last time he'd been this excited. Not even when he'd won the jade crown, not even when the Sevastos had been delivered to the palace.

This was something much greater.

Roke led the first of the thralls into the tunnel behind them, and the echoes of so many pairs of feet disoriented Sapora. He tried to ignore it and focus on where he was going. Thankfully the tunnel was smooth and narrow, and led only in one direction.

When he reached an opening in the wall, Sapora realised the stone door that had once sealed Veynothi's chambers was on the floor. It was covered in a thin layer of dust, and he frowned. He supposed Amarah, Antar, and whoever else had been with them had broken the door down. It angered him that they hadn't seen fit to replace it.

Stepping over the door, Sapora finally entered the chamber.

Having already visited Malashash's tomb twice before, he knew what to expect here. The stone plinth was as he assumed it would be—in the centre, near the back of the room and missing the blade his Valendrin now carried— with deep, narrow channels dug into the chamber floor leading to it. Unlit sconces lined the walls, but the Valendrin's light helped Sapora see that which he had travelled so far for: Veynothi.

She was lodged in the back wall, her face a grimace, her hands outstretched. Clearly she'd been in the middle of a battle when she'd been sealed away.

What patience she must have had to last five thousand years alone in this place.

'It's time.'

Sapora stepped forward and approached the plinth. He grasped it with both hands and the sconces burst into flame

—a vibrant white gold that threw a bright light on the entire chamber. He looked back to Veynothi and his heart skipped a beat.

She watched him with eyes that matched the flames.

'Roke. Bring in the first thrall,' Sapora commanded.

His personal guard obeyed at once, hurrying forward and dragging a middle-aged Ittallan woman with him. She wore dirty rags and her hair had been loosely tied up, but Sapora could still see the grime in it. Roke thrust her at Sapora's feet and stepped back.

This was not the time to hesitate. Drawing one of his scimitars, Sapora slashed, killing her in one, swift strike.

She didn't even have time to scream.

The woman fell forward, blood flowing from her slashed throat, pooling along the stone and into the wells beside Veynothi's plinth.

As the first well filled, a tiny blue flame flickered above it.

Sapora stood tall and brushed off his clothes. 'Lead more in. Two or three at a time.'

He'd known it would take an awful lot of blood to unmake the seal.

With every person he killed, more wells filled, and the small flames grew larger and larger. He could no longer even see the blade of his scimitar, it had been coated in so much crimson. Still he slaughtered. Still he descended further into the blood magic of his people—for a greater purpose.

He kicked bodies out of the way to approach the plinth every time, and every time he put his hands on it, the flames flickered, but Veynothi did not breathe. 'Valendrin,' he said, when he had killed every last prisoner Roke and his captains brought with them.

'You must add yours, too,' the blood mage instructed.

The wells were completely full. Corpses littered the

chamber, masking the floor. Sapora watched Veynothi, and she watched him.

He took his scimitar to his own arm and held it above the dish directly underneath Veynothi, where all the blood from the channels flowed. As he grit his teeth against the pain, the blood mage chanted once again.

Sapora didn't know what words he spoke, but he recognised some from when he'd used the griffins to locate Veynothi. Some kind of spell to reveal what had happened before, perhaps. The flames above the wells and in the wall sconces shifted colours, burning green then bright blue. He remained crouched above the dish, his wound dripping, his energy sucked away by the magic of the ritual. Or by Veynothi herself.

Dizziness gripped him, but he stayed where he was. As the Valendrin continued to chant, his wound began to heal.

And then Veynothi flickered to life.

The Ark sent forth a sudden burst of energy, sending Sapora, Roke, and the Valendrin flying backwards.

Sapora leaped back to his feet in time to see Veynothi step forward.

Her skin was still grey, as though the stone itself moved. But as the seconds passed, he watched it shift from stone to scaled flesh.

She took slow steps forward, the flames on the walls beside her burning more brilliantly, shifting from blue to red as she moved past them. Her lips parted slightly, and her long, black forked tongue tasted the air. '*Naja*.'

The Valendrin and Roke both dropped to their knees in reverence, but Sapora was a king. He didn't bow to anyone.

Veynothi wore no clothes, her bare skin shifting constantly as she breathed for the first time in five thousand years. Her loose hair trailed down almost to her knees, and she surveyed her chamber with eyes of molten gold.

When she reached the plinth, she raised one hand. The remaining five blades that had been stuck into the rock tip-first dug deeper, splitting it into a hundred pieces. One sword flew from the plinth to lay flat against her extended arm. The others lifted and sped to her back, crossing their points and holding themselves there, pressed to her skin.

Sapora had no idea what was going on. Nothing he'd read about Veynothi suggested her powers were anything like what he had just witnessed. He watched as the final blade lay horizontally across her lower back, where the points of the other swords kissed.

She surveyed the room again, her gaze lingering on the dead bodies littering the floor. She looked almost bored.

Sapora suppressed a shiver when he realised she had absorbed all the blood from the wells.

At last, she looked upon Sapora. Though he met her gaze for a moment, he lowered his head in respect. Though not a full bow, he also didn't want to insult her. 'Veynothi. I am Sapora, King of the Varkain and Ittallan. I have returned your sword to you, after thieves stole it.' He reached for her final blade, and the Valendrin hurriedly handed it to him.

Sapora raised his head and proffered the sword to Veynothi.

She flicked out her serpentine tongue to taste the air again. Her energy bristled, and the flames in the chamber flickered. She made no move to take the blade.

Sapora lowered his hand, keeping a firm grip on the hilt. He didn't know what to expect, so he decided to be patient and observe.

Veynothi lightly stepped over the bodies on the floor, closing the distance between herself and Sapora in moments. She reached forward and touched his cheek with one outstretched claw. Taking great care not to cut him, she trailed her finger down his neck and along his shoulders as she circled him.

Her tongue flicked out again.

And then she hissed in disgust. 'Half-breed. Mongrel. How *dare* you step into this sacred place?'

Sapora blinked. The hatred and contempt in Veynothi's voice took him completely by surprise.

'You killed all these people for your own gain. Disgusting, blood-thirsty creature.'

It didn't take Sapora long to regain his composure as Veynothi scowled at him. 'You will help me locate your brethren and begin acting out my plans for the control or decimation of Linaria's dragons. And you will destroy the Arillians.'

'You do not command me, *mongrel*. I listen only to Prince Karekis.'

Sapora let out his own hiss in frustration. 'You are indebted to me.'

'For what? Anyone can kill willing—or unwilling—victims. All you've shown me is that you're a killer. Not a king. I owe you nothing.'

Sapora almost growled. He'd managed to find and revive one of the most powerful creatures in Linaria, and she insulted him. She was like Tacio, but worse. Bored, irritated, and she radiated power unlike anything he'd ever experienced before. 'I have *earned* my title! Proved myself in the pits of Sereth; conquered and rule two countries; brought riches and freedom to my people; command the Imperial Fleet; killed one of the Old Guard.'

'Notable achievements for a mongrel.'

Her words bit deep. It was exactly the thinking that he and Isa had decided to wipe out.

He and Isa were of royal blood and that was all that

mattered. The Arks needed to obey him or it would all be for nothing.

The Valendrin's words of warning popped into his mind briefly, but Sapora ignored them. '*And* I control a Sevastos. The very one who put you in your tomb. I can just as easily have it return you to stone, should you insult me further. So yes, you *do* owe me, Veynothi. As will the other three Arks. In fact, all of Linaria will show me the respect I deserve.'

35

I t was full dark by the time Amarah broke the lock on the cell's gate.

In part, it was because she wanted to be sure Traego and the others would be near the city. But it was also in part because the damned lock was too old and stiff to be picked.

She'd used the oldest trick in the book—hiding lock-picks in her hair. The guards may have taken her garments, but they hadn't searched her at all. Even Morgen had done a better job of taking her tools off her when she'd been arrested in Niversai.

It showed her the true importance of the Arks and how valuable they were to Sapora. And now she had confirmation the snake wasn't in the palace any longer, it gave her more confidence in her plan to escape. And they could help themselves to whatever they found in the palace that would be of value as payment for their troubles.

Kylos might not have liked it, but Kylos wasn't her employer. Technically, Princess Isa was. At least as far as the jailbreak was concerned.

By the time Amarah reached the end of her patience,

she'd snapped two picks and was on her third and final one. In the end, she snapped the lock from the inside—using the pick to dig deep and shatter the rusted parts of it, splitting it open and unlocking the gate.

'Done,' she said. It was rather unnecessary. Solvi had watched her throughout her work, adding an additional layer of pressure that Amarah could have done without. 'We need to get the others out, then find Lathri and Isa.'

'As long as Sapora didn't take them to Veynothi,' Solvi said. But she didn't hesitate when Amarah threw open the gate and they both slipped out.

'Keep as quiet as you can. Don't want to bring the guards down if we can help it,' Amarah whispered.

Solvi nodded her assent. 'Yfaila. We'll get you out, now.'

Amarah took a few steps to look into the cell beside theirs. Yfaila was indeed an old Ittallan. She had the look of a proud woman who'd lost her confidence. She sat in the back corner of the cell, her hair tangled around her, her clothes torn and dirty. She didn't even look up when Solvi spoke.

'Yfaila. Can you stand? Walk?' Amarah asked.

The old woman shook her head. 'Leave me to my fate. Linaria has no place for a traitor like me.'

'Yfaila, do not say this. Everyone can be forgiven.' Solvi kept trying.

Amarah was less interested. If she wanted to stay here and rot, then let her. She was here to free the princess and Lathri. If anyone else wanted to come, they were more than welcome, but she wasn't going to force people who didn't want to leave. 'Come on, Solvi. We don't have time.'

Solvi shook her head. 'But we can't leave her!'

'Yes we can. Do you want to help your princess or not?' Amarah knew it was harsh, but it could take all night to

533

convince the miserable woman to come with them, and they didn't have that kind of time to spare.

At her question, Solvi looked back to the woman. 'Please, Yfaila. When Sapora comes back, he will kill you. Leave this place. Come with us.'

Yfaila hugged herself more tightly and looked at the wall.

Even in the dim light, Amarah could see the tears streaking trails of dirt down her cheeks. She knew a lost cause when she saw one. 'Come on Solvi. You wanted to help me, so help me now. Let's find the others.'

Amarah didn't give Solvi time to argue. She simply turned and hurried down the passage to where she'd seen Antar, Judd, and Oris taken several hours earlier. She rounded the corner, half-jogging, half-running, in her haste to reach her comrades. She heard Solvi following behind, keeping up with Amarah's run.

She skidded to a halt when she saw two Cerastes standing guard at the end of the corridor, by a crossroads. She cursed herself for not thinking there would be more guards down here, too.

Solvi didn't hesitate. She crouched as light engulfed her and she transformed in the blink of an eye. She growled low, her mottled grey and white fur bristling as she sized up the two guards in her true form—a snow leopard.

Amarah kept back. She didn't want to get in the way of her massive claws.

The young Ittallan rushed the guards, easily overpowering one with the speed of her attack. Her jaws could crush his skull, Amarah had no doubt, but Solvi simply knocked him into the stone wall, rendering him unconscious.

The other Cerastes managed to avoid Solvi's strike, and Amarah was on him before he could sound the alarm. With his focus on the enormous snow leopard, Amarah managed to grab him by the throat and wrestle him to the ground. She held him firm in a choke hold until he went limp in her arms. She would have held him tighter still, squeezing the life from him, but let him go when he passed out.

She blamed Moroda's influence and stood up, making her way to the crossroads and listening intently. There were no other guards coming, no cries of surprise, no alarm raised.

They were good.

Amarah helped herself to the ring of keys on the guard's belt as she looked around.

A narrow set of stairs peeled off to the left, leading deeper into the dungeons. 'Lathri and Isa might be on the lower levels,' she said to Solvi, who had transformed back and hardly looked tired at all.

'It is possible Lathri and the princess are down there. More secure?' She sniffed the air tentatively. 'There is blood, too. I think Lathri is there.'

'Let's get Antar and the others first. More of us can cover ground quicker.' Amarah hurried straight on. It was a guess. But with most of the cells empty following Sapora's departure, she didn't think it would take very long to track down the other sky pirates.

Amarah hurried along, trying to ignore the fact that her bare feet touched the filthy dungeon floor, while she sought her comrades.

'There are people ahead,' Solvi said.

She was right. Amarah ran past empty cell after empty cell until finally they reached the one where Antar, Judd, and Oris had been placed. 'Finally found ya.'

'You took your time,' Antar said, leaning through the bars, perfectly relaxed.

'Is everyone okay?' Solvi asked, looking into the cell. 'No-one is hurt?'

Judd had been sat with his back against the wall, and he stood up gingerly. His joints cracked as he got to his feet and he yawned. 'All good, thanks. Do you know where Lathri and the princess are?'

'We have an idea,' Amarah said. She immediately got to work on the lock, and found this one to be in an even worse condition than the one of her own cell. But with the key to hand, she had the gate open in less than a minute, and the three pirates were outside.

'How many guards are here?' Oris asked, closing the gate behind him.

'Don't know. We saw two on our way here. Might be more guarding the princess,' Amarah replied. 'It'll be easy getting to them. Getting back out will be tricky.'

Amarah and Solvi led them back to the crossroads, the two Cerastes still unconscious and strewn about the passageway. They ignored them and headed downstairs while Oris remained at the top to keep watch.

Solvi took the lead from that point onwards as she followed the smell of blood.

If Amarah had hated the dungeon floor upstairs, downstairs was even worse. All manner of grime lined the cold stone, and she almost wished she'd gone into the palace to find her clothes and boots before looking for Lathri and Isa. Unable to do much about it now, she carried on regardless, following Solvi through winding passageways as they drew closer to Lathri.

After a minute or two, they reached a cell at the end of a narrow corridor. Even Amarah could smell blood here, and she definitely didn't have an Ittallan's nose. There were other smells, too—various bodily fluids—and she wondered just how long Lathri had been left down here to suffer.

'Lathri!' Solvi called when they reached her cell.

The woman inside looked even worse than Yfaila had.

536

Amarah had seen tramps and beggars on the streets of Niversai who looked cleaner and healthier than she did. There were three others in the cell with her, and though they had also been tortured, none of them were as bad as Lathri.

Amarah immediately unlocked the cell gate and Solvi rushed past to get inside.

'Solvi. It...it can't be you?' Lathri said. Her voice was thin and frail, like an old woman's on the brink of death. Her filthy rags hung loosely from her and she struggled to stand. She rested a hand against Solvi's strong body and heaved herself gingerly up to her feet. 'How can you be here?'

'Jailbreak courtesy of Kylos and Princess Isa,' Antar said. 'We're here to get you out.'

Lathri wobbled on her feet, even with the support of Solvi. 'And the others?'

Antar grinned. 'We're gonna save Princess Isa, too. And whoever else we can. These three the only ones left?'

'Princess Isa!' Lathri gasped.

The other three women looked up and hope glazed their eyes.

'Can you stand?' Judd asked, entering the broken cell and approaching the three.

They nodded, their voices either hurting too much to speak or lost. One had deep auburn hair that reached her shoulders in tight curls, and the other two were blonde, like Lathri. All three were thin and afraid, and reminded Amarah of mice.

Judd eased them to their feet, where they appeared far less wobbly than Lathri. Although they'd been permitted to keep their rags, none of the women had shoes.

'Who else is here?' Amarah asked. 'Every cell we passed was empty.'

Lathri trembled. 'Prince Tacio came and cleared out the cells. All my followers and friends, taken.'

Amarah worried she'd burst into tears, but Lathri's resolve was far stronger than her clear physical weakness. 'If the dungeons are empty, no point us being here. Where's Princess Isa?'

'I didn't know she'd been arrested. I have not seen her in...I do not know how long.'

That didn't bode well. Then again, even though Isa was a prisoner, she was still a princess. If most of the people in the dungeons followed her, then seeing their true queen in a cell might have stirred too much disorder and chaos.

Better to isolate her somewhere else. It's what she'd do in the same situation with a highly influential, possibly dangerous prisoner.

'Well the job ain't finished until we find the princess,' Amarah said. 'But first we need to get our things back. I dunno about you but I don't like walking around in the muck.'

'There's usually a storage room near dungeons where they keep what they take from prisoners. We need to find that,' Antar said.

'Main entrance to this place is back near our cell,' Amarah said. 'Don't think there's no more guards down here or they'd have been on us. Gotta expect more upstairs. Palom and Kylos will be waiting, let's go.'

'Palom?' Lathri whispered, her voice lifting in excitement.

Amarah nodded, then hurried back the way she'd come, with Antar beside her. Judd and Solvi helped Lathri and the other three prisoners, and were able to keep up with them. When they clambered up the top of the first flight of stairs, Oris said everything had been quiet. He helped Judd with the women as Amarah led them back to her cell.

She gave the old Ittallan woman another chance. 'Yfaila. We have Lathri and the others. We're going to get the princess now. Are you coming?'

The old woman approached the bars of the cell slowly. She peered at them through bloodshot eyes. 'I will slow you down.'

Amarah snorted. 'Look at Lathri. Look at the others. They're still fighting, and I bet they're hurting a damned lot more than you.' She didn't have time to wait, but she also didn't want to leave anyone behind. Isa probably wouldn't take it well if she left someone alone in the dungeons to face Sapora's wrath when he returned.

Yfaila lowered her gaze.

Lathri said in a thin, weak voice, 'Yfaila. You aren't dead yet.'

That made the old woman look up.

Amarah gave her one last chance. 'We need to get outta the palace now. We're going to Estoria, far from the snakes. Our ship's waiting.'

Yfaila held her left arm at the elbow. 'This is going to kill me. It bleeds all the time.'

Lathri let go of Solvi and hobbled across to the bars. 'Let me see.'

Yfaila hesitated for a moment, then lifted her arm to Lathri's waiting hands.

Amarah watched, conscious that they were wasting too much time.

'You're a healer!' Yfaila gasped as Lathri's fingers gently massaged her arm. The flowing blood dried and Yfaila trembled.

Lathri dropped her arms, panting. 'There. I cannot heal it completely. Not now. I am...too weak. But I will help you recover, if you come with us.'

That sealed it. 'You would help me? After everything I've done?'

'We don't have time!' Amarah snapped. She unlocked the cell and threw the gate open. 'Solvi. Can you get her out?'

Yfaila took a step back, then cautiously made her way over the debris and out into the passageway. 'I owe you so much.' She steadied herself on Solvi's other side.

'Save your thanks for the flight.' Antar pushed forward. 'We need to get away.'

Amarah liked his determination and followed him up the last flight of stairs.

Antar stopped by the door, his knees slightly bent as he listened. 'All quiet outside.'

'I'd hope so. If anyone was there, they would have heard us by now.' Amarah pressed her ear to the door to verify it for herself. Satisfied there was no-one near, she and Antar forced open the door together and burst out onto the pristine marble hallway.

Back to back, they checked both directions.

Amarah saw an open door only a few feet from the dungeon, and poked her head inside. 'Looks like this is that storage room you said.' She hurried in and tore through the bundles of clothes left haphazardly in a pile. She threw on her old clothes and boots plus a hardy cloak. Their weapons were there, too, strewn across the racking and treated with little care. Except Veynothi's blade, of course.

She considered grabbing some of the armour but decided it would slow her down too much. She'd be carrying whatever she found to loot, and speed was of the essence on a job like this.

A moment later, Oris, Judd, and Solvi came through the door with the five Ittallan women.

Once they were rearmed, Amarah said, 'Solvi, Oris. Take

540

Lathri and these three to the ship, quick as you can. You can get up the tower, right?'

Solvi nodded, her pupils dilating and her whiskers twitching.

Amarah tried to ignore how strange it was that a giant animal could listen and understand her. 'Antar, Judd, come with me.'

They split off, each group going in a different direction, and Amarah's heart continued to pound. She'd much rather have to fight her way through waves of guards. Running through deserted halls and corridors simply made her more anxious that someone would suddenly jump out to attack her.

'Where are we going, Amarah?' Judd asked, when they slowed their sprint to a fast walk.

'Looking for the princess.' She glanced into every open door and pushed on those that were closed. 'Can't leave without her.'

Amarah had hoped they'd all be in the air by now, and had no way of knowing how much time had passed since she'd broken out of her cell until now. She'd only been in the palace once before, and although she'd explored parts of it, she certainly didn't know her way around as well as she'd like to.

But at least she had her scythe again.

They reached a wide staircase and Amarah headed straight up. She had no idea where Isa might be locked up, but if it wasn't at the bottom of the palace in a dungeon, then she might be locked in a suite somewhere upstairs. There were plenty of towers that were more easily guarded. It was possible the princess might be in one of those.

They skidded to a halt when the hallway veered off in two directions. The left appeared empty, but Amarah saw the red and gold livery of the Imperial Guard to the right.

541

Antar saw them too. He said, 'No point having guards unless they're guarding something.'

Amarah had to agree. The three of them ran down the hall, using their speed and surprise to overpower them.

But the Imperial Guard were trained soldiers, and even though they'd been caught off-guard, they drew their swords and met the charge with an aggressive defence. The clash of metal on metal as their blades met set Amarah's ears ringing. Blood spilled onto the marble floor as one of Antar's daggers opened a soldier from cheek to collarbone, and he dropped like a stone.

Another soldier attacked Amarah, his sword slashing at her. She ducked to avoid it, but felt the sting of the sword as its tip sliced across her lower back. Judd slammed into him and knocked him to the ground, and Amarah dropped the bottom of her scythe into his nose. Blood exploded from his face and she hit him again on the forehead. He didn't get up after that.

When she turned her attention to the other soldiers, the skirmish was already over.

'You ain't killing 'em, are ya?' Antar asked. He held a dagger in each hand, blood dripping from both.

Amarah rolled her eye. 'Don't ask.' She straightened and then winced when her back protested. It felt as though it had been torn wide open and she cursed her lack of a shield. 'I think the hangar is down that way,' she nodded.

Antar studied the hallway for a moment. 'Yeah, I recognise that tapestry.'

'Good. You two head down there. Get my warship and Isa's other class five. Might as well take what we can.'

Judd narrowed his eyes. 'What about you?'

'I'm fine.' She turned to go back to the door the Imperial Guard had been standing by. Her back burned with pain.

'You're hurt!' Judd said.

542

Amarah gritted her teeth. 'I'm fine. Get the ships and go. Ground team'll be waiting for us.'

She took a few more steps and then felt the trickle of blood down her back. Adrenaline had clearly worn off and the pain increased.

'Let me come with you,' Judd said. 'I can help.'

'Go to the ship!' Amarah snapped. Judd stopped mid-step, eyes wide. 'Once I find Isa, the two of us'll be fine.' She wanted them to hurry up and go so they wouldn't see her bleed, wouldn't see her weakness.

'Let's go, Judd,' Antar said. His order was enough to get the pilot to leave her, though she could see how reluctant he was.

Amarah waited until they were out of sight before she fell against the wall. Heat flushed her cheeks and stomach as the searing pain grew in intensity second by second. She grit her teeth and leaned forward trying to force down the vomit that suddenly rose in her gut.

When she'd taken enough of a breather, Amarah grabbed hold of the door handle, only to find it locked. Cursing, Amarah tightened her grip on her scythe, drew it back, then hacked at the door.

Every swing was agony. Her back screamed in protest. Her knees trembled with the effort. But she'd dropped her lockpicks and had no time to try and find the key. Now it was time for the blunt approach.

On the sixth swing, the wood splintered. She twisted the blade, ripping away chunks of wood and cracking the door's handle.

Amarah pulled the door apart and stepped through, only to be faced with another staircase. She took a steadying breath and made her way up, pulling herself along by the banister in one hand, and using the scythe as a walking stick in the other.

She tried to count the steps as a way to fight through the pain, but lost count around twenty-five. Her thighs ached, and she desperately wanted to stop for a breather. But Amarah knew that if she stopped now, she'd never have the strength to get back up again. She began to count again, and managed to count all the way to forty-seven, when the stairs ended at a narrow landing, and another door.

Taking deep breaths, she tried the door handle.

Locked.

'Dragon's above,' she snapped. Just as she readied herself to smash her way through a second door, the handle twisted back in response.

'Hello?'

It was Princess Isa.

'Isa!' Amarah gasped, still out of breath.

'Who's there?' Isa called through the thick door.

Amarah shook her head, trying to laugh but in too much pain and exhaustion to. 'Who d'you think? It's Amarah!'

'Do you have the key?'

Amarah shuddered. The back of her shirt was soaked in blood. 'I've got *a* key. Stand back.' She didn't wait. She slammed the edge of her scythe into the wood, where it dug in with a dull thud. This door had to be twice the thickness of the one at the bottom of the stairs.

Amarah pulled at her weapon, but it had wedged itself in deep. Amarah cursed her luck.

'Wait! Wait!' Isa called through the door.

Amarah didn't need telling twice. She leaned heavily on the handle of the scythe where it protruded from the door, sweat dripping down her forehead.

A few moments later, she heard the sound of a knife chipping at the wood. Amarah pressed down on the scythe, using it as leverage, and the door began to split apart. With

544

both scythe and knife attacking the wood, the two of them managed to break it open.

'I thought you'd have just used that blast of energy, like before,' Isa said, peering through the large hole in the door to Amarah.

'Sorry. Don't have it no more.' Amarah could hardly look up.

'Dragons above, what happened?' Isa gasped. She wrenched at her blade to widen the hole and pulled herself through. 'You're bleeding!'

Amarah blinked slowly as Isa darted back into her room and returned with sheets of fabric—presumably from her bedding. Isa tore it into strips and lifted up the back of Amarah's shirt.

Amarah winced as the princess staunched the flow of blood as best she could, and then bound her wound in strip after strip of bedding.

'You need a medic!' Isa returned to her room and then reappeared with a heavy bag full of weapons, parchment, clothes, and various bundles that Amarah couldn't discern.

She was impressed at her preparation. 'You've been ready to go?'

Isa nodded. 'Since I was arrested. I can't thank you enough for coming.'

'Don't thank me yet. Sapora's gone. He emptied most of the dungeons, took that filthy old Varkain and left for Veynothi.'

'Oh no, the Valendrin? We're too late!' Isa said. 'I've failed.' Her shoulders dropped in resignation.

Amarah scowled. Why was everyone so damned negative? 'Not you, too. I didn't get myself arrested for nothing. Everyone that's left is free.'

Isa frowned then. 'Everyone?'

Amarah winced as she struggled to make her way back

downstairs. They'd dallied long enough. 'Kylos and Palom are managing the ground team. All your followers are waiting for you, now.'

'Palom, too!' Isa hurried down and steadied Amarah as they gingerly followed the banister downstairs.

'You know, Sapora's a damned snake. He was always gonna do it. Get the Ark. But me being here means you're free to lead the fight against him. I ain't giving up. You can't, either.'

Amarah felt Isa's grip on her shoulder tighten at her words. At least she still had guts.

'I'm sorry you were hurt on my account,' Isa said. 'I'll repay you.'

Amarah smiled at that. She had no doubt Antar would have raided the palace before getting to the hangar and taking her warship. 'Yeah, you will.'

When they reached the bottom, Isa helped Amarah through the broken door. She looked down at the Imperial Guard and the puddle of blood on the floor and didn't react. 'Where now?'

'Need to get back to the tower above the dungeon. On the east side.' Amarah's breathing had become laboured during the descent. She prayed to Rhea that there were no other guards left in the palace, but she didn't want to get her hopes up, either. No job was ever that easy.

'Right. Follow me.' Princess Isa took charge, and led the pair of them down the hallway.

At least the princess knew the palace like the back of her hand.

Amarah followed as quickly as she could, but it didn't take long before every step opened the wound on her back a little more, and the burning pain was almost too much to bear.

546

'Almost there. The door to the tower stairs is just at the end of this hallway,' Isa said.

'Stay right where you are.'

Amarah had known it had been too good to be true. There had to be more guards, more people, ready and waiting to stop them. She could only hope that Solvi had reached the top of the tower with Lathri and the others, and Antar and Judd had made it to the hangar.

'Tacio. Get out of my way,' Isa said.

The Varkain at the end of the hallway was the same one who had been drinking next to Sapora when they'd first arrived. So *he* was the other prince? Sapora's brother? And Isa's too, come to think of it.

Amarah wasn't sure she could stand for very much longer, let alone fight.

Thankfully, Isa appeared more than willing to take him on.

'You traitor.'

Isa didn't smile, didn't frown. She remained emotionless at his words. 'Yes, but you've known that all along, haven't you? Clever Tacio.'

'Now you've been caught, you talk back?' The Varkain laughed, cold and mirthless. 'Sapora wants you kept alive, but he isn't here to enforce that right now. I think I'll enjoy slicing you up. You and your filthy pirate friend.'

Amarah struggled to keep her breathing straight. Isa looked ready to fight, but Amarah had no idea of her battle prowess. Or Tacio's, for that matter. If either of them were anything like Sapora, she didn't know who to put her money on.

'Come and try, snake.' Isa crouched and pulled out a pair of short daggers from the top of her boots. 'Let's see if you've actually got fangs.'

Amarah had to admire her spunk. Few people insulted a

Varkain and lived, but considering all the problems in Taban Yul, she assumed there had been an awful lot of political strife in the palace between these two.

What surprised Amarah was the fact Tacio stood his ground alone. He had no Cerastes with him, no Imperial Guard providing reinforcement. Perhaps the palace really had been emptied, save them. That, or Antar, Solvi, and the others had killed any who had been left.

Sapora really *would* be pissed when he returned, Ark or no Ark.

Tacio drew a sword from his hip and levelled it at Isa.

The prince and princess lunged at each other, covering the distance between them in seconds, blades drawn and ready. They struck at one another which such force that their blades sent off a high-pitched whistle every time they connected. Tacio attacked furiously with stronger blows than Isa was able to deliver. But Isa, shorter and lighter, danced away, stepping to the side, forwards, and backwards. She constantly moved, constantly forced him to over-reach or hack into thin air because she'd dodged a moment before.

She stepped inside his guard, nipped at him with her blades, and forced Tacio to retreat. Only when he managed to meet her blades could he then press his advantage, only to be turned away a few strokes later because of her superior agility.

Amarah had seen plenty of fights before, but almost all were street brawls. These two were masters of their weapons and even more deadly than the thugs and pirates she was used to battling. When she watched more closely, she saw that Isa never blocked Tacio's sword with her own dagger. She parried it, flinging it off to the side and redirecting the strength of his blow away from herself.

She had no idea how well Isa could hold her own in

battle, and her respect grew as the princess deflected Tacio again and again, darting in to slice at him when she spotted an opportunity and went for it.

Isa stepped in close, her chest pressed against Tacio's. She plunged her dagger into his side and twisted as she pulled it out. She thrust the dagger forward again when he stepped away and slammed the pommel of his sword on the back of her head, and lurched backwards.

Tacio clutched his side with one hand, and it came away red. 'You!'

His blood covered Isa's hand and dagger too, and she glared at him. Amarah saw her pupils abruptly constrict into slits, her breathing increase, and her pulse quicken. The veins in her throat bulged.

Amarah swallowed. 'Isa...?'

The princess either didn't hear or didn't care. She lunged forward again, dagger raised and ready.

Tacio parried her, slashed again, and met her barrage of attacks with steadily weakening blocks. Blood stained the floor and their footsteps carried it as they tackled one another.

Amarah wasn't sure who the better fighter was, but Isa was certainly more aggressive.

The princess threw herself into the fight, attacking relentlessly with seemingly no care for herself. She screamed, a gurgled cry of fury and emotion as she attacked over and over. Isa forced Tacio into a corner of the hall, and he almost cowered before her.

Amarah used the chance to hurry past them and get to the bottom of the tower stairway. 'Isa! Come on!'

But Isa was more interested in attacking Tacio than listening, and she didn't so much as turn her head. She continued to attack, her blade coming back more and more red as it found its mark in Tacio's side, arms, and legs.

'Isa!' Amarah cried.

Tacio roared back and kicked out, catching Isa by the knee and dropping her to the floor.

Amarah *felt* Isa's head crack on the marble.

'You disgusting creature!' Tacio hissed, panting heavily. He spat blood. 'Look what you've done to me!' He raised his bleeding hands, his jewelled fingers sore and dirty from the fight. 'You don't *deserve* to be killed by me. You're the lowest of the low. The kitten princess who sleeps in the hay like a common peasant!'

He kicked her and she groaned, daggers forgotten.

Tacio stumbled forward, many of his wounds bleeding heavily, his gaze locked on Isa. 'You tried to poison us with your betrayals. Now...now I'll show you what happens to traitors. And this time, there's no Sapora to protect you.'

Amarah froze where she was, one foot on the first step, her body half-in the doorway. 'Isa! Get up!' She was in no condition to rush forward to Isa's rescue. Her scythe was a walking stick at best, and her own wound forced her to hobble.

While Isa coughed on the floor and tried to get to her hands and feet, Tacio took several moments to catch his breath. He tried to straighten and dust off his clothes and used his fingers to slick back his hair again, though he left bloody streaks in it.

Amarah knew what was coming. 'Isa!' She pleaded.

There was no-one else, no-one left. And the princess had clearly stunned herself when she'd collided with the floor.

'Do you have any last words?' Tacio hissed.

And then Amarah watched her second ever Varkain transformation unfold in the hallway.

Tacio's true form was a cobra, like Sapora. But where Sapora was grey-green with flecks of black, Tacio was brown, almost copperish, with bands of grey stippling along the length of his body. His eyes had darkened from gold to red, and he filled the passageway with his coils.

Amarah whimpered. This was her nightmare. The damned Varkain of Niversai had beaten that fear into her, and now she had to face it.

Isa had managed to stand up in the time Tacio had taken to swan about, insulting her. She bent down to pick up one of her daggers, although Amarah wasn't sure such a small blade would be particularly effective against Tacio's true form.

Tacio moved slowly, his coils twisting in the small space. Amarah couldn't accurately say how long he was. Sapora had been thirty feet and filled the grand ballroom of the palace. Tacio had to equal him, at least, but in the confines of the corridor, he had far less room to move and manoeuvre.

'Isa!' Amarah called again.

Her shout caught the princess's attention that time.

Tacio struck, his fangs extended as he lunged for Isa.

The princess rolled out of the way, easily quicker than the enormous snake.

Although Isa's incredible speed had saved her, Amarah knew they didn't have time to see this fight through to its end.

'Go. I'll hold him back.' Isa's voice was the deepest growl Amarah had ever heard.

She winced as another wave of pain laced her lower back. If she waited any longer, she'd collapse. Trusting that Isa would follow, Amarah clambered up the stairs, using her scythe to keep her standing upright. She had no idea how she was going to fly *Otella*—or if she could even reach the top of the tower.

She knew her face had paled, that sweat rolled down her

neck with her effort, but she soldiered on regardless. She had to get Isa to safety. *Had* to.

With Sapora and Tacio in power, peace would never come to Linaria.

But with Isa, they had a chance. She had to keep that chance alive.

Amarah stumbled several times, but she pulled herself up and continued on when she faltered.

Thankfully, the door at the top of the tower was wide open, and the cool night breeze kissed Amarah's skin. It was more paradise than Estoria had ever been. When she looked up, she saw the silhouette of someone at the top of the stairs.

'Amarah?' Solvi.

Thank Rhea. 'Yes, it's me. Isa's coming...I hope...'

'You're hurt!' Solvi gasped. She grabbed Amarah and looped one arm under her shoulder.

'Is everyone...there?' Amarah asked, leaning against Solvi more than she'd thought she'd needed to. 'Lathri, everyone...?'

'We're all here, waiting for you! Can you fly the ship?'

'I'll be okay.' Amarah gratefully walked with Solvi up the last few steps, out the door, and onto the tower roof. *Otella* still sat where she'd left her, and several faces looked down at her from the ship's deck.

Solvi helped get Amarah up the ladder and onboard *Otella*. 'Anyone seen...Antar? Judd? Any other ships?'

'No-one until you,' Oris said. He helped Amarah to the ship's wheel and controls. Amarah switched on the engine, the propellers whirred into life, and the ship's sails unfurled. 'Where's the princess?'

'Coming.' Amarah panted. Her back and legs were going numb, and blood squelched everywhere when she sat down. But there was nothing she could do about that now.

'Lathri and the others are below. Thought it best to keep them outta sight,' Oris said.

Amarah nodded, unable to do much else, and desperately wanting to just lie down and sleep.

'It's the princess!' Solvi cried.

Footsteps pounded, then scrambled up the ladder as Isa got on board. 'Get in the air! He's right behind me!'

The entire ship shuddered as the enormous snake struck at the hull only seconds behind Isa. *Otella*'s side sails tore in his fangs as he ripped them apart.

Amarah took another breath, pulled a lever, and then turned the wheel as *Otella* half-fell off the tower roof and into the sky. Tacio's angry hissing followed them into the darkness, but he couldn't follow.

She knew the ground team would be waiting for them, and Tacio would pursue them as soon as he could get to his own warships. She had to hope there weren't too many pilots, nor ships, otherwise everything would have been for nothing.

And she had to hope that Traego was near and would be able to provide cover fire.

'The royal docks are still recovering from the attack on the palace,' Isa said, making her way over to Amarah. 'We have a window while they try and get a couple of warships together. I don't think he has enough Cerastes of Imperial Guard left for a full chase.'

Amarah nodded at the good news. Her arms trembled where she held the wheel, and *Otella* listed to the side. She struggled to keep the ship level, but she was so exhausted she could hardly keep her eye open.

Oris came to stand beside her. 'We need to head south.'

She struggled to adjust the wheel at his words.

Oris said, 'Amarah, you're bleeding. A lot.'

'I know.' Blood trickled down her seat and onto the deck,

where it pooled beneath her feet. If it was the last thing she did, she'd get *Otella* to the ground team. Even if she couldn't fly, Lathri, Isa, and the others could get on her new ship, or her warship, if Antar managed to get out.

Even if she crashed *Otella*, Traego would have her new ship as recompense.

That would make things fair, wouldn't it?

Oris didn't know what to say to her admittance of bleeding out. He went for something somewhat practical and as positive as he could manage, 'We'll be back in Estoria soon. It won't be long.'

Amarah grunted. He was trying to be helpful, she knew that.

But she wouldn't make it until morning, much less a two day flight back.

Amarah wiped sweat from her face and grabbed the wheel again, struggling to hold it tightly enough. She couldn't stand, not now.

The city walls were easy to see, at least. But she couldn't discern the moons nor stars to navigate. 'Oris. Where...?'

Oris grabbed the wheel as it slipped from her hands, and guided *Otella* south. The Rio Neva forest, Feor Mountains, and Jato's thunderstorm appeared on the left, but that was about as much as Amarah could make out.

Her body convulsed and she cried out, unable to hold the pain back any longer.

'Amarah! Someone help!' Isa cried. She steadied her and shrugged out of her short cloak to try and dab at the blood.

Amarah knew it was too late, of course. She'd lost too much blood, took on too big a risk. And for what? Freeing a princess and a bunch of prisoners?

They passed over the city's walls, and Amarah managed to turn *Otella*'s nose down, descending on the wide plains outside Taban Yul. She knew Kylos, Palom, and the others were waiting on the edge of the forest, but she wasn't sure she actually had the strength to land safely.

At Princess Isa's cry, Solvi rushed into the cabin.

The ship groaned as it dove, steeper than she'd have liked. The ground rushed up to meet them and Amarah tried but couldn't reach the lever to fan out the side sails. She gestured weakly towards it.

'Take her. I'll land,' Isa said.

Oris and Solvi didn't need telling twice. Between them, they lifted Amarah off the seat and carried her away from the controls, as Isa grabbed the wheel. A moment later, she'd corrected the steepness of their dive and slowed their speed.

Amarah felt herself being laid down on the deck, felt the warmth of the blood as it poured from her. She had no strength left.

Now, she only felt cold.

'Stay with us,' Princess Isa whispered.

What was the point?

Amarah's vision went dark as her breath slowed. She closed her eye and exhaled.

36

Palom stared up at the city wall, his heart pounding. He and the others of Lathri's resistance had taken up position on the edge of the Rio Neva forest and used the trees for cover. Only a couple of weeks ago, he'd been waiting for Amarah in Tum Metsa, on the edge of the world. Now, he'd joined a rebel movement intent on overthrowing Sapora and putting Isa on the throne. More than that, he was going to see Lathri again.

Leillu crouched at his feet, Captain Chyro stood to his left, and Kylos had hidden herself in the trees somewhere to his right.

Behind him, at least sixty armed Ittallan waited. They spoke quietly among themselves, a constant murmur that Palom tried to drown out.

The moons were high tonight, and bathed Taban Yul in silver. Palom had taken up his position that afternoon, and watched the sun set and the three moons rise while he waited for Amarah to be successful. His stomach clenched and unclenched at the thought of Sapora's claws in Solvi, Lathri, or Amarah. He was so close, so close, to freeing Lathri. He could almost see her.

Leillu turned her head and let out a warning growl. Palom followed her gaze and saw Kylos approach from the shadow of the trees. She was so light that Palom couldn't even hear her footsteps.

'Any movement?' Kylos asked in a low voice.

Palom shook his head. 'Your brother will see before we do.' He stared up. Despite the bright moonlight, he couldn't spot the eagle.

But if he couldn't see Aetos, then none of the snakes would be able to see him, either.

He'd always thought he was patient. You had to be, if you were a blacksmith, but this wait was sorely testing him. He'd managed to buy extra supplies in town—clothes, weapons, and armour mostly—and felt as prepared as he could be for flying away from Val Sharis.

Seeing Captain Chyro again had been a pleasant surprise. The young captain had explained he'd wanted to follow Solvi to Taban Yul to keep an eye on her. Palom suspected there was a little more to it than that, but he appreciated the sentiment. He doubted his niece needed much looking after, but knowing there were others watching out for her was added peace of mind. And from Chyro's post at the city gates, he'd been able to help more rebels enter and leave Taban Yul, right under the snakes' noses.

The young captain had wanted to remain loyal to the Imperial Guard, but after Sapora released Mateli, Chryro saw Isa as the true leader of Val Sharis. He'd put himself in terrible danger, but he said the ends justified the risk.

Palom could understand everyone's hatred of the Varkain—he couldn't stand them either—but after their devastating losses during the Ittallan-Varkain war and subsequent attack on the palace, few of them were keen to actually take up arms. Especially with a Sevastos at Sapora's control.

But Palom was ready for a battle. He wore mail under his shirt, leather gauntlets with brass knuckles, longsword on his back, and two fighting knives on either thigh. Chyro, though young, was a clear hunter and eager to fight. And Lathri trusted Kylos and Aetos, so he did, too.

'Is Odi still with you?' Palom asked.

Kylos shook her head. 'He went back to the others to keep them ready. When the ships get here, there won't be time for stragglers.'

Odi had plenty of charisma. It made sense that he stayed with the others instead of on watch.

Palom was about to head back into the trees to check on the others for himself, when an eagle's shrill cry made him pause. Aetos's warning.

Leillu flexed her wings and lashed her tail, agitated at the noise.

'Is okay, *Leillu*,' Palom said, trying to calm her.

The silhouette of a warship came into view above the city walls. He struggled to tell the edge apart from the night sky, and gasped when he realised it was hurtling towards the ground much too quickly. 'Take cover!' He roared.

Kylos and Chyro leaped in opposite directions, and even *Leillu* stopped growling. She backed away slowly, but Palom jumped forward to scoop her up. He held her close and dived for the nearest tree. He covered her with his body and the tree, and braced for impact.

But it didn't come.

He peered around the tree to see the massive warship hover just above the ground. The wind from its propellers send leaves, twigs, and debris flying. Amarah had said they'd be on a ship called *Otella*, and while Palom couldn't see the ship's name, he could tell it wasn't one of the Imperial Fleet.

Still clutching *Leillu* to his chest, Palom stepped out and glanced to the side.

Kylos nodded. 'That's *Otella*! That's them!'

'Bring everyone through!' Palom yelled. 'Chyro, help me get them onboard.'

Kylos disappeared at his order, and Palom raced forward, throwing *Leillu* in front of him where she stayed in the air with a single beat of her wings. She immediately flew up the side of *Otella* and disappeared from view when she landed on deck.

Palom skidded to a halt at the bottom of the ladder, then turned back to face the way he'd come. Kylos led dozens of Ittallan, and he held his arms out to take their bags and boxes as they scrambled up. Chyro mirrored Palom, and the two of them pulled up the Ittallan's supplies as quickly as they could.

'*Kali!*'

He looked up as the last few Ittallan reached the bottom of the ship. 'Solvi!'

'Amarah is in bad shape!'

The panic in her voice cut through him.

'Go see her. I'll sort out these last few!' Chyro said, waving him up.

Palom didn't hesitate. He grabbed onto the ladder steps and heaved himself up. Already the Ittallan on board were charging around, securing their belongings and taking up positions along the side of the ship. A small crowd had gathered outside the captain's cabin. The scent of blood filled his nostrils.

Thoughts churned in his mind. Had she been bitten by one of the Varkain? It seemed the most likely option.

'*Kali!*'

He glanced at Solvi as he marched towards the crowd.

'Bring Lathri. I do not know if she can heal their venom, but—'

'Lathri cannot!'

'What?' Palom whirled around.

Solvi shook her head. 'I will bring her, but she is very weak. The Varkain, they...'

A cold dread seeped through his chest. 'Take me to her.'

Solvi pursed her lips and hurried off towards a small door underneath the quarterdeck. Palom followed her through it, then pulled up short. Yfaila sat on the bench at the back of the wide cabin, a blanket draped over her knees.

And Lathri nestled into her shoulder. She'd pulled the blanket up over her shoulders, and even from several paces away, Palom could see how she trembled.

He ignored Yfaila, refused to acknowledge her, his attention only on the healer.

'Lathri...' He could hardly speak, the surge of emotion was too strong.

Solvi sat beside Lathri and rubbed her shoulders. 'Look, Lathri. My *kali* is here. Palom.'

At the mention of his name, Lathri's eyes flickered open. 'Palom...? Is it really...you?'

Palom sank to his knees in front of her and took her hands in his own. 'You're cold.'

Lathri smiled. 'I am weak. Tired. My energy...has been drained.'

Palom gently stroked her hands, tried to warm them with his. 'It is okay. You can rest. We are going to be in the air any minute now. Away from these snakes.'

Lathri coughed and leaned into him.

Palom wrapped his arms around her as she all but fell into his embrace. He'd been expecting her warmth, her energy. But all he felt under the blanket was skin and bone, the frail body of a woman close to death. 'Oh, Lathri. You have been through so much. I should never have left you.'

Her shivering lessened as she hugged him. 'I should...never have been so harsh. You wouldn't have left...if I'd been kinder.'

Palom shook his head, burying his face in her shoulder to hide the tears. 'I was fool. You were right. You were always right. I am sorry. Can you forgive me?'

Lathri laughed, then. At least, Palom thought she did. She relaxed into him, and they shared each others' warmth.

'Lathri? Solvi? Amarah's not going to hold on—'

Palom looked over his shoulder at the sudden voice. 'Princess Isa?'

The princess stood in the doorway, bloody and bruised, but still standing strong.

'Palom! Amarah's been cut by a sword. There's so much blood. I don't—'

'Lathri is too weak,' he said. He tightened his hug as if it would protect her.

Isa swallowed, visibly uncomfortable. 'I can just about land this ship, but I can't fly it. I only have class fives. If Amarah doesn't get up, we can't get away.'

'It's okay, Palom...' Lathri all but whispered.

'No! It is too much for you!' Palom replied, sterner than he would have liked, but unable to keep all of his emotions in check. They needed to get away or they'd be sitting ducks for Tacio, the Cerastes, and any other Varkain he had at his command.

'Let me stand,' Lathri said.

Reluctantly, Palom straightened to make room for her. Although unsteady on her feet, Lathri managed to stand unaided. 'Lathri, you cannot...'

She wouldn't *really* heal her, would she? Surely she knew

how weak she was? Using any more healing magic would be too much for her. Lathri herself was barely clinging on.

'I must,' Lathri replied, ever defiant.

Palom looked to Solvi for support, but his niece simply held Lathri's arm in case she fell.

Desperate, he looked at Yfaila. The old Ittallan had lost an arm since he'd last seen her, but he had no sympathy for whatever had happened while she'd been in Sapora's clutches. She said, 'Lathri is the only one who can help us.'

'No!' Palom bellowed, the strength of his voice rattling the walls. 'Lathri if you heal Amarah before you are recovered...you...' He couldn't say it.

Aided by Solvi's steady grip, Lathri took a shaky step forward. Then another.

'You will die, Lathri!'

When she reached Princess Isa in the doorway, Lathri looked back at him. 'If I don't heal her, we will all die.'

Palom's vision blurred, and he blinked away sudden tears. 'Lathri! No! I cannot lose you again! Please!'

But she left the room, Isa on one arm, Solvi on the other.

When Palom raced onto the deck, the small crowd had grown along with the smell of blood.

He saw a flash of blue and made a beeline for the young dragon. '*Leillu!*'

The crowd parted at his voice, but Palom stopped in his tracks when he saw Amarah. She lay face down in a pool of her own blood. The back of her shirt was caked in it.

And she wasn't moving.

Lathri had crouched beside Amarah, both hands pressed on her back, the blanket still around her shoulders.

His knees trembled. She gave her life energy to others when she healed them. *Ra*, she'd called it. Few Ittallan were able to study at the University of Berel, something to do with *Ra* and *meraki* not working well together. But Lathri had been one of the handful to master the art. She'd always used the magic for good. To help others. To save lives.

And now, here she was again, giving everything to a pirate.

'Lathri.' His voice broke. He couldn't shout, couldn't scream.

He sat cross-legged next to her, steadied her, rested his strong arms along hers and wished she could take his life energy instead of her own. Wished she could pull from his strength and not hers.

But that wasn't how *Ra* worked. *Ra* was life. Taking life from someone else was the opposite.

Palom allowed his tears to fall freely, and watched as Amarah's foot twitched.

Lathri went limp as the energy flowed from her and into Amarah, and Palom suppressed a sob. He pulled her into his arms, resting her upper body in his lap and gently stroked her face.

The Ittallan around him gasped, spoke, cheered. Palom ignored it all, his focus only on Lathri.

Feet thundered past and in front of him, more boots than he could count. People spoke but she couldn't understand what they said. It all blurred into one overwhelming mess. Bags and bundles were thrown about, and bottles rolled away on deck when they were dropped.

Amarah shivered.

Leillu chirped: a high-pitched noise she made whenever she was excited.

But it didn't mean anything.

Lathri's chest fluttered like a bird. She'd given too much. Even healing a stubbed toe would have been too much in her condition.

Amarah let out a muffled cry, burying her face in the deck.

563

She must have been on the brink of death. Perhaps even walking down the path to Rhea.

Palom rocked slowly, hoping to ease Lathri's pain. His thumb stroked her cheek, brushed loose strands of hair from her face. He leaned forward to kiss her on the lips, on the nose, on the forehead. 'My Lathri. *'Onia omor*, Lathri. *Onia...*' He slipped into his mother tongue as he held her close.

With a shaky hand, Amarah pushed herself up onto her knees and straightened. Blinking, Amarah looked around. 'What...?'

Amarah turned around, and her mouth dropped open.

Palom spared Amarah the briefest of glances before turning back to Lathri. Her haggard breaths came short and uneven, Amarah's drying blood covering her hands.

Amarah was on her feet in a second. 'Lathri! Palom!'

Great tears streamed down his cheeks as Palom cradled Lathri and rocked her gently from side to side. He couldn't say anything more.

Lathri had been utterly exhausted when she'd reached *Otella*. Now, she'd brought Amarah back from the brink of death.

Lathri's breathing quickened suddenly, and Palom adjusted his hold on her. He stroked her hair gently with one thumb and continued to rock.

Amarah, alongside Isa, Solvi, and the other Ittallan who had followed Lathri from the very first day, watched in silence as Lathri took her final breaths and died in his arms.

Palom's broken sobs punctuated the still, night air.

He knew they needed to get away before Tacio gave chase. But he couldn't bring himself to say anything.

Palom leaned forward to kiss Lathri's cheeks over and over. He pressed his forehead against hers and stroked her hair. His body shuddered with his sobs.

Amarah sank to her knees and cried.

The enormity of Lathri's death weighed heavy on him. She was the leader of the resistance. The driving force for the people against Sapora, Tacio, the Arks, everything. She'd brought Isa to their cause, had shown her for the true leader she could be. She'd taken on Sapora and lived, had survived through Tacio's brutal torture and kept Isa safe.

She'd united the Ittallan and shown them a better way forward.

But their work wasn't over yet. They were still on the outskirts of Taban Yul. Tacio would be after them any moment, and Sapora might return with his Sevastos soon as well.

Solvi crouched by her uncle, cuddled him and pressed her own head into his massive shoulder. She cried, too, but silently. In solidarity of Palom and in grief for Lathri.

They'd done everything they could. Amarah had been summoned by Isa to free Lathri and get her safely from the palace. She wasn't supposed to die. No-one was supposed to die.

'Ships incoming.'

Palom wasn't sure who shouted the warning, but it took him several seconds to process. When he eventually looked up, there was a warship and a tiny class five approaching.

It was a signal to keep moving. They couldn't wait around.

'Amarah. We need to fly,' Princess Isa said. Her voice wavered slightly.

Amarah pushed herself to her feet. She took a few shaky steps forward and patted Palom on his other shoulder as she made her way back to *Otella*'s wheel. Blood had slickened the floor, but she walked through it anyway. 'Is everyone on board?' Her voice was flat, monotone.

Palom shuddered. He'd need to fight if Tacio was on

their tail. He sniffed and shifted Lathri's weight to Solvi. 'I need to speak to Amarah.' His own voice was as flat as the sky pirate's had been.

Solvi didn't argue, and he heaved himself to his feet. *Leillu* remained by Solvi and Lathri, and he didn't try to make her follow.

He followed Amarah into the captain's cabin, one hand resting on the hilt of a knife. He stared past her and to the approaching ships. There was no flurry of activity, no orders to fire. Perhaps they weren't Tacio's soldiers.

Palom lingered in the door to the captain's cabin. 'These are...your friends?' His voice was thick with sadness.

Amarah nodded slowly, as though she were in a daze. 'This is *Otella*. It belongs to Traego, an old ally of mine,' she said. 'You remember my warship from the battle with Aciel?'

Palom glanced towards it, then nodded.

'Jato took *Khanna* from me. That ship there is my new one. Traego's flying it.'

Palom studied it for several moments. 'What is new ship's name?'

Amarah sighed and shook her head. '*RaKhanna*.'

37

Amarah followed *RaKhanna* in *Otella*, with her warship and Isa's class five on either side. As Amarah expected, the mood aboard was sombre, although there had to be a good sixty or so people crammed together on the airship.

She had thought their grand escape would be full of cheering and laughter that they'd outwitted Sapora, Tacio, and all their snakes.

Of course, she hadn't expected to make a mistake.

She hadn't expected to *die*.

Or come however close to it as she had.

It wasn't just that she blamed herself for Lathri's death. She'd *caused* it.

If it hadn't been for her, Lathri would still be alive.

Oris looked through the longscope Judd had used on their way to Taban Yul and occasionally called back to Amarah, making her aware of things he saw. 'Amarah. We've got trouble.'

She sighed. 'What now?'

'Ships from the palace. I see two. No, three.'

'They'd be fools to attack us,' Amarah said. Three warships against two, plus her *RaKhanna*, and Isa's little one. If they kept out of range, it wouldn't come to a battle at all.

Princess Isa ran into the cabin. 'Amarah—'

'Tacio's ships, I know. Oris saw 'em coming.'

'I doubt they'll send more,' Isa said. 'The Imperial Fleet was decimated.'

Amarah smiled. 'I've had more ships on my tail for treasure half as valuable as you. Don't worry.' She increased *Otella*'s speed, and her allies' ships matched it.

'I'm amazed you pulled it off.'

'Pulled what off?'

Isa looked at her, eyebrows down. 'Saving me. Rescuing the others.'

Amarah snorted. 'Any thief worth their salt could do that.'

'I'm sure they could. But most would grab what they could and then make their escape. Why would they burden themselves with the injured or weak?'

Amarah snorted again. 'Didn't get everyone, did I, though? Lathri...'

Isa pursed her lips. 'You did exactly what I asked.'

Amarah glanced back to keep her eye on Oris, who watched the approaching ships with the longscope.

Isa continued, 'I wish you weren't a pirate. If you put your mind to it, Amarah, you could do some good in the world. Rhea knows Linaria could do with good, competent people who want to make the world a better place. There are too many Tacios. Too much greed. People who take too much and leave a barren, lifeless husk in their wake.'

'Speaking of Tacio,' Amarah said, changing the subject, 'you fought him like a demon.'

Isa blushed and looked away.

'So? What's all that about?'

'I'm *well-versed* in combat.'

The princess was putting it mildly. And here Amarah had thought that all Goldstones and nobility did was go to fancy dinners, wear expensive clothes, and order other people about. She supposed Isa wasn't a typical Goldstone, much less a typical princess.

'They're gaining on us, Amarah!' Oris said. 'Are we fighting or not?'

Amarah was in no mood to fight. Not after everything she'd been through that night. Lathri might have healed her and restored her strength, but in her death, Amarah had lost a chunk of her motivation. She'd always been able to see her way out of a bad situation, always been able to find the opportunity.

But Lathri's death was so final, so absolute, that she struggled to see a way through it.

In the end, she carried the lives of everyone onboard. She couldn't lay down and die, not now. So she sighed and resigned herself to another battle. 'Isa. Wanna grab the scope? Oris, get to the cannons. Maybe the smell of *dragon's breath*'ll drive 'em off. Fire them straight away, I'll get *Otella* in position.'

Isa didn't seem to appreciate the order, but she relieved Oris of the longscope and the youth happily made his way below deck to his usual position as gunner. Amarah reached into the drawer under the wheel and pulled out the torch with the green splotch of colour painted on the front: *attack*.

'Gonna need you to signal to Traeg and Antar,' Amarah said. She grabbed the wheel and pulled to the left until it locked into place, turning the ship-mid air. If Tacio wasn't done fighting yet, then she'd give him a damn good reason to run back to the palace with his tail between his legs. 'You reckon Tacio's on one of those ships?' Amarah asked as she handed Isa the torch.

Isa lit it as she walked to the side of the ship. 'I very much doubt it. He wouldn't be seen bleeding, not by servants.'

That made Amarah laugh. After everything that had happened, Tacio's half-hearted attempt at pursuit seemed like child's play. Amarah kept a close eye on the three Imperial Ships as they gained on them, as well as the positions of *RaKhanna* and her warship.

As the other ships saw Isa's signal, they also paused in their flight and swivelled around to face the approaching warships. Often when it came to sky pirates, simply standing and challenging was enough to get someone to flee.

She wondered if all their forces would be enough to dissuade the few remaining members of the Imperial Guard. They can't have had an easy night with everything that had gone on right under their noses.

'Everyone hold on!' Amarah shouted. Better they were prepared than not. 'Come on, Oris...'

'Tacio's ships are almost on us!' Isa yelled.

Otella lurched forward as Oris fired the pre-loaded cannons. A collective gasp went up from the Ittallan on board as they saw several of Malot's fire dragons fly across the sky, beating their wings to hurtle themselves towards their target. The air filled with their roar, and the resulting explosion of impact lit the night in yellow and red.

Samolen magic always gave you the edge, and *dragon's breath* was no different.

Amarah didn't know why she'd even been worried. The "sky pirating" part of the job was always going to be the easiest.

'Whatever that is, I need it on my ships!' Isa said, her eyes bright with reflected light from the attack. 'Brilliant way to get rid of people.'

'Well I'm sure you can talk to Malot about all your requirements when we get to Estoria, princess.'

The roar of the conjured dragons echoed as wood took to flame, cracking and splintering in the immense heat. Smoke plumed into the sky, bringing with it the awful stench. Amarah covered her mouth and twisted the wheel. Now she needed to get away as quickly as possible. She couldn't stand the smell of *dragon's breath*.

With Tacio's ships dealing with fire and smoke, Amarah wheeled *Otella* and powered away. The old warship was far from the fastest thing in the sky, but with a decent head-start, she was sure they could put a fair amount of distance between themselves and Tacio's ships. And after withstanding the first round of cannon-fire, she very much doubted they'd be interested in tackling a second attack.

'Looks like Antar's coming in,' Isa said.

Sure enough, the huge warship flew close to them—closer than Amarah would have liked. She adjusted her altitude slightly to ensure they didn't collide. When she looked up, Antar waved at her, the biggest grin on his face.

Amarah shook her head, but she couldn't keep the smile completely off her lips. Damned Estorian.

Oris resurfaced, almost giddy with excitement. 'Tell me those shots weren't spot on?'

'They were good shots.' Amarah would admit that. She didn't want to stroke his ego too much, but credit where it was due. 'Don't think they'll be trying that again anytime soon.'

When all the ships were back in formation, Traego pulled ahead on *RaKhanna*, then turned slowly so they all faced his broadside. The signal for "wait" went up from on deck.

Amarah frowned and hovered *Otella*, unsure why they weren't tearing off at full speed. Her eyes widened when she saw the canon holes open and the guns roll out. 'What...what is he...He's not going to fire on us, is he?'

She grabbed one of the levers, ready to plunge *Otella* into a dive if she had to.

She didn't have time to react, though. Traego fired and *RaKhanna* lurched in the air as several small, round projectiles hurtled towards them. Each one slammed into the ships, but Amarah hardly felt a thing.

Confused, she looked around. Oris and Isa shrugged.

And then she saw the thin haze float up, covering the deck, masts, and sails.

She saw a small flash light up *RaKhanna*'s deck for an instant, and then it disappeared before her eyes.

'*Thief Shrouds*? Malot made more!' Oris gasped.

Amarah loved the ingenuity of it. The Kalosuk had managed to engineer a shroud that could be fired from an airship's cannon. Normally sky pirates would just carry a few of the little grey balls in their pockets, and then deploy them to hide whatever they wanted—from something as small as a basket to as large as a mountain. She'd never known shrouds as good as Malot created, and now they would be invisible to their enemies.

It had to be the simplest getaway she'd ever experienced.

But when she considered all Lathri had sacrificed, it was also one of the hardest.

'Amarah. I do not see the ships.' Palom entered the cabin again. He looked hollow, somehow like the ghost of himself.

'It's a little sky pirate trick. We use 'em to hide things.' It was the quickest, simplest explanation she could give.

'And we are now flying to Estoria?'

'It's outside Sapora's rule. Safest place anywhere near.'

Palom seemed to ponder over her words for a while. He briefly glanced to Isa before saying, 'I want to kill Sapora. And Tacio. For...for what they did...to...' His voice cracked. '...Lathri.'

'So do I,' Isa said, her voice hard. 'Tacio was the one who tortured people. Sapora didn't much care.'

Palom glared at her. 'Sapora *permitted* it. Sapora let torture happen. Sapora released Mateli. They are both *emonos*.'

'I do question the safety of Estoria,' Isa said. 'Sapora may not be able to send any of the Imperial Guard there, but there's nothing to stop him butting a bounty on our heads. Hiding among the most gold-hungry people in Linaria doesn't seem wise.'

'You got a better idea, you let me know.' Amarah shrugged. With the Arks released, nowhere in Linaria would be truly safe. Better they keep moving. 'We probably won't be in Estoria too long. I'll stay until Kohl gets back, anyway.'

Palom huffed at the mention of the Arillian.

Amarah cackled. 'Just like old times, isn't it? All of us getting back together. You and me and Kohl. We just need Morgen, now.' She'd last seen him in the far reaches of Corhaven. Funnily enough near where Sapora had just ran off to.

She hoped Morgen wasn't anywhere near Povmar.

Amarah said, 'In a way, Sapora's hunt for the Arks is what brought us together again. Maybe they ain't so bad after all.'

'This is not a thing to joke about!' Palom almost roared. 'The Arks are very reason there is hatred and divide between Ittallan and Varkain.'

Amarah shook her head as her poor joke died. It was a feeble attempt at humour to cover up their pain and sadness.

She sighed. Isa was right. She *had* been lucky. She'd had to bet on Veynothi being so important to Sapora that he dropped everything to find her. She'd hoped he'd be so busy with the Arks that he'd forget about her.

Isa, on the other hand, was another matter entirely. She was his blood. Royalty. And had a claim to rule. Both Isa and Sapora were half-Varkain, half-Ittallan, but Isa had far more support from the Ittallan than Sapora did. She had no idea how he'd react to his sister on the run, and she didn't much like the idea of Sapora bearing down on them with his Sevastos.

And then there was Aciel.

Even now, she remembered his voice commanding her. She was terrified that if she didn't pay attention, some echo of his power would compel her to do something stupid. If she didn't get herself incinerated by Sapora's dragon, first.

For all her joking about, Amarah knew she had bigger things to worry about than a damned snake.

～

BY MID-AFTERNOON, fatigue had begun to set in. Amarah hadn't slept in two days, if you didn't count nearly dying, and had trouble keeping her eye open.

They'd travelled south, following the line of the Feor Mountains to stay well clear of Jato's thunderstorm. Although it had meant smoother flying, it also meant longer flying. 'There's a little town down there. I reckon we land nearby and take a breather. Traeg'll need to be caught up with everything, too.'

'Makes sense. That town is Esta Cona. It's one of the

closest settlements to Estoria, actually.' Isa peered over the side of *Otella* with the longscope. 'Before you cross the sea, of course. But it's all wetlands here so mind where you bring the ship down. You're probably better off a few more leagues south. Then you won't have loads of townspeople coming out to see what's going on.'

Amarah followed the princess's advice and landed on a gentle, grassy slope that led down to a shallow beach and the sea.

The other ships landed close by, and Amarah stretched her arms above her. Every muscle complained.

She watched as Judd brought Isa's second ship to land on *RaKhanna's* deck. It made sense. No point having every ship in the air, and Judd was more useful as a member of the crew when he navigated.

Leillu was the first to disembark, leaping into the air and spreading her wings to glide gently down. Palom followed after the young dragon, and then Isa and her Ittallan were quick to get down, several bringing wood and supplies with them.

Amarah hadn't realised the amount they'd brought. She'd been face-down on the deck when everyone had embarked and spent the remainder of the flight glued to the wheel.

Solvi had wrapped Lathri in spare linens and blankets, and she and Palom gently carried her off.

Amarah frowned, but wasn't sure of the best way to ask just what they were doing.

'Palom wants her to be laid to rest in the mausoleum of South Galeo,' Princess Isa said, as though reading her mind.

'Why?'

'Tradition. Anahrik and Eryn are there, too. It's a prestigious resting place.'

But there was no way they could return to Taban Yul. Not now.

Another burial, then.

Amarah kept quiet as she watched them. For such a big man, Palom could be surprisingly gentle. He could easily carry Lathri alone, but he shared the task with his niece more than likely out of respect for her.

Tall storks with white feathers and long, red legs cawed loudly as they flew overhead, and all manner of insects chirped and buzzed near the abundant water. Small flocks of brightly coloured birds flew from trees and to the water nearby, their loud calls carrying for leagues. In a strange way, Amarah found it rather peaceful.

'You know, I can't say as I've been here before.'

'There's little here for anyone. Except fish, I suppose.' Princess Isa hadn't regained much emotion in her voice, and Amarah knew she had taken Lathri's passing very hard.

By the time they had enough wood for several fires, it was beginning to grow dark. Amarah was more than happy to spend the night here and head to Estoria early the next morning. Now she'd been reunited with Traego and Princess Isa, she'd follow their lead.

She was looking forward to finally taking her first flight on *RaKhanna*, and the new future she'd forge for herself on it.

The Ittallan who followed Isa were close-knit and looked out for one another. They sat huddled together, spoke openly, and helped one another with their food and fires. Amarah knew it sounded silly, but somehow it *felt* better than those who followed Sapora. The Varkain in the throne room had been lifeless, almost. They reacted only when ordered and didn't seem to have a single thought of their own.

And there was the Valendrin. That was a dark creature if ever she'd seen one.

Amarah sat down on the slope some distance to the right of the gathered people and watched them as they ate and talked. Princess Isa remained almost in the centre, with various Ittallan surrounding her, including Yfaila. They spoke at length and in detail about what had happened in the palace, the city, and how they'd all ended up here.

Palom remained alone, save *Leillu*, almost in the sea. He'd buried Lathri on the beach, gathered sticks and foliage, and lit them with dragonfire to mark her passing. He stood on the beach now, stoic as he faced the sea. The tide was coming in slowly, but still he didn't move, even as the water lapped around his ankles.

Amarah knew he and Lathri had loved one another, and Palom was simply trying to make his peace with what had happened. She wouldn't be surprised if he didn't sleep all night.

She scooped up a handful of sandy soil and let it fall through her fingers. Had Lathri not been so selfless, she wondered whether Palom would have buried *her* on the beach.

Traego made his way up the slope to where she sat, and Amarah didn't make any attempt to move. She didn't mind his company.

'Why ya all by yaself up here?' He sat down heavily and leaned on his knees.

'I've been with too many people. Just wanted some quiet.' It wasn't a lie.

'Want me ta go?'

Amarah shrugged. 'Do what you want.' Her scythe, slightly bent from the punishment she'd put it through in the palace, lay on the grass by her feet. 'How's my ship?'

Traego grinned broadly. 'She's a real beauty, that one.

577

But ya never did tell me what ya called her. Venin didn't know either. Don't have no name painted on it.'

'*RaKhanna*.'

Traego raised his eyebrows. 'Look at ya! Never thought I'd hear o' ya embracing ya Samolen heritage!'

Amarah shook her head. 'The name fit. So why not?'

'How much gold ya get?' Business as usual with Traego.

'Me? Nothing. I'll bet Antar got a lot.'

'Yeah. A full satchel. Crystal glasses and decanters, jewels, a tonne o' coin that apparently was just lying there for the taking. In an open chest.'

Amarah laughed. 'Happy with that?'

'A few hundred crowns worth o' gold and all my crew safe an' sound? Course I am.'

'Oris is coming along. Helped me get out the city.'

Traego scratched his nose. 'Yeah. He said something about that.'

Amarah closed her eye. She didn't want to talk to Traego about her near death experience. About how it was her fault Lathri had to be buried.

Traego seemed to sense her withdrawal, and he didn't push the matter.

Amarah wondered whether Morgen still carried his *Valta Forinja*. Worried whether he'd suffered under the damned thing's curse, too. Palom had dumped his somewhere, just like she had. Anahrik was dead. It just left Morgen's short sword.

She'd need to talk to Palom about that. Or perhaps Topeko. The Samolen kept themselves out of conflict and fighting for good reason. She was sure many wars would end pretty quickly if everyone who fought with a weapon went mad.

They listened to the waves as they lapped the beach, and

talk drifted up from the large, makeshift camp of mismatched Ittallan following their queen.

'So, what happens now?' Traego asked after several minutes.

Amarah shrugged. 'Sapora brings back three of the Arks. Takes over the world. Kills whoever don't bow to him.'

'Just like at the ball, then.'

Amarah bit her lip. He wasn't wrong.

From her time with Kylos, Isa, and the other Ittallan, she'd learned more than enough about the Arks for her liking. Five thousand years old Varkain weapons of war. If Traego had known what they were, he probably would never have gone on his stupid treasure hunt. Probably.

They were a bedtime story for Ittallan children—something to remind them to do as they were told or they'd be punished. For everyone else, they were a nightmare made real. A reminder of a time when the stakes were high and cities fell every day. When the daily battle against them was greater than both Arillian wars combined—in death toll and damage.

'And now we have Sapora's number one target in our midst,' Traego said.

'I hope you're not thinking of handing her over to Sapora!' His words shocked her.

'Get paid for freeing her. Get paid for returning her. Win, win?'

Amarah faced him to check whether he was joking or serious. 'Gold is great. But Sapora isn't worth it. Neither's Tacio. We're gonna see the fall of a kingdom because of these Arks. Maybe the world, unless something happens to stop them.'

Traego nodded, smiling. 'And who always comes up when there's falling kingdoms and war?'

'You do.'

'I do.' He laid back on his elbows and stared out to sea.

Amarah sighed heavily. Traego was always one to find opportunity in disaster and strife. She did, too, but never to the same extent. She'd lost an eye, gained a collection of scars, and almost died. Traego seemed to have put on weight and drunk too much rum. He was far too comfortable.

Right now, she didn't know whether it would be safer to stay with Traego and Isa in Estoria, or make her way back towards Jato to get her revenge.

And that was to say nothing of her goal to free Moroda from the Sevastos' crystal.

She shuddered as another memory of Aciel's voice came, unbidden, to her mind.

Perhaps Aciel would somehow break out first. It would save her the job of finding out how to free Moroda.

They'd just barely managed to hold their own against him before. The thought of fighting him again—and winning—didn't seem likely.

When Sapora returned to the palace with his Arks, Linaria would become a different place. Of that, she was certain.

She'd never really had much faith in Rhea before, but the Goddess had seen to it that she hadn't died when she'd been supposed to. She didn't think she'd ever be able to rid herself of the guilt she felt for living, especially not when she looked at Palom.

His grief was palpable.

Amarah didn't know exactly what the future would bring. Dangerous powers, yes, from Arks to the Sevastos, Aciel's will to wild dragons. And no matter how remote Estoria felt, one of those powers was bound to catch up with her before too long.

Her gut told her to keep moving, and to follow Isa.

There was no point running from everything—she

wanted to stand and fight. She told people often enough to do it. She had to take her own advice, too.

If Isa could overthrow the snakes, then she'd do everything in her power to help.

And whatever the future held for her, Amarah knew that she was going to survive.

End

NOTE FROM THE AUTHOR

Thank you for reading *Amarah*!

If you enjoyed *Amarah*, please consider leaving a review on Amazon and Goodreads.

Book reviews are crucial for indie authors like me, and even a couple of lines can make a huge difference. They're also the best way readers can discover new books!

Can't wait to get back into the World of Linaria?

Subscribe to my mailing list and you'll be the first to hear news, announcements, and special offers.

Plus, you'll also get to enjoy freebies, including a high-res digital map of Linaria and a free spin-off novella - *Rise of a Sky Pirate* - just for signing up!

www.llmcneil.com